Miriam Coles Harris

Happy-Go-Lucky

Miriam Coles Harris

Happy-Go-Lucky

ISBN/EAN: 9783743388833

Manufactured in Europe, USA, Canada, Australia, Japa

Cover: Foto ©Andreas Hilbeck / pixelio.de

Manufactured and distributed by brebook publishing software (www.brebook.com)

Miriam Coles Harris

Happy-Go-Lucky

A Novel.

BY

THE AUTHOR OF "RUTLEDGE;"

"THE SUTHERLANDS ;" "LOUIE'S LAST TERM AT ST. MARY'S ;"
"FRANK WARRINGTON ;" "RICHARD VANDERMARCK ;"
"ST. PHILIPS ;" "A PERFECT ADONIS ;"
"MISSY ;" ETC., ETC.

NEW YORK:

Copyright, 1881, by

G. W. Carleton & Co., Publishers.

LONDON : S. LOW, SON & CO.

MDCCCLXXXI.

CONTENTS.

[v]

HAPPY-GO-LUCKY.

HAPPY-GO-LUCKY.

CHAPTER I.

SEA BREEZES.

"But nature was so kind!
Like a dear friend I loved the loneliness;
My heart rose glad as at some sweet caress
When passed the wandering wind."

Celia Thaxter.

THE train stopped, without abruptness, the conductor called out "South Berwick," in almost a conversational key, to the inhabitants of the one passenger car that, with the baggage car and tender, formed the train. It had been crawling for hours along a flat country, stopping at intervals at stations that bore a family likeness to this, and then moving stolidly forward through more scrub oaks, and more sandy cuttings, and past more isolated and despondent farms. Sometimes a passenger got off. Less frequently one or two got on. At one place a man got off, and I watched him walk away, down a straight, long, sandy road that ran through a low pine wood, and seemed to have no ending. He was very tall, and seemed to dwarf the poor little forest.

He carried a bag, and was dressed all in black broad-
cloth, and the hat he wore was a sleek, well-brushed
beaver, which caught the rays of the morning sun, over
the tops of the pitiful trees, and shone illustriously.
We stayed so long at that station I watched him a good
way on his journey; but he did not turn back, or evince
any interest in what he had left behind him. I wondered
whether he was going to preach a sermon at a funeral
or to sell books out of his leather bag. But "whither
would conjecture stray?" Here we were at South Berwick, and my heart, which had been growing heavier
with each added mile of sand, went down with a sudden
precipitation as I heard the long-looked for announce-
ment, and, gathering up the child and the bag that fell
to my share, stepped out upon the platform.

It was a desperately dull and dreary place. One or
two men moved about deliberately, and seemed to be
taking care of our trunks and of the mail-bag, which
were all that they put out of the baggage-car.
Though it was the last of May, and though a bright sun
was shining, the wind was blowing from the sea, and it
was cold. I wrapped a shawl around Maidy, who clung
close to me and looked bewildered; Sophia (she was
maid, but she ought to have been mistress) set down
Baby on the platform, handed me the cord by which she
held the dog, and bustled about to see to the trunks. I
took Baby by one hand and Maidy by the other, and
walked up and down on the boards, and felt very sorry
for myself. What desolation, what dullness! and we
had taken a house here, and had to stay all summer. I
had been so long used to brick and mortar dullness and
desolation that this seemed very chilly.

"Don't go away with the checks," called Sophia

sharply, for I had walked down towards the old stage, the only vehicle in sight, and was trying to cheer Maidy by telling her it would take us away to the sea.

When the luggage was disposed of, and we were in the stage, wrapped in all the shawls the careful Sophia would allow us, we rolled away towards the village. It was no use to ask the driver how far we had to go, for he spoke without turning his head, and the wind took his words away from us. What a wind! But the sun shone warm on my shoulder, and the shawls were thick, and in a few moments we drove into a green and pretty village. The street was very broad, and the houses looked at each other across it with a cheerful recognition. There were vines about the doors, and the trees, through not very large, were green with the greenness of May. Two or three gray old houses stood with gable ends to the street, but more, all green and white, stood primly facing the public, not ashamed.

"Maidy, it's not so bad after all," I cried cheerfully, giving her a little hug, for there was a wind-mill in the distance, whose white sails were turning against the blue sky, and in a window I had seen some flowers. The little girl, tenderly responsive always to my moods, pressed close to me, and pointed, pleased, to a pigeon-house under the eaves of a barn, where pigeons, white and gray, were sunning themselves, and strutting up and down the little balcony. It was noon, and the school-bell was ringing, and a troop of children ran out upon the sidewalk and gazed after us. A horse was tied before the village "store;" an empty farm wagon rattled past us; this was all the animation that we saw, but the village, somehow, was not desolate; the sunshine and the greenness and the trimness made up for the absence of human stir.

We lumbered on through the village, pausing only to throw out the mail-bag at the post-office. The houses grew fewer and farther apart. We thought, as we approached each one, it was the one to which we were bound. I could see Sophia's hopes were set upon the trim boxes with white-washed palings. When all these were past, and we had only two low farm-houses between us and the blue line of ocean, which we now could see, I breathed freer. At the last of these two the stage drew up.

"Are you sure this is the house," I said, with a fear of some mistake.

"There ain't no other for it to be," he said, pulling open the stage door.

I sprang out, almost forgetting to take Maidy, who held out her arms to me eagerly. The little gray gate was closed. I was bending over the rusty latch, when Sophia recalled me to my responsibilities, and told me, in a hard tone, that the man was to be paid. After I had counted out the money for him, I said, laughing, "Sophia, I see you don't like the house; I am afraid you think it is a trifle old."

"Old," she sniffed, setting down poor Baby with emphasis, and jerking Rex's cord to keep him from under the wheels of the stage, but not looking at me nor at the house, as she followed me through the gate. "If any-body likes rats and cockroaches and ants and mildew—"

"It's perfect," I cried, gazing up at the gray shin-gles. "But how shall we get in? I thought Colonel What's-his-name was going to have it opened, and to send a woman to have a fire, and something ready for us."

"It all comes," muttered Sophia, "of taking a house without going to see it; and bringing children into the country at this time of year's an outrage. They're starved now, and there isn't a neighbor near enough to get a glass of milk from."

But at this moment around the corner of the house there appeared an Indian woman, brown and smiling, who said she had been sent to open the house and build a fire for us, and that there was bread, and eggs and milk within.

Sophia reluctantly followed her, and Maidy and I ran up the side steps that led to the balcony across the front of the house, and peeped in at the closed windows. I had a delightful feeling of possession; it was so long since I had had a delightful feeling of any kind, no one need have begrudged me this. I had been three years a widow, and had never been in the country since that dreary blight had fallen on my life, but had spent the time in stuffy city apartments, depressed by sorrow, harassed by poverty; many months of the three years prostrated by dangerous illness. It had been like a gleam of sunshine, when the doctor, touched by Maidy's pale cheeks, had proposed a summer by the sea for us, and had made the way plain by a communication with Colonel Emlyn, who owned two or three cottages at this remote place, and who was glad to hear of a tenant who would be contented with mildew and rag carpets, and who did not hanker for society. The rent was low, the air irreproachable,—that was all I asked; and with the first breath of the sea-breeze, life and youth seemed to come back to me. The zest with which I ran up the steps and counted the windows, and gazed at the narrow front door, with its rusty knocker and fan-shaped light above, contrasted sharply with the apathy with which I had taken possession of the rooms to which from time to time we had moved in the city. Sophia had had all the work of selecting and preparing them, and had been all energy and approbation in consequence. The case was reversed now, and Sophia's disapproval was the only cloud upon the sunny sky of our new life.

I loved the house from the first moment that I saw it. It was a dilapidated, unpainted farm-house, which Colonel Emlyn had bought as a speculation some years before, when he built his own house down by the sea. He had fancied it would be easy to rent it, and had spent a few hundred dollars in fitting it up. But it had been on his hands more years than off them ; and I suppose he often wished he had his few hundred dollars back, as no one enjoys an unprofitable speculation that is always in his sight. If the same amount of money had been sunk in an imaginary mine or on a collapsed railroad, he would not have given it a second thought. But here was his little mistake in view from every window of his house, and it fretted the good colonel, as I afterwards saw.

The house was built in an unusual way for that part of the country. The first story was stone, and in front, a few narrow windows let light into a kitchen and a mouldy sort of store-room ; the entrance to the kitchen was at the side. A flight of steps at one side led up to a balcony, which I believe was one of the colonel's improvements, but it was unpainted, like the rest of the house, and had turned a beautiful gray. A trumpet creeper, with a stem like a young tree, climbed over this balcony, and an ivy, with very small, glossy leaves, clung

against the not very firm shingles of the side towards
the sea, above the kitchen entrance. From the balcony
one saw the blue line of ocean above the low sand-hills
which skirted the beach. The fields between us and the
sea were perfectly flat, and there was not a tree in sight,
in that direction, save the old cedar that shaded our own
windows, and the few little sprigs that the colonel had
planted on the road that led to his own house. It was
about half a mile to the sea, from our cottage, but it
looked much less. We were the outpost of the farming
interest—the last house of the village towards the sea.

We could not get in at the front door, so Maidy and
I ran down the steps, and tumbled over Baby, who was
climbing up to meet us, and who, being set on her feet,
joined us in our researches in the yard. A thick bed of
periwinkles had rooted out the grass, and made a great
expanse of dark glossiness, and with exclamations of delight we pulled bunches of the dark blue flowers that
peeped above the leaves. Maidy found dandelions, too ;
she had a Park acquaintance with them, and was charmed
at the *rencontre*. The neglected old garden was full of
green things sprouting up : this, I knew to be a bunch
of hollyhocks, from the tall dead stalks that had survived
the winter's storms under the shelter of the house, and
stood up about the place of their nativity. These might
be artemisias for the autumn's joy, here was columbine,
morning-glory, the little heart-shaped leaves of a dark-
blue, scentless violet. And here, under an old box-tree,
grew a single stem of lily of the valley. There was
no trace of a path anywhere, nor of any flower-beds ;
dead grass lay about the roots of the new grass ; the stiff
dry stems of last year's vines snapped and broke as I
leaned down to look at the green soft wonders that were

springing up. Maidy was entangled in some fallen branches, and Baby stood waist-deep in ribbon-grass. I extricated Maidy, and lifted Baby out, and then we pushed on towards the empty barn-yard, and the colony of outhouses, dilapidated and unused.

"This, Maidy, shall be your playhouse," I cried, pulling open on its rusty hinges the door of an old workshop, from which a lean cat darted forth, scattering dust and some corn cobs that the rats had left.

"Whose is it now?" she said, looking wonderingly in.

"Ours, Maidy, all ours, even the big barn."

What a sweet feeling that was. We climbed over into the barn-yard, we pried open the barn door, we lifted the lids of grain bins, we revelled in the cobwebs and the dust-heaps, for they belonged to us. The poor little city babies followed me with eager, ignorant exultation. The sunshine was so warm and delicious, the verdure I looked out upon so new to my starved sight, a new current of life seemed setting through my veins.

I had led the children far down a narrow lane that ran past the barn-yard; I don't know where we meant to go. The children's arms were full of foolish treasures, my brain with fancies just about as worthless, when our wanderings were brought to an end by the shrill call of Sophia, who, out of patience and out of breath, had run after us, and had snatched Baby up, and was talking at me over her shoulder as she walked back towards the house.

"The child will be starved," she said "it's three-quarters of an hour since we got out of the stage, and here I have had her dinner ready twenty minutes, and it's stone cold on the table, while I've been hunting all over the old rookery for you, and calling and calling till I'm hoarse."

Baby didn't mind her scolding; she knew how little it meant, for she had been brought up on it. She stroked her nurse's cheek with her little soft hand, and pulled at the ribbon of her hat. Maidy and I turned meekly and followed towards the dinner which we certainly ought not to have forgotten. I took Maidy's treasures to carry, and lifted her over some rough places in the lane, and in many ways loitered to give Sophia a chance to get ahead of us and leave us to follow in peace. But great a hurry as she was in, she would not let us get out of hearing: we were to know what she had to say. It was her peculiarity: when she got worked up into a mood like this, it seemed inevitable that she should say just so much, and then a sullen and possibly repentant mood would follow, in which we had silence enough.

Sophia could not be considered like an ordinary servant. She had come to my mother's house a girl of fourteen, when I was not as old as Maidy. Every one knows the intimacy that grows up between children placed in such relationship. Sophia was my nurse, and waited on me, though she was scarcely more than a child herself, but I looked up to her with great respect, and loved her with great affection. She had an immense influence over me, and my whole childhood bore her impress. When I was married, she came to me, naturally, and my interests were hers. My mother could ill spare her, being near the close of her lonely, suffering life, but I was so very young, and was going so far away, it was tacitly conceded, Sophia must go with me.

As things turned out, it seemed a mercy that she

did. My husband and I were but a pair of children;
trouble and illness came fast enough; my whole married life was not three years. No sister could have
been more unsparing of herself, no mother more vigilant and anxious. Our ignorance, our slender means,
our youth, would have made us very helpless without
this lynx-eyed guardian. For many months after I was
left a widow, she had, single-handed to take care of me,
and of the two babies, with the barest purse, and the
darkest outlook. My mother had died a year before;
the little property that was coming to me was in litiga-
tion; I had literally no one to look to. What did I not
owe her! She had a right to scold me and to lead me
back to dinner in disgrace.

Rather better times were upon us now, and she
would probably scold the more in consequence. The
lawsuit had been recently decided in my favor, and the
small property that my mother left was now mine. It
was well invested; the income from it, though not large,
was as certain as such things can be. We should never
be called upon to go through the experiences of the
past two or three years, and with economy we could be
comfortable, and I could educate the children, and live
respectably, and not be oppressed with care for the future. It was heaven to feel this, after the long pressure
of anxiety, but though I had known the facts for two
months, I had not seemed to realize them till I had
breathed this air and got out of the surroundings so
associated with suffering.

When we got to the kitchen door, I remembered, as
I laid down Maidy's treasures on the stone, that I had not
yet been in the house, and I said this, with a little laugh,
to Maidy.

"It's fine housekeeping that begins with the outside of the house," snapped Sophia, settling Baby in a chair by the table, while the Indian woman put the omelette, and the bread and butter, and the tea upon the table.

"What a dear old kitchen," I said, going to look out a latticed door that opened into a sort of covered place, with one side open to the yard, and with the well just before it. "Maidy, I shall draw the well."

"It's more than I shall," cried Sophia, "and I'm inclined to think you'll find your kitchen dear, before the summer's over, sure enough, if you count all the help you'll have to hire to get your work done in it."

I did not dare admire it any more after that, but sat down humbly beside Maidy, and was served with a meal anything but cold, which we all ate with appetites which even Sophia could not disapprove.

CHAPTER II.

VIVAT REX.

"His very hair is of the dissembling color."
As You Like It.

TWO days followed, during which my pleasure in my new home was unabated. I continued to keep house outside, and Sophia, now somewhat mollified, to get in order the inside. It was on the afternoon of the second day; I had got my blue flannel suit out of a trunk (or perhaps Sophia had) and had put it on for the first time, together with a shade hat which she had trimmed for me when we first began to talk of the seaside. It was very odd not to be wearing a black dress, but it all seemed in keeping with the free, new life. Maidy admired me very much, and insisted upon kissing me. She was only five years old, but she had a great sense of the fitness of things, and had been distressed, I believe, by my great crape veil ever since we came to the country. She and Baby were fresh and pretty in their flannel dresses, and white sunbonnets, and thus we all went out for a walk, leaving Sophia at the gate, looking after the work of her hands with some pardonable satisfaction.

For were we not, in a sense, the work of her hands, blue flannel dresses and all? I always have believed the children would never have lived but for her care, and I

[20]

know I shouldn't. And as to the blue flannel dress and the coarse straw hat, I should never have had them but for her intervention. I had not wanted anything for the last three years but to be let alone to cry my eyes out under the crape veil supplied to me by fate. Susan leaned for a few moments over the gate and looked after us, with a softness in her black eyes; it must have comforted her to see me look so young and well again; and the children, for whom she had so labored, walked demure and prim beside me in the soft spring sunshine. I think she felt that afternoon as if the warfare were over, and the day of peace fairly risen in the sky.

Baby was but three years old, and had to be very much aided when we went to walk. I did not propose to go very far, but the temptation of a new road led me on, and long before I knew it, we were a good way from home across the level country, and the sun was declining slowly. Maidy was very fresh and bright, but Baby was beginning to lag behind and fret a little, and I began to think it was a pity that we had come so far. We had not reached the sea yet, though we were very near it, and could hear the waves breaking on the shore, though the sand-hills hid them from us.

We had been walking for some time on a road that ran parallel to the beach, and now I found myself on a narrow lane that crossed it and went down through an opening to the water's edge. The road was a little lower than the field, and I sat down on the bank, and took Baby on my lap, and pulled some wild roses from a bush beside me and ornamented her hat with them, and tried to amuse her and get her rested. Maidy strayed off in pursuit of more wild roses. Rex, the dog, lay at my feet and panted after his exertions. He was a French poodle, with soft, white, curling hair and lovely pink skin under it; he had a temper as infirm as Sophia's, and eyes as black, but much more tender in their expression. We loved him beyond language, but he barked nearly all the time, and was a great inconvenience. Baby now began patting him, and, rested, got up, toddled about on the uneven ground and pulled grass and flowers, and scrambled up one rail of the fence, and down again and up again, and so on. I clasped my hands around my knees and sat looking over the long line of fields across which the level shadows were stretching, breathing the air fresh from the sea, and listening to the roll of the surf beyond. The sunshine was still warm and delicious; some birds chirped about the bushes near me; Baby's happy little chatter sounded as intelligible; when Rex, starting from my feet, gave a furious bark, and dashed down the lane, along which a troop of cows, two loose horses, and a bull, were coming rapidly.

I sprang up and got Baby by the hand, and called vehemently to Rex to come back to me. He, instead, ran barking at the heels of the cows, who, frightened, kicked and ran and looked back at him, and kicked again, and the horses shook their manes and raised their heads, and looked as if they might do any fearful thing under such a provocation. The peaceful lane became suddenly a scene of great tumult and confusion. I don't know where the cows had come from, nor how they had got upon us with so little observation; I suppose I must have been very much lost in my revery; I did not dare to run down the bank after the dog, whose destruction seemed imminent, among all those hoofs and horns. I held Baby by the hand, and going as near the edge of the bank as I could, I called despairingly, and then tried to whistle. I could not whistle; I never could. I pursed up my mouth with effort, and no doubt made a very ludicrous face, but all the sound that came was a very faint affair, like an aspirated sigh, which of course the dog could not hear. I felt like crying, I was so full of trouble and excitement. At that moment, directly at my elbow, I found some one standing. I turned quickly, and looked into the face of a young man, who had come upon the scene as mysteriously as the cows.

"Shall I whistle for you?" he said, with gravity, though his eyes were very merry.

"Oh, if you only would," I cried, with no sense of the humor of the situation. "I am sure he will be killed, and I'm afraid of the cows."

Thereupon he whistled, a clear shrill whistle, that arrested the attention of the dog, who halted for an instant, turned his head towards us, and then dashed on, with renewed zest, after the bull, who was putting down his head angrily.

"He will be killed," I exclaimed, dropping Baby, and wringing my hands.

The stranger sprang down the bank, dashed in among the horns and hoofs, and, making a plunge at the dog, caught him by the hair, and bore him wriggling and barking back to me, and put him in my arms.

"Oh, thank you," I said, but I don't suppose he heard me above the racket that the dog and the cows were making. I struggled to hold him, and to keep him quiet, but Baby was tugging at my dress, and, looking across to the other side of the road, I caught sight of poor Maidy, who was, from the contortions of her face, probably crying loudly, but I couldn't hear anything but the yelping of the cur and the lowing of the cows.

I had forgotten all about her. She was clinging to the fence (the wrong side of it), of course, and in a very ecstasy of fear, for which there was much excuse, as the cows were upon her side of the bank, and she was really in danger of being walked over by the great creatures, even if they had no evil intention towards her.

"Shall I bring your little sister to you?" said the sedate stranger, who again accomplished the feat of fording the current of cows, and who sprang up the bank lithely, and stood by the terrified little child almost before I had taken in his question. He was small and slight; at the first glance I should have said he was eighteen, at the second, twenty-eight. He was close shaved, and his hair was very dark, and as short as it could be cut. He was very sunburned; his eyes were keen and dark; his nose was well cut, his mouth rather large. He was dressed in knickerbockers, with a blue flannel shirt and red belt, and wore a little, close-fitting cap, also blue, I think.

I looked anxiously to see how Maidy would take the approach of a stranger. She was a very timid child, and I was always prepared, from experience, to see her go into a frenzy of crying, if any one came near her whom she did not know. It was a comfortable surprise, now, to see her suspend her sobs, look up into the stranger's face, let him take her hand, and finally lift her up in his arms. She was small and light for five years old (such a pretty doll, with her long, loose, yellow curls, and large blue eyes). He lifted her up on his right arm, and drew one of her little hands around his neck, and held it in his left. He was talking to her softly all the while, with his face close to hers. She did not seem to be at all afraid

of him, nor of the cows, but listened with parted lips
and a serious look, the tears still on her checks.

The rear-guard of the cows was now passing us.
He waited a moment, then skirted the end of the procession, and brought her back to me. He set her down
on her feet on the bank beside me, keeping hold of
her little hand till she was standing firm, then, in a
graceful sort of way, stooped down and kissed it before
he released it. He lifted his cap to me, almost without
looking at me, and was gone. My eyes followed him
with a sort of wondering admiration of his light, quick
movements; a cart, which I had not seen in the mêlée,
seemed to be waiting for him in the road which I had
just left. He sprang into it, and the young lad who
was driving it looked curiously and amusedly towards
us, and I was quite sure was laughing at something
that he told him of us. The cart was one of those
two-wheeled joggling things, known as beach carts.
There were some crab-nets in it, and a basket covered
up with sea-weed. The horse was a nice-looking cob,
who in a few moments had joggled them, not out of
sight, that would have been difficult in a country
where one could see one's friends coming to call three
miles off, but out of a critical neighborhood. That is
to say, they were soon so far away I couldn't tell
whether they were laughing at me or not. They drove
through the herd of cows as if they were not afraid of
them; the clumsy things scattered to right and left; I
began to see they were lean and high-shouldered creatures, who probably wouldn't have done us any harm.
The troop settled down into a comfortable jog, and
across the level landscape I could see them moving on,
marked by a little cloud of dust. I put Rex on the

2

ground, with an admonitory shake, and helped the children through the fence.

"What did he say to you, Maidy," I asked, as I wiped the tears off her face, and set right her somewhat distorted skirts.

"He said he would take me to my sister," she answered.

"Your sister, indeed! Well, what was he talking about all the rest of the time?"

"He told me not to be afraid of the cows; he said, they wouldn't hurt me. He held me tight."

"Ah, were you afraid?"

"No, he held me so high up, like the milkman."

I laughed. Maidy had a great liking for being lifted up in the strong arms of a man; poor child, she had had little experience of it, the milkman being about our only male visitor since she had been old enough to remember.

"Which do you think is the nicest, this gentleman who carried you across the road just now, or the milkman?"

But Maidy's feelings were hurt by my laugh, and she put down her head, and would not answer.

"It's all right, dear little one," I said, kissing her, and leading her on to join Baby. "You like to be carried, I know; you can't remember how Papa used to carry his little girl, hours and hours together, when she was a baby, and was sick, and couldn't go to sleep." And the tears rushed into my eyes at the recollection.

"Tell me about it," whispered Maidy, holding tight my hand. Dear Maidy; how she loved to hear those stories. She had been my only confidante, these sad years; twilight after twilight, while Sophia plied her busy needle, and rocked the baby, in another room, Maidy, in the dark, had lain in my arms, and listened to stories of the father whom she could not recollect. I don't know whether it was good for her or good for me. I almost fear these three years had been very morbid ones. I had acknowledged to myself no duty but the duty of keeping fresh the past; perhaps I had resisted the natural reaction that might have come if I had been passive. But, indeed, the circumstances of my life had been all against any such reaction; I ought not to blame myself too much. The dullness and gloom of my surroundings made me turn my gaze back into the past, where once there had been light. If in my grief there was selfishness, at least there was no rebellion. I only asked leave to hide myself and weep.

How far Maidy's timidity and frail health were the result of this treatment, I cannot tell. I did not think I was injuring her, Heaven knows. She was my only comfort. Sophia had such an acrid way of putting my duty before me that I unwisely discredited all she said. She left me nothing to do, with her tremendous energy and activity, and as to what she counselled me to feel, it was not surprising that I did not consider that she knew enough of the grief to know its remedy. She had loved poor Arnold almost as much as she loved me, but it was not her way to sit down and cry about anything, and it must be said, in this strait, there was not much time for the luxury of tears for her. If she had not bestirred herself, what would have been our fate? But it was an abiding subject of complaint with her that I took no interest in anything, that I was, as she expressed it, nursing my grief and making much of it.

"Tell me about it," murmured Maidy that evening,

as we walked home under the soft sunset sky. The grass was growing a little damp; sweet smells came up from the close-cropped fields over which we walked; the solemn monotone of the sea beyond sounded in our ears. I told her; but somehow 'the telling was not as it used to be, in the close-shut, dim room, with the low roar of the city coming up from below. Our grief was a sort of hot-house plant, that did not seem at home in this free air. Maidy vaguely felt dissatisfied. She looked up in my face again and again; she even twitched my dress once reproachfully when my eyes wandered to the sunset, and my narrative flagged in its flow.

"Don't let us talk any more, Maidy," I said; "I want to look at the sunset gates, and think about Paradise."

Then I felt a pang of self-reproach; I could not bear to be dishonest with the child; I was not thinking of Paradise; I was feeling the calm and hush of nature, full and sweet; the glories of God's lower world, where all the senses were fed with health and with content. The shadowy world into which we had looked from that dark, silent chamber, had receded far out of my self-accusing sight.

"I mean," I said, putting my arm about her neck, "I am tired of talking, and just feel like being quiet. Besides, I think I ought to carry Baby."

Baby was again getting a little cross—she was willful always, as different as possible from Maidy. She was tiny; with such hands! I think they were the prettiest things. She was all so perfect and so pretty. Her eyes were gray and her lashes dark; she had not much hair, but it was wavy and of a chestnut color. Her throat was very slender, and I never was tired of looking at the way she held her determined little head. Dear little Baby—everything she did seemed so wonderful, being done by a creature so minute. We were in the habit of thinking her a prodigy, but I suppose, really, it came from her being so much smaller than a child of three years ought to be.

It was not much of a trial to carry her, but I was glad to hand her over to Sophia, and to go into the house, which we did by the side door of the kitchen, where our tea was spread. In a day or two, when things were more in order, we were going to move up stairs to the room above, and take our meals on a thin-legged little mahogany table, which the Indian woman had spent some hours in polishing. The furniture of the room was rather scanty and the floor had a rag carpet on it; but there was a corner closet with a glass door, and a very small supply of blue china cups and saucers, and five plates. These atoned for the other defects and made it possible for me to feel I had a dining-room. Meanwhile, the kitchen was warm and snug, and each meal that we had eaten in it had seemed better than the other.

"Sophia," I said, dropping the sugar in my tea, "we have had an adventure. Maidy and Rex were almost under the feet of a herd of cows, and a young man suddenly appeared and rescued them. You may ask why I didn't, but the truth was, I was afraid; it was bad enough to look on."

Sophia did not appear to listen—she never appeared to listen; it was one of her characteristics to put her own occupations before the communications of others, though I don't think she ever lost much. She went on buttering Maidy's bread, as she stood over her chair, and pouring out Baby's milk, without even looking in my direction.

Maidy, with her mouth full of bread and butter, said, "He carried me," but Sophia only asked whether she'd have more hot water in her milk, with the pitcher suspended over her mug, and manifested no sort of interest in the matter. It was long years since I had presumed to find any fault with Sophia's habits, even tacitly, but the sea air seemed to be affecting me radically. I resolved she shouldn't know anything about the adventure till she asked about it. So I said the Shinnecock made beautiful muffins, and took another one, and then told her I should be almost sorry when we went up-stairs to dine, it was so pleasant in the kitchen. The tins shone in the light of the parlor lamp, which was on the table, the stove doors were open, and the fire within shed forth a cheerful glow. She was not pleased with me, I could tell; she shot a quick glance at me to see what I could mean, and was in a bad humor all the rest of the evening. As she was putting Maidy to bed, I heard her asking some leading questions, which resulted in Maidy's telling the story to the best of her ability. From that little point, perhaps, started her opposition to me in all that concerned my new life.

CHAPTER III.

"Thou hast my love; is not that neighborly ?"
As You Like It.

FROM the balcony, and in fact from all the south
windows of the cottage, I could see the house
of my landlord, Colonel Emlyn. He was, in fact, the
only summer resident of the place. He had several years
before, in a casual visit to the village, been smitten with
it, and, as rich men will, had built a house far too expen-
sive for the place, and then, vaguely conscious of his
error, had tried to remedy it by investing more money
in more land, and building two or three cottages to rent.
The cottages had never rented, the place was as far as
ever from being a summer resort. The colonel did not
go the right way to work. He was not fond of society
himself, but he supposed the two children whom they
were bringing up would soon be; and for their sakes,
he would have been glad of a neighbor or two who
would be agreeable, and he had had visions of seeing
the place become popular enough to bring back to his
pocket a very small percentage of what he had invested
there.

One chilly March day, when the cottages were first
built, a very important, fashionable woman had come
down to look at them, having heard of them from the

[31]

colonel himself. There was a high, rough wind, the
driver of the stage hadn't been over civil, the lady's head
ached from having got up so early, the shut up houses
naturally looked dismal and felt damp—she went back
by the next train in disgust, and told the story of her
journey at every dinner for the next six weeks. All the
people who had been asking questions about South Berwick were dismayed and gave up the thought. One
sheep having turned away and jumped over the bars, all
the others, with mutton gravity, jumped over too, and
left the colonel with his houses on his hands.

I had been wondering whether the Colonel and Mrs.
Emlyn would come to see me. It had seemed to me
that it would be very unpleasant if they didn't. I had
cast a great many curious glances over at the large
house whose outlines were so clear against the sky. I
could see figures sometimes on the piazza, though it was
impossible to distinguish them. Whenever the carriage
came out of the gate, I watched with interest to see
who was in it. The beach cart I knew belonged there,
and the young man who had picked Rex up by the
hair, and the young lad who had laughed at us. With
all my watching, I did not know any one else by sight.

The house was about half a mile from us, facing the
ocean. It was a large house, long in proportion to its
breadth, with a gambril roof and dormer windows, and
a great stack of chimneys in the center. The kitchen and
other offices were on the ground floor. A great veranda
ran all around the second story, and overlooked the low
sand-hills, which in this part of the coast skirt the sea
invariably. There was, at a little distance, a colony of
stables and outhouses. There was no pretense of keeping the grounds in order. The entrance was through a

plain gateway; a few trees had been set out, but had made little progress. The house honestly declared itself there for the sea and for nothing else, and it was sufficient reason for being.

One morning, not long after the adventure that I would not tell to Sophia, I sat on the balcony rather idly sewing, and looked, as people do in the country, idly across towards the house of my neighbor. I saw the carriage come out from the stable, and drive up to the door, and presently some one get in. I could see some drapery which did not belong to a man: I began to wonder if it were Mrs. Emlyn, and if she were coming to see me. I ran into the parlor and opened the windows to let more sunlight in, and looked in the glass to see if my hair were right, and then, a little flurried, came out again and sat down with my work. I heard the voices of the children, playing in the yard below, and wondered whether, if Mrs. Emlyn did call, she would ask to see them. It is quite agitating to have visits when you are not in the habit of having them. The carriage was now out of the gate, and coming up the road; it was certainly coming this way, but this way led to the village, to the post-office, to the station—to everything. It was coming quite fast, too; the stout, well-groomed horses made very good time, and the road was hard, and, it is unnecessary to say, level. The carriage was not very new in style, but comfortable and in good order. Yes, they *were* coming here; the horses drew up at the gate; behind the trumpet creeper I agitatedly watched a lady get out, after a middle-aged man, who, of course, was Colonel Emlyn.

The lady came in at the gate, the gentleman followed her, looking down at the latch, and feeling its rustiness

2*

with a landlord's touch. The lady was very tall, quite
an inch taller than her husband, and of a full and good
figure. She walked quickly, and with an erect bearing;
she was very near-sighted, and looked keenly through
her glasses. Her hair was almost white, in little curls
above her forehead; in contradiction, she had a young
complexion, and a soft color on her cheeks. Her manner was most decisive, while her voice was very sweet.
Her movements were abrupt; you were deadly afraid of
her till you looked into her face. When her face was
in repose, it was as sweet as a child's; but even when it
was ruffled, you soon concluded to take heart and hope
for happier times, which were on the way. When she
came up on the balcony it was with a firm tread, but
the foot that I saw, as she stepped up, was, by a natural
contradiction, small and pretty. She looked about her
for the bell or the knocker, not seeing me. I had
arisen, and was coming forward from the other end of
the balcony.

"Here is the young lady," said the colonel, who was
just behind her.

"Oh, where?" she said, peering around; and then
caught sight of me.

"I beg your pardon," she said, meeting me; "I
hope we shall find your mother at home." She did not
give me time to answer, but added quickly: "I suppose
we have the pleasure of speaking to her daughter?"

I colored very much and said who I was.

"You?" she cried incredulously. "I — I — well,
you must excuse me. It isn't your fault that you look
so young. People generally don't mind it, though."

Then the colonel came forward and she presented
him, and I asked them to come into the parlor. When

they were seated, she still kept talking of the question
of my identity, and smiling at the recollection of her
mistake.

The colonel said, " You must excuse us. It comes
of making up one's mind on insufficient premises. We
only knew through our friend, the doctor, what our
new tenant's name was, and that she was a widow."

(I wonder if he saw me wince.)

" The other day," went on the colonel, " Mr.
Macnally and Ned came home and told us they had
seen a young girl and some little children down below
the meadows, and we concluded that they were all the
lady's children."

" Besides," interrupted Mrs. Emlyn, " Ned said he
had seen an older — person — on the beach with the
children. We came to the conclusion this was she."

" That is Sophia, the children's nurse. She was my
nurse too ; she has always lived with us. She manages
everything."

This I said with a desire to make a greater show
of respectability. I had a feeling that the colonel
would want to cancel the lease, that he would not in-
trust his premises to such an unmatronly person. I
began to feel myself more insignificant than ever.
They had come to see me under a delusion. I felt it
an incongruity that such a person as I should be called
upon. Mrs. Emlyn looked so grand and imposing. She
had almost touched the ceiling when she stood up. She
was not so very far from it now that she sat down.

" I hope you like it here," she said, " and that it
agrees with your children—they *are* your children ? "
she added, interrogatively, doubtful of all her conclusions.

"Oh, yes," I answered, most uncomfortable.

"It sounds exactly as if Mrs. Emlyn looked upon you as a fraud," said the colonel, coming to my help.

"Not at all," she returned, with decision; "but when you don't know people, you must ask questions. You don't think there is any thing to object to in being asked questions, do you?"

I tried to say I didn't, but as it was a false statement, I don't believe I made it very forcibly, and it made me seem younger and more inefficient than ever. He certainly, I thought, will take the house away from us.

"You've been ill, some of you, I take it, since the doctor sent you here," went on Mrs. Emlyn.

She certainly had very small grounds to base her conclusions on, and was not to be blamed for wishing to enlarge them. I began to think it would have been kind in the doctor to have told them something about us, but he was a great and a busy doctor, and had to be content with sketching his good deeds in outline. I told her I had been ill a good deal for two or three years, and that the children were both delicate, particularly the elder.

"Are they girls or boys?" asked Mrs. Emlyn, and when I told their ages, she looked disappointed.

"But of course," she said, "they could not be any older—" and then she made a pause.

I struggled with myself; I wanted to put myself right with these so important people; my voice trembled when I said, "I am older than you think me; I was married when I was eighteen, that is six years ago. Now I am twenty-four."

"Ah!" she said with a sigh, and a look of compas-

sion. Then, regaining herself, she said, " I was hoping
to find the children old enough to be playmates for
Naomi. We have," she went on, in an explanatory
tone, "two children, a nephew and a niece, whom we
are bringing up. The little girl is lonely, she has no
companions; but she is twelve years old. Ned has his
tutor, who is about as much of a boy as he, and they
are always out and having a good time, but Naomi is
lonely, I wish the children were older."

"I don't think Naomi pines," said the colonel.
" She is always happy enough when I see anything of
her, racing about the beach, or driving Ruby before
the beach cart."

" Yes, and how often does she get a chance to drive
Ruby? Ned and Mr. Macnally have the cart all the
time, and Naomi has to amuse herself the best way she
can. If she weren't such a good little girl she would
be whining all the time. You really don't know anything about it; I would give anything for somebody to
play with Naomi. I had set my heart upon there being a little girl about her age."

And she looked at me reproachfully. The colonel
laughed, and I, agitated as I was, also laughed a little,
and then Mrs. Emlyn began to see the absurdity of the
matter, and laughed too ; a very pleasant, musical laugh.

"You don't suit at all," she said. " You are too
young for me and the colonel, and too old for Naomi
and Ned ; and the children are complete misfits."

This made things a little easier. The colonel got
up and walked around the room and examined the wall
paper and ceiling critically.

" It isn't so damp as one would think," he said, looking around and drawing a deep breath, as if critically to test the atmosphere.

"We don't think it damp at all. I have a little fire lighted every evening in the Franklin. I am so glad there is a Franklin."

"Ah, you like it?" he said. "I had the chimney opened, and that stove brought down from the attic; the old people who owned the house had stuffed up the chimney, and put in an air-tight."

"And isn't that little corner cupboard in the dining-room nice?" I said. "Don't you want to come and look at the dining-room?"

So we went into the dining-room, and I showed them the cupboard and the little, long, narrow closet by the walled-up fireplace, and all the improvements that I had made in the arrangement of things. I am afraid the dining-room, so called, was a dismal old hole, but I liked it very much, and said so.

"Ah," cried Mrs. Emlyn, shrugging her shoulders, "I don't want any old houses to live in. I should smother in this room. Why don't you take the sashes of the windows out? They don't open more than five inches. If it weren't for being afraid of the rain I should take the sashes out."

She was much interested in everything, but she kept outside the door and did not do more than look in.

"You need some more china," said the colonel. "Penelope, can't we spare some of that old blue, like this?"

"Oh, I don't know anything about the china. Ask Rachel, she can tell you. I do not think, myself, there is any more than we can use."

While I was protesting, frightened, that I didn't

need any more china, she explained herself with gestures.
" You know there isn't any use in promising what we
haven't got. It is just like a man to make promises.
My own impression is we are rather short of blue, but
if we're not, there's no objection to your having what
you want. Only there's no use in making promises." .

The colonel didn't seem to mind at all, and said,
" We'll see," and then fell to promising me some more
piazza chairs, when we walked out there; and Mrs.
Emlyn said there was a hammock that was not being
used, if I cared for having it. She did not seem to be
exactly consistent about promising, for she pledged herself to send me, besides the hammock, an extra mattress
and two tables.

" You might as well have them," she said. " They're
doing nobody any good, and lumbering up the attic."

That took off the load of the obligation, certainly.
The colonel walked about, quite as if it were his house,
which seemed odd to me. He was a short, rather thin
man, with a prominent nose, kind blue eyes, bushy eye-
brows, a high forehead, and grizzled hair that curled
yet. One feels as if grizzled hair would have forgotten
to curl, particularly when it is thin on the top. He had
an alert manner, but in some way gave you the idea of
philosophic quiet. He dressed with scrupulous neat-
ness, but in rather old style. When they went away I
accompanied them to the gate, and felt as if we were
old friends. The children, not perceiving the august
visitors, came running around the corner of the house.

" Ah !" Mrs. Emlyn said, looking at them, " these
are the children ? They are very pretty, the eldest one
particularly. I am sorry that they're not old enough
for Naomi."

But the colonel took them up and talked to them, and seemed to like them. When they got in the carriage Mrs. Emlyn leaned out and said, " We'll send you the things when the man can be spared to bring them. And you must come and see us if you *aren't* the right age, any of you."

And then she laughed again, and they drove away.

CHAPTER IV.

ON THE SANDS.

"Upon the wings of wild sea-birds,
    My dark thoughts would I lay,
And let them bear them out to sea
    In the tempest far away."

                                    Faber.

A DAY or two after that I went down to the beach, with Sophia and the children, for the whole afternoon. Sophia took the children and sat behind the bank, and turned her back to the ocean, which she despised, and sewed. The children naturally did not stay with her, but wandered over to where I sat, close by the waves, with a great gray blanket spread out on the sand, enveloped in shawls. It was the first warm day of the season, but the wind was strong, and cool enough to make all the shawls acceptable, sitting still.

"Sitting still, and doing nothing," I know that was what Sophia was saying to herself testily as she pricked her fingers and looked over the bank at me. That was always what I seemed to be doing. Considering that the children's summer clothes were not even yet cut out, perhaps it was rather shiftless. But I was not thinking about the children's summer clothes, nor yet their winter ones. What was I thinking of as I sat there hour by hour, while the great waves broke at my feet, sucking the sand back in their retreat, and then spread-

[41]

ing it smooth again before me, while the little bubbles
burst up through it, and the sand fleas scampered across
it? I watched the blue horizon, across which, at far
intervals, a white sail drifted. I gazed up and down
the long stretch of beach, lonely and bare, and noted, at
either point, where my vision ended, the pillar of cloud
that the spray made against the far sky. I don't think
a sand-piper ran along the sand that I did not notice,
nor that a gull swept above the blue tide that I did not
follow out of sight, nor that a wave broke at my feet
that I did not curiously scan. I did not think about
the past; I did not speculate upon the future; I had
no great thoughts such as the sea seems to give to others;
I did not want any one to read or talk to me; I did not
want to read or talk myself; I liked to see the children
playing a little way from me, but it annoyed me to have
them come and prattle by me, and make demands upon
my attention. When a great wave, green and crystal,
came thundering in from sea, and burst upon the beach,
I had no greater thoughts than speculation whether the
next incoming one would be as high and would rush up
as far upon the sand. I made a pillow for myself of a
shawl; I drew another over me; it was delicious and the
sun shone warm; I lay content and idle while the half
hours lapsed away. I don't know whether it was exactly
right to be so vacant and indolent, but it seemed just
the medicine for my sick and thought-sore mind.

The afternoon wore away; the children were still busy
at a great hole which they had spent two hours in making broad and deep, when I idly saw them reinforced
by a third child—a tall, slight, girl of twelve, perhaps,
with a great profusion of yellowish-brown hair upon

her shoulders, and a sun-burned, pretty face, blue eyes, and a bang that reached nearly to her eye-brows.

"This is the melancholy Naomi," I thought, but a great wave rolled in that moment, and I returned my gaze to it, and wasted no more thought upon her. By and by the children's voices at my elbow forced me to abandon a sea-gull to its fate, and look up. Naomi stood shyly before me, with a child in each hand, her face radiant with happiness.

"Mayn't they go home with me?" she said; "it isn't far; they want to see my rabbits."

"Ask Sophia if there's time," I said, smiling up in her pretty face.

They ran over to Sophia, Naomi carrying Baby part of the way. Sophia evidently took the opposition, for Naomi and Maidy both looked extinguished, and Baby was crying and stamping with her little foot, and pulling at Naomi's hand, in the direction of the house, which rose behind the sand-hills, not quarter of a mile from us along the beach. At first I thought Sophia very cruel, but then changed my mind, and reflected how far the afternoon had waned. Certainly we ought even now to be getting ready for the march. But Sophia should settle the matter; she didn't mind breaking their hearts as much as I did, and I looked away across the opal-tinted sky and sea, and lost myself again in revery.

Not for many minutes—a whoop, a shout, I don't know what, sounded from behind the sand-hills, and looking back in the direction whence it came, I saw the young man, whom I had come to recognize as the tutor, emerge from behind them, waving his hand to Naomi, and trying to attract her attention. The beach was very wide, and I was down at the water's

edge. I pushed the shawls back, and listlessly sat watching them all; the jerks of Sophia's head, the stamps of
Baby's foot, the faces of the disappointed children, the
gestures of the new-comer, who could not get them to
see him. He was dressed as when I had first seen him;
now he carried a gun, and a game-bag slung over his
shoulder. At last he succeeded in catching Naomi's
ear, as he approached her along the top of the sand-hill.
She dropped the children's hands and flew towards him.
What he had to say to her pleased her very much, for
her face brightened, and she gave a gesture of delight.
But then her eye falling on the children, she looked
disappointed again and pointed to them. He made a
suggestion; she pointed to Sophia, and shook her head.
He shrugged his shoulders: then they both looked towards me, and after a consultation, she sprang down the
bank and came running towards me.

Meanwhile the young man threw himself down on
the beach grass and took out the charge of his gun, and
busied himself about something in the bag at his side.
Naomi breathlessly said, as she stood before me:

"Oh, please can't we take the children home in the
cart? Mr. Macnally has just come for me to go to the
village, and he says they can go too, if you'll let them.
And we'll take good care of them, and we'll leave them
at your house when we come back. Please let them
go; I'll hold Baby, myself, so she sha'n't joggle out,
and Maidy shall sit on Mr. Macnally's lap—Ruby is
very gentle, and Mr. Macnally is such a careful driver.
Please."

It certainly was a great deal the easiest way of getting them home, and I consented. Sophia wouldn't
like it, but neither would she like carrying Baby all the

half mile, home. It was only a question of degrees of disapprobation, and it seemed for once as if the children might have the benefit of the doubt, and do as they asked. I only hoped they'd let me alone and wouldn't bother me any more about it. By the arrangement, I should get a half hour more by the waves, so I pulled the shawls about me, and lay down a little more on my elbow.

But more bother was to come. Sophia came laboriously across the heavy sand to me, to utter her protest; the children looked after her in keen suspense, the young man began to take an interest.

"You don't mean to say," she said, as soon as she could speak, for panting, "that you told that strange girl that the children could go home in the cart with her and that—that—man, there?"

"Why not? Yes, I told her they could."

"I suppose you want them killed? I should as soon think of turning them adrift in a sail boat. That—man always drives as if he was pursued, and the cart's nothing but a death-trap. I won't take any responsibility about it."

"Oh, I don't ask you to. Nothing will happen to them, I'm sure; but if anything does, I won't blame you. I've told her they might go—I can't take back my word. One must be civil to one's landlord, you know."

"I know," returned Sophia, with a sort of hiss, setting her lips very tight, and turning away. I only feared there would be another reference to me, there was so prolonged a conversation, but at last I saw them go away, towards the house, Baby in Mr. Macnally's arms, and Naomi and Maidy close at his heels. They were all gazing at him with intense approbation. He was tossing Baby over his head, the last I saw of them, as they disappeared on the other side of the sand-hills. Sophia gathered up her work and went her way, without a word, leaving me to get the shawls home as I could.

CHAPTER V.

" His limbs were well set, an' his body was light,
    An' the keen-fanged hound had not teeth half so white;
    But his face was as pale as the face of the dead,
    And his cheek never warmed with the blush of the red;
    An' for all that he wasn't an ugly young bye,
    For the divil himself couldn't blaze with his eye,
    So droll and so wicked, so dark and so bright,
    Like a fire-flash that crosses the depth of the night!"
                                    Samuel Lover.

FROM that day, Naomi spent almost as much of her time at the cottage as at Happy-go-lucky; her aunt must have been gratified at the kindness with which she took to the little misfits. She put Baby to sleep, she taught Maidy her letters, she went to house-keeping with them both, out in the lilac-bush; they had tea in the barn, on the balcony, under the box-tree, everywhere, in fact, that tea could be taken. She went home, by strict orders, to the superior meal of dinner, and naturally had her breakfast before she came to us, but tea in some form and on some part of the premises, she always took at the cottage. She was a delightful little mother, and so perfectly happy in her position that even Sophia was reconciled to the intrusion, particularly as it gave her so much more time for those terrible summer clothes. She could be entirely trusted

[47]

with the children, out-Sophiaing Sophia in regard to damp grass, and being a perfect martinet in the matter of manners.

We were favored tenants. All the promised things were sent, and a great many more. The carriage stopped nearly every day to bring some vegetables from our landlord's early garden, or some fish or crabs from the bay, or some addition to our rather slender kitchen furniture. Once or twice I had gone down to the gate and received the gifts out of the carriage window from madame herself. The colonel had come in twice about the kitchen chimney, and altogether we felt that we were very comfortably placed. Our letters were brought from the mail every night by some one from Happy-go-lucky: we seemed quite taken under its wing. When it stormed, the man from Happy-go-lucky stopped to take our orders to the grocer: when we were "out" of anything unexpectedly, we had no hesitation in hailing him as he passed to the village, and making him our messenger. I had not yet paid my visit there; two rainy days and a headache had prevented.

A third rainy day was just ending; the children had been reinforced by Naomi, who had come across the fields, all water-proofed and India-rubbered. They had had their tea, in a spirit of adventure, in the garret. I had had mine alone, in the little dining-room; the wood fire in the parlor was blazing, and the lamp was lighted; I was sitting beside it with a nice book. The children were below with Sophia in the kitchen, when I heard a step on the balcony outside, and then a knock at the door. I knew it was the mail, and hurried to open it. Mr. Macnally stood there, very dripping, with a package of letters and papers in his hand, which he was assorting.

"I beg your pardon," he said, looking up and seeing me. He tried to take off his cap, but the wind did it for him, and also distributed some of the letters on the floor, as he stooped forward to catch the light, and a little stream of water ran across from the door to the oil-cloth on the hall. The gale put out the parlor lamp at the same moment.

"It's too bad," he said; "I think those are for you, but I can't be sure. If you'll let me, I'll look at them by the firelight."

So he shut the door against the blast, and, coming into the parlor, knelt down and examined the letters by the blaze from the fire, while I hurried to re-light the lamp. Just as this was accomplished, and he was handing me the letters that belonged to me, the children rushed up stairs and into the room, headed by Naomi.

"Mr. Macnally," she cried, "I thought it was you. Aunt Penelope told me that I must go home with you, or whoever brought the letters. *Can't* you wait a little while, just a little while? Please, can't he? Sophia is going to let us pop some corn; we've got it all ready. The children want to see it so—they haven't ever seen anybody pop corn—they'll be so disappointed. Won't you? Don't you think he might?"

The little ones added their clamor; in the midst of a rather embarrassed parley which they took for an assent, they, with gestures of delight, flew down-stairs and in a moment returned with the corn and with a shovel.

"It's to be done here, is it?" said the tutor, putting his ulster in the hall. "That looks as if you wanted me

3

to help you.   But I thought people popped corn in the kitchen."

"Only when they can't get a parlor to pop it in," cried Naomi, going down on her knees by the fire. "Besides," lowering her voice, "the kitchen's much more particular than the parlor here."

That was soon evident. The parlor wasn't particular. The ashes were dragged over the hearth, up to the very verge of the rug.   The half-burned sticks broke in two and rolled to the sides of the Franklin, the smoke puffed into our faces, the sparks scintillated around our hands.   The coals, which had been piled into a heap in the center, grew gray, and fresh pine and more wood had to be put on.   It was surprising how much had to be done to get things in condition to begin.   I had to find paper, Naomi had to go down-stairs for kindling wood.   We all crowded around the fireplace, and as the plot thickened, went down on our knees upon the rug.   I held Baby in my lap, and tried to keep her from getting into the fire.   Naomi held the shovel over the coals, and Mr. Macnally put in the corn and stirred it.   Maidy crowded in wherever there was least room, and looked over the lowest shoulder.   When at last the right heat was obtained, and the first grain of corn yielded to the pressure, and burst suddenly into a pretty white blossom, Maidy gave a shriek of delight, as if at a feat of jugglery.   Mr. Macnally laughed, and, pulling her into the circle, took her before him on his knee, and put the stick into her hand with which he had been stirring the corn.

"You poor little Cockney," he said, "aren't you glad you've come to the land where the pop-corn grows?"

Whenever a grain popped, both the children shrieked,

and Naomi, who was a blasé popper, laughed with pat-
ronizing freedom. The tutor held Maidy by brute
force, or she would have thrown herself into the coals
in her excitement, and it was only by a firm hold that I
kept Baby from grovelling in the ashes. By the time
the last grain had blown into whiteness, all the faces of
the party were scorched, and everybody's hands were
grimy from the ashes.

"There, Maidy," I said, "that's the last one; now
you must really get further from the fire," for Maidy,
being the stirrer, was of course in the forefront.

No, Maidy didn't want to get back; she wanted
more, and she began to cry, and say Naomi must go
down to the kitchen and get more corn.

"Why," said the tutor, withdrawing her a little
from the heat, "now's the time to eat the corn. Naomi
will get a plate."

"Mr. Macnally, why did you tell her that? Sophia
never would consent. Popped corn is highly in-di-gestible," cried Naomi, with importance. "You have spoiled
it all."

"I'm awfully sorry," he said. "At the risk of being
disingenuous, Maidy, then I must tell you it is highly
in-di-gestible, and we never do anything with it but
play it is a snow-storm. *Shall* we play it is a snow-
storm?"

Maidy was not appeased, only perplexed by the hard
words; at this moment Sophia appeared in the doorway.
I began to feel the ignominy of being on the floor, with
three untidy children and a strange man. I don't know
why Sophia's presence should have roused these feelings,
but it did; I was not accountable to Sophia. I got
upon my feet in some way, and put Baby on hers. Mr.

Macnally did the same, and as his back was towards Sophia he made a funny gesture of straightening a cravat which did not exist, and smoothing down his hair, of which there was a growth of about an eighth of an inch. Undoubtedly this was meant for Naomi's amusement, for she seemed to understand him, and giggled.

Sophia disdained to look at any of us. With her eyes averted, she told me she had come to take the children to bed. Maidy began to cry violently and cling to Mr. Macnally, in whose arms she still was. Baby struck out at her, and said "go 'way, bad thing," and held tightly the skirt of my dress.

"Isn't it pretty early?" I said, hesitatingly. "Can't you let them stay a little longer?"

I caught an amused smile flit over the stranger's mouth; his eyes were discreetly on the ground, and I could not see their sparkle. The sight of the smile emboldened me to say, "They can stay up for twenty minutes more, if you'll come back for them then."

Sophia went away without a word. It was all very well for Naomi and Mr. Macnally to look relieved and merry; it was I who would have to take it to-morrow.

"Now for the snow-storm," cried Maidy's friend, setting her upon his shoulder, and giving her a handful of the corn. Maidy showered it down with great satisfaction over every body, while Naomi gathered some of it up industriously for repetitions of the storm. By and by the supply grew short, so much of it was lost among the chairs and tables; Maidy looked dissatisfied.

"These second-hand showers, Maidy, are apt to run short. It's the worst of them. Can't we do something else to make ourselves happy?"

And her cavalier was proceeding very gently to take

her down from his shoulder, when she began to cry, liking her position.

"For shame!" cried Naomi, "when Mr. Macnally has been so good to you!"

"These second-hand mothers are hard upon little girls, ar'n't they?" he said, kissing the little hand that clung about his neck, and not offering to take her down. Naomi blushed.

"Sophia always tells me to make her mind. She wouldn't trust her to me if I didn't."

Thereupon Baby, seeing how much was to be got by crying, cried, and demanded to be taken up upon the other shoulder.

"You see," exclaimed Naomi, "somebody must be firm."

The tutor and I both laughed; I evidently didn't count for much in my household; but though I laughed, I did not like it very much.

"If your great-grandmother Naomi will permit," he said, with a bow in the direction of that young person, "I shall be very happy to have you on the other shoulder."

"Oh, yes," cried Naomi, forgetting her wrongs in a new thought. "And dance an Irish jig with them, as you did that day on the beach! Please, Mr. Macnally, it would be so jolly. Please, mayn't he? He won't make much noise."

"Why don't you ask Sophia?" I said. She was flying off, taking me seriously, when I called her back. "It isn't necessary to ask Sophia this time," I said.

"Then he may? Oh, what fun. Mr. Macnally, you will, won't you?"

"I must ask you to excuse me," he said, rather shortly.

"But the Baby?" said Naomi, snubbed. "Won't you let her have a ride on your shoulder, anyhow?"

Mr. Macnally knelt down like a camel, while I put Baby on his other shoulder. He held each one by the hand, and rose up, balancing them carefully. They screamed with delight while he gave them a ride through the circuit of our apartments. There was a great row while they were out in the dining-room; I didn't know but that the Irish jig was beginning, but they were all subdued and respectable when they reappeared in the doorway of the parlor. To get through this door, it was necessary for the camel to go down on his knees again, which he did with great ease. He had the sort of figure that gave you the impression it would be no inconvenience to him to roll himself up like an India-rubber ball and be shot off the moon; he would surely land on his feet in South Berwick if he meant to appear there.

"Now," he said, after another tour of the disordered little parlor, going down on one knee before Naomi, "if your great-grandmother will have the goodness to bear a hand—"

"I don't think that's fair," muttered Naomi, a little nettled. "I've had the care of them a great deal—"

"I know," he said, kissing one little scorched face and then another, as he set them down, "and now I think, Naomi, if you'll get your cloak and hat we will say good-night."

Naomi, and the children after her, ran down-stairs to the kitchen, which seemed to have served for Naomi's dressing-room, and where, no doubt, the judicious Sophia had put her wet water-proof before the fire when she first came in.

The stranger and I began to feel a little awkwardness, after the children went away. We had really not addressed each other directly, except in the matter of the letters, all the time he had been here. He had a down-looking, rather shy way when it came to talking to me, that seemed like a very young man. And yet, he was not a very young man, unless twenty-six or twenty-eight is very young; one felt sure he was as much as that. His lithe, slight figure, in the inevitable blue flannel clothes, made him look very boyish, but his face, when you took that into account, gave a different estimate. His cheeks were flushed now with the fire and with the romp; his eyes were keen and bright, when you could get a gleam from them; his mouth was restless with mirth that it seemed an effort to subdue, and yet I had a feeling that I was talking to a man who was at least my equal in age, my senior in experience of life.

I attempted some commonplace, as a woman is sure to do, first, while he stood by the table, looking down, attempting nothing. It was about the storm, no doubt, and when it was answered, there was another pause. The disordered room seemed to strike him.

"It has been rather unconventional for a first call," he said, not looking up, but a smile spoiling the decorum of his face. "Like a first call from a hurricane," he added, moving a chair back against the window, and setting straight a little table that had been whirled out of its corner by Naomi.

"I don't mind," I said. "It keeps Sophia in good humor to have plenty of things to put in order. It's the best thing that can happen."

"Far be it from me, then," he said fervently, putting the chair and table back to a fraction of the same angle in which they had been standing. He had a delightful little accent, English or Irish, or perhaps Canadian ; I quite liked to hear him speak, and found myself speculating as to whether I couldn't speak that way if I tried. Then Naomi and the children came tumbling into the room again, and waterproofs and umbrellas and overshoes were all that came into discussion. As the tutor knelt down to light his lantern at the fire, Maidy came up and pressed close to his side and slipped her little hand under his arm, and watched him silently. It was such an astonishing action for the shy child. When he went away, she followed him to the door and held up her face to be kissed, though the wind nearly swept her back into the room. Then she ran to the window and pressed her face against the pane, and watched the little spark as it wavered along through the darkness, in the direction of Happy-go-lucky's hospitable lights.

CHAPTER VI.

TEA, TREATED UNCONVENTIONALLY.

" 'Twas nice, of course, to hear from you
    About their wild, Bohemian ways;
  One likes to know how people do
    Who are not in the world.—"

Olrig Grange.

I HAD meant to go to pay my first call at Happy-go-Lucky, a mountain of crape; even getting out my best dress and veil from the damp little closet in the wall where they spent their days. But it was too incongruous and absurd; I could not fancy myself dragging them through the dust of the road and the damp of the grass, and appearing with dignity to make a visit of ceremony upon my landlady. So I gave the Shinnecock my flannel dress to brush with extra care for the occasion, and taking Maidy for companion, went unconventionally across the fields in the direction of the house. When we went in at the gate two or three great dogs bounced out at us, sending Maidy into paroxysms of fright, but as many men came out from stable and garden and carriage-house and called them off.

When I got to the steps of the house, I was again in doubt. Every stage of the visit had been attended with doubt; whether I should come morning or afternoon, whether I should wear crape or flannel, and now whether I should go up the front steps or the side steps, or where.

For wide flights of steps led to the broad veranda on each side of the house, and I could not distinguish any definite "front-door." In fact, the house seemed all doors and windows, mostly open ones. We went finally up the western steps, trusting, when there, to light upon a knocker or a bell or some distinguishing mark that visits were in order. The veranda was very wide, running entirely around the house; there was a roof only over certain portions of it, forming porches on each side. These were in shade at some time or other of the day, and were amply provided with chairs, hammocks and settees. At the windows unshaded by them, the sunshine streamed into rooms that, so near the sea, were all the better for it. The western porch was now flooded with the afternoon sun; no one was sitting there; if there were a door there, it was not distinguishable from a window, and was wide open. I went rather uncomfortably to the rear, where the veranda was connected with a platform that led out to the crest of the sand-hill overlooking the sea. Visitors could not reasonably be expected to enter from the ocean, so I went back and tried the north, or, more properly, the front side of the house. But here more open casements, more disarranged and untenanted chairs, and no bell, no knocker. The veranda was inclosed below, and formed the kitchen, laundry, and servants' rooms. Here I could distinguish the servants' voices, and laughter, and sounds of work. How could I make them hear me? I tried to knock on the floor with my umbrella; it probably sounded like the tap of a woodpecker, and elicited no reply. It would be unpleasant to have to pin my card to one of the posts of the porch, and go away.

As I walked up and down nervously, wondering what I ought to do, Maidy suddenly dropped my hand and went towards the western steps. She had caught sight of somebody she liked, who, however, had not as yet seen her. Mr. Macnally came up the steps three at a time, whistling, and carrying a crab-net over his shoulder. He started when he caught sight of Maidy, made a gesture as if he would scoop her up in his crab-net, and then hurried to her and stooped to kiss her. '

" What's my little lady doing here alone?" he said. She took his hand shyly and pointed with the other towards me, as I came around the angle of the house. He took off his cap to me, which he hadn't done to Maidy, worse manners.

"I'm trying to find a bell or a knocker, or a front door."

" Have we ever a front door," he said. "I never thought of it before. No, I don't believe we have. We go in—'promiscuous.' We don't have many visitors. There are not many to come, you know."

" All the same, it's awkward for them when they do. It's the first time I've been, and I ought not to be too unceremonious."

" Certainly, a first call ought to be conventional : I know it." And he took his cap off again and stood with it in his hand, and his eyes on the floor, and an unspoken jest hovering on his lips.

" How can I find out if Mrs. Emlyn is at home ?" I said, nervously, after a pause of about a minute, which seemed to me much longer.

"Might I take your card to her?" he said, and, I can't tell how, he transformed himself in a moment into the sleekest of Jeemeses, with his cap tucked under his arm, holding out an imaginary salver to take the card. All this time he didn't look at me; but the expression of his face, his attitude, the slight serving-man accent with which he pronounced the words, were a livery and knee-breeches.

"I haven't got any card," I said, almost too uncomfortable to be amused.

"Oh! then," he exclaimed, with a look of relief, resuming his natural expression, "it isn't to be strictly point device. Perhaps you will come in, this way, through the dining-room."

We went in through an open casement, and he gave me a seat, and went away to find the lady of the house. It was an immense room, running the whole length of the house. I didn't wonder Mrs. Emlyn could not breathe in my dining-room, if she were used to breathing in this. It was about forty-five feet long, with a width of twenty-two or twenty-three. The staircase went up at one end, and in the center was a great fire-place bricked up to the ceiling, with a fire even now smouldering on the hearth. The furniture was heavy and old-fashioned; one or two nice pieces of tapestry hung against the wall, and between the windows, on the panels, were crossed some swords and guns, a helmet or two, and a few pieces of armor that perhaps wouldn't bear scrutiny, but were quite effective. The floor was bare, except a rug and footstool at the head of the table. The mahogany of the table was polished very bright, but on it was the *débris* of a lunch which some belated one had recently been eating. The colonel's pipe-box, a very rude affair, was nailed up between the fire-place and a tapestry that must have cost a pretty penny. The tutor had set down his crab-net in a corner as if it were the place in which it belonged. There were fishing-poles and creels and reels in another, and under the stairs, in full view, hung cloaks and shawls and coats of all descriptions, and a perfect colony of hats and caps. The windows, which were very wide, were opened full to the strong wind from the sea and the sun now "sloping to his western bower." On one side of the fireplace was a box for wood, on the other a basket for Naomi's little Blenheim, who always slept there. A table in a corner was piled high with school-books; under it was a croquet box with the mallets sticking out from the half-closed lid. The silver on the sideboard was shining beautifully, and the window panes were crystal clean, but on the sideboard stood a dripping glass jar of sea-weeds, and before one of the windows a great tin pan, in which crabs and scallops and star-fish battled about, dismayed at their imprisonment. A pool of water, gradually widening on the handsome wood floor was not likely to improve its polish. It certainly was not an untidy room, but if one might say so, a most liberal one. All crafts and tastes seemed to have the freedom of it, and everything was tolerated but dust and dirt.

There had been sounds of knocking at many doors upstairs, and presently Mr. Macnally came down.

"I am sorry to say there is nobody in the house. I don't know where Mrs. Emlyn and Naomi have gone. It is possible that we may find them on the beach."

So while Maidy clutched his hand, I followed him out upon the veranda and across the platform to the

sand-hill, whence we could see up and down the beach.
The beach looked wide and lonely, not a human being
in sight. Maidy looked disappointed. "I want to see
Naomi's rabbits."

"Next time; we must go home now," I said, feeling
uncomfortably that I was making a call upon the tutor.

"Next time sounds a great way off. Mayn't she
come with me to see the rabbits? I will bring her back
to you in a little while."

That was not objectionable; so going down on the
beach, to be off the premises and beyond the imputation
of paying him a visit, I sat down on the sand and waited.
The afternoon was perfect, the sky and sea blue, the
breeze fresh, the air sun-dried and warm. I had just
got soothed into a dreamy forgetfulness of my recent
embarrassments, when a great shout from the sand-hill
made me turn around; Naomi was springing down, followed by Maidy, and the Colonel and Mrs. Emlyn stood
on the top, waving to me.

"You're to stay to tea!" cried Naomi, panting.
"Aunt Penelope says you are, and she's come out to
fetch you. Oh, such fun!"

And she caught Maidy in her arms, and whirled her
round till they both fell, exhausted, on the beach. Meanwhile, I got up, and hurried up the sand-hill, to meet
my host and hostess. They renewed the invitation to
tea, and Maidy and Naomi danced a war-dance around
us till the matter was settled.

"What will Sophia say; you always go to bed at
seven, and how shall we get home if it is dark?"

"Oh, we'll see to that; we'll make Mr. Macnally go,
or Ned, if he is busy. Come, Maidy, come and see the
rabbits."

Then the colonel asked me to walk around the place with him, and see the water-works, and the garden, and the stables. The hostess excused herself, and went on the piazza to read, while we went to look at these improvements. It is always a doubtful pleasure to be dragged about country places to look at improvements. It is only possession that gives a charm to rams, and wheels, and forcing-beds, and model stables. The colonel was glad to find a listener; he did not let me off from anything. He had evidently spent a good deal of money, which nobody would have guessed if he hadn't told them. The lawn looked as if it would have been the better for a little of the attention that was given to the calves and colts, and a tithe from the water-works ought to have been exacted to make a better gate and fence. But those things showed, and could take care of themselves; the things that did not show and were practically useful were what the colonel set his heart on bringing to perfection. It was a very amiable trait in the colonel's character. All the same, I was glad when the tea-bell rang, and we went back to the house. Not, however, without some pauses and procrastinations as the water tank was passed. We were so long on the way that when we reached the dining-room the lady of the house was already at the table, looking a little severe and pouring out the tea. It was past seven o'clock, but the days were at the longest; I remember it was

"St. Barnaby bright,
  The longest day and the shortest night."

The sky was brilliant with the sunset, through all the west and north windows of the dining-room, standing open. The tea-table looked very pretty, with nice

old blue china and heavy silver, but it seemed to me a
happy accident, for I never saw a table less carefully
arranged. The dishes seemed principally congregated
about the colonel's and some one else's plate, which I
later found to be the tutor's. Naomi, who had followed us in, reached across and put a glass of ferns and
daisies as near the middle of the table as she could get
it. Her hands were very dirty; her aunt guessed,
rather than saw, that they were, and told her to go and
wash them before she came in to tea. Naomi said
Maidy's were dirty too, so they made up a party, and
went off quite cheerfully to wash them.

I had a seat with my back to the fire-place, and my
face toward the windows. It seemed to me I had never
seen a room so delightful, nor windows so satisfying.
One looked over miles of green and level country, dot-
ted here and there with farm-houses, buried in thick,
low trees planted to keep off the winter winds. The
white sails of a wind-mill caught the eye; or, in the
distance, the tall church spire of a neighboring village. Beyond, against the horizon, rose a long low line of
hills, purple in the evening light. This was what one
saw of earth, but of sky, where, ever, did one see so
much? To one brought up among the hills, or bred in
city streets, it was like a revelation. It was an arch,
not a patch; a firmament, not a strip.

All this while the colonel was carving a chicken
with concentrated interest; Mrs. Emlyn was arranging her tea-cups, and I was between sky and earth,
now gazing at the glories of the west, now filled
with chagrin that Naomi did not bring back Maidy,
and feeling somehow, that the ignominy of the re-

tarded tea belonged to me. It was not a convivial thing, this sitting down three to a table laid for seven.

"I am so sorry about the children not coming," I said timidly to Mrs. Emlyn.

"Oh, I am used to it," she said. "They all know what they have to expect. If they are half an hour late, they wait on themselves. I will not keep servants on their feet all night."

Presently the tutor came in, and then the little girls, and last, just as the clock struck the half hour, Ned, a handsome, sunburnt lad of fifteen, whom I had not seen before. He gave me a shy, pretty bow when he was presented, and took his seat between his aunt and me. The servant looked up at the clock, and stolidly took her departure. It must be acknowledged she was no great loss, her services had been merely nominal before. Mr. Macnally alone looked a little anxious as she withdrew, and glanced with curiosity towards Mrs. Emlyn, I suppose to see if she were not intending to make an exception, as they were not alone. But there was no such intention. I don't think the Princess Dolgouruki would have had an exception made in her favor, in that household.

"There isn't any marmalade," cried Naomi, in a disappointed voice.

"I told you," said her aunt serenely, "that unless you asked me for it when I was in the store-room, you should not have it. I can not be interrupted at my meals."

Naomi refused to be resigned. "Maidy wants some, too," she said.

"Maidy wants nothing of the kind. You are trying to put her up to it."

"Maidy, don't you want it?"

"Mamma," said Maidy in an embarrassed whisper, "what does she mean? What is marmalade?"

Then we all laughed, and Naomi grew red.

"Never mind, Naomi," said the tutor, "we can't always be certain of our witnesses."

"*You* want some, I know. Aunt Penelope, Mr. Macnally wants some marmalade."

"What is it? I don't know even what it's like."

"It's like what you ate half a jar of last night, and that's the reason that there isn't any now."

"My fish!" cried Ned, stung by a sudden recollection. He hadn't got as far as marmalade yet, but was eating chicken and potato salad with a ravenous appetite. "My fish have been forgotten. Aunt Penelope, the cook promised them for tea. Mayn't she send them up?"

"No, that she mayn't. You know as well as I do that it's half-past seven o'clock."

"Then I suppose I'll have to go and get them for myself," and he got up and disappeared in the direction of the kitchen stairs.

The colonel watched him with a look of admiration, but I noticed he always spoke to him with a sort of severity, as became a man and a guardian. He lived over secretly in the handsome boy his past youth and its pleasures. While Ned was dishing his fish in the kitchen, Mrs. Emlyn had been brooding over the disappointment to Naomi in the matter of the marmalade. With all her majesty, she had the tenderest heart, and it destroyed her comfort to think the child was denied anything.

"You don't mind how much trouble you give," she exclaimed at last, getting up, unable to bear the rank-

ling thought any longer. Everybody had forgotten
about marmalade by that time, and while she hunted
for the right key on her bunch, and walked away like
Lady Macbeth, we all wondered.

"Aunt Penelope!" cried Naomi, divining, "I don't
want the marmalade. I wish you wouldn't get it."

And full of compunction she sprang up and ran after
her aunt, who did not look back at her.

"Macnally," said the colonel, "did I get you out
that Sauterne yesterday? No? Then while the store-
room is open, and I think of it, I'll go and look for it.
You'll want it with your fish, if Ned should ever bring
it up."

And the colonel pushed back his chair and went
away in the direction of the store-room. Mr. Macnally
glanced round the table at the four chairs pushed back,
the four napkins lying in various outspread attitudes,
the four unfinished plates, and cups of tea; and then
his eyes met mine with a look compounded of apology,
deprecation, and very keen amusement. I was very
glad he did not say anything, it would have seemed dis-
loyal. No doubt his instincts could be trusted, for I
don't suppose he thought of speaking, from the way in
which he applied himself to Maidy's entertainment
across the table, but I did not know him enough to be
sure he wouldn't, at the first moment. It was such a
situation, most men would have felt at liberty to make
a joke about it, particularly a man who seemed to have
lisped in comic numbers, if one could judge from the
habitual expression of his eyes.

Meanwhile Maidy was eating a great deal more than
was good for her; she was not used to such a bewilder-
ing profusion of nice things. I had been rather too

much embarrassed to enjoy my tea very much, but I had
enjoyed the sunset opposite me, and the novelty of
everything, and the study of human nature, though I
had not reached the stage of knowing that I studied it.
First Ned came back, bringing his fish, then the colonel
with his bottle of wine, then Mrs. Emlyn and Naomi,
each with a jar or two of marmalade. The fish seemed
such a temptation that they all began again. All except the lady of the house, who, by a contradiction that
seemed inevitable, always ate less than other people, notwithstanding her grand proportions.

"Naomi," said her aunt, "why don't you eat the
marmalade you've given me such trouble to get out for
you? You haven't even opened the jar."

"I didn't know there was going to be fish," said
Naomi, a little abashed.

"And Mr. Macnally and Maidy, that were in such
a state for it. I think it was all a conspiracy to get me
to the store-room."

"The fish was sprung upon us, Mrs. Emlyn; we
didn't know there was going to be fish. It's all Ned's
fault, he should have given us warning. Colonel
Emlyn, I'd like another slice of it, if you've no objection."

Colonel Emlyn seemed to like nothing better than
supplying those two hungry plates, and filling up the
tutor's several times empty glass; he looked severe,
but his eyes were kindly and affectionate. Mrs. Emlyn
had taken up her knitting, and sat half pushed back
from the table. Naomi's appetite was at last appeased,
and Maidy would no more of jelly and cake. Ned and
his tutor were still eating and chaffing, while they all
looked on and occasionally joined in the skirmishing.

It had been a very prolonged meal : the sunset had died down into a yellow glow that overspread the sky, but did not illuminate the room.

"Naomi, if these young gentlemen are going to eat all night, you will have to light the candles."

"Not for me," cried Mr. Macnally, "I can see my way to the Santerne, and that is all I ask."

"Well, then, she'll have to light them for me, for I've only just begun."

Naomi grumbled at having to do anything for her brother, but her aunt put her down promptly, and she spent a good deal of time in lighting the candles in two silver candlesticks with three or four branches apiece, and in setting them on the table. Maidy got down from her chair when Naomi rose to get the candles lighted, and in an innocent fashion made her way around to the other side of the table, where the tutor sat. He lifted her upon his knee, and pushed his plate back, and occupied himself thenceforth in low engrossing chatter with her, into which she entered with a sedate interest that was very pretty. Finally Ned declared himself satisfied, and as the waitress had come back, her own meal being ended, and had begun languidly to take the tea-things off the table, we moved away.

Then I was introduced into another room, that I found only second to the dining-room in interest. This was the parlor, which was separated from the dining-room by a curtain. It was on the ocean side of the house, about half the size of the dining-room, the other half being the bed-room of Mrs. Emlyn, into which this opened. It was a more civilized room than the dining-room, having walls stained a sort of old gold, with cedar wainscoting and mantel. There were several good pictures, a piano, and plenty of well-worn easy-chairs, and one or two sofas. A large square table with a lamp on it was covered with books and drawing things. To this the children naturally gravitated, as their territory; a smaller lamp and a smaller table, in another corner, seemed the quarters of their aunt. The colonel, evidently less gregarious, established himself in a great chair between the fire-place and the dining-table, on which the maid had put another lamp, and smoked and read the paper, or listened to the chatter from the other room as seemed him good. Mrs. Emlyn invited me to go out on the piazza, and we walked up and down together for a few moments.

"It is good to get the glare of the lamps out of one's eyes," she said, "and the noise of those children out of one's ears."

It was, indeed, a change from the lighted room to the solemn starlight of the dark skies, and the deep monotone of the sea breaking on the beach beyond us.

"Youth is good," she said, "and high spirits and the ferment that they bring; but at my age, one has to have frequent silences to rest one from them. You, I suppose, like it, and it doesn't tire you?"

"I am not used to it," I answered. "It might tire me, for very long. It pleases me now, because it's such a novelty."

"Wait till your children are a few years older, and you'll have enough of it. It seems a great way off, I suppose, but it will be here before you know it. When Naomi and Ned first came to us—it seems but yesterday—they were babies in the nursery; and now they are such great creatures, with wills of their own, and individuality developing one way or the other fast enough to frighten one. I'm quite easy about Naomi, she's sweet-natured, and good-brained, and a comfort. But Ned is such a strong young colt, I feel as if none of us could hold him in, or turn him, if he got started in the wrong direction. And, who knows how soon he may? It is a great thing that we have got such a man as Macnally for him. He is like a boy with him; but I am satisfied that he keeps his authority in spite of it, and that Ned studies as he never did before."

"Has Mr. Macnally been with you long?"

"Only since January. Ned had been at school, but, to tell you the truth, we had to take him away. He wouldn't study, and he would get into scrapes; silly boy scrapes, with not much harm in them, to be sure; but we were worn out with pulling him out and starting him fresh. It was all waste time, base ball and secret societies. So the colonel advertised for a tutor, and this one turned up, and he seems the very man for us. We dreaded it very much. Naomi's governesses had always been such a nuisance in the house. But really I don't know now how we could get on without Macnally. When Ned has to go, I think we'll have to have Naomi prepared for college, just to keep him."

"He is an Englishman?"

"No, an Irishman. Didn't you notice his accent? He had only been in the country a few weeks, I believe, when he came to us. I've often wondered why he came away from home. Everything about him, his clothes, and toilet things, and all that, without being dainty exactly, look like a petted sort of son. But he's a reticent fellow, after a certain point, up to which he is frankness personified. I only hope we never shall be disappointed in him."

"Ar'n't you afraid he will upset the lamp?" I exclaimed, rather irrelevantly, for I had been gazing into the room, and it was impossible not to tremble for the furniture, with what was going on.

"No," said Mrs. Emlyn, calmly, "I'm used to it. They have broken one or two, but the oil is non-explosive, and it won't hurt the floor. I've taken the rugs away from that side of the room, and there is no cover on the table. If they spoil their own books and drawings it is their look-out."

"But if they burn up my Maidy?"

"Oh, there isn't any danger; Mr. Macnally keeps her under his arm. I should always be willing to trust him with children; he seems to love them. There is one thing about him, he can always stop an uproar by a word. They don't often go too far."

We watched the uproar, till it was quenched, as she had predicted, in a magical sort of way, and Naomi picked up the sofa cushions, and pushed the hair back from her flushed face; and Ned shook himself, and got his loose flannel shirt straight above the belt, and took up a paper and settled himself to read. The tutor, meantime, did not seem to have lost his care of Maidy, who was looking elated, but a little frightened; he led her over to the piano, and took her on his knee, while he played some soft melody, and whispered songs, I should think, into her ear. Mrs. Emlyn and I walked up and down in the starlight for a little longer, and then went in to get ready for my going home.

"I am sorry to trouble anybody," I said; "it isn't very dark; I don't think I should be afraid."

"I'll go," said Ned, getting up, and looking awkwardly polite.

"You've got to study your Latin," said Naomi, officiously. "Mr. Macnally said you had. He said he'd have to take Maidy and her mother home himself; that you must study all the evening."

Ned's eyes said, mind your own business, and a good deal else, but he did not dare to be more explicit, before me. I didn't think the tutor looked particularly pleased with Naomi's zeal in the arrangement of affairs; he got up from the piano and, putting Maidy down, said Ned could be excused for the little while that he would have to be gone.

"I'm so sorry to have to trouble any one," I said, stooping to tie a handkerchief on Maidy's neck.

"You see how much you got by it," muttered Ned, as he passed by Naomi to hunt for his cap.

The colonel was fast asleep by his lamp in the dining-room, so we tried to be very quiet as we went through the room. They all accompanied us to the steps of the piazza.

"I want you to go," said Maidy, pulling at the tutor's hand.

"Didn't you hear," he whispered, "I've got to study my Latin lesson?"

Naomi went with us to the gate; Mrs. Emlyn and Mr. Macnally were satisfied with saying good-bye on the steps. Maidy was dissatisfied, and looked back reproachfully while she could see her friend by the light from the windows, and when she couldn't she began to fret and say she was tired, and wanted to be carried. Ned offered to carry her, but she wouldn't consent, and clung to my dress peevishly. I am afraid we were not so agreeable as to make Ned glad he had come, except in so far as he felt that he had circumvented Naomi.

4

CHAPTER VII.

BRINGING THE MAIL.

" This is the curse of life! that not
  A noble, calmer train
Of wiser thoughts and feelings blot
  Our passions from our brain;
But each day brings its petty dust
  Our soon-choked souls to fill,
And we forget because we must,
  And not because we will."

Matthew Arnold.

THE next evening, as I sat by the lamp in the little parlor, I heard the latch of the gate opened, and the tutor's light, quick tread upon the balcony steps. The door stood open, so he could not knock, but took a step into the little hall, and paused, in sight from the parlor door, open also. He lifted his cap, and said he had brought my letters, or, to be more accurate, my paper.

"My mail never amounts to much," I said, getting up and taking the paper, in its stale-looking wrapper, and sighing a little as I thought of how I used to watch for the coming of the mail. "All the same," I added, correcting the sigh to a smile, " I'm very much obliged to you for bringing it. Won't you come in?"

He was a little better dressed than he had been on the occasions on which I had met him; that is, he had

a coat on, and a white shirt, and a cravat. This led me
to think that perhaps he had meant to come in.

"Perhaps I ought to pay Miss Maidy a visit," he
said. "She has earnestly requested it."

"She has gone to bed; I am sorry not to give you
the excuse."

"I don't want an excuse, but a permission," he said,
taking the chair on the other side of the table, while I
sat down again. As on the other occasions when we
had been alone together, his manner lost its confidence,
and he became, though always well-bred, shy and rather
piquantly embarrassed. He seemed to need the defense
of the children to get on well with me. When he was
throwing pillows at Ned the night before he had not
seemed to mind me much, though, to be sure, I had been
on the piazza, and not actually in the room; and at the
tea-table he had not shown much embarrassment while
he ate all that fish and tortured Ned about his Latin.
These reflections made me a little less embarrassed myself; it made me feel older than he. Besides, that passing shade of thought about my want of interest in letters
that might come to me now, had its effect in making me
—what shall I say—dignified, self-respectful, apart.
The past cast this faint sort of shadow upon me, and
made me appear what was not quite natural to me, and
what I had not appeared before since I had been in this
place, devoid of old associations.

"It is quite a walk for you to the office; do you
go every night?"

"Ordinarily, I like the walk after tea. I would
rather leave Ned wrestling with his Anabasis than be
present during the struggle."

"It isn't always a victory, I'm afraid."

" Scarcely a victory, poor boy. I don't think I ever saw anybody who hated study as he does."

" Do most boys feel that way ?   Did you ?"

" I ?—ah—well, I don't know.   I liked play a good deal more than work, of course, but I took hold better than Ned.   I hadn't the same temptations as he, everybody watching me, and being so important.   There were such a lot of us there wasn't much account made of how we felt about it ; we hadn't much chance if we didn't work ; we had to strike out pretty well or we'd have gone down, and nobody to cry about us either."

" You mean at home ?"

I suppose this was passing that certain point where, according to Mrs. Emlyn, Mr. Macnally's frankness ended and where his reticence began, for, with a slight contraction of the forehead he said—yes, among his brothers and some young cousins who were brought up with them.   Then he went back instantly to Ned, and the disadvantage that it was to a boy to be made too much of.

" That seems to me the mistake about the bringing up of children in this country, in the better classes, I mean.   Whether it is that the people are new to wealth and don't know how to manage it, or are simply trying to correct the errors of their own less favored childhood, and are going too far the other way, I don't know. But it strikes me all the time that too much is being done for children ; they're not only being pampered and stimulated in their pleasures and amusements, but they're being worried over and experimented upon in their studies.   I don't mean this as regards Ned and Naomi's guardians ; circumstances have made the trouble with them."

" I don't believe I know enough of the bringing up of children here or anywhere to judge."

" I taught a little while in a school before I came to Colonel Emlyn, and I saw a great deal of it." This did not seem to be a pleasant recollection, and we had evidently again reached the point alluded to by Mrs. Emlyn. We seemed bringing up against it all the time, and I wondered whether I was catechetical, or what. I certainly did want to know something about him. He piqued my curiosity all the time. I had often found myself wondering about him ever since the day he picked Rex up by the hair. I had not made up my mind whether I thought him handsome or not, whether I thought him covertly amused at everything American, or not; whether I thought him very humble, or very proud, or secretly chafing at his inferior position; whether he thought everything the Emlyns did was perfect, even to the way they had the table set, or whether he condemned them in his supercilious British heart. I did not even feel that I knew what his opinion was of my intelligence; but I felt with a certain feminine intuition that he did not disapprove of my appearance.

" People are so hard upon American children," I said. " I suppose I ought to be studying up the subject to prevent my two from being like the rest of their relations. I've read Herbert Spencer, and Miss Sewell, and Miss Edgeworth, and I approve very much, in turn, of what each one says about the bringing up of children; but, somehow, it doesn't seem to make any difference in the way I bring mine up. Maidy has her own individual way of being naughty, and I have my own individual way of getting her over it, and none of the examples seem to fit."

"Then Maidy is sometimes naughty? I shouldn't have thought it of her, the pretty little atom."

"Yes, I suppose there is the germ of the worst American child in her."

"Heaven forbid! I am sure it is the germ of a bad little Irish girl. I can trace it in her, now you speak of it."

"Well, little as I know of American children, I know less of Irish."

"Except your washerwoman's. I didn't mean your washerwoman's, though that's the general standard of the nation here, I find."

"Naturally, when only washerwomen come here."

"It doesn't show a strong imagination to be satisfied with believing in a nation of washerwomen."

"Oh, as to that, I don't suppose anybody does believe in that, but it's difficult always to keep up a faith in what one doesn't see. Now, when one has been strengthened by seeing an Irish gentleman in the flesh—"

"If the *mise en scéne* isn't too great a strain upon the credulity," he said, and I fancied a flush passed over his face as well as a quick smile. We got out of that somehow, and back upon the mail, the post-office, the post-master, and the late hour that the train came in.

"It's absurd," he said, "having the morning paper at this hour of the night, when it might be here at noon."

"If it did not come till to-morrow night, I should not care."

"Then you never read the papers?"

"I don't care much about them, and as for letters, I get almost none. I would cheerfully sign off my interest in the post-office till September for a very small sum. I hope they don't tax me for the support of the post-office? How *are* post-offices sustained?"

"That shows, indeed, that you don't read the papers, and that you're not informed about the 'institootions' of your country. But it surprises me less to hear that, than to hear that you don't care for letters, and are not counting the hours to mail-time from the moment you get up."

"South Berwick contains all that interests me; I can't think of where a letter could come from that could interest me in the least."

"Somebody might leave you a fortune."

"They wouldn't know where to direct it, if they did."

"I suppose the lawyers would keep it in a pigeon-hole till you got back in September from your exile."

"It isn't exile. I'm no more out of the world here than I am in the city. There's nobody to take the trouble to write to me, that is the plain truth. I haven't any members of my family left; the few friends I had, when I was a girl, live so far away I have lost sight of them, and interest too, I am afraid. And as to the relations of my—my children, they are equally remote from here, and I never have known them well. I came to the city a stranger, and all the time I have spent there I have been absorbed, and selfish perhaps—a great deal of the time too ill and too unhappy to seek friends, or to endure them if they had sought me."

I felt viciously candid. I had an impulse to show him I was insignificant, and that there was no mystery about my past, only obscurity. I did not look at him, so I did not know at all how he received these unnecessary statements. I sat leaning back in my chair with my hands in my lap, looking into the fire, which now and then blazed up, and now and then sent out a little shower of sparks. Sophia had bought a cord of hickory, and the kindling was of drift-wood, which the children helped her to gather on the beach. Though it was June, we never failed to have a fire at night.

"So you'll understand," I said, taking my eyes from the fire and glancing at him with a smile, after a silence of several minutes, "why I am not likely to get many letters while I am living at South Berwick."

He was not looking at the fire, but at me, intently, but he glanced away.

"I understand," he said, in a forced sort of voice, as if he had not expected to be called upon to speak that moment; "and that you won't be overcome with gratitude for what I may bring you from the office."

At that instant a stick broke in the middle, sawed in two by a sharp little persistent blaze beneath, that had not intermitted. One end rolled across the little hearth of the Franklin stove, and toppled over on the rug. We both sprang forward; Mr. Macnally caught it by the uncharred end and threw it back upon the andirons.

"We haven't any fender; it is—"

"A burning shame," said he, shaking the ashes from his hand.

"Yes, a burning shame; I hope you'll tell the colonel and he'll have to hunt one up for us, or take out a new insurance on his house."

"I am afraid fenders are at a premium. I have

heard a good deal about it since we have been here. The colonel has bought all the old chests of drawers and three-cornered chairs and andirons within a radius of six miles; but it strikes me he has failed to find a fender."

"Perhaps, outside that radius,—don't you think he may be persuaded? I think I'll try myself."

"Should you like to go? Perhaps we might organize a fender hunt."

"Oh, that would be delightful. Meanwhile, Mr. Macnally, you are not making that fire up properly, if you'll let me say so. The stove is too shallow for a back-log; it smokes the moment that you put one on. You are used to the Happy-go-lucky chimneys, which are built on more extravagant principles."

"They certainly ought not to smoke; that dining-room affair has had enough spent on it to build an ordinary house. From what I can learn, the colonel devoted three years of his life to it."

"And does it ever smoke now?"

"Rarely; it may be said to draw fairly well, except, of course, when the wind's in certain quarters."

"The dear colonel! Isn't he nice?"

"I'm glad you think so; nobody could be nicer." This he said gravely, and with a certain earnestness.

"And Mrs. Emlyn," I said. "I think she is different from any one I ever knew. I am so unused to strangers, I was inclined to be very much afraid of her. But now I think I entirely admire her and feel almost at home with her."

"She is so devoid of self-consciousness and so genuine, she ought to inspire confidence in any one she wants to please."

4*

"I hope she will always want to please me. I should not like to be any one she didn't want to please. As you say, she is so genuine, it wouldn't occur to her to disguise the fact."

Mr. Macnally laughed a little, but he did not say anything. It annoyed me that he should think it necessary to be so discreet. Loyalty, I suppose, he would have called it, but it seemed to me only an unnecessary discretion. I concluded we would not further discuss people to whom he felt himself so bound as not to be natural in speaking of them.

When he went away, Sophia swooped in and began to bang the shutters almost before he shut the gate, and to put out the lights.

CHAPTER VIII.

IN RE BRASS.

"Le coq français est le coq de la gloire,
    Par le revers il n'est point abattu ;
    Il chante fort, s'il gagne la victoire,
    Encore plus fort, quand il est bien battu."

IT was a cold, bright morning; I wrapped myself in
a warm shawl, and walked up and down in the sun
before the house, and watched the children at their play.
Their noses looked a trifle blue, as they frisked about in
their stout little coats and tried to open the gate with
their be-mittened little fingers. Sophia was busy about
some household matter, and had left them in my charge
for an hour or so. The sun was growing a little warmer,
and when I was tired I sat down on the horseblock outside the gate, and rested. As to the children they never
seemed to tire, but purred about in contented little
games into which, I am ashamed to say, I did not even
try to enter. It rather bored me; and when I had
opened the gate *ad nauseam,* and had found Baby's
mitten for the twentieth time, I distinctly admitted to
myself that I wished Sophia would get through her work
and take the children off my hands. A good brisk walk
would have been much more to my mind.

I was sitting on the horseblock, harboring these
discontented thoughts, when I heard a shout of greet-
ing behind me, and turning, saw the beach cart, with

the children and their tutor, drawing up to the gate. Mr. Macnally threw the reins to Ned and sprang out, coming towards me. He looked quite handsome as he stood, cap in hand, before the horseblock.

"That fender-hunt," he said. "We have come to see if you will go with us to-day."

I think he was afraid of a refusal; he looked quite earnest and a little shy, and as if he were prepared to have to urge it very much. When he saw the delight which lighted my face at the prospect of getting rid of opening and shutting the gate for Baby, and assisting at Maidy's little tragedies, he looked much relieved.

"I should like nothing better," I said, "if only Sophia will come and take the children. I promised her to keep them till she got through some stupid work she's set her heart upon."

I ran in to see. Of course, she wasn't through; of course, she couldn't have them for an hour, at least.

"Oh, Sophia, you'll *have* to!" I cried, made bold by my desire to go. "It isn't every day I get a drive. You'll have to let the things wait, or bring the children in."

I didn't look at her; I knew she was desperately angry, and I ran away to get my gloves, feeling very selfish and very young. When I came back I found Baby in Naomi's arms and Maidy in her friend's, the tutor's.

"Won't you let them go too?" said the latter.

"Oh, no!" I exclaimed. "Baby has to take her nap in half an hour. It would be insupportable. It would spoil the drive."

"Then let me go, mamma—let me go. I'll be so good!" cried Maidy, in trembling suspense.

"Impossible, Maidy; you know there isn't room for you. You'll stay like a good girl and play with Baby, and I'll bring you home some wild flowers if I find some."

Maidy hid her face on her friend's shoulder and sobbed heart-brokenly. Baby meanwhile was screaming and scolding and slapping all in a breath.

"Let Maidy go, won't you?" said the tender-hearted tutor, sotto voce. "There is room, and I'll take care of her. She won't be any trouble, if you don't mind."

"It would be rather unreasonable in me to mind having my own child. Well, if you don't, she can go."

Then Baby alone remained to be disposed of. I took the poor little termagant from Naomi and ran in to give her to Sophia. But Sophia would not even turn around from the closet shelves, which she was putting in order, and look at me. I had to kiss poor Baby and set her down on the floor, and call out my directions to Sophia, without any response. Outside the door I paused, half minded to give up the drive, and go back and take the Baby up. But through the door I caught sight of the gay-looking cart, and the horse with his best harness on; Maidy's radiant face, with her arms around the tutor's neck; Ned's picturesque suit, Naomi's gypsey hat; no—I couldn't give it up. As soon as we were out of sight Sophia would pick up Baby and put her to sleep; why should I let her stubbornness spoil everything? So I went out, but with rather a troubled look.

"This seat is the most comfortable," said Mr. Macnally, putting me in the front seat. "Ned, who's going to drive?" he added.

Ned hated the back seat and being with Naomi, and showed very plainly that he wanted to. "Very well, don't break our necks for us," Mr. Macnally said, putting Maidy in at the back, and jumping in after her.

Ned got in beside me, and took the reins as if he felt a little ashamed of having been so selfish. But that didn't last long; he was too familiar with the sensation to be oppressed by it.

"It's awfully cold," he said, putting a blanket over my lap; he meant to make up by being very considerate to me. The tutor had already muffled Maidy in wraps, and held her on his knee. Naomi was holding on with both hands. I am sorry to say that was what people on the back seat had to do in that cart, when it went fast.

"How about school?" I said. "Isn't this an unusual hour for you all to be going on a lark?"

"Oh!" cried the tutor, "didn't we tell you? Well, it is an anniversary—we have so many feasts of obligation at Happy-go-lucky, it is difficult to remember. But this is a birthday, or something of that sort. For so small a family, we have a great many birthdays. This is the third since we came down from town, if I remember right."

"But they weren't all birthdays."

"They were all holidays, however, and very imperative. I don't think we could have existed if we hadn't taken holidays."

"But whose is this?"

"Shall I tell you?" cried Naomi in jerks, for we were going very fast.

There was a sound as of the suppression of these jerks.

"It isn't a birthday," said the tutor. "It's an anonymous sort of celebration; it's of doubtful origin--an apocryphal event; it isn't generally noticed in the family; but the day was fine, Ned's lessons were unusually hard, and Naomi hadn't written her French exercise. Ned, if you drive so fast I sha'n't be able to articulate another word."

"I don't see the use of articulating fibs," said Ned, bumping fast over a bridge going out of the village.

"I'll tell you; it's Mr. Macnally's birthday if you want to know," cried Naomi, in gasps, from the rear.

"'However' did you find it out?" I asked her, looking back. We slacked up now going up a hill, and Naomi was able to express herself quite audibly.

"I'll tell you all about it."

"Not if I can help it," said her tutor, throwing an afghan over her head. The smothered explanations from under it didn't enlighten me much, and Ned, who was out of reach, said, "Naomi found it in one of his books when she was snooping about his room."

"I didn't snoop!" cried Naomi, getting her head out of the afghan. "Mr. Macnally sent me up to find a book on his table, and the window was open, and a perfect gale, and all the things blowing about, and his prayer-book and his portfolio on the floor. And I picked them up and the fly-leaf was loose and I put it back and it had the date on it, and I couldn't help seeing. I don't call that snooping."

"No harm done, Naomi," he said. "We shouldn't be here but for that fly-leaf and that gale. It's an ill wind that blows nobody good."

"I told Aunt Penelope about it, and she said we should have a holiday, and Mr. Macnally didn't want to, and got quite in a pet about it, and talked to Uncle, and said he couldn't do us any justice if we had so many holidays, but Aunt Penelope wouldn't give it up, and said she'd—"

"Come, Naomi," said the tutor decisively, "tattling's as bad as snooping. We're here, and that's enough."

"*Where* are we, please? For I don't think I've ever been out on this road before."

We were now in a sandy road leading through a forest. The wind could not get at us, and it was quite warm and sheltered; and having to go slow on account of the sand, Mr. Macnally and Naomi got out and walked along beside us. I also think they were glad to be excused a little while from the back seat. The foliage of the trees was not very heavy and the sun came down warmly through them. The woods were full of ferns and squaw-vine in bloom, and huckleberry and blackberry vines in blossom, and new leaves of all sorts of pretty shades. Naomi had the happiness to find a strawberry, nearly ripe. Maidy got down too, and walked. At last the road grew harder and Ned insisted that they should all get in again, "if we wanted to get back to-night."

The wood seemed endless; but I, being on the front seat, didn't want it to end particularly.

"Turn to the left, Ned," said the tutor. "There's a hamlet over in that direction that I want to beat up for fenders."

Presently we came upon a little opening in the woods, and then a field or two, and then, on slight rising ground, we came in sight of a large, old-fashioned farm-house, with a fence around the front half of it, and the rear half open to a road, which led up from the highway. There was a colony of out-buildings, more or less shabby; but the front of the house was trim, and had box-wood borders to the path, and some flowers in raised beds, and some hydrangeas in big green boxes on each side of the door. The small panes of the windows, and the fan-shaped light over the door, at each side of which there were little fluted pillars, all looked like pre-air-tight antiquity.

"I am sure they must have fenders here, if anywhere."

"'Just the place for a snark,'" the tutor cried, leaping out. We all waited anxiously while he knocked respectfully at the door.

"Louder, louder," called Ned and Naomi, after we had waited a great while.

They called louder, and he knocked louder, till one would have thought the panel of the door must yield.

"Try the other door." The fence that separated the front from the back of the house was a high picket; the gate was barred.

"No connection with the corner store," said the tutor. "They live here in the morning, when they do their work, and in the front in the afternoon, when they have their 'good clothes' on, and they don't speak to themselves if they meet in the passages."

"Try the other door; it's too cold to wait all day," cried Ned. He put his hand on the fence, and leaped over it, and scrambled through long grass and many shrubs, to the front door. He pounded long and loudly there, but got no answer, and came back at last, shaking his head.

"They know what we've come for," he said, "and they've barricaded themselves in up in the attic. I can see a frieze of fenders through that little dormer window, and the end one is all bristling with andirons, and tongs and shovels. All such lovely brass."

"You don't half knock," said Ned. "If you'll come and hold this horse, I'll make 'em hear."

"Very well," said the tutor. "You may try your fist at it and welcome. Mine's used up."

So he sprang back over the fence, and stood by the head of the horse while Ned got out and went up to the door with the valor of fifteen. While he was furiously knocking, Mr. Macnally sprang up and took his place beside me,

> "Qui va à la chasse
> Perd sa place,"

he said, as he gathered up the reins; "come, Ned, they've all gone to a funeral, even the dogs and cats. It's nothing but a waste of time." When Ned turned around and saw the trick that had been played upon him : "All right," he said good humoredly, as he got up behind; "I'll pay you up for it yet." Not a dog had barked at us, the house was as deserted as if no one had ever lived in it, and yet we saw a thin curl of smoke issuing from one of its chimneys as we drove past and looked anxiously back at it. The next house to which we came was a miserable, unpainted little place. Ned had only got down when a woman and a troop of untidy children came out to see what brought us.

"We are looking," said the tutor blandly, "for a brass fender. We thought perhaps you had one to dispose of."

"Lor, no," said the woman, deprecatingly, as if a brass fender were a patent of nobility. "We haven't

got none of them things. Did you try to the Squire's
jest above here?"

"We tried, that is, we knocked—a little—at the
door, but we think they must be out—or something.
Nobody came to answer."

"The three girls is deaf. You should a knocked
quite smart and lively."

"Ah, yes. That possibly was our mistake. We must
try again. In the meantime, perhaps you have something to dispose of—"

"Early potatoes, do you mean, or garden sass?"
asked the woman. "Well, not now, but we shall have
next week or thereabouts."

"I didn't mean in that line, exactly. We want
something old-fashioned, you know—something in
brass. You haven't any candlesticks or snuffer-trays or
andirons or even bellows with brass noses? Anything
in brass, you know. Even a warming-pan, if you should
have one that you didn't use."

The woman shook her head. "We haven't got
anything but one brass candlestick that one of the
Squire's girls give me last housecleaning, and that's
been broke and sodered up again, and broke again."

"Oh, let us see it," I cried. "Do you think it
would do for a birthday present?"

"Depends upon what kind of a birthday it was;"
returned the woman.

"If it wasn't much of a birthday, do you think it
would do?" said the tutor, insinuatingly.

"Might."

"Please bring it," I cried. The woman brought it,
while the children in the cart tittered, and the children
by the gate gazed, open-mouthed. She certainly had

not undervalued it. It was very lame and battered, but I bargained for it, and carried it off at twenty-five cents. We all agreed it was best to go back to the Squire's, and wait till some one appeared at a door or window, whose attention could be arrested, and then appeal to some other sense than that of hearing.

"I'm prepared to camp out in the front yard," said Mr. Macnally. "Maidy and I can live on very little. We could fast for a week without much inconvenience. In that time, some one would, no doubt, come to the window."

We went back, and again drove up to the rear door of the house. Ned, for form's sake, got out and began to knock a little, faintly. Very promptly the door was opened, and a tall, grizzled old man appeared in the door-way. Ned was so taken aback he could not speak, and the old man looked inquiringly from one to the other of us. He was so dignified and well-mannered that we-were quite unnerved.

"This is brazen, indeed," said the tutor, low, while Ned stammered, something, helplessly. "I should as soon think of asking the colonel to sell me his water-wheel, or his favorite calf."

"Somebody must help him," I murmured; and then, in despair, leaning forward, I said quite loud:

"Oh, please, sir, if you will excuse us for troubling you—but we're greatly in need of a fender for a Franklin stove. Somebody told us you had some old things of that kind, and we took the liberty of coming."

He came forward and said he should be very glad to oblige us; he thought perhaps he had such a thing in the garret; he would go and look. The girls, he said, were a little hard of hearing, but perhaps we'd come inside and wait. We declined this offer, and he turned into the house, followed by Ned, who did not think it would be polite for everybody to say no. The host showed him into a sitting-room, and then closing the door, went up into the attic for the fender. The sitting-room was not empty; an elderly woman, with a cap on, sat darning stockings by a stove. When, at last, she saw Ned, she got up and apologized, in a very low voice, and said she was a little hard of hearing, and sat down again to her work. She looked up at him occasionally in a pleasant manner. Ned felt restless, and as if it weren't very civil not to be making a little conversation with her, when she looked so pleasant. He was embarrassed, and overlooking the fact that she couldn't hear him, the next time he caught her eye, he said, in reference to a mosquito-bar at the window, which he had been looking at: "Are you much troubled with insects here?"

She looked perplexed, got up and came softly to him, and said very low: "I'm a little hard of hearing," and put the left side of her cap quite near his mouth.

Ned regretted very much that he had looked at the mosquito-bar, or had caught her eye; but he bravely repeated his insipid question, and repeated it again; but all without effect. She shook her head softly, and said she must go and call her sister Betsey—she couldn't understand.

While she was gone out of the room, Ned almost resolved he would go out and get into the cart, and leave it to somebody else to do the shouting—but he was still afraid of being impolite, and stood his ground, though redder in the face than was usual with him.

Presently the old woman returned, accompanied by

her sister. This one was shorter and broader than the other, and had a large hooked nose, with which she took snuff.

"Abby is a little hard of hearing," she said, below her breath. "She didn't quite understand; what was it you was saying?" And she also put her ear very close up to his face.

"I only said, are you much troubled with insects here?"

She indicated by a nearer approach to his mouth and a questioning motion that she wanted it repeated once again.

He repeated it once, twice; she shook her head. Abby, looking on anxiously, shook hers too.

"I can't quite catch it," she said. "I must go and call my sister Phœbe."

So she bustled out, and Miss Abby stood by, perplexed and watchful. If she hadn't been there, there is no question that he would have escaped by the front door. But she stood quite close to him, with her troubled old eyes on his face.

"It's very inconvenient," she said, in a low tone, "very inconvenient, being hard of hearing."

"It is, very," groaned Ned; but he wouldn't be entrapped into saying anything more.

By the time Miss Betsy returned, accompanied by Miss Phœbe, the beads stood on Ned's forehead. There was such a hoarseness in his voice that no wonder Miss Phœbe had to ask him to repeat the hideous formula over and again. She was quite young, compared with her sisters, not more than sixty-five, with a very insinuating smile, and quite a color on her cheeks. She evidently was less deaf than they, for she got a word at last.

"Troubled?" she said. "Just try again. Troubled? our dogs have got at your sheep? No! Something about the mowing machine, perhaps? No! Just say it once more, if you please!"

The two others stood close up to them, with wrinkled faces full of solicitude. Every time Miss Phœbe shook her head, indicating failure, Miss Abby and Miss Betsey shook theirs in sympathy. It was a dreadful situation. Ned groaned and glanced despairingly around, and gathered himself up, and gave one final shout. It seemed to him the words did not mean anything; he hated them; he would have liked to have dug them out of the dictionary; it was like a night-mare.

"Are you much troubled with insects here?" He put his mouth quite up against her yellow old ear, he roared, bellowed, thundered the words into it. "I only said, 'Are you much troubled with insects here?'"

Miss Phœbe heard; she dropped off from him, for she had laid her hand upon his sleeve, and said "Oh!" in a tone of mingled contempt, relief and incredulity. She repeated it to Miss Betsy, who said "Oh!" too, in a tone expressing exactly the same feelings, perhaps the contempt a little accentuated. Then it was repeated to Miss Abby, whose "Oh!" was more contemptuous, relieved and skeptical than her sister's, as her suspense and anxiety had been of longer duration. She turned her back to him and picked up her darning, and sat down almost with a jerk.

"I'm very sorry," began Ned, hot and wretched; but when Miss Phœbe projected her ear at him, he turned and fled. When he got outside, he found us embarrassed with our riches. A fender barricaded his way into the cart ; a pair of andirons occupied his seat. I held a shovel and tongs, and Mr. Macnally had a warming-pan over his shoulder, mounted very high. The polite old Squire (whose hearing was perfect) was trying to find a place for a spinning-wheel between Naomi and Maidy. Naomi had a brass candlestick in each hand, and looked a little anxious for her personal safety.

" It'll ride there," said the farmer.

" But where'll I ride ?" muttered Ned, anxious for unspoken reasons to get in.

" What's the matter with Ned ?" cried Naomi. He said something that sounded like " Hold your tongue, can't you ?" but it wasn't loud enough for anybody to be sure, and left ground to hope that he was not such a brute.

" I hope you'll call again," said the Squire, with mild politeness, bowing us off.

" I know there's some of us that won't," muttered Ned ; but it was not till we got down the hill and out of sight that we heard his reasons for not wanting to. When we drove through the village with our spoils, we were the objects of much friendly comment. I think no more absolute nonsense was ever talked than during that last two miles, and no more riotous laughter ever heard. We were in what the country people call a " gale," and none of us had a right to be over sixteen. When we reached the gate of the cottage Rex flew out at us furiously, and refused to recognize us.

> " If I be I, as I do hope I be,
>   I've a little dog at home, and he'll know me,"

said the tutor, as he got out, trying, with the butt end of the warming-pan, to protect his knickerbockers from the infuriated little poodle. While the others were unloading my share of the plunder, I caught the dog up and ran to incarcerate him in the dining-room. Naomi followed me up the balcony steps and into the parlor with the candlesticks.

"Here are all three," she said, "the broken one and all."

"Oh, that reminds me, I want you all to come and take tea with me to-night, you and Ned and Mr. Macnally, to celebrate the birthday, you know. Here's Baby, just awake, bless her little heart; I can't go down again to tell them, for I've got to take her. Remember, you must come at half past six o'clock."

Naomi screamed with delight, and ran headlong down the steps of the balcony, and didn't stop till she got outside the gate.

"Mr. Macnally, Mr. Macnally, listen!" she cried. "I've got something to tell you. A message, hear—"

I was holding Baby, by the parlor window, quite out of sight myself. Mr. Macnally was standing out by the edge of the road, and Naomi at the gate. He dropped the warming-pan, and a pair of andirons which he was putting in the cart, and put himself in an attitude and laid his hand on his heart, and gazed at Naomi, waiting for the message.

"We are invited," she said impressively, "invited here to take tea to-night, to celebrate your birthday. Do you understand?"

. He made a somersault, and came up on his feet, just before Naomi, with his hand on his heart and in the same attitude of abandoned devotion. He said

5

something which I did not catch, and then Naomi cried, " Well, I'll go and tell her."

She came and shouted up the stairs, " We're all coming; I've got to go now, so good-bye."

I watched them drive off, and said to myself " The mystery is solved. *The trapèze !*"

CHAPTER IX.

KEEPING A BIRTHDAY.

"Alas, the happy day ! the foolish day!
Alas, the sweet time, too soon passed away !"
William Morris.

"———the sense
Of exile from Hope's happy realm grew less,
And thoughts of childish peace, he knew not whence,
Thronged round his heart with many an old caress."
Lowell.

"SOPHIA, the children from the other house are coming to tea.

"What, that long-legged boy ?"

"Why, he's long generally. I don't see anything out of proportion in his legs. What can we have for tea ? They have such lots of things for tea down there, I don't know what they'll think of ours."

This assured us a good tea. I could not confess to her that the tutor was coming, for I knew she actively detested him, but I smuggled an extra plate and cup and saucer on the table when it was time for them to come, and I left it for her to suppose that his coming was unpremeditated, and that he had been invited after he came in, as was no more than civil. Notwithstanding her disgust and anger at his presence and at my selfish conduct of the morning, she did not manage to depress us very much. We had a very merry little tea,

[99]

with Maidy and Baby both at table, and Ned enough at home to eat as much as he wanted. After tea we had the pleasure of building a fresh fire in the Franklin and of trying the new fender.

"'Four feet on a fender,'" said Ned, leaning back in a low chair and putting a pair of very dusty shoes upon it.

"What's the objection to hind feet?" said Naomi, who was sitting on the rug and holding Rex, and she put his hind paws up beside the dusty shoes.

"What's the use of always trying to be so deadly clever?" snarled Ned, giving the dog a push with his foot.

"It's you who were trying," said Naomi, enfolding the dog in a motherly embrace.

"Let dogs delight," said the tutor. "Celebrate my birthday by an absence of rows to-night."

"Talking of birthdays; where's the candlestick? Maidy, go and fetch it. I left it on the table in the hall.

Maidy brought it. "I tried to clean it," I said, "but it hasn't a great luster."

"It puts my eyes out," said the tutor, shading them.

"That horrid break," I said, "and the patching up. I wish I had a ribbon that I could tie around it. Here's one on my fan. I'll have to spare you that."

There was a bit of lilac ribbon by which my fan hung from my belt, so I loosened it and tied it round the candlestick in a pretty knot, and hid the defacing sodering, and all that; then we set it on the mantel-piece and lavished a great deal of admiration on it. The children were rolling about on the rug with Rex.

Ned had withdrawn his dusty shoes to the other side of the room, and was looking over some pictures at the lamp. Mr. Macnally put more wood on the fire, and opened the doors and windows, for it was growing warm. Naomi started up from the rug.

"Let's play cartoons, or consequences, or something, won't you? Mr. Macnally likes games; I assure you that he does."

"And his taste must be consulted on at least one day in the year."

"Well, but you *know* you like it; you've often said you did. We only want some paper and some pencils; please, dear hostess, and we'll tell you how."

We had altogether a very jolly evening; Naomi and Ned were both clever with their pencils, and as to the tutor, I abandoned the trapeze theory and concluded he was a member of the Royal Academy, collecting in disguise studies for the next year's exhibition. I have those cartoons yet, yellowed, dusty. I do not laugh when I look at them now, alas! . . .

The "gale" had expended itself; we could not laugh so many hours consecutively. The children were sleepy, and Naomi and I carried them off to Sophia to be put to bed. Nothing would have induced Sophia to come into the room, I am sure. When we came back we found Ned had settled himself into a book, and the tutor was standing with his hand on the mantel-piece gazing into the fire. I sat down in a low chair and Naomi knelt down on the rug and put her pretty yellow head against my shoulder.

"What a nice day we've had! I like holidays. When does *your* birthday come?"

"Oh, Naomi, don't ask me. I don't want to remember my birthday. I don't keep it any more."

I tried to speak lightly, but a quick expression of pain contracted my face. It was three years since I had kept my birthday with anything but tears and bitter recollections. All the joy and merriment of this day seemed frightful to me at that reminiscence. Had I grown childish; had I lost all sense of my bereavement in this sudden lightening of heart? No wonder Sophia despised me and avoided me; I hardly knew myself. I could scarcely keep back my tears; I trembled and was pale. I had an impulse to go into the dark room where the children slept and take them in my arms, and cry over them and ask them to forgive me for having forgotten for so many careless hours.

Naomi went on prattling; Mr. Macnally walked over to where Ned sat at his book, and talked with him about it. Naomi's questions were torture—Where were you your last birthday, where were you before? Did you use to get many presents? Was that little turquoise ring you always wear one of your birthday presents? It was the prettiest little ring. How many years since the birthday that you got it? There were two stones that were turning just a little green; it must be a good while that you have had it on. How long do you think? What does it mean when a turquoise turns green? Does it mean you have forgotten about the person that gave it to you, or that they have forgotten about you?

"Naomi," said the tutor, a little quickly, "Ned's found a picture of that basket-fish that washed up on the beach the other day. Come and look at it."

"In a minute," said Naomi pensively; "I'm looking at some rings. Do you believe—"

Naomi loved sentiment more than she loved natural history; she wouldn't have made the exchange so promptly as she did, if the tutor's voice had not had a tinge of authority in it which she and Ned knew better than to disregard.

"Yes, but I want you to come now, while I am explaining it to Ned. You bothered me enough about it when you found it, when I hadn't any illustration of it."

He made the explanation a tolerably long one, and I had time to recover a little from my agitation. It was probably the reaction from a long day of excitement, and the great change from my ordinary days, and my nerves were not yet as strong as I supposed them. When Naomi made a move to come back to the fire, Mr. Macnally took out his watch, and she understood, from his gesture, that she must go and get ready to go home. Even this little sympathetic help, and the sense of being shielded from what was really such a trifle, unnerved me. I must have cried if they hadn't gone without many more words, which happily they did. But a good night's sleep restored my nerves, and a day or two brought me back to the common-sense basis of being happy when there was so much to be happy about.

From that time, there was a great deal to be happy about. The returning tide of health, the absence of care, the friendship of good people, the companionship of quick and clever minds, the exhilaration of an unrivalled air, the stimulant of beautiful scenery, formed a pretty good foundation for a happy summer. It was not very gradual, the intimacy established between the

cottage and the big house.   We were not long in finding out that a day was incomplete when there were no
hours spent in common.   Two days in the week I read
German with Mrs. Emlyn.   I was the most indifferent
German scholar in one sense, but no one could read
with her, and be indifferent in interest.   Her mind
was so quick and her love for language so enthusiastic,
she inspired even the dullest and most timid.   It was
like being pushed along by a swift skater, the exhilaration
made one forget the ignominy of not being able to do it
one's self.   My enjoyment gave her pleasure and
made her pardon my inefficiency and want of training.

I was a favorite with the colonel, who often took
me with him in long drives about the country.   Mrs.
Emlyn feared horses, and hated driving, and when
Naomi was in school and could not go with him, he
was always glad to come for me.   In the afternoon,
when the children and Mr. Macnally were free, we
often went on excursions, long sails on the bay, crabbing or fishing expeditions, walks when it was cool, or
more often drives to distant villages, which did not end
till after dark ; and when there was no question where I
went to take my tea.   I had long ceased to care by which
door I entered the hospitable house, or what time I came,
or in what apparel.   There was a high chair for Maidy
always standing in the dining-room now ; even Baby
had her private establishment in that generous apart-
ment, and knew under what table to look for her box of
blocks and picture-books.   Rex no longer barked when
at home the tutor came up the balcony stairs three
steps at a time, or when Ned thundered at the door and
shouted " Fenders !"   Naomi could pull his ears, and
Mrs. Emlyn tread on him in her near-sightedness with

perfect freedom. He understood the consolidation of interests, and behaved much better than Sophia, who would not allow herself to be drawn into the vortex of intimacy which had engulfed her betters. I am sure she could not have helped being gratified with the improved health of the children, nor with her own exemption from care and labor; but she never acknowledged it, nor ever ceased to fret for the time when we should leave this mouldy shanty and go back to the city.

I remember particularly the effect one of these tirades had upon me. It was a lovely July morning, warmer than most days in that bracing climate. A strong breeze from the sea tempered the heat of the sun. I was on the balcony with my work, Mr. Macnally was sitting in the hammock, with his gun leaning against the railing, and a game-bag over his shoulder; Naomi was playing with the children at the foot of the steps; Ned was busy loading some shells on the horse-block, Rex was lying on the edge of my dress, newly washed, and white and fluffy, with a blue ribbon on his neck. The sunshine fell on the gray floor of the balcony through the leaves of the trumpet-creeper, and here and there lighted up one of its long red blossoms. The roll of the sea sounded far off and dreamy; its blue line was faintly seen across the green and level meadows. The children's voices were a happy music in my ears. The wind that kissed my cheek was soft as velvet. I leaned back in the low chair in which I sat, and drew a long breath of content. At that moment in the doorway appeared the spare figure of my faithful Sophia, to present to me the other side of life.

Sophia was about middle height, spare of flesh, and

5*

quick of movement. Her complexion was dark, her eyes of a dull black, but very penetrating. I always felt as if I had done something wrong when I met them, not that she always meant to be accusing me, but there was something in them that stirred an uncomfortable sensation in my whole being, which I wrongly perhaps, attributed to the workings of conscience. She had an uncomfortable power over me, of which she was quite unconscious. Whether it were her stronger will, or some psychological influence that we have not yet got a name for, she could at any time, when my health was not at its best, make me do anything that she chose. And even when I was in my best estate, she could throw a blighting shadow over very happy hours. My face clouded as soon as I saw her standing in the door-way, and found her eyes fixed on me.

Sophia was rather a good-looking woman. I often wondered whether, to other people, she was not quite pleasant to look at. The children loved her, and they would not certainly have loved her if she had not been pleasing to them. I fear it was with me an antagonism of temperament that put us both at our worst. Her black hair was slightly mixed with white, but she wore it neatly, and she was always dressed rather above her station, though with simplicity. Her forehead was low and her hair grew off from it in a cowlick, which prevented it from being parted in the middle. Her nostrils were thin, and moved with every breath and every emotion; indeed, they had much more active expression than her eyes.

"Well, Sophia, what is it?" I said, for she stood without speaking.

It was no matter, she had thought I was alone.

"Oh, Mr. Macnally will excuse us. Is anything wrong?"

"Nothing but these," she said, bringing forward two or three pairs of the children's shoes, covered heavily with green and yellow mould.

"Oh! why don't you put them in the sun to dry. It was a pity to have shut them up."

"They have only been two days in the nursery closet. And it is about that that I came to speak to you. That room's not fit for the children to sleep in. The paper's peeling from the walls. I've taken up the carpet and hung it in the sun three times this summer, and yet it's always cold when you tread on it. I never saw anything but a cellar that compared to that room for dampness."

"It seems to agree with them particularly well however, they've never been so well in all their lives before."

"You'll have to speak to Colonel Emlyn to have the chimney opened, if we stay here till the end of August. I wouldn't undertake to bring baby through those damp August rains without a fire to dress her by."

"The poor colonel! He has spent the rent twice over on the kitchen floor and the pump and the roof of the wing; I shouldn't have the face to ask him about the nursery chimney, Sophia."

"As you please," said Sophia, with nostrils flaring.

"You can bring her into my room to sleep," I said, "and dress her there. It is always warm and comfortable."

"About these shoes. Are you going to have them half-soled? If we stay here six weeks longer, they will just about last them through; but something must be done; you can't get anything to fit them here."

" Then can't we send to town ?"

" For six weeks?—that wouldn't be worth while."

She gave me a searching look. I felt the little shoes were only an excuse to fret me ; she knew much more about the nursery properties than I, and never consulted me but for purposes of her own.

" I'll take them to the shoemaker in the village to be mended," I said, and took up my sewing. Mr. Macnally met my eyes as I looked up in a moment to assure myself that she was gone. They asked me a question so plainly, that I answered involuntarily.

" I can't help it, I owe her everything ; and if I didn't, I shouldn't dare to say a word. What should I be, left without her? People must pay the penalty of being inefficient."

" You're not going to let her take you away from here in six weeks?" he said.

" Well, if she does, she may prepare to bury me, for if I go back to that horrible city and live the life I have been living there I shall die. We won't talk of it," and I gave a sort of shudder.

" But the first of September; it is such tyranny;" he repeated.

" I shall die; that will be all," I said.

" We shall all have resort to the happy dispatch," he said, getting up, and lifting his gun to go. " Have you any idea," he added, pausing as if irresolute, and, to occupy the irresolute moment, bending back the barrel of his gun and looking into it, " have you any idea how much you yield to this sort of pressure? I have often wondered."

" I suppose everybody thinks me weak," I said,

biting my lips, and pushing the needle in and out of
my work, aimlessly.

"I don't know what everybody thinks; and I don't
suppose you mind what I think."

"Why shouldn't I mind? I don't know so many
people."

"Well, in a very small world I suppose I might
count for one," he answered, with a compression of the
lips, perhaps from the effort of snapping the gun back
into its place, still standing half turned from me.

"Oh, you count for a great deal more than one, in
my world. You would be lecturing me, if you knew
how much more. You ought always to tell me what
you think, if it isn't too bad."

"My thoughts always honor you," he said, with a
sudden strange sincerity, more startling from the contrast to his ordinary gayety of manner. This time he
turned quite away, and, stooping to pick up his cap
which had fallen to the floor, he went towards the
steps. We were on the sort of terms when goings and
comings were not necessarily attended with much
explanation. We should probably meet two or three
times again to-day; so while he went down the steps, I
silently resumed my sewing, and pondered deeply on
the few words that had escaped him, beginning with
the question, Had I any idea how much I yielded to the
influence of Sophia? It was very unusual for him to
say things like this. I could scarcely remember when
he had said anything so personal before. He needn't
have told me all his thoughts honored me, for I knew
it. He had put me on a very high pedestal, I felt.
With all our intimate freedom of intercourse, there
was always a silence about myself, that was a sort of

homage I vaguely liked. He could listen; I was almost capriciously confidential sometimes, for he was a person who inspired you to talk about yourself; but he did not respond; he did not ask me questions, he did not lead me further by any words. I felt a great liking for him, a great interest in him. He was cleverer than any one I had ever met before; he was the gayest, brightest element that had ever come into my experience. Delightful as the life was at Happy-go-lucky, it was impossible not to see that it was he who gave to it its greatest charm. In some ways of looking at him, he seemed the embodiment of youth; in others, there was a man's intensity and reticence. I sat with my eyes on my work, when Naomi called up to me:

"Aunt Penelope said you were to come to tea to-night. Did Mr. Macnally tell you?"

"No. Why to-night especially?"

"Somebody is coming up from town, who, I can't remember. Mr. Macnally, what's the name of the company that's coming up to-night?"

But Mr. Macnally and Ned were already off, out of hearing. It was Saturday, and Ned was very jealous of infringements of his holiday. His tutor had a sort of conscientiousness about him that one could not help respecting. He probably hated to go tramping off in the sun; but the care of the boy never seemed out of his mind.

"I'm paid for it," he said once, when I reproached him with leaving us. He had not been bitter about it, rather jolly, looking back and saying from over his gun:

"My own convenience counts as *nil:*
It is my duty, and I will."

CHAPTER X.

EN GRANDE TENUE.

"For innocence hath a privilege in her
To dignify arch jests and laughing eyes."
As You Like it.

SOPHIA'S unhappy jealousy of the other house did not prevent her desiring me to appear my best when I went there, and though she often looked as if she were capable of powdering the peaches with arsenic, she was always careful that everything should be in the best order, when they came to us. I have known her to work a whole day to prepare a good tea for them, when it seemed as if she hated every member of the family with bitterness enough to kill them. That afternoon, therefore, it did not surprise me to find that, having overheard the invitation Naomi gave me from her aunt, she had spent an hour pressing out a pretty white muslin dress that had been in a trunk all summer, and which was the work of her own hands in the early spring, when we had first talked of coming to the country. She had wonderful skill in such matters, and could reduce a fashion-plate to fact unerringly. The afternoon was so unusually warm that I had slept, and was just arousing myself to the necessity of getting ready to go, when she entered the door with the dress on her arm.

"Should I better wear that?" I said.

"I don't know why not," she said, putting it on the bed. "It's the only warm day we've had, and we mayn't have another. Goodness knows, if I'd thought we were coming to such a place as this, I shouldn't have spent a week's work on your dress."

"It's sweet," I said, touching the flounces affectionately. "Come in by and by and fasten it on for me, won't you? I can't manage that handkerchief alone."

When my hair was dressed and I was ready for her, she made some excuse and came back into the room, and lifted the dress over my head and fastened it on for me. It was picturesque and pretty, though very simple, made with a short round skirt, with ruffles at the bottom, a round waist, sleeves to the elbows, with ruffles, and a handkerchief of the same material folded across the bosom. I was slender and tall enough to make it becoming; it was so long since I had seen myself in anything that was, that I flushed with pleasure as I stepped back, and saw the whole effect. Then I glanced guiltily at Sophia to see if she had seen the flush, but she hadn't; she was looking with an expression almost of satisfaction at the details of the dress. Then she went away, and brought me a pair of slippers from the trunk.

"They'll be dusty by the time I get there," I said insincerely; it really gave me pleasure to think of putting them on.

"You can see yourself what a figure you'd make, with walking boots, in that short dress. Be careful and walk in the path, that's all that's necessary."

Then she raised her eyes, and began to criticise the part that was not the work of her own hands. "You've got your hair too high," she said, and with both hands, not ungently, she pressed down the light-brown mass, till the contour satisfied her correct eye.

"You're the only woman," she said involuntarily as she looked at me, "that I ever saw that could spend twelve hours out of the twenty-four in the hottest sun that blazes, and not have your skin the worse for it. Your throat's just as white as your shoulders, and your face isn't a shade darker than it was when you went to school. Baby's going to have a skin just like yours."

"And poor Maidy's always scorching up; her very eyelids burn."

"That's like her father; she's got his light-blue eyes, and that same sort of hair—but Baby's eyes are grayish-blue, like yours, and her lashes are long and dark, like yours. She'll be the prettiest, if she's spared."

Sophia was always conscientious about that clause: she ended every allusion to the children's near or distant future with a proviso about their being spared, as if some hideous gardener were cultivating the earth, with a prejudice against children, whom he weeded out with a liberal hand, and as if it were only an oversight when one here or there was "spared."

She went again to the trunk, and came back with a parasol. "You'd better use that thing up," she said, "it's getting yellow."

I had forgotten its existence; it was a piece of my wedding finery, a broad, pongee parasol, with a deep ecru lace around it.

"What care you take of things," I exclaimed. I should never have thought of it again. Ah, Sophia, what should I do without you?" And the tears swam in my eyes.

"Much you care," she muttered, going out of the

door. "As long as things come ready to your hand, it's little odds who slaves for you."

Probably the sight of me again in girlish dress, and perhaps the words I had just said, had upset her, and she took refuge in her habitual rudeness, but I was too hurt to think so then.

The afternoon sun was low in the west when I started for Happy-go-lucky, with the broad white parasol over my head, and a light chip hat in my hand. I had broken off a bunch of a yellowish pink geranium that grew in one of the garden-beds, and fastened it where the handkerchief crossed on my bosom. There had been a rain the night before; it was not dusty; the heat of the day was over, but the air was still soft and warm, and the wind had fallen. It was a delightful walk.

When I came up the steps at Happy-go-lucky I heard voices on the south piazza, and going around the corner of the house, I found the whole party assembled. The heat of the day had probably been the cause of their being at home, and the coolness of the porch facing the ocean had drawn them together. Mrs. Emlyn was sitting with a stocking bag on her lap, and a heap of dictionaries on a chair beside her, in whose company she had evidently spent the afternoon. Naomi was swinging in a hammock, with a story-book in her hand. Ned was cleaning his gun at a distance of two or three feet. Mr. Macnally was sitting on the step, leaning his head against a post. The colonel and a stranger were seated with their backs to me, looking out over the tranquil, pale sea. The wind came faint and soft from the ocean, the waves broke on the beach with scarcely any sound. Ned was the first to discover me as I approached them.

"I say!" he cried, jumping up, "I'm going up-stairs to dress myself this minute."

"Oh, how sweet you look," cried Naomi, rolling out of her hammock, her rough flannel dress much disordered from the long afternoon's nap there, and her hair tumbled over her eyes. This called every one's attention to me. I hadn't put my parasol down, but held it back over my shoulder, and stood in a kind of stage fright at finding myself the center of so many eyes.

> "There she goes,
>   Pretty as a rose,
>   All dressed up in her Sunday clothes,"

roared Ned.

"Ned!" called out his uncle, reprovingly, seeing my embarrassment. All the three gentlemen were on their feet. The glasses were on Mrs. Emlyn's nose.

"Why not?" cried Ned, stoutly; "she looks awfully pretty, and I've never seen her dressed up before. I couldn't help it, you know; I just couldn't."

"You're a rude boy," said his aunt, decisively. "I'm not at all proud of your manners. Take that dirty gun away, and go and get ready for your tea."

Ned rather sulkily gathered up his blackened rags and rods and boxes and went away, leaving me in a worse state of agitation than before.

"Don't scold Ned," I said, confusedly.

"No, on my honor," said the colonel, "I think his aunt was too hard on him. I don't find it in my heart to blame him;" and he bowed significantly.

"I shall go away," I said, between laughing and crying.

"I should think you would," cried Mrs. Emlyn, "as from a company of savages. If this aberration of good breeding occurred very often, I should go myself."

"But," urged Naomi, pressing close upon me, and fondling the ruffles on my sleeve, and gazing at my slippers, "but what did you do it for? Why did you put your good clothes on to-day?"

I was driven into a corner; I was desperate; I didn't know what I did.

"You told me there was company," and with an impulse half shy, half defiant, I lifted my eyes to the group standing before me. A woman is rarely mistaken when she commands admiration; perhaps my courage rose and a faint flutter of coquetry inspired me as I met, one after another, the eyes fixed upon me. First the colonel's, kindly and mirthful, then the strange blue eyes of a strange man, then the deep, keen gaze of Mr. Macnally, who stood behind the others.

"Ah, my dear sir, you are the excuse, we owe it to *you*. Allow me, madame, to present to you the Company," said the colonel, with great enjoyment of his own observations.

The stranger bowed. Mrs. Emlyn, who did not understand coquetry, and imagined me more unhappy than I was, said, "I think we have been quite rude enough, all of us, and I propose to let our visitor have a seat now, and to talk of something besides the way she's dressed. It is so warm, you did well to put on something thinner," she added, as I sat down beside her. Thereupon they all laughed, and the colonel said,

"Why don't you begin, my dear?"

This did not please her, and she simply frowned.

The stranger did not sit down, but stood before me a few feet, leaning against one of the pillars that supported the piazza roof. He was a tall man, rather imposing in figure and carriage. He was probably between forty-five and fifty. His features were good; he had undoubtedly been remarkably handsome when he was younger, and still would be noticed for good looks. His blue eyes had a slow way of fastening themselves on your face, and then not being easily shaken off. The expression of them was not entirely pleasing. A heavy mustache covered his mouth, which might have been bad or good. His hair, which was thin on the top, was brown where it was not gray. His clothes were perfect, a great contrast to the old-fashioned trimness of the colonel's, and the rough carelessness of the tutor's. His hands and feet were *de la haute noblesse;* he threw the whole party into an inferior position. He had evidently been a man of the world from his youth; no easier and better manners could be imagined. One felt he always had

> "Sipped wine from silver, praising God,
>   And raked in golden barley,"

wine that had "grown fat on Lusitanian summers." Happy Mr. Boughton!

Mrs. Emlyn turned to me and began to ask questions about the children; why had I not let Maidy come?

"It's to be feared Maidy had no clothes fine enough to accompany her mamma to-night," said Mr. Macnally. The visitor transferred his eyes slowly from me to the speaker; I wondered what he thought of him, from his faded flannel shirt, and dusty knickerbockers, to the easy audacity of his manners, and the keenness of his dark eyes.

"I thought we had agreed to give up the subject of clothes," said Mrs. Emlyn.

"I didn't promise."

"Well, it's time you did. I won't have another word of them. It's a pity," she continued, "that a woman can't put on a pretty gown once in a summer, without being frightened back into flannel, before she's had it on an hour. For my part, I never want to see blue flannel again. We've had a surfeit of it. I'm glad to see you in anything so fresh and pretty."

We all laughed, no one more heartily than Mrs. Emlyn herself.

"There's a charm about you and your clothes, my dear. We all revolve around you and can't break away."

"I'm going up-stairs to dress," said Naomi, getting behind her aunt's chair, and asking in a low voice for permission to put on a white dress.

"The contagion of folly," said the tutor, shaking his head, and balancing himself on the rail of the veranda.

"You don't seem to have caught it, Macnally," said the Colonel.

"I've had it," he said; "you can't take it twice. Sometimes, however," he added, his eyes falling on and glancing off the polished boots of the stranger, "it takes a chronic form, though weakened, and you never get over it. Doctors call it cachexy, don't they? It's pretty serious then."

For the first time since I had known him I

found myself annoyed by what he did; I wished he
would get down off the rail, and stop talking utter
nonsense. It made me angry to see the deliberate blue
eyes of the new-comer measuring him. I wanted to
have him thought well of, and I felt sure he was not.
This was the first time that any stranger had come in
among us in our free and unconventional life. I had,
perhaps, not realized how great a part of our enjoyment
had come from the fact that we were all *d'accord;* that
we all sincerely liked each other. I was too sensitive
not to feel the jar of this new presence. He dislocated
everything. No one of us stood as we had stood
before. I lost my bearings, and began to criticise everything. I began to make apologies in my own mind
for what before had seemed to need no apology. I
wished for an opportunity to explain what had only
just seemed to call for explanation. I don't know
whether a similar distortion had taken place in the
minds of the others; but it seemed to me they were all
caricaturing themselves. The colonel was more prosy
and old-fogy than ever before, Mrs. Emlyn more unnecessarily candid and sharply plain-spoken, and Mr.
Macnally outdid himself in perverse disregard of all
conventionalities. What nonsense he talked, and what
applause he won from his host and hostess! Last night
I should have laughed, too, and that hour after sunset,
looking over the slowly-darkening sea, would have
been delicious to me. But to-night all was out of
tune.

Tea was late; it was almost dark when we were
summoned to it, and the candles were already lighted.
Ned and Naomi came down promptly; Ned had actually put on his Sunday clothes, and Naomi looked love-

ly in her best white dress, and a bright ribbon in her hair.

"Where will it end?" cried Mr. Macnally. "It is the dawn of the reformation."

"You are the only one not affected by the movement, Macnally," said the colonel.

"I am sorry," said Mr. Macnally, bringing rather prominently forward a sunburned hand and a flannel sleeve, in some unnecessary act of civility at the table, "I am sorry to be a memento mori—showing you what you were yesterday and what you'll without doubt be to-morrow."

But Mr. Boughton, the visitor, was seated by me, and I was quite willing to take his attention from all this, and he talked to me when he could make me hear above the voices of Ned and Naomi and the rest. When we went out from the tea, of which I don't remember much, except his unwavering blue eyes on my face, and his persistent low voice in my ear, I was for a moment alone by the parlor lamp. The gentlemen had gone out on the piazza to smoke, Ned was busy with his dogs, whom he was feeding at the door, Naomi was carrying something to the store-room with her aunt; I stood alone at the parlor table, with a little contraction of trouble on my face—which I suppose the light beside me brought out pretty clearly. Mr. Macnally came in from the piazza and came up to me, without the audacity and merriment of ten minutes before.

"I am afraid," he said in an eager, appealing sort of way, "I'm afraid something has happened to annoy you. I'm—I'm awfully sorry if I've had anything to do with it but you know I didn't mean to, I needn't tell you that."

I was silent—what was there to say ?

" Was it about that stupid dress ?" he said, not looking at me. " I ought to have seen ; but I own I didn't think you'd mind."

. "It isn't very pleasant to be made so absurd before a stranger," I said, with a taint of insincerity which was half unconscious.

"I'm sure you're right," he answered, " and I can't tell you how ashamed I am. But he seemed so tiresome, such an old muff, with his shiny boots and his slow ways, I really didn't feel as if he were in the way of our talking just as we always do."

This vexed me ; I don't at all know why ; but I said, " One sometimes gets tired of—buffoonery—all the time—"

"I'm sorry," he said, faintly. I looked up hastily into his face. He had flushed painfully, and now the color was going back, and the expression was as if he had been wounded physically. I was ashamed before I had actually said it, and now I was frightened. What had I done ? It is no light thing to call your friend's raillery and wit, buffoonery. Men don't ordinarily say that sort of thing to each other with impunity ; and from a woman, how much harder to bear. And a woman, too, who had been treated with such unvarying homage and delicacy. I had heard the children say that his quick Irish temper kept them in awe of him in school-time, and I could well imagine that such eyes as his could sometimes burn with sudden anger. But he was not angry now ; it was something a great deal worse.

6

He was very pale, and he turned away with the instinct of hiding his emotion.

"I am very sorry," he repeated, but in a low and uncertain voice. "I have not had any idea that that sort of thing offended you. I—I have been altogether mistaken in—in—"

I tried to say something to extenuate my rudeness, but at the moment that I began to speak, Mrs. Emlyn and Naomi came into the room, and Mr. Macnally left it.

"What is the matter with Mr. Macnally?" she said. "Is he ill? He looks pale," and she followed him to the door and called after him, but got no answer.

The few days that followed this are too uncomfortable to recall. I was not given to self-analysis in those days, or I might have found that my unhappiness meant more than I should have liked to admit. I thought I was only uncomfortable from self-reproach. I was so absorbed in my own feelings that I think I must have made a sorry companion in the walks and drives to which I was doomed by my landlord and landlady, who seemed more than ever intent on having me with them. The tutor had in some way fallen out of our programmes and Mr. Boughton had taken his place. We hardly saw him save at the table, and then he was so silent as to be forever jeered at by the colonel and by Ned.

There was sailing, driving, walking, for the entertainment of the guest; I remember little about it, but that he was always by me, and that if he had patience with my abstraction and dullness, he must have been a good-natured man. I had just one fixed idea, and that was, to get a chance to make my peace with Mr. Mac-

nally, whose pale face and averted eyes haunted me
continually. But the chance was not easy to get. He
was not always at meals, and he kept far out of my path
at other times. I was frightened, too, when I did see
him, and it was almost impossible for me to look at him
or address him.

The table was dull: we all languished. Mrs. Emlyn
sometimes yawned, and wondered if it were the weather
made her feel so stupid. The colonel roused himself
to talk, and didn't mend matters. He was not a con-
versationalist. Ned and Naomi sparred a little, but even
they seemed to have lost their zest. Mr. Boughton had
the floor a good deal of the time. He talked well, I
suppose. He had a nice voice. He had been everywhere.
He told little incidents very charmingly. (I don't mean
anecdotes, Heaven forbid!) It was very pleasant to him
to be listened to, and we all listened pretty well. But
somehow it was not very vivacious, and in the midst of
it Mrs. Emlyn would yawn, or Ned would interrupt, or
the colonel think of something about the water-works
that needed his personal attention.

The light had been put out, and I had put it out,
and I felt sore about it all the time. What would I give
for five minutes to beg his pardon in? I begged it all
night long, when I lay restlessly awake, and all day
long, while Mr. Boughton talked melodiously to me,
and I didn't listen.

At last the day came when I got my five minutes.
We had been off on a long drive, the host and hostess,
Naomi and Maidy, the guest and myself, in the three-
seated open wagon. It was a bright day, and we had
stayed much longer than had been planned.

When we came back it was an hour and a half after

dinner-time, but it did not seem to disturb our entertainers very much.   There was only one thing that troubled me about it, and that was that Ned and his tutor would probably have taken dinner by themselves, after the manner of that free-and-easy household, and gone away with their guns. When we drove up to the house we saw, through the dining-room windows, two blue flannel backs bending over the table, and a servant languidly bringing in dessert.   Only Ned turned his head to see us as we passed the window.   Mr. Boughton carried my shawls into the parlor, and left me, called by the colonel to some irrigation consultation. Naomi went with her aunt to get out the dessert.   I called Maidy, and sent her into the dining-room to say to Mr. Macnally that I wanted to speak to him for a moment in the parlor, when he should have finished his dinner.   I heard her little baby voice deliver the message, and then I sat down with a very agitated feeling and waited for him to come to me.

I heard Ned push back his chair, and invite Maidy to come with him to feed his dogs, and remind Mr. Macnally that in ten minutes they ought to be away. It seemed to me a good while after they had started down the steps that I heard him get up, and come towards the door of the parlor.   It was probably my own impatience that made it seem so long ; now that he was coming, what, after all, did I mean to say to him ? Now that he was standing before me, I hardly had composure enough to look at him.   I was sitting on a sofa by the window and had been pretending to read ; I pushed my book away, and asked him to sit down, that I had something to say to him.   He sat down, not on the sofa, but on a chair exactly by it, and waited for me to speak. But it seemed simply impossible for me to speak. I bit my lip and tried to command my voice, but it would not come.

"I'm afraid," he said at last, rather low, "that it troubles you to say what you want to; and I hope you won't bother about it, if you do it simply for me."

"No," I said, gathering voice, "it's for myself more than for you. It didn't hurt you,·perhaps, that I was so rude the other night, and said such an unpardonable thing, but it has hurt me and made me really wretched."

"That's foolish," he said, with a trace of his eager manner. "I hope you'll put it out of your mind and never think of it again."

"Will *you?*" I said, looking at him.

"Yes, as much as I ought," he answered, with a faint smile, looking away.

"That's it; you'll remember it and be influenced by it, and keep it between us, and yet forgive me. I'm quite sure you forgive me; I've been sure of that. If you only had been angry. Why wouldn't you be angry? It would have been a blessing."

"You ask impossibilities."

"And I suppose it's just as great an impossibility for you to forget?"

"Oh, no; believe me I could forget it, if—if you really meant me to."

"Well, I do mean you to. I do ask you to forget I ever said what wasn't my thought, what was totally against my feeling, what was utterly untrue. It was just the result of a foolish discord in my feelings,—I cannot understand it. I was all out of tune and peevish. I—I—*wish* I hadn't said it."

"Why?" he asked, eagerly. "Because you think it—troubled me?"

"Yes; and because I think it will make you different; that we sha'n't have the same happy times again, and that you'll never feel the same towards me."

"Oh!" he said, and a deep flush passed over his whole face; "you are talking about impossibilities again."

"If it only might be an impossibility! You've always been so nice. Don't think I haven't appreciated it. I can't suppose you will ever be able to have exactly the same respect for a person who could do such a wantonly rude thing; but you'll try and *like* me just the same, won't you?"

"I'm afraid I shouldn't have to try," he said, with something between a smile and a setting of his teeth together, as if he wished I'd stop.

"It would be all the better if you didn't have to try," I answered, not understanding him, and rejoicing only in my own lightened heart.

Ned's tramp was heard across the north piazza, and he gave a nervous start and rose.

"Thank you," he said, hurriedly, glancing towards the door by which that young barbarian might be expected to come in; "thank you for what you've said to me."

"I hope I'll never have to say it to you again, that's all."

"I can't say I hope it. Kill me again to-night, if you will bring me to life to-morrow, as you have done to-day."

He had turned to go out of the piazza window to get his gun, which stood there; he leaned towards me as he passed me, and said it too low for Ned to hear, who was already on the threshold looking in.

CHAPTER XI.

CATECHETICAL.

"I seek no copy now of life's first half !
Leave here the pages with long musings curled,
And write me new my future's epigraph."

E. B. Browning.

THE next afternoon I had the pleasure of a long conversation with Mr. Boughton on the piazza. It was not an unalloyed pleasure, as I knew Macnally and the children had gone down along the beach to look at something which with much philanthropy they hoped might prove a wreck. I had not the courage to go off and join them, leaving Mrs. Emlyn alone with the visitor. After they were quite beyond recall, Mrs. Emlyn got up and went in the house and didn't come out again. It was a great nuisance. She would never know the sacrifice that I had made; why had I not gone? However, I made the best of it, and was as polite and patient as I knew how to be.

I knew that Mr. Boughton was a very recent widower. I knew that he was very rich. These were the two points of his personal history that I possessed. They were not, unhappily, points that could be made use of to furnish conversation. I could not ask him anything about the late Mrs. Boughton. I could not ask him how it felt to have as much money as he wanted. On this last head I felt much curiosity, but

[128]

naturally I couldn't even distantly allude to it. It is a singular restriction of good manners, that we can't ask each other what our income is. It's a subject of such universal interest; a touch of income makes the whole world kin. It did really seem hard that I couldn't talk to him of the only thing about him that was interesting. I wanted to ask him how it felt to know that if he wanted anything, from a house to a story-book, he could have it by saying so, and taking out the money. I wanted to know if it made him stop wanting things to know he could have them. *I* wanted so many things. I was always rushing forward making plans, and then coming crash up against the dead wall of insolvency. Fancy having a road clear before you as far as you can see, and no limit to the making and carrying out of plans, but the desire to make them and to carry them out. It would have been very entertaining to have had his experiences about it, but, alas, it was impossible. He seemed equally anxious to get at some of my experiences. His conversation took a vaguely, politely personal turn. It's sometimes quite fascinating to have the conversation take a personal turn, if it's vague and polite enough. Mr. Boughton understood how to do it very well, but somehow I did not feel inclined to tell him much about myself, vague and polite as he was.

The afternoon wasn't quite as bad as I anticipated, and wore away much quicker. When we saw the wrecking party coming back along the beach, we walked down to meet them.

"I have a great curiosity," said my companion, slowly, "to know what your impression is of that young fellow, whom the Emlyns treat with such familiarity. They are so unconventional and so benevolent, one doesn't expect them to be discriminating too. But for you—how does he strike you?"

" I'm afraid I'm unconventional as well as they, and perhaps benevolent!"

"Not undiscriminatingly benevolent in this case, let me hope." And he fastened his slow blue eyes on my face.

" I must say, I like him immensely,—even on the top of a flagstaff."

For Macnally was at that moment plain in view, going like a cat up the pole before the Coast Guard house, with Ned after him, who necessarily, having only ordinary legs and arms, was very much behind.

"He's agile, I admit."

"Is that all you admit?" I said, my eyes following the now descending figure.

" He has a glib tongue and much audacity. I'm not settled as to what I think his walk in life has been. Perhaps he has enlightened *you*. The colonel doesn't seem to have much knowledge of his past."

" Well, I'm sorry that I haven't either. I only know we all like him so much as to forget whether he has had any past or not. Ah! He's got down safely. But poor Ned has got a tumble!"

Naomi by this time came tearing up to us, looking like a tomboy. I couldn't help thinking what a trial we must be to Mr. Boughton, one and all of us. After tea, the colonel took Mr. Boughton away to smoke, and Mrs. Emlyn went out for her usual walk on the piazza. The rest of us closed in around the parlor lamp; it was on a wide, bare table, of which the mahogany shone. Naomi settled down to her drawing; I sat with my embroidery on my lap, my work-basket on the table.

Mr. Macnally sat just beyond me, pulling out the gay-colored worsteds and making patterns with them on the mahogany. Ned had his back to us, reading intently a Waverley novel, and not looking up even when he was spoken to, which wasn't often. A happy sort of quiet had settled on us, which was broken by Naomi saying,

"How much nicer it is since you came here to live in the cottage! I think it is just as if you lived here at this house, and had the cottage too. Mr. Macnally, don't you think we have a great deal nicer times since the middle of June?"

"Since the middle of June? Why, wasn't it before that that we had our great haul of blue-fish? I don't think I've had a bite since then. And as to the snipe, the little beggars haven't looked at us for a month or more. We had prime luck when we first came down."

"Oh, nonsense. I don't mean that. I mean at home here, all the time, and going to drive and all that. It mayn't make any difference to you and Ned, but I know Aunt Penelope and I like having her," and she leaned over from her chair and gave me a little kiss.

"Thank you, Naomi, dear; and I like being with you."

"Who do you come to see here?" she said. "Aunt Penelope is so much older, and I am so much younger; I *wish* you came to see me. As to the others, they're as bad. Only Mr. Macnally. He is near your age. *Aren't* you, Mr. Macnally? Tell me truly, are you older than she is, or younger? No, you *couldn't* be younger."

"Not if I tried!"

"But, do you really think you are his age? You don't come to see him, anyway."

"I never thought of it before, Naomi. It is rather embarrassing. I actually don't know whom I come to see."

"I know," said Ned, tipping back in his chair and looking over his shoulder at us. "I know, and I'll tell you something if you'll all promise not to tell."

"I pledge myself for one," I said.

"Well, now, honest, though—Mr. Macnally, and Naomi, you. I heard something this evening, just before tea, while I was asleep in the hammock—Mr. Boughton and uncle were sitting there talking, and I couldn't help hearing; they ought to have looked out if they hadn't meant me to hear 'em."

The boy's face shone with mirth, and he twisted himself around on his chair and put his elbows on the table. "The first I heard was uncle saying, 'She is a charming young creature, all tenderness and sweetness,' or some such stuff as that; and then old Boughton said in a spoony sort of way, 'She's perfectly unconscious of her beauty; she's the only woman that I ever saw that was.' Then uncle said she had always lived in a very quiet sort of way, but, that generally women found out they were good-looking if they lived in the backwoods. Then the old fellow knocked the ashes off his cigar, and said (oh, if you could have heard him! with a sort of swell): 'Col. Emlyn, she would adorn any station.'"

The boy doubled himself up with laughter.

"What were they talking of? What is the fun of it?" I said, bewildered.

"Oh, you don't see? Good for you. Adorning any station. I suppose the old cad thinks his station is the tip-toppest one to let just about now. I wonder if there is a woman alive that would be fool enough to take him ?"

" Plenty ;" I said, sagaciously. " He isn't so very old ; he's very handsome, or he has been, anyway. And his manners are so gentlemanly and quiet. A woman might do worse, Master Ned. I wish you may have as good a chance as he, when you are forty-five."

" Whew," said Ned, " I begin to be afraid to tell my joke."

" I don't see any joke so far," said Naomi.

" Nobody expected *you* to," said Ned, casting a contemptuous glance at her over his shoulder. Then he turned to us, and went on sotto voce, with glances at the window to see if any one were coming in : " He's in earnest, he's awfully in earnest, and it's coming very soon, I shouldn't wonder. But no matter. I couldn't be quite positive about when he's going to speak. He was asking all particulars of uncle. He wanted to know how old, about, she was, how long her husband had been dead—whether there were any relations that would be any way objectionable—whether there was a possibility of any other attachment being in his way—"

" Ned," said the tutor in a voice that made him start, though it wasn't any louder than his own ; " it's bad enough to listen, but to repeat what you have heard's a little too bad for even schoolboy morals."

Ned flushed, and looked both angry and sulky.

" You didn't seem to mind at first," he said, with a sharp look at his tutor's face.

" I wasn't paying much attention when you first began," he returned, meeting his eye with a glance that sent it down.

"I know!" cried Naomi, dropping her pencils, and leaning forward with excited eyes. "He means you! Tell me, *does* he mean you? Did you know he—he—felt that way? Tell me, did you know it?"

Naomi had never been as near as this to any matter of the heart before; she felt awed, one might say, by the proximity of a proposal, even though it came from a man of forty-five or over. Her sentimental ideas of love were suffering a little distraint from the recollection of the scantiness of Mr. Boughton's hair, and the fact that he had been married before, but nevertheless it was the most thrilling moment of her life. She pushed back her drawing things, and slid down on her knees beside me, and put her hand upon my shoulder.

"Do you mind it," she said, in a low voice, " that he has been married before?"

I had grown red and white a great many times since this revelation, and was bending over my work, trying to steady myself to speak when I should be called upon. I hadn't attained any great composure of voice and manner when I was obliged to answer Naomi's very searching question.

"If I had anything to do with the matter," I said, "I should mind it. But I haven't."

"But he meant you," cried Naomi; "Ned says he did. Don't people generally know when—when—other people are going to ask them—for their hand?"

Naomi had read Miss Austen and the Waverleys, and felt she was correct in her phraseology, though it didn't sound quite right when used in the light of common day. Ned snickered, and Naomi blushed scarlet, but even her mortification could not withdraw her thoughts from the fascinating subject.

"I should think," she said, softly, "that you would have known."

"I should not be likely to think of what would be an insult to me."

"An insult! Why, I thought people thought it was a very high compliment—an honor. I don't see how it could be anything else. Do you mean," she went on, after a moment's pause, "do you mean because you—had—been—been married before?"

I signified an assent in some way.

"Tell me just this one thing," she said, earnestly; "do you think it isn't nice for people to get married again?"

"I am sure I don't think it is nice, Naomi. I wish you wouldn't talk to me any more about it."

"Just this one thing; just answer me this one question and I won't bother you any more," and Naomi's eyes filled with a strange intentness. "Would you ever get married again? Would anything induce you?"

"No, Naomi, I would not; nothing would induce me."

"I am so glad," cried the child, clasping her hands around her knee, and gazing up into my face. "I didn't think you would. I don't see how any one can do it; any one, at least, that has really been loved."

The woman's heart was stirring in the bosom of thirteen. It was not Miss Austen and the Waverleys this time.

"Tell me one thing more—"

"No, Naomi, not one thing more. You promised me," I said, very low.

Ned had gone back to his book, but he was not reading very much. His eye furtively studied all the faces in turn around the table. I don't think he got much out of Mr. Macnally's, who made and remade the worsteds into patterns on the table, and never once lifted his head. I was struggling so hard to command myself that I suppose I looked unnatural. I heard a moving back of chairs upon the piazza, where the colonel and his guest were smoking, and then my plans for escape took sudden shape. In a moment more they would be in the room, and Mrs. Emlyn too. And then the going home; it was possible the colonel would lend himself to some plan for giving his guest an opportunity for seeing me alone, perhaps this very evening. I pushed my work into my basket rapidly and got up.

"I'm going home," I said, as quietly as I could. "Say good-night to your aunt, Naomi."

"Aren't you going out on the piazza to speak to her? Won't she think it's queer?"

"I don't want to call her in; I must go. Tell her Sophia was going to the village, and I had to go to stay with the children. Good-night."

And I hurried into the dining-room, where my wraps had been hung. Mr. Macnally had got up when I did. I got my things down from the pegs below the stairs, and hurried out upon the porch, just as the gentlemen from the other side of the piazza were entering the parlor by one of the windows. I almost ran, and was half way to the gate before I found I was followed by Mr. Macnally.

"You have dropped one of your shawls, or perhaps it's Maidy's little cloak," he said simply, coming up beside me.

"It's Maidy's; oh, thank you," and I stopped and took it, panting a little from my flight. "I—I sha'n't need any one to go home with me," I added, as he walked beside me. "Indeed, I'd almost rather be alone. I hope you won't think me rude, but I'd rather."

"It would make me very uncomfortable to think of your going by yourself," he answered. "It is a lonely road."

"I don't mind it. It's not far. And there is a moon."

"Therefore you don't need a man." And when he made this poor joke, he gave a short laugh, which grated on my ear. There was a moon, in a clear, calm sky, and by it I saw, as I glanced at him, that his face had a contracted, hard look, unlike himself. It seemed to me everything was reeling out of place in my poor little world. I felt frightened.

"Don't you think it's a little unreasonable," he said, in an altered tone, very ordinary and controlled, "to avenge on all of us, who haven't offended you, the offense of another person, who, you consider, has?"

"I don't want to avenge anything on anybody, but I'm in a hurry. I want to get home to the children. I—I think I'd rather go alone."

"I hope you'll let me go with you," he said, earnestly. "There are often strange, rough-looking men about. There is now a schooner unloading over in the bay. I didn't like the look of some men of her crew who have been about the village through the day."

We had got to the gate by this time, and I passed out of it, and paused for an instant as I saw he stood still.

"Have this much consideration for me," he said. "I will not go if you forbid me, but I shall be very uncomfortable if you do."

" Oh, you're very kind. I shall not be afraid; but if you want to come—I mean, if you think it best to come, I shall, of course, be very much obliged."

So he swung the gate shut after us, and walked beside me silently. The night was serene, and the sky brilliant with stars, and with a great full moon. There was a smell of salt in the air, and the wind was soft south-west. The grass was a little damp, and we made our way out into the road. We met no one; the only sound was the slow beat of the surf upon the shore, away from which we were walking. Across the level fields I could see the light in the window of our cottage.

For a long while neither of us spoke; then I said, with a suddenness that must have been rather startling to my companion,

"I have a question to ask you. Will you answer me honestly, whatever you may think?"

He did not reply at once. After a moment, he said, "I can think of but one question that I wouldn't be willing to answer you honestly, and I don't believe you'll ask me that. What is it that you want me to tell you?"

"You heard, I suppose, what Ned said to-night. Granting it to be true—for I don't think he is old enough and bad enough to have invented it—I want you to tell me—do you think I have done anything to have deserved it? You have been here all the time, you are very observing, and it seems to me you must know if I have."

"I don't understand. What do you mean exactly? Have you deserved what?"

"Why, this mortification, this humiliation, this talking me over as if it were a possible thing that I—that—"

"I suppose I understand what you mean. But you must excuse me if I say I can't look at it as you do. I can't see anything in what Ned said to mortify and humble you. I can understand that it might make you angry to feel that any one whom you didn't favor had presumed so far. That a woman must always feel, I suppose. But I don't see any cause for feeling humbled and degraded by it."

"Then, if you cannot understand, I cannot hope to make you. But I will put my question plainer, and you can surely answer it that way. Have you ever seen anything in my manner, at any time, to justify any one in thinking that—that I would—that it would be possible for me—to marry again?"

A perceptible shudder ran through me, as I forced myself to say the words. A long pause followed; we walked on slowly; my companion hit the heads off several daisies with his stick, as they shone up at us in the moonlight; I loosened the clasp of the cloak about my neck, for it seemed to smother me.

"I promised to be honest," he said, at last, "and I will be frank as well. If it is presuming, please do not blame me. I never should have dreamed of offering you my judgment, if you had not asked it of me."

"Yes, I know. Well?"

"My judgment isn't so very awful; you needn't be alarmed. You are young, to begin with, and very natural. When you are happy, you are happy; when you are pleased, you smile upon whoever

pleases you, and don't make a disguise of it. No
one could misunderstand you, who was capable of
discriminating. It doesn't seem to me possible that any
man could connect the idea of coquetry with you. But
that doesn't help the matter much ; in the world, one
never knows who one's judges are. One's got to be
prepared for misinterpretation. This gentleman who
has presumed to think of you : how can one tell whether
he is true and simple enough to know truth and simplicity
when he sees it, or whether he carries his conceited and
tainted judgment with him wherever he goes ? Of one
thing I can assure you ; I never saw you give him a
look, a smile, a word, upon which, in my judgment, he
could have founded the very faintest hope."

"That's all I wanted to know," I said, drawing a
deep breath of relief.

"But it's not all I wanted to say," he pursued, after
another pause. "We are on the subject, and I want
to say one word more before we finally dismiss it. I
don't know what right I have to presume to give you
counsel. I have never fancied myself having the
temerity to do it, but Ned's eavesdropping seems to
have *bouleversé* everything. May I say to you just one
thing ? I warn you that you may not like it, and that
you may think I am presuming."

"Of course it is right for you to tell me if you see
me doing wrong ; we have known each other well
enough for that."

"It is not in my creed that you could possibly do
wrong."

"Ah !"

"But that you might, from the excess of some good
feeling, be led into what would be fatal to your happi-

ness. If it were only wicked people got themselves into a mess, it would simplify affairs exceedingly. But it's the ones like you—let me beg your pardon—who do it quite as often. Let me say it quickly, for I know you won't like it. You are making a mistake about yourself, and putting yourself in a wrong place. How can it be wise for you to expect to go through the world as if you were something sacred—to expect to be treated as one apart from the ordinary walks of life? Believe me, people won't understand you; the world doesn't acknowledge such distinctions."

"Then I will go away from the world; I will shut myself up from people if they will not let me go my way."

"Well, if you think that the best and wisest thing for your two little girls. Won't it be bringing them up to rather a dreary sort of life? Would it be good for Maidy, especially, to be brought up cheerlessly?"

"That depends upon what you call cheerlessness."

"Well, to be shut out from the world, from all healthy young society."

"They needn't be that."

"They will have to be, if their mother refuses to be philosophic about occurrences like that which led us into this conversation. If she is unable to school herself to take a cheerful, natural part in the society in which she happens to be placed."

"It will be time enough to think about that when they are a little older."

"It doesn't seem to me there is anything gained in putting off lessons, when we once acknowledge that we've got to learn them."

"But I don't acknowledge—"

"Oh, I think you will, when you have thought it

over.   Won't you do me one favor?   Put all this out
of your mind; forgive this presuming gentleman; of
course, you needn't see him again, but let him go in
peace; you may well believe he won't stay very long;
and then let things go on as before, and don't bother
about anything in the future.   You don't want to make
Ned and the colonel and Mrs. Emlyn wretched, I am
sure, by making too much of the matter."

Clever reasoner, ingenuous listener! Before we had
reached the cottage gate and lifted its rusty latch, my
tumultuous feelings had been sensibly reduced, and I
was almost brought to feel ashamed of them.   I went
and sat between the children's beds in the little nursery,
and watched beside them while Sophia was away at
the village.   I certainly had made rather a fool of myself, and I wished sincerely that I hadn't said so much.
I promised myself to be wiser in the future.   I could
act upon my resolutions, but there was no use in talking about them, even to the friends whom I knew best.
Mr. Macnally undoubtedly felt that I was weak and
womanish.   No one enjoys being thought weak and
womanish.   He had been very kind, but it was plain to
me that he would treat any display of my exceptional
views with deep though silent, contempt.   I felt sure
he had wanted to laugh at me all the time, though he
had been so deferential.   I promised myself that I
would let things go on exactly as before; only I would
be on my guard if any more middle-aged widowers
strayed into our peaceful pastures.

CHAPTER XII.

SECOND THOUGHTS.

" They are dangerous guides the feelings——"

MRS. EMLYN was very much distressed about the matter, which Naomi did not fail to repeat to her in full. The result was I was allowed to remain in quarantine for several days, and the widower was discouraged at second-hand. He went away, as might have been expected. Mr. Macnally, it is probable, suggested that nothing be said to me about the matter, and so, though I had had several visits from everybody but Ned, who was *en penitence,* there were no allusions to the subject. It was a little awkward, as nobody dared to make a joke of it, and it wasn't the kind of thing to bear serious treatment. It must have been a constant temptation to Mr. Macnally, but he was so very honorable, I never detected a smile on his mouth, or a twinkle in his easily ignited eye. It is disagreeable to feel one's self the object of such circumspection. One distrusts nothing so much as what one's friends do not say to one.

A day or two after the gentleman's departure, I was, by a little stratagem, got to Happy-go-lucky for dinner, and once the ice was broken, everything went on as before. There was no change, except that every one was kinder than ever, and that my dear host, in-

[143]

stead of resenting my objection to his plans for my happiness, made more of me than ever, as if to atone for having unwittingly given me even an imaginary cause of pain. We slid again into the old life, and no one, married or single, came to disturb our easy, pleasant days. Only once did the colonel propose sending for some friends to pass a week.

"An' you love me, no," cried his wife. "Life's too short for that sort of thing, not to say the summer. It gives me indigestion to be civil to people for whom I do not care. I simply will not have them."

So she simply did not have them, and we were happy. I read German as usual with her. I drove with the colonel. I went crabbing and fishing and sailing with the children and their tutor. Maidy and Baby were lugged about with unfailing patience and good-nature by Naomi and Macnally, and even by Ned. I don't know how I could have fancied I deserved half the kindness I got, or have been comfortable under it. But it all seemed the natural order of things, and I was happy.

The summer had worn on now to the latter half of August. It was Saturday, I think the third Saturday in August. Saturday was always a festival in the Happy-go-lucky calendar, because there were no lessons. Very soon after breakfast the cart had driven up, for Maidy and me to go crabbing. We spent all the morning on the bay, Maidy and I drifting along in the boat, and Macnally, Naomi and Ned plunging about in the water with their nets, shouting, splashing, dripping. Rex sat in the prow of the boat, shivering if a drop of water fell on him; Maidy dipped her hands in the little ripples of waves that the south-west wind made as it came

across the sand-hills from the sea. The sunshine was
now and then obscured by fleecy white clouds

"—shepherded by the slow, unwilling wind,"

which moved across the deep blue sky. The wide
stretching country looked green and ripe with the late
summer vegetation. Beside the bay lay long acres of
unfenced meadows, among the damp grass of which grew
meadow-pinks by millions, and where snipe fed and
fluttered. From the boat, where I rocked idly, I could
see, across the level stretch of fields, here and there a low
farm-house, with its environment of trees: here and
there a distant sharp white steeple pricking up into the
sky from its surrounding village. The wind-mills waved
their white arms in the sunlight; in a field near by, the
men stacked the sheaves of corn beside a wagon loaded
with great golden pumpkins. The ducks along the
shore dived and paddled and quacked; once and again
a white gull darted down from the heights above, dipped
in the blue water for its prey, and flashed away victori-
ous. I liked the smell of the seaweed lying on the
shore; I liked the sights around me, and the sense of
security, and the idleness and the feeling of health that
the fine air gave me. I watched the crabbers, now led
far away from me, now back almost beside the boat.
It would have bored me very much to have been as
muddy and wet as they, but it amused me to watch
them. I held Maidy's dress in one hand, to keep her
from tipping over into the water, and I talked a little
to Rex to keep his spirits up, and so the morning
passed. When it was time to go, they put the baskets
of crabs in the boat, and Macnally and Ned, up to their

7

waists in water, drew us along the shore, half the length of the bay, to where we had left the cart.

"It's quite a march of triumph," I said.

"Especially to the crabs," said Mr. Macnally.

It wasn't quite so much of a march of triumph when we had all, wet and dry, to get into the cart.

"Which will you be neebor to, me or the crabs, shure?" asked Macnally, as he stood by the basket of crabs, the most abominable object, his bare legs covered with sea-weed and mud, and his trowsers, rolled above the knees, dripping with water.

"I'd much rather get out and walk than be neighbor to any of you."

"I say, Ned, we are a most disreputable lot," he exclaimed, as that vagabond came up. "You and I and the crabs must hang on behind the cart, while Naomi gets on the front seat. We must trust to them to drive. Life is *always* uncertain."

A more disreputable lot certainly never drove through the peaceful village; Sophia's nostrils were justified in their expression of contempt, as she flounced away from the front door of the kitchen, where she was sitting with Baby, when we drew up before the gate. She would not look upon us.

"It's only to get Baby," called out Naomi. "They are all going home to dinner with us."

But it was useless calling to her. Naomi had to go and get Baby and find her sack and her hat. Sophia would none of us. Mrs. Emlyn, even, thought Macnally and Ned ought to be ashamed of their costume, or their want of it, and she sent them up-stairs, sharply reprimanded, to make themselves respectable for dinner.

"There is a limit," she said, with a severe look upon the four shoes left standing on the threshold, and the four barefooted tracks across the boards of the piazza.

Ned only rectified matters by a clean suit of his ordinary blue flannel, but Mr. Macnally came down a petit maître, the daintiest little man I ever saw. Nobody had ever known he had such clothes. He looked as handsome as possible; his hair, which had grown since June, was parted fastidiously. His clothes were of rather a light gray, and of the best London make. The children howled around him; even Maidy seemed to understand the joke, and clapped her little hands when the colonel turned him round and round to look at him. Baby dived into his pocket and tore out his fresh and most distinguished-looking handkerchief.

"It's embroidered; it's got initials on it;" cried Naomi, catching it from Baby. "How many letters— L—what is it; isn't that an L? I didn't know you had a middle name."

But Macnally flushed and seemed annoyed, and, putting out his hand, took it back peremptorily, and pushed it out of sight in his pocket; then he kissed Baby with a brightening of the face, as if to beg her dear little pardon for being annoyed at anything which she had been remotely the occasion of. Mr. Macnally was very swell all through the dinner, though with the slight disadvantage of having Baby on his knee the whole time. She refused to leave him, and he would not permit her to be taken away. It was a more informal meal than ordinary, even; we had not been expected quite so near the regular dinner hour, and things came up rather intermittently. It was quite immaterial to us at what stage the farcied crabs came; they got a little mixed up with the dessert, but we ate them all the same, together with some belated sweet potatoes, which appeared contemporaneously. Naomi left her pudding to run out and get a flower for the tutor's button-hole. Maidy insisted upon going round the table and sitting beside him, and having her peaches and cream carried around after her. My discipline at home was indifferent, but at Happy-go-lucky it faded out of sight. The colonel encouraged the children in all sorts of liberties, and Mrs. Emlyn snubbed me when I remonstrated.

"Your children are well enough," she said. "You must let them alone a little; that is all they need."

We all sat on the piazza after dinner, Macnally sitting in the hammock, and the babies and Naomi all tumbling about him, swinging him and being swung alternately. Mrs. Emlyn had her stocking bag and her dictionaries in a chair beside her.

"You don't get on much with your German," she said to me, shaking her head.

"Dear Mrs. Emlyn," I cried, "if you only knew how lazy I am!"

"Well, it's good for you, I suppose, but I should think you would get tired of it."

"I'm not tired of anything here. I only wish it might go on forever."

"Somebody's walking over your grave, Mr. Macnally. You shivered," cried Naomi.

"My 'good clothes' are too thin, perhaps," he said, rolling up Baby into a little ball and burying her in some shawls in the hammock, at which Rex barked and made an uproar.

"Seriously," said Naomi, "do you believe in that?"

"Believe in what? My good clothes? Of course I believe in my good clothes; you would too if you'd paid for them. They cost a lot of money."

"Oh, you know what I mean; shivering when people walk over your grave, and all that."

"Nonsense, Naomi," said her aunt, "you're getting superstitious as well as sentimental. Where do you learn such things? A year ago you never talked such nonsense."

"I heard my uncle say that," said Naomi, doggedly.

"We shall have to be careful what we say before you."

"Oh, you'll soon get tired of that. But why should people say so if it isn't true?"

"What ague-fits the old Romans must have had, Naomi, with their graves along the roadsides. I should think they would have shivered all their bones out of joint," said her aunt.

"They did have ague-fits sometimes; I read of it."

"But these must have been continual, with the steady tramp of multitudes. All business must have been suspended, for every one in Rome must have been chattering, from the least to the greatest. I think, Naomi, we'll have to dismiss that theory for the want of proof."

Naomi looked a little ashamed. "What made *you* shiver then, Mr. Macnally, if it wasn't that?" she said, persistently.

"I'm very delicate, you know, and I think I feel a little draught."

As we were holding our hats on our heads for the gale, even Maidy laughed.

"Aunt Penelope," said Naomi, quite ready to

change the subject, "you promised us we might have tea on the beach some night this month. This is just the night."

"Because the wind is blowing a gale?"

"The men on the beach said it would fall at sundown."

"What do they say about the shivering business?"

Naomi pouted. "Mayn't I go and tell the cook to get things ready for us, Aunt Penelope?"

"Better see first if anybody wants it but yourself."

Naomi fell upon me with kisses, and begged me to say I wanted tea on the beach. "And you too, Mr. Macnally, say you want tea on the beach."

"I would rather have tea on the beach, Miss Naomi, than inherit a fortune—yes, than have an offer, or than be elected President, or than have a pair of diamond earrings, or than find out where my grave is going to be—"

"You see, Aunt Penelope, they all want it—may I tell the cook?"

The cook was told, the preparations began. Naomi was full of business. Mr. Macnally and she and the children and I were to go along the beach and select a "site." Ned was to follow later in the cart with the pots and kettles and the things to eat, and then was to go back for the colonel and his aunt.

CHAPTER XIII.

TWO GRAY EGGS IN THE SAND.

" And oh, those days beside the sea!
 The skerries paved with knotted shells,
The bright pools of anemone,
 The star fish with its fretted cells,
 The scudding of the light foam-bells
Along the stretch of rippled strand
Spotted with worms of twisted sand,
 The white gulls, and the shining sails,
And the thoughts they all brought from the Wonder-land!"
         Olrig Grange.

IT was an afternoon to be remembered; the sky and sea were gloriously blue, the wind was fresh, but not cold; a storm had just spent itself out at sea; the surf ran very high and burst in marvelous glitter and magnificence at our feet. The delight of that beach always was its loneliness; there was rarely a human footprint on it; the sand always lay smooth and pure up to the very banks; now and then the little three-pronged print of a sand-piper's claw, or the winding trail of a snake from among the tufts of beach-grass, would mark it.

We found the place where we meant to make our encampment. It was a spot where the beach was widest, and where we were well sheltered by the sand-hill. We spread down our shawls and blankets; the children went off to gather drift wood for the fire, Mr.

[151]

Macnally to drive in the stakes and find the cross-piece
for the kettle. I wrapped myself in the shawls, and lay
dreaming, with the sound of the surf in my ears. A
tuft of beach-grass grew at my elbow, with the mysterious little circle in the sand around its base; and beyond it, idly looking, I saw, in the grayish-yellow sand,
two grayish-yellow eggs, laid in a sand-made nest.
The eggs were so near the color of the sand, and the
depression in which they lay so slight, it was almost
matter of surprise I had discerned them. The little
hollow was lined with small, smooth pieces of shell, well
worn by the beating of the waves. Trusting little
creatures, committing their treasure to the mighty One
who rules the tide crawling to its bounds beside them,
and the deep sky with its hidden tempests of wind
and fire and water, spread above them!

The little nest gave me many thoughts as I bent
over it. The eggs were still warm, so I moved my
blanket a few feet further away, and lay very still, that
the mother might come back and hover them with her
soft breast. She did not come, as long as I watched,
and my eyes wandered away to my two little ones, committed to God's care as blindly, with the waves of death
washing up beside them, and the firmament of destiny,
with its manifold and hidden powers, spread over them.
Nothing between them and the vastness of life's possibilities but my feeble, fluttering heart's protection and
God's omnipotence. With tears dimming my eyes I
watched the little figures moving about upon the
sand, and pledged myself in my own heart to live
and, if need be, die for them, who had no other earthly
guard.

I was startled from my revery by a step beside me. It was Mr. Macnally, with his axe over his shoulder.

"I am tired, as becomes a gentleman ; I'll do no more menial service in my good clothes," he exclaimed, throwing down his axe upon the sand.

I gave a cry. Alas ! the poor little nest was buried beneath the cruel steel.

"What have you done ?" I exclaimed, starting up. "Ah, the poor, poor little nest !"

And I lifted the axe from the crushed and scattered eggs. In my afternoon's revery I had identified myself so with the little guardian of the nest, that I could not keep back my tears. "The miserable little mother," I cried, looking into the beach grass for her.

"A plague upon my carelessness," he cried ; "it was a nasty thing to do."

I went into the beach grass, peering down ; a plover, with a piercing cry, flew up and darted away. "The miserable mother !" I repeated, gazing after her through my tears, which could not have seemed otherwise than silly, to a man.

"Upon my word, I'm sorry," he said, with a little harshness in his voice. I glanced at him, and his face showed pain enough to make me ready to forgive him. I don't know whether it was my tears or the bird's sharp cry that had given him the pain, of which, however, he seemed genuinely ashamed.

"I know you didn't mean to be careless, of course ; but I had been watching it for an hour, meaning to warn any one that came near, and to propose that we move away from here, not to scare her ; the poor, poor little mother !"

7*

" I hope she won't lose her mind," he said, testily.
" One hears of being as crazy as a coot; perhaps a plover
might go insane as well."

I looked at him reproachfully, which only added to
his irritation.

" You're so unhappy," he said; " and yet I'll be
bound you ate an omelette for your breakfast."

" If I didn't know you were sorry, I shouldn't forgive you," I said, sitting down on the heap of shawls,
and turning my face away from him.

" I *am* sorry," he said, in a softened tone, throwing himself down on the sand; " but I just can't bear
to see—anybody—cry. And it seemed to me such
a little thing to cry about—two gray eggs in the
sand !"

" It wasn't just two gray eggs in the sand; it was a
great deal more."

" Well, what was it; won't you tell me what it
was ?"

" It was my thoughts," I said, swallowing down
some more tears as my eyes fell upon the fluttering little white figures in the distance. His eye followed
mine, and no doubt his thought; for his mind always
moved lightning-quick, and his sympathy was as keen.
I felt he watched me covertly for a few minutes. It
made me restless, and I got up and said I was going to
bring the children back.

" Why should you go," he said; " I can make them
hear."

And he gave a peculiar, clear call, with which
Naomi was familiar. She waved her handkerchief in
reply, and went towards the little ones, playing beyond
her on the beach. I sat down again, and my compan-

ion resumed his position near me, only with his face seaward. The sun was sinking behind the hills at our back. The wind had fallen, as the sailors had predicted. Lovely tints from the sunset colored the sea and the opposite heavens. The tide was coming in, and the great waves, edged with white foam, rushed up the sands, ever nearer and nearer to us. Through openings in the sand-hills, when we looked behind us towards the sunset, there were beautiful glimpses of the green meadows and the blue Shinnecock Hills that bounded the horizon, and far, far on each hand stretched the wide, lonely beach, on which the ever-changing, yet ever-monotonous waves beat their long-drawn music out.

At last, through the opening nearest to us, came Ned's lusty shout.

"The ball opens," cried Macnally, starting to his feet. "No more time for sunsets."

"Do you want me to help you get the tea ready?" and I got up rather reluctantly.

"I'm sorry to say, I think it is your duty."

"Hurry up," cried Ned. "Don't you know I've got to go back for the others."

The cart was soon unloaded; such a lot of things, even to a jug of water and several bundles of pine knots.

"They didn't depend much upon the resources of the country," said Macnally. "I had found a spring, but I had misgivings about the drift-wood holding out. Better bring a few more bundles with you when you come back with the colonel and your aunt."

When Ned was gone, we lighted the fire and swung

the kettle, and spread the cloth on the bottom of an old " panny " that Mr. Macnally had found up in the beach grass high and dry, and had dragged down on the sand. It made an excellent table, except for a tendency to slope downward at the ends, so the things to eat had to be all put in the middle. The fire was just beyond on the sand, and was blazing brightly, and the kettle already throwing out its steam, when the children's voices were heard approaching.

"Oh, there," I said, as I, on my knees, was stirring the coffee in the little pot in which it was to boil, "I meant to have taken those broken eggs away. I don't want the children to see them, particularly Ned, who hasn't any principle about birds' nests."

"I'll go and bury 'em dacent," he said. "And sha'n't I bury the hatchet too?" he added, looking back.

I was a little ashamed of my sensibility by this time; the practical business of getting tea had restored me, therefore I didn't mind his lambent wit.

The children broke into exclamations of delight at the fire and the big cake on the table, and the biscuits and the cold chicken and the jar of marmalade. They hovered like little gnats around the fire, and with shrieks of delight laid on occasionally a modest splinter to increase the blaze. When the beach cart appeared in the opening with the dear colonel and the dearer aunt, we set up a great shout of welcome, and all ran to conduct them across the sand to the fire. The coffee boiled over, of course, as soon as I turned my back, so I had to hurry to it, and leave to the others the duties of hospitality. But it made a delicious smell that gave the colonel more pleasure than all our welcome or all the glories of the sea and sky.

The colonel sat on a barrel at the head of the table, with his overcoat on. He was very careful about not taking cold, and said, though we had heard it before, that eternal vigilance was the price of health. Mrs. Emlyn sat on the slope of the panny, at the foot; and Naomi, her yellow hair damp with the spray, but her cheeks red with the fire, and her eyes bright with enjoyment, ran from the kettle to the table ceaselessly, now handing up a cup of coffee to her uncle on his barrel, now carrying the biscuits to her aunt, or giving Ned, under protest, a second spoon for his marmalade.

"You know there's only one apiece; now Maidy and I will have to use the same. It's just exactly like you."

"Children, there's one spice we never lack at any of our meals," cried the colonel, shaking his head, but drinking his coffee with complacency.

"It's grown indispensable to me," said Macnally, buttering his bread with the carving-knife. "A meal wherein we vaguely feel there is some want, is a meal where Naomi and her brother don't give us any quarrelling."

"It's all very well for you to make a joke of it," said Col. Emlyn. "But let me tell you, such habits are bad tenants; they ruin the property, and you won't easily get them out. I may live to see Naomi nag her husband and Ned bully his wife."

"There is no danger," cried Naomi, tossing her pretty head.

"Not the least, for you," said Ned, in an offensive tone, which embittered the biscuit that Naomi had sat down to eat.

"I know what kind of a man I sha'n't marry," she said, with a mouthful.

"So do I, lots of 'em; in fact I don't know any other," returned Ned.

I was still kneeling at the fire, Rex beside me, pouring out the coffee—endless cups.

"You haven't had anything to eat," said the colonel, his appetite appeased. "Macnally, I'm ashamed of you, in your good clothes too. I should have thought you'd have had better manners."

"Don't reproach me," cried Macnally, "I've been feeding these children for the last half hour. One can't be nursery-maid and preux chevalier at the same time. I'm hungry as a bear myself."

The meal was a very long one. The sunset was gone, and a faint twilight begun, when the last appetite was satisfied.

"Now we must be going home," said the colonel, bustling about; "it is getting very damp."

"Oh, bother home!" cried Macnally, flinging himself down before the fire. "It's just beginning to be pleasant here. Let's stay till the moon rises."

"The children," I said. "I'll have to take them home."

"Oh, hang the children," he returned, profanely. "Or throw them on the fire."

Maidy thereupon climbed into my arms as we sat around the blaze, and Baby stared at him, standing behind me, with her chin on my shoulder. He looked a picturesque figure, lying stretched upon the sand, with the strong light of the fire on his slender, well-made limbs, his black hair, and his intensely shining eyes.

A compromise was made; the children went home

in the cart with the colonel, who was to send back the cart with one of the men. This man was to finish packing up the pots and kettles, and was to drive back such of the party as desired to drive. We were all grown very lazy since our supper, and nobody wanted to be post-prandial waiter or kitchen-maid. We pushed the panny, feast and all, into the background, spread our blankets near the fire, piled on pine knots, and sat down around the blaze, Rex with his nose almost in the ashes.

The night was still and beautiful, the sky deep and dark, full of sharp, clear points of stars. The tide had turned and was going slowly down ; the roar of the waves had lessened, or we were used to it. Where the fire-light reached the water there was a wonderful pageant, but, except that stripe of brilliance all was dark, and the unseen roar beyond seemed sullen.

" The moon's due in half an hour from now," said Ned, bending down to look at his big silver school-boy watch by the fire-light.

" Oh, Mr. Macnally," cried Naomi, who sat close beside me, with her hands clasped round her knees, a red shawl drawn over her head; "say something for us."

" Good-night, do you mean ?"

" Oh, you know I don't mean that."

" Well, what do you mean ? Do you mean you're too lazy to chatter, as well as to put the cups and saucers away ? Are you going to turn over your talking to me ?"

" I know you understand me. I want you to recite some verses for us—to say something that you know by heart. Please, now, don't make a fuss. Remember

what you tell me when Aunt Penelope makes me play
for company."

"Right, Naomi, that's a very good argument; Mr.
Macnally, you must begin at once."

"Exactly, Mrs. Emlyn; but where shall I begin?"

"Ask Naomi; she seems to know what you can
do."

"I know, I know!" cried Naomi, all eagerness. "Begin—right at the beginning of—'Shamus O'Brien.'"

"No, no, Naomi, that's not fair. You don't make
a good choice, either. Let me tell you the 'Pied
Piper.'"

"I don't want the 'Pied Piper.'"

"Then, have something about the sea—'Sir Patrick
Spens,' the 'Wreck of the Hesperus,' 'Inch Cape
Rock'—"

"I don't want any wreck or any sea. I want
'Shamus O'Brien.'"

"'Shamus O'Brien!'" we all called out.

And we _had_ "Shamus O'Brien;" in fact, we have it
still, for I don't believe any of the four who listened to
it will ever be able to forget it if they try. Naomi
was shivering and sobbing in my arms when it was
over; Ned took a long breath, as if he had not breathed
since it began; Mrs. Emlyn drew back her face from
the firelight, and did not trust herself to speak for a
long time; and as for me—but I cried so easily, it was
no great victory to make me cry. I think that victory
might have been won though, over tougher and colder
natures; I think there are few people who would not
have thrilled and shivered and wept at that marvelous
recital; at the wonderful pathos of his voice, the
wonderful power of his glance;—"fountain and fire;"

I could not analyze his empire over my feelings, then or ever; I did not even ask myself what moved me; I trembled and wept, and lifted my head and looked away, and tried to think of other things, as a child might.

He looked pale when, the recital over, he bent down and threw some more wood upon the fire.

"It will be gone before the moon arrives," he said, looking towards the east, where there was as yet no sign of its appearing. We all sat quite still ; nobody wanted to talk for a few minutes; Macnally went to see if the cart were coming. He did not return till Rex's sharp bark had warned us that it was.

"Who's going to ride?" said Mrs. Emlyn, getting up and shaking off her emotion.

"Better see for whom there's room when all the things are in," I said.

When the things were all in, there was barely room for two. I felt quite fresh and ready to walk, and so, after a good deal of protest, it was settled that Naomi should ride with her aunt, and Ned and Mr. Macnally and I should walk home along the shore. Ned didn't want to walk, and grumbled a good deal that he was not allowed to drive, and the man sent on foot, but his aunt would rather have walked to the Gulf of Mexico than have permitted him to drive her half a mile.

While we were raking out the embers, the moon came up; the last expiring blaze of the fire looked pitiful, in its sudden glorious light. We were quite ready, inconstant ones, to leave it, and start on our walk along the now illuminated beach. Ned kept with us for a long while—as long, indeed, as Mr. Macnally would sing with him. Ned had a good voice, but his

répertoire was not extended, and only that his and his
tutor's voices blended and sounded rich and strong and
mellow, would one have been contented to hear, over
and over, the same ineffable nonsense.   When Mr. Macnally halted, and dragged, and finally declined to go
further on such a monotonous strain, Ned betook himself off, by a short cut home, across the fields.   Rex,
draggled and damp with the spray and the dew combined, ran on before us, a white speck in the moonlight.

The sand was heavy, but we walked down close to
the waves, where it was wet and a little harder. Sometimes there was a silver mist over all; then that would
be swept away, and the full glory of the moon would
overflow the heavens and the sea.   Sometimes, when I
was tired, we would sit down on the sand and rest a
little while; we did not talk much.   It was the sort of
night that one feels can't come twice in a summer, such
a rare combination of cloudless sky, full harvest moon,
and balmy air.

"Under a harvest moon," said Macnally, as we sat
resting thus upon the sands, "one may naturally
moralize upon what one has been sowing through the
summer."

"This idle summer! I am afraid it would depress
me to think what I have sown, or rather what I
haven't."

> "We scatter seeds with careless hand,
>   And deem them ever past,
>   But they shall last ;
>   In the dread judgment they and we shall meet."

"Why do you say such things?" I said, shivering, getting up.

"I'm sure I don't know. One can't help thinking, a little—once in a while."

"I should have said you put the periods pretty far apart."

"Why? Because I couldn't cry over a bird's egg?"

"I thought that was buried."

The rest of the party had been at the house a long time when we got there. Mrs. Emlyn was walking up and down the piazza, and looking rather anxious.

"You will be tired to death," she said. "It was a great walk for you, through that heavy sand. I should have made you ride. I have kept the cart to take you home."

"Thank you. Then I won't sit down."

"No, you'd better not. It's getting late, and it is damp," she said, with characteristic frankness. "Besides, the man is waiting up, and he's been working hard all day."

"I'll drive you," said Ned, going down the steps. I kissed Mrs. Emlyn good-night, and went down after him. Mr. Macnally was standing beside the cart; I saw him put his hand on Ned's shoulder, and heard him say to him in a low voice,

"Let me drive to-night, won't you?"

Ned started, and looked not well pleased; he drew back and said, a little sulkily, "If you want to."

"That's a good fellow," said his tutor, low, as I came down the last step; and he put me in the cart, and sprang in beside me.

We drove on silently for a while. Nothing that he had ever said to me had ever startled me. What he had said to Ned did startle me. Why did he want to drive me home to-night? He always respected Ned's rights and position so scrupulously, and never asked favors. As he had said, one must think a little—once in a while; and I vaguely and uncomfortably began to think.

He stooped down to look at his watch by the moonlight. "The post-office won't be closed," he said; "sha'n't we go for the letters, before I take you home?"

"You'd better leave me, first," I said. "It's late; besides, I'm a little cold."

"Here are two shawls under the seat, beside the blanket. Tie my handkerchief around your neck. See, you can't be cold now. And we may never have another harvest moon. Besides, I may have some letters that—that I want to consult you about. Go with me to the post-office, won't you, please?"

It seemed perverse to say no, and I wanted to go, too. So I wrapped the shawls around me, and tied the handkerchief on my throat, and consented to drive on past the cottage, at the gate of which stood Sophia, looking out for me.

"I shall be back presently," I called, as we drove by. I am sorry to say she didn't give me any answer, but slammed the gate and went in.

"I shall pay for it to-morrow," I sighed.

"An hour of this harvest moon is worth a month of her bad temper," he said slackening the horse's gait. It *was* heavenly. The village looked asleep, save for a light in a window here and there, and a girl's figure now and then leaning over a gate, listening to some departing sweetheart's words. The white houses were picturesque flecked with the shadows of the vine leaves

growing over them. The trees threw long shadows on
the road. At the post-office there was a light still
burning.

"We are not too late," he said, springing out, but
he came back in a few minutes looking a little disappointed.

"There are no letters," he said, "only the colonel's
Scientific American, and some agricultural journals.
His ten acres ought to be pretty well worked up.
Every published light is thrown upon them."

"Have you no letter for me? For once I was expecting one."

"You?" he exclaimed. "I thought you never
cared for letters. You told me, I remember, that nothing coming from outside South Berwick could be of
any interest to you."

"*Nous avons changé tout cela.* I have an interest
now."

"Seriously?" he said, giving me a quick look.

"Very seriously."

"Don't make me uneasy," he said, rather low.

"Why should it make you uneasy? You don't tell
me about your letters."

"I would—I meant to, if you would listen—if you
cared to know."

"That's all very well. I've wanted to know all
summer and you haven't told me."

"Ah! I'm afraid you're not sincere to-night. It is
not like you to be insincere."

"At all events, I'll be sincere about *my* letters. I
am expecting—a pattern for Maidy's new set of aprons.
I can't sleep for thinking of it. I wrote two weeks
ago, and no word has come about it."

"Ah!" he said, with a sigh, "I believe that's all the interest that you have in life."

"Well, that and their fall dresses."

He had not turned the horse's head when we left the post-office, but was driving on through the village.

"Where are we going?" I said.

"Anywhere," he answered, "but towards home."

"Oh, please turn back. It's late. I—*want* to go home."

"To lie awake, pondering the pinafores, and the fall dresses?"

He saw that I was distressed and in earnest about it, and slowly turned the horse's head, and slowly drove back through the sleeping, silvered village.

"It has been such a perfect day. You might have added just a half hour to it, if you had been generous; you wouldn't have missed it from your pinafores."

"Yes, it has been a perfect day. How many, many we have had this lovely summer!"

"If this should be the last," he said, "should you be very sorry?"

"Why should it be the last? There is a week left of August. And Sophia may give us a respite for September, that is, if the nursery stove can be made to draw respectably."

I was so unused to fencing and parrying, and being, as he said, insincere, that the horse went much too slowly for me, and I feared every word that my companion uttered. He saw it, I think, and was silent. When we got out at the cottage gate, he exclaimed, with a little sigh :

"Well, it has been a nice day, if you haven't a good word to say for it."

Now I was inside my own gate, I felt at liberty to praise it. "It has been a nice day; I never denied it. It has been the nicest—in the world."

"It might have been half an hour longer, and nobody the poorer," he said, a little wistfully.

When he was gone, and I was alone in my room, I couldn't help thinking—a little, and my thoughts did not please me. What if I had been sowing, all this idle summer, that of which the harvest would be bitter and grievous? What did it all mean? I did not want to think. I untied the handkerchief from about my throat, and smoothed it out, with a strange sort of sensation, as my fingers passed over the delicate fabric. The initials I bent down to study by the light. They were entwined in a very intricate monogram. There were four letters; but how to arrange them I did not know. There was an M and a B. These were the only familiar ones. I had believed his Christian name to be Bernard; I had always seen him write his initials B. M.; here was certainly, in addition, an L and a C. Who was this man, who had come so near me; with whom I was on these familiar, easy terms of friendship; happy, if I could satisfy myself and him, that we were not on any other terms? A self-reproachful confusion reigned in my mind. I could not have told exactly what I reproached myself for; but it seemed natural, as things were wrong, that I had done something wrong as my share of the matter.

But these reflections, intangible, and, in a way, of the imagination, were swiftly put to flight. From the open door of the nursery came a sound, terrible always to my ear, the barking cough of croup. My heart sank, with a sort of sick faintness, as I threw down the handkerchief which I still held, and hurried to the nursery. I knew what it meant. Poor Baby's tea-party on the beach might cost her dear. Her little white dress I knew had felt damp, when I had put her in the cart with the colonel. Over it, she had had but a light flannel sack, which we had taken her out in at noonday. Of course her shoes must have been wet, for she had been playing close down by the waves all the afternoon. Against my self-accusations I had to put the fact that she had gone through the same exposure many times before, without any apparent ill result. I had grown careless because the children had been so steadily well all summer. I was tortured with the recollection of her, so bright and eager, in Macnally's arms, leaning down to put the last stick on the fire, before she was sent home. Her little white dress and red sack, and bare kicking legs, with short stockings crumpled down over the tops of her shoes, had made such a pretty, droll picture in the firelight. Then he had tossed her above his head, and carried her on his shoulder to put her in the cart beside the colonel. Pretty Baby! that was only three or four hours ago, and here she lay, fevered, restless, choked by this fierce, destroying malady.

"Sophia," I whispered in terror, catching her arm, for she was sitting by the bed, "tell me if you think she will get over it—"

"You won't deserve it if she does," she muttered, shaking off my hand.

CHAPTER XIV.

THE NEST IN THE CEDAR TREE.

" Oh, that the year were ever vernal,
   And lovers' youthful dreams eternal!"
                                    Song of the Bell.

" But all things carry the heart's messages,
   And know it not, nor doth the heart well know,
 But Nature hath her will; ——."
                                    Lowell.

I DID not take off my clothes that night, nor did
  Sophia. What made our watch the more anxious,
was the fact that we were alone in the house. The Indian woman, who was our cook and general servant,
had many calls from her family and her tribe, and was
continually asking leave to be away for a night or for a
day or two. The day before, she had gone, to be
away two nights and a day. We had felt always very
secure and comfortable, but this sudden visitation of
illness showed us how unsafe it was. Sophia was very
well skilled in the care of this disease. Baby had had
several attacks, more or less severe, during her little
life. She knew what remedies to apply, and had the
nerve to wait calmly for their effect. I was unnerved
and terrified, and begged her to go and get a doctor.
None lived near us; it would have been madness for
her to leave the child and go out at midnight for one.
And as for me, I could scarcely have brought myself to

8   [169]

quit the sight of the suffering little face.   I obeyed her
orders as calmly as I could, and submitted to give up
the doctor.

Before day-break, the child was much relieved.
When it was light enough, Sophia went away for the
doctor, leaving me with many charges what to do and
what to avoid doing.   She looked back uneasily more
than once, as if she scarcely dared trust the child with
me alone.   I couldn't blame her; I was in agonies of
self-reproach.

The remedies that she had applied seemed to have
been all-sufficient.   The doctor added nothing to what
had been already effected.   The morning was cloudy,
and finally rainy.   By noon the Baby seemed as well as
ever, sitting up in her crib, and domineering over us
all.   I was not allowed to feel easy about her, for both
the doctor and Sophia predicted a return of the trouble
after night-fall.   It was a wretched day.   I could not eat,
and even the watch of the night just past failed to make
me want to sleep.   I could not bring myself to leave
the nursery, nor to take my eyes off poor Baby.   When
I heard voices below, I shut the door, and sent Maidy
to tell whoever had come that Baby was ill, and I
couldn't leave her.

The rain pelted steadily all the afternoon against
the window panes; night gathered outside, and with
it thickened my gloomy apprehensions.   This time we
were not alone.   An Irishwoman, who lived in a lonely
shanty a mile or two away, often came to us to supple-
ment the Shinnecock ; she had the reputation of being
half crazed, but we had always found her industrious
and faithful.   She was persuaded, after her day's work
was over, to stay with us all night, and be ready to go

for the doctor, or render any assistance outside the room. I do not think she slept much, though she was given a bed in the garret. I heard her moving about at intervals all night, and, once when I went down into the kitchen for hot water, I found her there, muttering to herself, and mixing some unknown substances together in a bowl. She gave me a suspicious look when I came in, and directly threw the mixture out of the open window, by which, notwithstanding the rain, she stood.

" I don't half like Ann Day's look to-night," I said to Sophia, when I came back to the nursery with the hot water. "Don't people say she's unsettled in her mind ?"

" She's got more sense than half the people that think they've got their wits," returned Sophia succinctly, and dismissed the subject.

The night, which had begun with such gloom and apprehension, wore on to midnight, and then to dawn, and still Baby slept peacefully. When the faint light of day crept into the eastern window, and I felt the cool moisture on her little forehead, and listened to the even breath that passed her parted lips, I almost cried for joy, and for relief from terror. Sophia had acted all night as if another attack were inevitable, and now the day had come, and she was well. I threw myself on the bed beside her, and, worn out by my two nights of watching, fell asleep.

When I awoke it was broad day ; Maidy was dressed, and eating her breakfast by the window ; Baby was sitting up in her crib, unnumbered toys before her ; Sophia was tidying up the room, not in the quietest manner.

Maidy ran to kiss me : "Mamma, we have made all sorts of noises and you wouldn't wake."

I took her in my arms and kissed her, and leaned over to kiss Baby. The past hours of dread seemed to me all like a black nightmare. Had there ever been a danger that I should lose one of these, my treasures? But in the rebound I did not lose the consciousness of what I had resolved, and promised to myself ever to keep before me. Baby, with an unwonted tenderness, laid her soft cheek against mine, as I leaned over the rail of the crib. Maidy patted Baby's chestnut curls, and then smoothed my disordered hair. "My pretty mamma," she said, putting an arm around my neck. "My pretty babies," I murmured, holding them in one close embrace.

"Come to your breakfast, Maidy," said Sophia, in a sharp key. "These things can't be kept about all day."

I kissed her again, and she slid down from the bed, and went submissively to her bowl of bread and milk. She looked back at us rather wistfully, however. Sophia did not quite dare to send me away, but she threw dark glances towards me, as I sat on the bed, leaning over Baby's crib, and playing with her. I can't say Sophia felt defeated; that would be saying a harsh thing, for she loved Baby most devotedly. But she felt as if my punishment had been a petty farce, compared with my deserts; I had been let off too light by fate. She had grown so jealous, I think she was jealous of the favor that she thought I seemed to have found with Heaven.

I could afford to be magnanimous; so I got up soon, not to annoy her further, and went away to dress myself. The weather outside was dull and gray. The storm had subsided in the night; the wind had dried the earth a good deal; but now it had fallen, and a silence brooded, and a sullen sky frowned overhead; it was anything but joyful, but my heart was so eased I did not feel it.

Later in the morning, Sophia put Baby to sleep in her crib, turning me and Maidy out of the nursery. We went into my sleeping-room, which was in the rear of the parlor, and I sat by the window with some work, while Maidy played with her dolls beside me. Presently Sophia looked in to say that she had to go downstairs to prepare something in the kitchen; she had left the nursery door ajar: I could listen. The nursery was on the opposite side of the house, behind the dining-room; to reach it, one had to cross an open sort of place, unceiled and rather dark. There were beams overhead, and the sides were boarded up; several old wooden chests stood in it, in which we kept blankets and bedding. A flight of stairs descended to the kitchen from it. Across this dark space I made my way, once and again, to see if Baby were all right. Once I almost stumbled over Ann Day fumbling about outside Baby's door, who said she had been looking for the clothes-pins.

Baby slept long and peacefully. I went back to my sewing by the window. The air came in from across a leaden sea; Maidy leaned her head down on the window-sill; we were watching a nest of king-birds in a scraggy cedar tree that grew a few feet from the window. The scant foliage of the cedar was supplemented by a Virginia creeper that had grown over it, and hung from all its twisted limbs. In one of the crotches of this tree a pair of king-birds had built a

nest and reared a brood. Two only of the young ones
were left in the nest. We had watched them from the
window often. While we were talking about them, I
heard a gate opening from the farm-yard, and steps approaching. There was a lane which led up from Old,
Town Pond, about a mile away, which crossed our
empty farm-yard; not unfrequently people came that
way, and crossed our premises. The place had been
unoccupied so long, the villagers had got into the habit.
So I did not look up or notice till Maidy called out, as
the steps paused below the window, and her eyes turned
from the tree to the ground,

"Oh, there's Mr. Macnally and Ned; mamma, mayn't
I go down?"

"No, no," I said quickly, then looked out. Mr.
Macnally stood with his cap off, making a low salaam to
Maidy. He had his fishing-rod over his shoulder, and
a creel. Ned had the same indications of his calling.
He contented himself with saying good-morning, and
tramped away across the garden, and went towards
home.

"I hope Baby is better," said Mr. Macnally, standing below the window.

"Oh, she is almost well, I hope; she's asleep now."

"You had a great fright, I am afraid."

"Yes, indeed," I returned, drawing a long breath.
There was a little silence; I was thinking what an age
it seemed since we had driven home in the moonlight,
and of all, inward and outward, that had passed since
then. He was thinking—who can tell what? He did
not seem exactly his easy, merry self, though he tried
hard to counterfeit it.

"I have brought you something, Maidy," he said,

after a minute; "a lot of treasures from the beach that I picked up this morning—a baby horse-foot, two little crabs, and the prettiest scallop shells you ever yet beheld. See, they are all here in my creel. I haven't caught a fish, while Ned has got a dozen."

"Oh, mamma, let me go down and get them!" cried the child.

"No, no, Maidy, it is too damp for you. Mr. Macnally will leave them on the front steps, and Sophia will bring them to you by and by."

"Sophia will break them," cried the child, all in tears. "She threw away the last shells that he brought me; she said I never should bring one of them in the house if she could help it."

A swift red overspread my face, while I tried to stop the child's tears.

"I'm sorry," said Macnally, coloring, I fear, a little too. "I'm sorry that I suggested them. See here, Maidy, you can reach them if you try."

He swung himself up into the old cedar, and, sitting on a branch that brought him about on a level with the window, reached out his hand and gave her, one after another, the beloved treasures. She stretched out both little hands and grasped, first the crab, then the horse-foot, then the scallop shells, one by one, laughing, almost shrieking, with delight, the tears still shining on her cheeks. Macnally looked eager and happy while he was gratifying her; he stretched forward, steadying himself by one hand on a branch above, a lithe and graceful and almost boyish figure.

But while he was giving her the last shell, we became aware of a tumult in the tree above his head. Sharp cries from the parent birds filled the air; first one, and then the other, flew at him, grazing his head in their flight, pecking at him, and obliging him to defend himself with both hands.

"The little vixens," he cried. "What are they about?"

"The nest, the nest!" screamed Maidy, her smiles extinguished.

"There's a nest with two young birds just above your head," I explained.

"I'm trespassing, am I," he said, letting himself down to the ground lightly, and looking up. "I'm afraid they're the ghosts of the plovers' eggs. *Ma foi*, but that smallest one has got a temper! I think her first name must begin with S," he exclaimed, dodging another attack.

"Why must her name begin with S?" demanded Maidy, open-eyed.

"Because she's savage," he returned.

It was really a curious sight, the wrath and courage of those two tiny creatures defending their young. Mr. Macnally drew back a little from the tree, and gathered up his rod and creel. At this moment Ann Day came out from the rear door of the kitchen, with a basket of clothes to hang out. One end of the rope was fastened to a branch of this same tree. As she approached quite near us, I said,

"Take care, Ann; don't shake the tree; there is a nest of young birds in it, and the mother bird is afraid that somebody is going to hurt her young ones. She is flying about in such distress; listen to her; poor thing, it makes my heart ache for her."

The woman was a low, thick-set Irishwoman; her features were coarse, but her expression kindly. She

had light-blue eyes, which were restless, but not ex-
pressive, ordinarily. She looked up when I began to
speak, with her usual uninterested manner, but when
she saw the nest, and the birds circling above it, and
heard my explanation, a deep flush came over her face,
and an angry light was emitted from her eyes. She
stooped over her basket of clothes, muttering to herself.
Her hands shook; I almost thought I heard a curse,
and drew Maidy back from the window. She pulled
out some article from the basket, and attempted to hang
it up upon the line, but, not succeeding, tore it down
and threw it upon the ground, scattering the box of
clothes-pins at her feet, and with a lowering look towards the birds, went muttering away.

"Have I done anything to offend *her?*" said Macnally, with a gesture of despair.

"Oh, no," I said smiling, looking after her, as she
disappeared from sight behind the barn.

"Who has done anything, and what, may I ask,
does it mean?"

"Poor Ann!" I said, with a sigh. "She has had a
sad history, as far as I can gather it. She has told me a
little, and the Indian and Sophia have got more from
her. She went to the West Indies when she was a
young woman, to wait upon an officer's wife, and naturally, after a year or two, married a soldier."

"And quite as naturally, after a year or two, he deserted her, I suppose."

"Exactly; leaving her with one child. I don't know
how she happened to come to the United States; but
for some reason she did. The child was a great burden
to her, though I am sure she loved it very much. I
fancy her great desire was to earn money to go back

8*

to Ireland, and the child was in the way of her going out to work by the day, and if she took a place at service, she couldn't get wages enough to do more than support it at board. Then somebody suggested to her to put it in an institution of charity. I can't get out of her what the name of it was ; I don't believe she really knows herself. At any rate, she put it there, wherever it was, and took a place at service, and earned good wages for a year or two, and put the money into a savings-bank. Poor soul ; she has the bank-book now, and showed it to me. She won't use it, for she thinks it is blood-money."

" What does blood-money mean, mamma ?" said Maidy, pressing eagerly against me.

" I had forgotten you, Maidy. Well, it meant this time, that it was the price she paid for her little girl's life."

"Did she sell her ?" said Maidy, in awestruck tones.

" Not exactly, but she feels as if she had. For, one day, when she got liberty to go and see the child, she found it had been dead for several weeks, and was buried in the pauper burying-ground."

" Poor soul," said Macnally, with a sigh.

" They hadn't taken the trouble to warn her of its illness, though they had her name and address. And some underling told her it had been ill-treated and neglected, which may have been true, or may not. All that was left to her was the little bundle of clothes which the child had worn when she took it there. This they gave her back, pinned up, and marked systematically with her name. She brought it over one day and opened it and showed me the clothes. There was a little faded pink calico frock ; she stroked it with her

hands, and said, 'me foine ghirl ! me foine ghirl !' She
never went back to her place, but wandered about the
streets for days, carrying the little bundle; her intellect
quite shattered. I suppose she must have been taken
up by the police and committed to some asylum. After
that she doesn't seem to be able to give any account
of herself that is at all coherent. She is quite reasonable on every other subject, and is an excellent worker.
I suppose they found she was fit to set at large, and so
dismissed her from the asylum."

"How did she wander up here?"

"I can't imagine. I have often wondered. But it
was the very place for her; the quiet and the total absence of all associations. The neighbors are kind to
her, and she gets a good deal of work. Her tumble-
down little house, though, is in an awfully lonely situation. I've feared sometimes some tramp would murder her for her little hoardings. Ann loves to hoard,
poor soul; her calamity didn't cure her of it."

"Is she capable of doing a servant's work? Can she
understand orders given her, and all that?"

"Oh, yes, as well as any one; except when something
upsets her—seeing children, or something like that, she
is quite the best servant that I've had in a long time."

"What has set her off to-day?"

"Well, I have an idea that yesterday she was stirred
up by hearing Sophia talk of Baby's illness, and seeing
my agitation; and just now, it was the sight of the
mother bird's distress about her young ones. I saw the
blood rush into her face the moment I called her attention to it, and her poor dull eyes grew so troubled, and
then so fierce. I'm sorry I spoke to her about it. I
ought to have known better."

"I don't see how you possibly could have known better, or, indeed, could have guessed what troubled her at all."

"You would see, if—if you were a mother," and I stroked Maidy's head as she leaned out of the window.

"The maternal instinct, I confess, baffles me in some of its developments—that, for instance," he added, as one of the birds swooped above his head again. "What have I done to call for that?"

"Leaned against the trunk of the tree, I am afraid."

"Ah! Well, I don't seem to be popular here. I think I'd better be taking myself off."

And shouldering his rod, and kissing his hand to Maidy, he went away through the garden, leaping the fence, and striking off across the fields.

That afternoon, late, Sophia came into the nursery, where I was sitting with the children; she held out two dead birds, with necks wrung, heads dangling. "See what I found under the nest," she said, with a tone of triumph. Maidy gave a cry, and bursting into tears, hid her face in my dress. "Sophia!" I cried, reproachfully, "how can you torture the child so?"

"Oh," she exclaimed, tossing her head, "I didn't kill the birds; you needn't reproach me. Go to them that did."

"I should, with pleasure, if I knew whom to go to. It was a cruel thing. The poor mother bird, how she must be grieving now!"

"Well, you won't have far to go."

I knew, by a certain inflection of her voice, that always made itself apparent when she spoke of Macnally, that she meant him. I could almost have laughed at her persistent malice. I soothed Maidy, and insisted on Sophia's taking the birds out of sight at once. I did not feel that I ever wanted to look out of my window again, at the old cedar tree. A little thought made me sure to whom the poor birds owed their death.

CHAPTER XV.

A DAY OF RECKONING.

" Who is spendthrift to passion,
Is debtor to thought."

AS the day drew to a close, it grew duller rather
than brighter. I felt a longing for fresh air,
after my two days' confinement to the house. Baby was
as well as a baby could be, and was having her tea in
the nursery with Maidy. There was nothing to keep
me in the house ; so, wrapping myself in a rain cloak,
and drawing the hood over my head, I went out into
the twilight. I purposely avoided the road and the
direction in which I might possibly meet any one, and
followed the lane that led to the Old Town Pond—a
lonely enough lane, with neither tree nor habitation on
its whole length. A quick walk in the damp wind
seemed to me what I needed to steady my nerves and
shake off the overpowering depression that I had been
feeling all day.

The landscape was almost shrouded by the twilight
and by a faint mist blowing in from sea. Walking ex-
hilarated me a little ; I went on and on, till I reached
the pond, and the road that led from it down to the
sea. This road I followed, and soon stood on the sand,
and heard, rather than saw, the waves that, under the
mist, were rolling in upon the beach. The tide was

[182]

low; the wind was off the shore, and was beating down the surf, which broke on the sand with a sort of wail.

It was a lonely spot, a mile from any house; but I wasn't in a mood to feel afraid. Some fish-houses stood a little back from the beach; my walk had tired me, and I sat down in the shelter of one of them to rest. The reaction from my rapid walking, the moaning of the sea, and the dreary loneliness of the spot, overcame me, and putting my head down on my hands, the tears that I had been fighting against all day came to my relief. Yes, the harvest was ended, the day of reckoning had come, and I was wakening from my long and happy dream. No more summer seas for me; no more blue morning skies, and tender-tinted evening ones. Life must begin again in bitter earnest. The sea might well make moan for what was gone.

As I lifted my head for a moment with a despairing sort of weariness, I heard voices: one was a woman's, so I had no sensation of fear, but only drew back more in the shelter of the fish-house to escape attention. I listened rather anxiously, however, till they should pass, and I be free again. It was unexpected seeing any one here in so lonely a place. Presently the voices came nearer, and paused not four feet from me. I recognized the colonel's voice, and Mrs. Emlyn's. It was not unnatural that they should be here, as they were both good walkers, and often went on foot several miles from home together when the weather was as cool as this; but it was unfortunate that they should have come here. How could I command my voice, and not show traces of my not yet past emotion? I sat still, hoping they would pass on and not see me. Mrs. Emlyn gave a long breath of fatigue, and sat down on a boat just around the angle of the fish-house. We could not see each other for the mist and darkness, but their voices would have been distinct if they had whispered.

"How long have you suspected this?" said Mrs. Emlyn.

"How long? Oh, I can't say. Ever since Boughton was here, I think. I believe he put the idea in my head originally."

"It's a wretched piece of business. Why haven't you given me a hint of it?" she said, testily.

"I should think that, being a woman, you could have seen it yourself."

"Well, I'm not a woman to go about, poking into other women's hearts and imagining love affairs. I thought you knew me well enough for that. How should I be likely to think that a woman who couldn't bear even the faintest allusion to the fact that she was a widow, and who didn't seem to care for anything but her little children, was ready to be fallen in love with by the first man she met?"

"One sees plenty of that sort of thing in the world."

"Well, thank heaven! I'm not in the world, and never mean to be. It's a man's judgment you've made, not a woman's. I don't believe she has an idea of this sort of thing."

"I wish to heaven she mayn't have, but I'm much afraid I'm right. Macnally's a taking sort of fellow; we've shown the poor young thing scant kindness in throwing them so much together."

"I should as soon have thought of being afraid of Ned. One seems about as much of a boy to me as the other."

"Ah, well, you *are* discriminating."

" There's such a thing as being too discriminating. I, for one, believe you've made altogether a mistake, and that she's no more idea of his infatuation than I had, till you told me."

" Time will show. If she had only, now, taken it into her head to like Boughton. There was a capital marriage for her. But women's fancies are unaccountable."

" Hers would have been, if she had fancied him."

" How if you find she has fancied Macnally? Can you account for a woman in her senses, old enough to be married and have children, sending off a man of position and wealth, like Boughton, and setting her heart upon a fellow, like Macnally, about whom she knows absolutely nothing, except that he hasn't twopence over and above his salary as tutor?"

" Macnally's a gentleman, and a much more thorough one than Boughton, even if I'm not discriminating. I can understand a woman liking him, and I can't understand her liking the other."

" Macnally's a fascinating fellow, I suppose; women always like that sort of man. I confess I've a great liking for him myself. He's the best tutor that we've ever had, and an agreeable companion. But there are some things that I acknowledge I don't like about him. His want of confidence in us, first of all. What do we know of him? Absolutely nothing. He answered my advertisement; I was taken with him instantly. It's the first time in my life I ever did such a thing—I don't know whether I told you—I didn't ask any reference of him."

" You didn't tell me, indeed; I should never have

heard the last of it if I had taken a servant in that way."

"Well, what's done is done. I never have been troubled about it till this perplexity came up, and I began to feel some responsibility about this poor young widow. We've all been so fond of him, it was natural she should take him as one of us. We've done wrong, I'm afraid. I shall always blame myself."

"Wait till you know whether there's any harm done."

"I can't understand," he went on, "how, if things were all right with him, he shouldn't occasionally speak to us of his people, and allude in some way to the past. But it's all a sealed book. I don't believe he's ever dropped a word."

"Nobody's ever asked him, maybe."

"I've given him chances enough. Only to-day I took occasion to approach the subject; I got nothing by it. He seemed almost irritated. I verily begin to think the fellow's nothing but an adventurer. *What* do we know about him?"

"We know that for ten months he has been faithful to his work, and a gentleman, and irreproachable in all his conduct; he has commanded our respect and won our affection. Adventurer is a hard word, and I am glad I'm not a man, to pass so easily a judgment so severe."

And she got up and moved away.

"It isn't my final judgment," said her husband, following her. "But you must confess things are not as clear as day."

And their voices were lost to me as they walked

away towards home. They passed within two feet of where I sat, crouched down in the shadow of the fish-house. I had not had the daring, nor, indeed, the strength, to go away after I had found they were talking about me. I was so trembling and agitated, I could not have got away without being recognized, and the idea of making my nearness known by speaking to them was quite beyond my courage. It all passed so quickly, too. I felt numb and paralyzed. Even after they were gone, I felt unable to get up and go towards home.

When at last I went, it was quite dark. I could scarcely see the fence before me when I reached the lane. The ground was wet with dew; the mist came palpably against my face; the stones and ruts hurt my feet, as I blundered along through the lane; briars caught my cloak as I pushed through the narrow opening in the fence. It was all unspeakably miserable; a feeling of shame sickened me; a sense of disappointment made a physical weight and load about my heart. They need not have been worried about me; I had found out what they guessed, and had made my resolution in the dark hours of Baby's illness. But, oh!— but, oh! that they might never know — !

Before I got upon my feet and started on my walk home, I had come to one conclusion; the *something to be done*, that is the only solace in troubles such as this, was to get away from the place as soon as might be. I had even in my mind written the letter to the agent about the rooms we wanted; I had decided the number of days it would take to hear from him, to dispose of the packing, to prepare the children's clothes. If it hadn't been for the stimulus of this, I don't quite know how I should have got back along the length of that dark lane.

When I entered the house I left my damp cloak in the kitchen, and went up and tried to warm myself at the parlor fire. The Shinnecock, now returned to her duty, brought up a tray of tea, and set it for me on a little table, near the fire. The children had gone to bed; I heard Sophia singing to Baby through the open nursery door. I didn't heed my tea, which stood untouched, steaming away its fragrant cheer, but pulled out my portfolio, and sat down by the light to write the letter to the agent for the rooms. I had not finished it when I heard Macnally's quick, light step on the balcony, outside, and a knock, though the doors were open. I said, come in, and he entered with a brighter, more eager look than he had had in the morning. In his hand he carried quite a package of letters.

"I'm sorry," he began. "I don't think the pinafore letter has arrived, but here is your paper. The colonel has got quite a budget;" he added, his face almost imperceptibly losing its brightness. Something that he had meant to say, he had not said. His quick eye, no doubt, had taken in, at a glance, that there was some trouble; the neglected tea, my unhappy face, the careless condition of my hair and dress; and, worse than all, the inevitable constraint of my manner.

"You were writing, and I disturbed you," he said, drawing back a step or two.

"Oh, no," I returned, with a changing color that the words did not call for. "I have nearly finished my letter; it can't go till to-morrow morning."

"Is it about the pinafore? Or has something else

turned up, of interest enough in life, to write a letter for?" he said, with a little smile, emboldened, perhaps, by the fluctuations of my color. My face must have showed that he had unwittingly said something that gave me a sharp pain, for he added quickly, and in a voice very tender with feeling,

"I am afraid Baby is worse. I am afraid you think me very careless, but indeed I hoped that was all over, and she was really well."

"Baby is well," I replied, recovering self-possession. "I really am quite over my worry about her. I suppose I feel a little nervous and unsettled still, but a night's rest will put that all right, no doubt."

"I must not keep you, then," he said, uncomfortably, looking at his watch. "It is past nine o'clock, and you have been awake two nights."

He pushed away the chair before him, refusing to sit down; a stick rolled forward on the andirons, and he stooped over and put it in its place; he stood for a moment, resting his hand on the mantelpiece.

"I had something to say to you," he said, with his face turned to the fire, speaking with a little constraint. "But perhaps I'd—I'd better put it off till you have more time to listen."

I didn't answer; it seemed to me he must have heard the beating of my heart. But he heard nothing, I suppose, and the silence must have sent a chill through him. He did not even turn and look towards me, or he would have seen an agitation that, perhaps, would have seemed less cold. At last, he said, in a husky sort of voice:

"I was speaking to you the other night about expecting letters. Those I had looked for have arrived to-night. There was one of them I wanted to—to tell you about—and show you. Would you care to see it?"

As he said this he lifted his head suddenly and bent on me a look that seemed to devour me with its intensity. I had a feeling of terror. I looked this way and that. I wanted to escape. I believe I gave a kind of gasp, and then bent down my head over the portfolio which I still held in my hand.

"I will not force it upon you," he said, in an unsteady voice, as he crushed the letter in his hand. "I will not force anything upon you."

And when I raised my head again, and looked up, he was gone.

CHAPTER XVI.

THE SEA MAKES MOAN.

" Therefore I crave for scenes which might
My fettered thoughts unbind,
And where the elements might be
Like scapegoats to my mind."

Faber.

NAOMI stood at the nursery door knocking the next morning.

"May I come in?" she said, as Maidy, stretching up to the latch, opened it a little way.

I gave assent with less good-will than I had ever done before to my pretty little neighbor. I was taking care of the children while Sophia ate her breakfast and did many things about the house before coming to relieve me. She insisted that Baby must still be kept in her room, though I felt certain that the necessity was past. The weather was quite settled now: the house was intolerable. I was so irritable that I could scarcely speak peaceably to the little emissary from Happy-go-lucky, and the children's many demands upon me nearly drove me wild. Another night of sleeplessness had put my nerves almost beyond control. I feared Naomi's eyes, and her dear little questioning tongue. If she had only known it, I loved her better than ever then, as a part of my lost and ended summer, but still I was afraid of her. Then passed a few moments of security, while she kissed and caressed Baby, whom she had not before been permitted to see since her illness. She gave her a doll she had dressed for her, and to Maidy, a little picture she had painted, that no feelings might be hurt. Then she came up beside me, and laid her hand on my chair.

"We've missed you so," she said, stooping down and giving me a kiss. "We've had dismal times since Baby has been sick, and it's worse than ever now, for Mr. Macnally went away this morning, to be gone almost a week, I think. It's nice to have holiday, of course, and Ned's got all sorts of plans for having a good time. But it's not so nice at home without Mr. Macnally. He's always saying something makes you laugh. Don't you think he's very funny? And somehow uncle doesn't seem in a good humor with any one this morning; he's scolded all the men since breakfast, and I think said something cross to Aunt Penelope, though I don't know what. Aunt Penelope often says things to him, and he never seems to mind; but it's something new for him to speak to her in that way—don't you think it is?"

"I'm sure I don't know, Naomi, how should I? And I don't think your aunt would like you to talk about these things to me."

"You're just like one of us," said Naomi, caressingly. "I feel as if you were my cousin, or something. Aren't you coming down to dinner to-day."

"Oh, dear, no. I mean, that is, I can't leave Baby for a great while yet. Poor little girl, she'll have to be looked after very carefully now, you know."

"Can't Maidy come? It's awful lonesome; you don't know."

We compromised on Maidy, and I was left alone.

No answer came from the house-agent. I would not tell Sophia that I had written till I had certain plans to offer. I packed quietly many of my own things, which would not attract her attention. I spent diligent hours over the children's clothes. I paid little bills about the neighborhood ; if I could not have been busy, I should have been very much more unhappy than I was. I had fortunately been out, once or twice, when the colonel and his wife called, and Baby's illness answered for excuse for my not going down to Happy-go-lucky.

It was the fourth night after Naomi had brought her little budget of home news. I longed for the sea ; my head ached ; and it seemed to me to stand on the sands and feel the wind blow, would cool and cure me. After the children were asleep, therefore, I wrapped myself up and went out. It was twilight ; a gray, faint mist hung between heaven and earth, and hid the stars. There was a "moist, whistling wind." When I reached the shore I stood still, feeling it blow upon my face ; but it did not seem to cool the fever in my blood. The waves rolled in monotonously at my feet ; but the sound did not soothe me. There was no one on the lonely beach ; but the solitude did not help me, and, restless and disappointed, I turned back.

I could see the road a good way before me ; the white dust of the well-worn track, however, was all I could see, at any distance. The gray fences and the little spindling trees, set here and there along the roadside, were all invisible in the twilight. It was a good half mile from the beach to the cottage.

On my right, after I had walked quarter of a mile,

the road turned off to Happy-go-lucky. Its windows were shining with hospitable lights. Ah, dear, bright lights of Happy-go-lucky! What feelings they stirred in me! I could not hope to see them many times more. The best that I could hope was, that, by and bye, I might come to remember them with love and gratitude, and not feel bitter and ashamed. I leaned against the fence for a moment, looking at them, and then took up my way towards home, walking, not in the road, but in a narrow, faintly-beaten path close by the fence.

Some sort of a sound, not wave, and not wind, reached my ear, and I began to feel afraid, and hurried forward. I don't know what I was afraid of; it was a sudden agitation, the result of my ill-used nerves, no doubt. Along the path, coming rapidly near me, I saw a figure, dimly. I stopped in a sort of panic, irresolute which way to fly. Before I had time to move out of the way, the man, for it was a man, confronted me. The dim light, my dark dress, and his own preoccupation, made it as unexpected to him. We both gave a start, I a little involuntary cry of fright.

"I beg your pardon," he said, not knowing me, and stepped aside. I recognized the voice of Mr. Macnally. It was not remarkable that he didn't know me. I had on a long gray cloak, with the hood drawn over my head, which, I am sure, he had never seen me wear before.

"I was frightened, for I didn't know you," I said, hurriedly.

"You!" he cried, with a start.

"I'm glad you've come back," I said, not knowing exactly what I said or did. "I—I—thought you

weren't coming back for a good many more days yet—"
and I put out my hand.

He caught it and held it for a moment. We stood so
near together I could feel the strong pulsation of his
heart. He could not speak, nor could I. I withdrew
my hand, remembering, as I did it, that it was the first
time that he had ever touched it, except sometimes,
perhaps, in getting in or out of the carriage, and very
rarely then. He had taken very little advantage of our
constant intimacy—this adventurer. He dropped my
hand, and turning walked beside me.

"Are you just come from the train?" I said, at last.
He assented. "Naomi told me you were going to be
away a week."

"I meant to stay longer; forever, if I had the courage, but I hadn't." He spoke in a quick, low voice, but
perfectly distinct. "I went away in a great fury with
myself and you, like a hot-blooded Irishman, as I have
the ill-luck to be. Since I've been away, I have had a
thousand thoughts. Heavens! If one could stop thinking! The other night—were you only sorry for me,
and only angry that I dared to want to speak to you?
I thought I saw something else in your face, and I've
come back to ask you what it was. I hope you won't
be insincere. It isn't like you to be insincere. You
won't say I haven't any right to ask? Remember, I am
very unhappy. Tell me if there was anything that
would give me any right to hope?"

"No," I said steadily, after a moment. "I cannot
see that there was anything."

"Remember that this is life and death," he said,
standing still.

I was so near the fence that I put my hand out on the rail, and supported myself, as I stood trembling.

"It is life and death to me. You will be sincere. How can it be that—that you haven't any feeling for me? You have liked me, I know that well enough. You have been glad when I came, sorry when I went away. You have found it dull without me. We read each other's thoughts, we know each other's fancies, we choose the same path to walk in. Is that only liking? Or what is the great gulf that is fixed between the two? Is liking one thing and loving quite another? I don't ask you to love me with the vehemence of my love for you. It isn't in your nature, it wouldn't be fit. But I ask you to look well into your heart, and to be sure that you are right in sending me away to such a dark and miserable loneliness. Haven't you built up some morbid and unreal obstacle? Isn't it the past that you are trying to foist upon the present? Don't think me harsh. I believe that you are deceiving yourself. If I thought you knew your heart and could give an honest answer, I would go away in silence and take my fate like a man. But it tortures me, it unnerves me, it makes ruin of all my resolutions, to feel I am fighting with shadows; that it is a dead hand draws the circle into which I may not step."

"It is not that," I said steadily; "you are mistaken. I would tell you, if it were as you believe."

"Then what is it?" he cried passionately. "I have been humble enough, and reverent in all my thoughts of you, and patient in waiting for the feelings that I trusted to inspire. I never believed that I could speak in this way to you, but the fire has burned its way out, and you must let me speak. Give me my answer and

I will go away. Tell me, as before Heaven, what is it stands between us?"

"Why is it necessary for me to say more than I have said already?"

"Why? Because, if you don't, I shall never believe in any one again. I shall feel that you have been insincere while I have been believing you divinely true and clear. It will have been a deception that will do me deadly harm."

"Don't talk about deception. What have you been making *me* believe? Why did you not tell me before what—what you have told me now?"

"Because I waited till you should be prepared to hear it. But my secret outgrew my strength to hold it. Heaven help me! If I had but kept it!"

I made a movement to go on, but with a gesture he prevented me. The wind was strong and beat my dress and cloak against the fence and held them, and I leaned back upon this rough support. My limbs were so weak, I hardly think I could have stood without it.

"If I had waited," he said, "till you had grown more accustomed to the thought and sight of me—if I had given your prejudices, your resolutions, time to weaken and decay— I will wait now. It shall be as if I had not spoken; things shall go on as they were before. You will forget this folly, won't you? You must not give me my answer. I don't want it. You shall only give me hope by being silent. See! the worst is past. I begin to live again. We will be friends; just the sort of friends we were before. It shall not be your fault if I deceive myself. I only ask reprieve."

I shook my head. "You know that is impossible. Don't talk of what can never be. This is the very end. We—you, I mean—must make the best of it."

"Why I—why I alone ?" he said, eagerly catching at my altered sentence. "Oh, if you would but speak, if you would but tell me this one truth—is it I alone who suffer ? *Don't* you care for me ? How can it be ; how can I have been so deceived ? I have lived on this one strong hope always, since I knew my feelings towards you. I have known there would be a hundred obstacles, but never this. If you had had a troop of suitors I should not have feared them. When that padded, pompous creature came to see he wanted you, I never had a thought of jealousy. I never counted his money and his good position worth a thought. I knew you would abhor him. I felt sure, sure of your heart when you came to know it. And now you say you know it — "

The wind was blowing stronger every minute.

"I am cold—let us go home," I said, faintly.

"One thing—one word more, and this is ended. If I could be so duped by my own desires, if I could be so at fault in all my judgments—but no, everything reels! I cannot bring myself to believe you different from what I have believed you. I won't ask you the question that I meant to. I would rather believe you true and simple, and all you have been in my imagination, than have you for my own, and know that I had been mistaken."

"If you mean," I said, incoherently, "to ask whether I care—whether there is any one else—"

"Well ?" he said, sharply, drawing his breath quickly, as I paused.

"There isn't anything like that," I said. "You might have known there wasn't."

"Then, what is there?" he cried, in a pleading voice. "What is there that makes you treat me so? What is there that makes you forbid me to wait, and try, and hope a little longer? What is there that has changed your nature so? So good and gentle always, so afraid of making other people suffer. How can you —kill me—in this way? Have you reflected; do you know what you are doing?"

"Yes, I know," I cried, putting my hands before my face "It doesn't do any good to be sorry."

"Why doesn't it do any good to be sorry?" he murmured, bending towards me. "Listen to your heart this time. It will tell you true."

I lifted my head, and through the dusk his eyes shone like stars.

"There is no use," I said. "I cannot give you any other answer. If you waited a hundred years, it would be just the same."

He gave me a long, despairing look. "Then God in His mercy help me!" he said, putting his head down on his folded arms upon the rail beside me. How long we stood there I don't know; the wind swept by with a moaning sound, now lifting a little the gray, dusky mist, now gathering it thicker round us. I heard steps approaching, and the rough voices of men.

"Quick," I said, "let us go, some people are coming; I'm afraid of them."

He did not seem to hear me, and did not move at all. I had to repeat what I had said, and then to touch his arm, before he lifted his head, and understood me. By this time, the men, a party of sailors, had passed along. They were on the opposite side of the road; they did not seem to notice us. Their voices grew faint in the distance, as I walked slowly on along the path; Macnally walking silently and mechanically beside me. We were not very far from home; in a few minutes we reached the gate. He only went with me to the foot of the balcony steps. The kitchen windows were open, and a strong light came out from them across the path; as it shone for an instant on his face, I saw that it was white and very haggard. I don't know whether he said anything as we parted; I to go up the steps, and he to go out of the gate again.

When I got into the little parlor I found it cold and dark; the fire had gone out; the lamp had not been lighted. I shivered, and lay down on the sofa. I had such a feeling of physical fatigue and languor, that I could only think of the bliss of dying, and going to sleep forever. It seemed impossible even to imagine suffering anything more. After a few moments, Sophia came in, bringing the lamp. I knew it was overwhelming curiosity that brought her, and not a care for my comfort. She had, no doubt, seen Macnally's haggard face, as he passed the kitchen window. When she saw me lying white and faint on the sofa, she came near me, with a cold, hard look.

"You have been out late," she said, "and you have missed a visitor. The young lad from the Emlyns came and brought you a letter from the office. And his teacher called a little after, on his way, I should think, from the cars."

"Yes, I met him."

"I supposed you did. I know he came home with you now."

I didn't answer, only lay with my eyes shut. Her wrath smouldered awhile, in these trivial explanations, and then burst forth unstifled.

"I've been wanting to say something to you for some time—"

"Don't say it now, Sophia, I don't feel well enough to talk."

"You've felt well enough to talk, for the last half hour or over, with that man that's just gone out from here. You can hear me, I think, a little while at least. I'll do the talking, and you can do the listening. I've lived with your people ever since I was a little girl: it doesn't become me to say what I've done for you and for your children. If your husband had lived, I should never have thought of giving up the children, no matter what had happened. I am sure it will cost me hard to leave them that I have brought up. They are like my own to me. But if they were my own, they would not keep me, if I once made up my mind to go. You may make what arrangements you think best for yourself and for the children. I have made up my mind to one thing, either *that man* stops coming to this house, or I go out of it. I will mind your children and do my duty by the house as I have always done, for their sakes, and for their poor dead father's, if this thing is put a stop to, here and now. You can choose your choice. But I cannot, and I will not, see those children that I have nursed so long brought to disgrace and shame by a heartless mother. I will not see it, I say. I will go away and hide myself and try to forget it all. It is enough that this thing is the talk of all the village. If they were little boys it would not be half so bad ; but

9*

girls that's got to grow up shadowed by their mother's reputation!"

"Sophia!"

"Yes; I mean exactly what I say. It makes my flesh creep when I think of their poor father, only three years in his grave, poor fellow! When I think of what he was, and what he would have been to them, and then think of what's in store for them. Poor babies, they would be better in their coffins, where they would have been, if *you* had had the care of them. A woman that can forget a man like *that*, and take up with such a one as *this*, what right has she to have the care of children? A wild Irishman, turning somersaults in the village streets, shouting his songs and nonsense in the ears of decent, quiet people, that's a man for a lady to take up with. Folks say they don't know even what his name is; it's handy to have two or three, sometimes, I've heard. He's likely to have need of all he's got. The Emlyns will be sick of him, perhaps, sometime. He gets a little money now from teaching, but where'll the next bit come from, I should like to know. I suppose he thinks he knows, and that he's sure of a shelter and a crust if he plays a good sharp game, down here. But remember, now's your time to choose. I'll only wait another day to have this matter settled, and know exactly what you have made up your mind to do. For the children's sake I'll stay, if you break with him entirely; but for no earthly sake will I stay if he comes in the house again." I did not attempt to answer her, but got up, and almost staggered towards the door.

"Are you not going to answer me?" she said, fiercely. "Maybe you'll repent it if you don't."

I shut the door of my room, and left her talking still. The foul and muddy flood seemed to have washed out everything pure and lovely in life. I think, I simply longed that moment to die, and be hidden from all human sight.

CHAPTER XVII.

IN THE BROODING DARKNESS.

> " —— Did heaven look on,
> And would not take their part ?"
>
> *Macbeth.*
>
> "O God ! could I so close my mind,
> And clasp it with a clasp !"
>
> *Eugene Aram.*

THE next morning Naomi's pretty face appeared at the nursery door again, but this time disfigured with scarcely dried tears. She beckoned me to come out, and had scarcely a word for her little playmates. I put down Maidy, who was in my lap, and followed her into the parlor. She threw herself into my arms, and began to cry.

"Mr. Macnally is going away to-night," she said, between her sobs, "never to come back again. What can make him go ? Something is the matter. Uncle is all upset about it, and Aunt Penelope sent me out of the room, and won't talk to me. Ned, even, feels sorry that he's going. What shall we do without him ? I like him better than anybody I can think of. Oh, why, why does he have to go away ?"

"Why does he say he has to go ?" I asked, sitting down and drawing her down beside me.

"I don't know what he says to uncle. I know uncle thinks he ought not to go, and leave us, before the year is out. Aunt Penelope answers short, and won't give me any satisfaction. And he—oh!—he looks so dreadfully. It makes me think of Shamus O'Brien, 'For his face is as pale as the face of the dead.' He's the handsomest, and the best, and the kindest! Oh, what will it be at home without him? Ned quarrelling all the time, and nobody to stop him—and no jokes, and no fun—and nobody to take my part! I wish we could go to the city right away. I don't want to stay here any longer. Did *you* know he was going away to-night?"

"No, Naomi, I didn't."

"I wonder why he didn't tell you. Did you know he meant to go at all?"

"I knew he might go. I didn't know when he'd go."

"Has he heard any bad news from home, I wonder? I think it's so hard, Aunt Penelope won't tell me. They treat me like a child. As if I couldn't be trusted to know such a thing as that. I care more than any of them, and yet they act as if it wasn't any interest to me. He's all packed up—he's telegraphed for passage on the steamer that sails to-morrow. He's given Ned his gun, and me some books. He's just as nice as ever. He tries to talk the same and be like himself, but it isn't natural, and his face is so pale, and his eyes so hollow. The chambermaid says he didn't go to bed at all, but just walked about his room all night. At breakfast it was horrid. He couldn't eat anything, though he took lots of things on his plate. He tried to make believe he did. But all he took was a cup of coffee, strong enough to kill him. Aunt Penelope made it for him so, I guess, because she saw he couldn't touch his breakfast. She didn't even try to talk, except to stop me if I said anything, good or bad, to anybody. Oh, it was a horrid breakfast—but to-morrow will be worse."

And poor Naomi hid her face in my lap, and cried abandonedly.

"Don't cry, Naomi. You know people can't always be together. When you get older you'll be used to partings."

"I thought you'd feel badly too, you've always seeemed to like him so."

"I do feel sorry, ever so sorry. But you know I'm older than you, and I've said good-bye to so many people."

" Then I don't want to get older, if I'm going to feel that way about things. I could say good-bye to a hundred thousand people, but it wouldn't make me used to saying good-bye to him. If he was going away happy, and all that, it would be bad enough. But to know he's in trouble—and not to know what the matter is! And to keep thinking all the time it may get worse, and not to know for certain anything about him! I didn't think you'd be that way. I thought you'd feel like me about it, he was such friends with you. Why, that ridiculous old candlestick you gave him with the ribbon around it on his birthday, he packed it up the very first thing, for I went up to his room to take him some things that the laundress had forgotten, and he was packing it into a box all with tissue paper around it. And Maidy's little Cinderella was in the tray of his trunk. Poor Maidy! She won't have him to carry her on his shoulder any more. But she'll soon get over it, I suppose, she is so little."

I stroked Naomi's yellow-brown hair, and would

have smiled, if I had had the heart. I petted and comforted her as well as I could, and she soon went home,
to hang around her tutor's closed door, to be snubbed
by her aunt, snarled at by Ned, ignored by her uncle,
and to have her honest grief most entirely disregarded.

The day passed heavily enough with me. After
Naomi's visit, nobody at all came near me. I felt
very sure he would not go away without seeing me.
It seemed to me probable he would come the last thing
before he went away.

The train went at nine fifteen. At eight o'clock he
had not come. It was a warm, close night, not a breath
of wind stirring. All the parlor windows were open,
and the doors. It was not hot—it never was hot at
South Berwick—but there was to-night a quality in the
air that made it abominable: it weighed you down like
lead; it oppressed you like a trouble: you opened a window and no freshness entered; you fanned yourself, and
were not the better. I sat down by the parlor lamp
awhile, then walked restlessly about the room, and then
went from one room to another, trying to occupy myself, but listening intently all the time. All the doors
and windows were open; it seemed as if everything
were laid under a spell, not to be banging and fluttering in the usual gale.

Sophia had taken her work, and was sitting in the
dining-room by a small shaded lamp. She often sat
there in the evening, to be near the children. The
dining-room, as I have said, was next the nursery, and
communicated with it by a door. This door was shut,
however, to keep out the noise and light. Sophia trusted
to her sharp ears to hear them through the hall which
led into the sort of unfinished garret into which the

nursery opened. The parlor and my sleeping-room were on the other side of the hall, all opening, in the same way, on this unceiled, ill-lighted space. Stairs to the attic led up from it, through a door; stairs from the kitchen led up to it from below. I should think it was about sixteen feet square. You could touch the beams by slightly lifting your hand; they were cob-webby and dusty, notwithstanding Sophia; across the floor she had laid strips of rag carpet from the stairs to the different doors, that the children might not be roused by steps on the bare floor.

I stood for a moment by the open window of my room, looking out into the starless night; then crossed this chamber, and went softly into the nursery. A shaded lamp was burning in one corner; the door was open, and the window. The room was all in the scru-pulous order in which Sophia always left it when her day's work was done, and her nurslings were asleep. Here lay Maidy's little shoes, beside the chair on which lay her folded clothes; there Baby's; there the bath-tub, with its sponges and towels on the rack beside it, the soap and powder box and brushes on their little table, close at hand. Before the unlighted stove hung the bath-ing blankets, and two little wrappers. There was not a thing out of place; all told the story of monotonous nursery life. That was the life that lay before me; that was what was to satisfy my soul henceforth. I took the lamp in my hand, and went and stood below the two little cribs, where the light fell upon the two children in their peaceful sleep. I gazed long and steadfastly. Yes, it ought to satisfy me; it should satisfy me. I thought of the agony that wrung me

when only a few nights before I had seen Baby lying
in that same crib, so ill. Was I the same woman?

I put back the lamp, and went and stood between
the two cribs, and bent first over one and then over the
other. Yes, I loved them best; it was enough; I was
satisfied. Baby lay with one hand under her cheek, the
other grasping a little battered fleecy lamb, with a faded
ribbon on its neck, and a tiny tinkling bell, with which
she always went to sleep. Her soft chesnut curls were
moist on her forehead, as was the little band of embroidery on the nightgown round her throat. With a
tender care, I turned back one of the light coverings
of her crib, and stooped to kiss her pretty, pretty, little hand. Maidy gave a sigh and turned over on her
pillow; "Dear little Maidy," I thought, gazing down
at her sweet face, as she lay with her arms crossed on
her breast, and her eyelashes on her cheek; "you and
I will be companions, and live together always. Baby
will go away and marry. You and I must love each
other very much; there is a long road before us." I
caressed her fair curls, and spread them out upon the
pillow, and lifted one to my lips and kissed it. I
thought of the time when she was a tiny infant, and
when her proud young father first held her in his
arms. "Dear Arnold," I said, in a whisper, "brother
for all eternity; I will be faithful to your children."
Then I knelt down, with bowed head, between my two
babies, and commended them to God's gracious care
and keeping; and for myself I asked fortitude and
patience.

With a heavy heart I got up and walked to the
open window, through which the stagnant air crept in.
For a moment I had forgotten the outside world, while

I had been on my knees beside the children; now I heard a wagon pass, and it recalled me to the present, and I went restlessly out of the room. It could not be that he would go without seeing me again. I walked up and down the parlor, and up and down the balcony, and then sat down by the lamp with a sort of resolution that I would not get up again. It was now nearly half past eight; I might as well face it, the wheels I had heard were his. He was going without seeing me—perhaps it was best. What good could come of saying good-bye; what solace could there be in half an hour out of a life-time? Separation might as well begin now, as at nine o'clock. I must begin to school myself; I would not get up, I would not listen. I would read, and turn my thoughts away. I heard the gate-latch lifted, and a step outside. I did not raise my eyes till some one stood in the door. It was Macnally. I got up, and said:

"Naomi told me you were going to-night. I began to think you weren't coming to say good-bye to me."

"Oh, no," he said, "Ned has gone on to the train with my luggage, and will get the checks. I have— half an hour."

And he took out his watch.

"You can't walk it in fifteen minutes," I said.

"Easily, in ten," he returned, with a faint smile. "But don't be uneasy. I shan't get left, or, if I do, I can catch my steamer by the early train to-morrow. It's a well-bred steamer, and doesn't sail till three o'clock."

"Then, if you have so much time you might sit down, I think. Here is my very nicest chair. You look as if you were dreadfully tired."

"Do I?" he said, passing his hand over his forehead as he sat down. "I don't exactly know what I am to-night."

"It is so close," I said, moving restlessly my fan. "We haven't had such a night this Summer."

"No, I am sure of that," he returned, with an almost imperceptible gasp.

"It suffocates one," I went on. "And in September, too, when one doesn't look for suffocation."

Rex came pattering in at this moment, having heard a friend's voice. He wagged his tail gently and walked across the room and put his paws on Mr. Macnally's lap.

"Poor Rex, poor fellow," said he, stooping down and patting him. But Rex could not be satisfied with this. He sprang up on his knees, and put his nose in his face.

"That's an unusual attention, old fellow," he said, in rather a low voice, as he held him off. "You know I'm going away, I see."

"Don't let him trouble you," I said, getting up and going to take him from him. "You're so tired. You must not be bothered."

"I shall have time enough to rest on the steamer," he answered, leaning back in his chair, a sickly whiteness passing over his face as for an instant he closed his eyes.

"You are ill," I said, standing before him with the dog under my arm. "What shall I get you? I *wish* you didn't have to go."

"I wish to Heaven I didn't!" he cried, with a bitter little laugh, rousing himself and lifting his head. "I am not ill; you must not worry. I am, as you say, awfully tired; just fagged out. It will pass. You mustn't worry." I ran to the dining-room and got a glass of wine, braving Sophia, who sat there sewing. When I came back he was standing up.

"You must drink it," I said, in an agitated way, standing before him. "Won't you? It may do you good."

He took the glass from my hand, and drank off the wine.

"Now sit down and rest," I said, wheeling the chair close up to the table and shading the light where he sat down. "You have twenty-five minutes. You can rest a good deal. Rex, lie down, lie down, sir."

Rex lay down at his feet, with his head on the floor, his black eyes fixed with a keen attention on his face. He wagged his tail occasionally, but made no other movement. There was a silence of a moment or so.

"You *are* better?" I asked, bringing a light chair and sitting down near him beside the table.

"Oh, yes," he said. "I am better. I asked you not to worry about that."

"The voyage may do you good, and the change. I think it often is the best thing. And you'll let us know all about it; you'll write—to—some of us."

"I just promised Naomi."

"Be sure you write soon, just as soon as ever you are landed. We shall want to know."

Then I opened my portfolio, lying on the table, and said, "Here's a photograph I got out for you this morning. I thought perhaps you'd like to have it. It was taken in the Spring. It's better of me than of the children. Baby wouldn't sit still, as might have been expected, but Maidy's is pretty good. And on the outside I have written an address which will always reach me—some time when I mightn't be near the Emlyns—at any rate, I put it down."

He took the little picture and leaned over it to look at it by the light. An expression of great pain passed over his face. I faltered, " I thought you'd like to have it, though it isn't very good."

" I shall like to have it one of these days, no doubt; but I don't like to have it now. It is so little for a man to have when he wants—everything."

He leaned down on the table with a sort of groan, and put his hands before his face.

" I'm sorry I gave it to you," I said, almost crying. " I don't seem to know how to do the right thing. I wish you wouldn't—feel so—"

" Forgive me," he said, lifting his head, and putting the picture in its envelope in the pocket of his vest without looking at it again. " Forgive me ; I know this is unmanly, and I don't blame you for reproaching me. Yes—as you say—the voyage and all that sort of thing is apt to do one good. And you—when shall you go away from here ?"

" Oh, very soon, I hope ; as soon as ever we can go. Next week perhaps. I have begun to pack."

" And you will be—in the city after this ?"

" I suppose so, I don't know. It all depends upon the children. If they keep well, we might as well stay there as anywhere ; but if they're not as strong, I've sometimes thought it would be better for us to have some little place in the country where we might live all the year."

Involuntarily I looked up at the clock, and his eyes followed mine. " I have ten minutes more," he said, with a bitter smile for a moment on his lips. "Don't begrudge them to me. I have no doubt I shall live forty-five years more, at least; we're a long-lived family. Nothing ever kills us; there are no bullets for us, no rotten sleepers, no misplaced switches, no defective boilers. I don't believe we should be hung if we committed murder! Don't begrudge me my ten minutes; turn your back upon the clock, and trust me to get myself away in time."

The tears swam in my eyes, and I looked down.

"Ah, don't!" he exclaimed, with frantic irritation in his voice. "You don't know what you're doing. A man can't stand everything at once."

Then he got up and walked once or twice across the room. "You are sorry for me?" he said, stopping before me, his voice full of the deepest tenderness. "I am ashamed that I have made you cry. I will go away and put an end to this; good-bye."

"Don't go till it is time," I faltered. "You don't seem to think I care, but you might know I do."

"How should I know it when you've told me that you don't!"

"I haven't told you that. We can't go all over it again, but you ought to understand. It makes me very unhappy."

"Yes, because you are sorry for me. Isn't that all that makes you so unhappy?"

"I shall be very lonely, you must see that. I haven't so very much pleasure in my life. It makes me very uneasy and anxious to know you feel so bitter and unhappy. Won't you promise me to get over it, and to be like yourself again? I wish this summer could be blotted out."

"Ah, well, it can't be, that is all. Good-bye."

1 got up now; the hands of the clock pointed at five minutes of nine.

"Good-bye," he said, again, turning towards me, and holding out his hand.

I put mine in his, and he held it, and looked into my eyes with an intent and searching look.

"Why must I go?" he said. "What is the need?"

"There is a need," I said. "You must go, but oh, don't go without being friends with me. Indeed, it isn't my fault."

"Whose fault is it?"

"Whose? How can I tell? Fate's—"

"Shall I tell you what it is? It is your children stand between us. You cannot say it is not. You aren't willing to trust them to me, whatever you might be willing for yourself. I can't blame you. I have led an idle life; but you needn't have made it final—you might have let me try."

"It must be final. Do not let us talk about it any more. Only be friends with me, and believe I am unhappy too."

He did not let go my hand, nor take his eyes from my face, but grew whiter and whiter.

"Good-bye," I said, pale and trembling. "You ought to go—you will be left."

After a moment more he released my hand; his lips moved—I don't know what he said. We were standing near the parlor door; Rex jumped up, and began to lick his hand. He took a step forward towards the hall, then turned back.

"The children are asleep? mayn't I look at them before I go?" he said, in an unsteady voice.

He knew the way to their room. I stood in the parlor door and watched him go along the narrow hall, into the open garret that led to the nursery. He was gone three minutes, perhaps; when he came back, he looked deadly white. He did not offer to take my hand again or speak to me as he passed me, but the look in his eyes was one that I fain would have forgotten.

He was gone: the gate latch fell for the last time after him, and I began to feel the full weight of the thing that I had done. I went out on the balcony, and walked restlessly up and down, and tried to think over all the good and sound reasons that had seemed sufficient for me, half an hour ago. But they didn't seem to me good and sound any longer; nature cried out against them. What had I done? I had sent him away from me in the state of mind in which men do rash and awful deeds. There might be a bullet for him, though he had said one never had been found. I thought of his hot Irish blood; I was afraid for him. What right had I to spoil his life in this way? Didn't his love for me make some duty for me? Were the children and the past all that had any claim upon me? Hadn't I made some grave mistake?

I saw Sophia go stealthily in from the balcony to the dining-room. She had been listening outside at the open parlor window, to our parting words. Ah, well, she might listen now. She would never hear anything more. It was all over—it was all over! I said it again and again to myself, leaning my head against the little pillar that supported the balcony roof, where the trumpet creeper twined. The night was utterly starless, and yet there was no mist. There was such a stillness. The surf on the beach was low and faint, like the pulse of a dying man. I heard no sound at all but that, and for that I had to listen keenly. We were so far from the village, no bustle reached us, if there were any there. I counted the minutes, and wondered if he would reach the train. Oh, if he might not! If he had to come back, I should tell him that he need not go. *Why* had I let him go? I prayed that I might have another chance to see him; it was not all over, it should not be all over; I would write, and tell him to come back. Ah, where should I write? I remembered he had left me no address; it was even possible, in the haste of his going, and the displeasure at his departure, he had left none with the Emlyns; it seemed to me as if his brief and bright presence had been like a star in those black heavens, suddenly shooting down and being lost in darkness.

The minutes passed; the village clock had long sounded out nine, and still no coming of the train. It was late; he would make it; there was no longer any hope that he might miss it. It was nearly twenty-five minutes after nine when the whistle sounded, sharp and piercing, through the still air. I held my breath during the few moments, till it sounded again; he had said good-bye to Ned, he had gone into the close and dimly-lighted car, and had thrown himself into a seat. Yes, it was all over, for the train was moving, the whistle sounded clear and distinct across the plain. I could see the lights of the train as it moved along the level country, for half a mile distinctly in my sight. Everything was dark but that moving chain of lights, creeping in silence from me, further and further every instant. A sort of oppression seemed to overpower me, and when the last

10

light wavered and was swallowed up in darkness, I sank
upon a seat, and, burying my face in my hands, said
some passionate, incoherent words aloud.

Sophia's figure appeared in the door-way; she approached me. "Did you call? Do you want anything?" she said.

I lifted my head and leaned it back upon the vine
by which I sat. "No, I did not call you. I don't
want anything."

She looked at me keenly and went back to her sewing. She might look her fill now. I did not care who
knew. Ah, what had I done? Had I not been influenced by others? Why had I not listened to my heart?
I had thought it was all steadfastness and duty, but how
much of it had been concession to the world's opinion;
fear of this terrible strong woman who domineered me
so. They had called him an adventurer; how that
word had stuck in my mind! I could not get rid of
it; it was coming up continually. If there had not
been any such word, I wondered if I should have sent
him off. How weak I was, how paltry and poor I
looked to myself; how strong and grand his love looked
when I compared it. A woman who did not even
know her own mind, who could deceive herself so,
who could think herself so firm, when her purpose
was like shifting sand! What was the past to me? I
hated it, it wearied me to think of it. Arnold—a dear
brother, nothing more—what feeling had I ever had for
him that compared to this? How dull, how shadowy,
how pale the past all looked. How childish and immature the hopes and pleasures of that time. Why had I
not been a woman, and resolute, and known that a love
like this had its demands, as well as memories like

those? It had been puerile—it had been like a girl in a story-book. I had not risen to the occasion that had come upon me. I had courted self-sacrifice, and had forgotten that I was not sacrificing myself alone. Yesterday it had seemed to me the height of heroism to say I would live for my children and put aside all that could make life bright to me; to-night it seemed contemptible. Why could I not have lived for them, and saved him, too, from misery?

The cold counsels of yesterday had said it would be cruelty to them to link their future with one of whom I knew so little; to risk their certain daily bread in the uncertain fortunes of a nameless adventurer. Through much struggle and many straits I had brought them on so far in their life's journey; in the Providence of God I had now a reasonable certainty of competence and comfort for them. I had no right to throw this away, and put in jeopardy their future: I was bound to give them, being fatherless and helpless, my best care, my whole love. This new protector, with his shrouded past, his uncertain future, his versatile talents, his hot blood—what would he make of their lives? What part even of myself could I give to them, having first given myself to him?

All this to-night seemed ungenerous and unworthy. It all seemed to me tainted with a suspicion of his honor. If I had believed in him thoroughly, how I could have listened to such reasoning. And I did believe in him; what spell had been upon me to decide against him? I could always have trusted him with my own fate, why not with my children's? Why had this conviction come so late? What was duty, what was right? How could I know what God meant me to do

ever, if upheavals of purpose such as this came over
me ? Ah, poor children, you have a sorry guardian,
strong in naught but her repentances !

I sat still, leaning my forehead against the vine
stem : the tears, usually so ready, did not fall to-night:
a weight of lead was on my heart, a fire of suffering in
my brain. Each moment that passed took him further
and further from me ; the distance between us grew
with every second. I stretched out my arms into the
thick, dark night ; I prayed God to let him come back
to me ; to save me from this devouring anguish. How
could I bear my life ; how would this wound ever heal ?
All was so still, so heavy, so fixed, so fated. The air
itself stood still ; it seemed to me the ocean, too, was
dead, for I heard no longer its faint pulse upon the
shore.

Once only I heard a little sound that startled me.
As I leaned my hot forehead against the vine, below
me, there was a faint rustling of the lilac bush that
grew beside the path, and an instant after, the gate
latch was softly lifted, and as softly dropped into its
place. I raised my head and looked down, but it was
like looking into the eternal abyss ; there was nothing
but black darkness a foot beyond the house. I roused
myself enough to walk along the balcony and glance
into the dining-room. It was not Sophia ; she sat
bending over her sewing, slightly rocking, her lips
tight pressed together. She had not heard the sound ;
it must have been light, indeed, to have escaped her
ear. It did not trouble me long ; it must have been
some trespasser passing across the yard, coming from
the lane. I went back to the chair in which I had been
sitting ; physically, I was so weary and overstrained ;

mentally, I was so far from any ability to rest or calm myself. The conflict of feeling did not abate as the night in her swift course moved on.

Ten o'clock struck; eleven; twelve. I felt as if years of trial had passed over me, and yet the hours were not slow. A bitter feeling seemed to grow upon me. At last I forced myself to rise and go into the house. I hated the thought of the house, and the four walls pressing in upon me. The black, midnight sky had seemed less gloomy. But I must take up the burden of daily life and nightly care again. My lip curled with a bitter contempt for my puerile round of duties, having left the great one so undone. I must put out the parlor lamp, lock the front door, see that the windows on the balcony were fastened. But as I passed the dining-room, I saw that Sophia still was there, by the lamp, stitching relentlessly, and not looking up. I knew she often sewed half the night; it was not unusual; fall clothes for the children were now in hand, and she bent her whole mind upon the work of each season as it came. Still, I knew she would not leave me up; suspicion, curiosity, both would oblige her to see me fastened in my room.

When I came into the parlor, I sank down into the large chair by the table that I had wheeled up for Macnally to sit down in. Three hours ago! It seemed a lifetime, and yet but a moment. The irrevocable three hours; what a gulf of space that had put between us, widening every moment; he speeding on into the night, in that chain of moving lights; I purpose-weak, bound, left behind helpless in the dark stagnation of the life that I had chosen. The hands of the clock moved on another half hour. The lamp took the law into its own

hands and went out. Only a faint light came in from
the dining-room across the hall. Sophia, who had moved
restlessly about to attract my attention for some little
time, now came in at the parlor door.

"Ann Day went away without her money this evening," she said, in a hard, practical way that grated on me
unbearably.

I was leaning back in the chair, my eyes shut. I
did not open them, but said "did she?" in a tone of in-
difference that seemed to make her angry. She went
about slamming the shutters, fastening the door; presently she said, taking her lamp in her hand:

"It is half past twelve o'clock."

"I heard it strike," I answered, not moving, nor
even opening my eyes. She went away angry. I de-
fied her so far as I was capable of having any feeling
toward her. She had done me all the ill she could;
she would never trouble me again. My long strain
had exhausted me. I lay back listless in my chair:
several minutes passed, I heard her moving about in
the open chamber outside the nursery, closing the one
small window in it. Then I heard her go up the attic
stairs, and walk across the bare floor to the end of the
rough, empty space, where the Indian woman slept. I
knew she always went up there, before she went to bed
herself, to see that the woman had put out her light
and left the scuttle safe in case a shower should come
up in the night. She came down, and shut the door
of the stair-way. Then she went to the door of the
kitchen stair-way, and tried it. I heard her mutter
angrily something about the woman having left it open.
She shot the bolt with wrath, and then went on into
the nursery.

A moment, perhaps two, passed, and then a shriek, the most agonizing and blood-curdling that human voice ever uttered, smote my ear. I started bewildered to my feet and grasped the table for support. Another, and another, then a silence; I could not move, my limbs had no power in them, I seemed under a spell. Another moment, and Sophia stood in the door-way, holding a light in her hand; her face was horrible to look at, white, stricken, with eyes that blazed with evil, evil fire.

"Come and see," she said in tones that hissed, "come and see your lover's work."

I did not move. She darted towards me seized my wrist with a grasp of steel, and dragged me on into the open chamber.

"Come with me, come with me and see," she kept repeating wildly.

But at the nursery door her grasp relaxed, she fell down shuddering in a sort of swoon; the light fell with her and went out. I stood on the threshold, in utter darkness; I could not even see the outline of the nursery window, though it had stood wide open. It was the nursery lamp that Sophia had held: that in the dining-room she had put out. My thoughts would not come; where were the matches kept, how should I get a light? A sort of paralysis came over me, I didn't know what to do, I could not have done it at that instant if I had. I didn't know what I feared. I grasped the door-post with my hand—my feet were against the senseless body of Sophia lying stretched across the threshold. There was such a stillness, such an inky darkness. I don't know how many minutes it was before I regained intelligence and force enough to decide where and how I should get a light. I could remember no place where the matches stood but in my own room. I put out my hands and guided myself by the rough boarding across the chamber, to my door. I stumbled over something lying just inside it; trembling and almost senseless with fear, I put down my hand. It was only an overturned foot-stool. I was in the presence of I knew not what horror; my hand might touch it the next minute. I groped along to the dressing-table where the match-box stood; too bewildered to be careful I guided my hand badly, and struck over a china vase which fell with a crash to the floor; the sound seemed frightful to me in my excited state. I listened for some terrible result.

"It will wake the children," I thought; but a heavy, dumb silence fell. I could hear the beating of my heart. At last I reached the matches, but my hand shook so, I could not make a light till I had tried many times. The candle stood near—another moment—and the faint, reassuring light flickered under my eyes. I looked around. There was the overturned footstool and the broken vase; there was nothing else out of place. I must go to the children. It was in the nursery that Sophia had uttered that first awful shriek; ah! what was I to see? The children—I must get to them.

I made my way back across the open chamber to where Sophia lay. Where was Rex? why did he not bark? why was it so awfully still? As I went, the faintly-lighted candle flickered with the motion, and threatened to go out. I put my hand before it. Sophia had struck her arm as she fell; there was a little trickle of blood across the hand that lay outstretched upon the sill. I stepped over it, and stood inside the room. Breathlessly I held up the candle, and glanced around. It was all in the order in which I had left it four hours before; nothing seemed out of place. There were Maidy's shoes upon the chair, and Baby's snowy, folded clothes, and the tiny sack hanging on the back; the sponges, the towels, all as I had seen them then. Had Sophia lost her reason? What mystery was I surrounded by?

I drew a deeper breath, but with a palpitating heart came near the children's cribs. I saw the blankets were disarranged; Baby lay half-uncovered. I went in between the cribs, and stooped down eagerly, holding the candle low.

There lay my Baby; her little head thrown back upon the pillow, her lips apart, her limbs drawn up; around her slender throat a slight darkening of the flesh, as of a violent, compressing hand. The arm that lay upon the coverlid was strangely cold. I put my hand upon her heart; the flesh was cold; there was no motion. I held the flame before her lips; it did not flicker.

. . . .

Maidy's body lay outstretched, her face down upon the pillow, which was bent about it, as if it had been held together; her curls were tangled and torn, a great handful of loose hair lay upon the blanket; her arms, relaxed, lay at her sides. She was quite cold.

10*

CHAPTER XVIII.

THE COURT-ROOM.

" From its intensity of aim
    Our whole life aimless seemed ;
The very stern reality
    Made us almost think we dreamed."

Faber.

" COLONEL, we're all ready now, if you'll tell the carriage to come round ; it is quite time," and Sophia opened the door, and put her head into the next room to the one where I sat. It was a large, old-fashioned room, with a low ceiling. The furniture was common and plain, such as one usually finds in country inns. An air-tight stove filled with hard coal, made the air detestable. It was quite unnecessary, for it was only October, and the day was not unusually cold. It had been lighted, however, for my comfort, and I did not think of making a complaint. The colonel came anxiously forward into the room, followed by his wife.

" The carriage is at the door," he said. " Now take my arm. Do you think you feel quite able ?"

Mrs. Emlyn was looking at me with unspeakable solicitude. Sophia went upon the other side of me, her eyes upon my face with leaden scrutiny.

" Put that other bottle of salts in your pocket," she

[226]

said, looking back at Mrs. Emlyn, who had fallen be-hind; "it's best to be on the safe side; we might get separated."

The colonel leaned down every minute to look at me. It gave me a feeling of dreadful irritation to be so watched. When we got into the lower hall, and were going towards the front door, Sophia took hold of my veil.

"Aren't you going to put it down?" she said.

My arm was over it. I held it tight in its position, and made no answer. Outside there were only a few people standing about; they had not known that we were there. The colonel put me in the carriage, his wife beside me, Sophia and himself on the seat oppo-site. The fresh air revived me; I leaned back and looked out. It was a strange village, or rather town; the county town, in fact; there were a good many shops, and some pretentious houses with cupolas and bay-windows close to the street. It seems all very quiet; there was very little stir.

"Did she eat any breakfast?" said the colonel, in a low tone, to Sophia.

Sophia shook her head. "She won't make the effort. There is no use in talking to her."

Mrs. Emlyn made her an imperious sign to stop. She was the only one who understood that I needed to be let alone. My eyes rested on Sophia's face, while she covered her annoyance by busying herself taking a key off a bunch that she took out from her pocket. Her black clothes made her face look very pale, and her hair, which, a month ago, had been but very slightly gray, was now as white as snow. There were dark circles round her eyes; her face was most striking;

her lips had a feverish look; there were deep lines about her firm-set mouth.

The kind colonel looked aged and worn. His manner was a little flurried, though he spoke with great coolness and precision. Mrs. Emlyn had a look of such intense self-repression that it was painful to meet her eye. She spoke little, and seemed ever to be guarding me from the words of others.

When we approached the court-house, I saw why the rest of the town had seemed quiet. Vehicles of all sorts and kinds stood thick around it; all the posts, and fences, and trees in sight, had horses tied to them. Men were coming and going in through the wide open door, boys were swarming round the windows, looking in. We drove to a side door, and no one noticed us. An officious deputy in black clothes, who had been waiting for us, came forward alertly, and opened the door of the carriage.

"All right, this way," he said.

I put down my great sweeping crape veil, and Sophia looked relieved.

"This way," he said, going forward. "Would the lady like a glass of water?" he added, as we entered a sort of ante-room. I shook my head.

"It's always handy in the court-room," he said. "I always keep it handy. You've only to look at me if you feel faint, and you'll have a glass of water quick as wink."

"She isn't going to feel faint," said Mrs. Emlyn, standing between him and me.

"Of course not, of course not," he said. "Only it wouldn't be to wonder at after all she has gone through."

Then he went forward and cleared the way for us;

he seemed to do everything with so much satisfaction
to himself, with such a clerkly zeal. I don't clearly
know what happened for a few moments after this.
My veil was so oppressive that after, in a great hush, I
had been led to my seat, with the colonel on one side and
Sophia on the other, I verified their prognostications,
and began to feel deadly ill.

"It is only the veil," I tried to say to the colonel,
who bent nervously over me.

"Take the d——d thing off," he whispered hoarsely to Sophia, who was thrusting sal volatile in my
face.

She threw the veil back ; the deputy rushed forward
with his glass of water. Somebody opened a window
beside me : in a moment I was better. I motioned to
Sophia to sit down. She twitched the colonel's coat
and he sat down too. There was a great hush again.

We had come in through a side door, and were led
along in front of where the jury sat, past the raised
platform of the judge, to some seats in a railed-off space,
corresponding to that in which they sat. Between us
and the jury was the judge's platform. I could not see
the faces of the jurors. On each hand of the judge sat
a side judge, a justice of the peace. Below this platform, on a level with us, was the clerk's desk. In front
of this, and running half the width of the room, was a
long table, at which the lawyers sat. All this was railed
off from the room ; beyond were tiers of seats, packed
with people, rows and rows of faces turned towards us.
The aisle was filled with men and women standing;
the door-way was crammed with heads.

It was the second day of the trial. The day before
the prisoner had been arraigned at the bar ; had pleaded

not guilty; the day had been consumed in the impan-
elling of the jury. This morning the examination of
the witnesses was to begin.

The first witness called was Sophia Atkinson.
When her name sounded, I began to come out of the
haze of confusion consequent upon my faintness, and
the entering upon such a strange scene. Sophia grew
a little white, and I saw her nostrils dilate convulsively;
but she got up without looking at any one, and walked
with a firm step along in front of the lawyers' table to
the witness-box, which was at the right of the judge's
platform, in front of the jury. This was raised somewhat above our level, but not to the height of the
platform. When she took her seat, however, I could
still see her face. The prosecuting attorney stood up
in his place, which was at the right end of the lawyers'
table, and began examining her. She answered in a
firm voice, from which, after the first sentence or two,
all huskiness of agitation disappeared. After being
sworn and giving her name, he asked her place of residence.

"South Berwick, in the old house known as Detmold's, on the main road, half a mile up from the
beach."

"How long have you lived there?"

"Since the nineteenth of May last."

"What is your occupation?"

"I am a nurse."

"How long have you been in the family in which
you now live as nurse?"

"Since my fourteenth year; I am now thirty-three
years old."

The lawyer, who was blond and bland, waved his

hand: "Only answer the questions put you. You have been there nineteen years then, I understand?"

"Nineteen years," said Sophia, briefly.

"Look at the prisoner at the bar, and tell me if you know him."

I followed Sophia's glance; it went straight to the table where the lawyers were, at the end near our seats. I had not seen him before, in the confusion of faces and voices around me. Her eyes and mine fell on him at the same moment. He sat with his back towards the railing, against which the people pressed; his head was bent down; he leaned a little on the table; his face was turned towards the witness-box. She must have met his glance full, but she never quailed.

"I know him," she said.

"How long have you known him?"

"Since the second or third of June last."

"How often have you been in the habit of seeing him since then?"

"Every day; sometimes two or three times a day."

"Have you seen him in the house, or in the street, or where?"

"I have seen him principally in the house, where he came every day."

"Can you tell me why he came there every day?"

"To see my mistress, I suppose."

"When did these visits begin? As early as the second or third of June?"

"They began then, but they did not become daily till a fortnight later, I should think."

"Did he generally come alone?"

"Sometimes alone, sometimes with the Emlyn children, whom he taught."

"How did he occupy himself during these visits at the house?"

"Laughing and talking with her and with the children; more often with her alone."

"Did she go out with him alone?"

"Never that I can recollect."

"How did your mistress seem to receive these visits?"

"She seemed to like them; she was always friends with him."

"Did she have any disagreement with him ever—any quarrel?"

"Never any quarrel that I can remember."

"State anything that you can recollect about what occurred at any of these visits; what you noticed between them; in his manner to her, for instance."

"Well, he was always making excuses to come; he was always bringing her her letters from the office, or shells or things for the children, or some message from the other house. He always seemed to be following her about with his eyes, and to be trying to keep her attention to himself when there was anybody else in the room. He acted like a man that wants to make a woman like him."

"How did she treat him—kindly?"

"I object," said the prisoner's counsel, rising.

"On what grounds?" the judge asked.

"On the ground of irrelevancy; it is too remote, at least."

"What have you to say in favor of your objection? I will hear you on that point, Mr. Hardinge."

"Well, sir, in the first place, what has this lady's treatment of the prisoner got to do with the murder of these children? The lady is not on trial here. This is the trial of Bernard Macnally. If she treated him well, that does not show us any motive for the killing of her children. My learned brother doesn't offer to show that she and the prisoner were at enmity. He has proved the contrary by this witness. In his opening yesterday, he disclosed no purpose of that sort. This evidence is too remote. It puts the mother of the murdered children on trial. I am not retained to defend her."

The blond and bland prosecutor looked nettled. He had a skin that showed his emotions; besides, his country breeding gave him less hardihood in argument. His opponent, the prisoner's counsel, was a lawyer of eminence, a close thinker, an adroit pleader, hardened by years of city practice. It was like putting half a dozen green, strong, strapping, country fellows against a trained, professional wrestler. He could throw them all into a heap, and walk unlimping off the field. Mr. Bell had plenty of help, but he knew he needed it, and he felt unpleasantly that his trials were beginning early, in the examination of his very first witness.

Mr. Hardinge was a man of middle size, rather slight than stout. He was probably not more than forty-five years old, though his moustache and hair were very grizzled, while his well-drawn eyebrows were still quite black. His head was admirably shaped, his features regular. His eyes were dark and very penetrating; he had a manner which, it must be confessed, was, professionally, offensive. There was a terrible hardness about him, and his opponents always prepared for the worst. The light-haired and suffused Mr. Bell felt belligerent to his fingers' ends. Mr. Hardinge seemed to feel nothing.

"Your Honor," said Mr. Bell, when the judge indicated to him that he would hear his reply, "I propose to show that this lady and the prisoner were on terms of intimacy; that that intimacy had ripened into an affection, which was mutual. I propose to show what was in her heart, as well as what was in his."

"There you propose to show too much," retorted Mr. Hardinge. "The jury will have to wait till the day of judgment to know that."

Prosecuting attorney. "My theory, if I can be allowed to state it without interruption, is that the prisoner at the bar committed this crime, to rid himself of the only obstacle in the way of gaining the woman whom he sought. I will show this before I have got through with the witness on the stand, if, as I say, I can be permitted to go on."

Mr. Hardinge. "This prosecution, your Honor, had its origin in a public clamor for the life of the prisoner; race prejudices are all against him, enemies have been fanning the flame, senseless stories have been set afloat, which it shall be my care to show at their true value. I am glad to see, at this early date, that the theory of the prosecution is breaking down by its own weight. No counsel, however ingenious, could carry far such a burden of, I will not say incongruities, but impossibilities, as is here presented to the jury. A man, in sound mind (I do not set up the plea of madness for my client, though my brother of the prosecution offers it to me so gratuitously), a man in sound mind, educated, refined, and of apparently high moral character, proposes to himself to take the life of a child, whom he knows to be a part of the very existence of its mother, to gain a stronger hold upon the affections of that mother! Your Honor, does this theory commend itself to your intelligence? I fancy the stubborn, solid, common sense of Sutphen county will revolt at this. I fancy it will take more legal ingenuity than the century has yet developed, to prove to the minds of this jury that a man might devise to himself the wisdom of cutting off the left hand of his mistress, that she might more trustingly put in his her right! The proposed testimony shows, at most, that the prisoner had no motive for the commission of the crime."

Prosecuting Attorney. "Then I contend it is admissible."

Defendant's Counsel. "On the contrary, *we* will prove the want of motive in the prisoner. That is our affair. You have no retainer from the prisoner to present his case. It is the part of the prosecution to prove an adequate motive for the commission of the crime, and the part of the defence to show a want of motive."

Judge. "I will sustain the objection so far as to disallow the question in this form. The witness can state what she has seen."

Attorney for the Prosecution. "State what you have ever seen or heard during his visits."

Witness. "Well, she always was pleasant."

Attorney. "When he brought her flowers or presents, was she much affected by it?"

Witness. "I don't remember that he ever brought her any."

Attorney. "When he didn't come, or anything like that, did she seem disappointed and unhappy?"

Witness. "I don't remember any time that he didn't come. He was always coming."

(A faint ripple of amusement through the court-room.)

I saw that, in a certain sense, Sophia was loyal to me. Much as she hated and desired to ruin Macnally, she would never degrade me, according to her view, to the attitude of having favored him; throughout she would make him my rejected suitor. The attorney asked her several more questions which I have forgotten, all aiming at establishing my preference for him. Sophia stubbornly put me forward as amiable and gentle, "kind to a visitor, as any lady would be," but her memory served her for nothing beyond that—nothing. He finally gave up the matter and told her to state where she was, and how occupied, on the evening of the second of September.

"State, in your own words, all that you remember of what happened after you had put the children to bed on the evening of that day."

"The children were both asleep before the clock struck seven. I put the nursery in order, as I always do. Then I went down-stairs, and told the Indian woman to go up to bed early, for she had been out late the night before, and looked very sleepy. She was sitting by the fire. The supper things were all washed up, and the kitchen looked tidy. I told her to be sure and shut all the doors fast when she went up. I generally tell her that. I trust her to shut up always. Then I took my sewing, and went into the dining-room, which adjoins the nursery, and sat down by the lamp. The door was shut that goes into the nursery from the dining-room, but all the other doors on that floor were open. It was a hot night. I shut that door because I didn't want the children to be disturbed by the light, or by any noise that I might make. About the time that it struck eight, I remember noticing that my mistress was moving about in the other room, the parlor, on the other side of the little entry. She went into the nursery after a few minutes and staid there a considerable time, I should think twenty minutes. Then I heard her come back and sit down in the parlor, and for a good little piece all was quiet. Then I heard the gate open, and somebody come up the steps. I looked out of the dining-room door, and saw the prisoner as he came in at the front door. He looked very pale and bad. I knew he was going away for good that night by the train. I had heard Naomi Emlyn say so. He went into the parlor, and I heard their voices, talking, for some minutes. I couldn't hear what either of them said, I was too far off. After a little while, my mistress came quickly into the dining-room, and went to the sideboard and poured out a glass of wine and hurried out with it. She looked frightened. I laid down my sewing, and went out on the balcony. I saw her give it to him, and saw that he was lying back in the big chair, looking very ill. She stood before him; I couldn't see her face, nor hear what she said, because her back was to the window, outside of which I stood, and they were over the far side of the room. Presently he seemed better, and she sat down by the table near him. She looked very sad, and as if she was sorry for him. He looked dreadfully cut up. They talked, but I didn't hear anything they said. Presently she looked

up at the clock, and then he got up, and then she. He
said 'Good-bye.' He looked awfully. They had then
moved nearer the window, and I could hear what both
of them said distinctly. I heard him say, 'Why must
I go?' I heard her say, 'You must go, but don't go
without being friends with me.' Then he said something that I didn't understand; and then he said, 'It is
your children stand between us, you cannot say it is not.
You aren't willing to trust them to me, whatever you
might be willing for yourself.' His voice fell then; he
said something that I couldn't hear, and she did too.
Then I heard her say, 'Good-bye. You ought to go,
you will be left.' He let go her hand, which he had
had hold of, and took a step or two into the entry.
Then I heard him say, 'The children are asleep?
Mayn't I look at them before I go?' Then I heard
him go through the hall, and into the room that leads
into the nursery. He was gone about three minutes,
I should think; it seemed to me a good while, but the
clock hadn't struck nine yet, and the train went at nine
fifteen. That was why I noticed. I thought he meant
to get left. When he came out, I was standing behind
the blind door, which was standing part way open—I
mean, not folded back against the house. He could
not see me. I looked through it right into the entry.
He came from the open chamber into the hall. My
mistress stood in the door of the parlor, half in the
hall, waiting for him. He looked as white as a sheet.
He did not offer to take her hand again, or to say good-
bye over, as I thought he'd have been sure to do. He
just looked at her, a kind of desperate look, and passed
right by her, and went out, pushing the blind door back,

and down the steps, and through the gate, and out into the road."

There had been the deep hush of intense listening over the whole court-room. As her voice dropped, and she paused, there was the faint sound of breaths drawn deep, of heads lifted—excitement at its climax.

"You say the clock had not struck nine then?"

"No, it struck just after he went down the steps. I thought he'd barely reach the train, I remember. I went back into the dining-room and took up my sewing. I forgot to say, just before he came into the house, it must have been half past eight about, I heard the woman go up-stairs to bed. I remember the time particularly, because I looked up at the clock and said to myself, she wouldn't have been in bed till ten if it hadn't been for the fair and festival of the night before. I wondered to myself when she came up the kitchen stairs, if she hadn't been too sleepy to put out the fire. I heard her go up the attic stairs; I heard her moving about over my head; she sleeps at the end of the garret that is over the dining-room. In a few minutes all was quiet, and I never heard another sound from there."

"Did your mistress go back into the parlor? Describe what followed the departure of the prisoner."

"She didn't go back into the parlor. She went out on the balcony. I went on with my sewing. I heard the whistle of the train as it went off; I sat and sewed a long time. Once or twice I got up, and looked out of the window. I didn't leave the dining-room that evening except once to go on the balcony and see if she wanted me. I heard the clock strike ten, then eleven, then twelve. I had a piece of work that I wanted very much to finish."

"Do you often sit up as late as that?"

"Yes, when I am busy with anything I have in hand; sometimes a good deal later."

"During this time you did not hear any sound about the house?"

"I heard nothing at all. It was a still night. There wasn't any wind. I have very quick ears."

"How about your mistress? Did she go in the house?"

"Never, once. If she had gone in, I couldn't have helped seeing her pass the dining-room door. If she had gone down the steps, I couldn't have helped hearing her."

"What was she doing there, all those three hours?"

"Sitting still and resting, I suppose. She couldn't have been reading; there wasn't light enough. It was a hot night. The balcony was the pleasantest place to be."

"Did she seem unhappy, depressed?"

"Couldn't say."

"Didn't you have any conversation with her; didn't you speak to her at all?"

"I asked her if she wanted anything; she said she didn't; that was all that passed between us."

"About what time did she go into the house?"

"A little after twelve, I should think."

"Relate what occurred after she went in."

"She went into the parlor and sat down. The lamp had gone out there; she sat in the dark. After a little while I got up and went into the room, and said something to her about the house, I think. She didn't seem to take much interest. Then I went about and began to shut up. I thought she ought to be going to bed;

it's bad for people to sit up so late, when they haven't any work to do and can just as well go to bed as not. After I had shut up the front part of the house, I went up-stairs, and saw the Indian woman fast asleep in her bed. Then I went to the rear of the open chamber, and fastened the window. It was then half past twelve. I had heard the clock strike, and had told her, to remind her it was time to go to bed. I found the nursery in order, as I left it. I moved around a little, putting away my work, and getting out something from the closet. By and by I lifted the lamp from the corner where it stood, behind a screen, and went over towards the children's cribs, to look at them as I always do, the last thing before I go to bed."

A choking sound rose in the woman's throat; she stopped speaking, bent her head down a little, and with her hand beat nervously upon the arm of the chair in which she sat. A low murmur of sympathy came from the women in the crowd of listeners. I knew she was making a stern fight for self-control, and I knew, too, that she would conquer. Presently she lifted her head, and went on in a steady voice.

"I went to the little one first; she sleeps on the outside, so I can get at her easiest; the oldest little girl's crib is in the corner; there is room to pass in between the two cribs. I saw—she wasn't as I left her. My first thought was she had had a fit or something. Her little legs were drawn up as if she had a hard pain, her head was way back on the pillow, her mouth was open —she looked as children do in convulsions, except that she hadn't that drawn look about the face. I put down the light and seized her in my arms. I felt as I touched her that she was very cold. I don't know what I did

11

then—for a minute, my thought was she had had a fit.
I didn't see the mark on her throat that I saw afterwards. I was in such a sort of taking for a second I
didn't know which way to turn. I had a feeling I
must get her in a hot bath. I was afraid to tell her
mother. I generally do everything for them myself.
I caught up the lamp and ran towards the stove to light
the fire. As I passed the crib where the other little
girl was, I don't know how it happened I looked at her.
I wasn't thinking about her. I saw something was
wrong with her—she was lying on her face—the pillow
was jammed about her head; she couldn't breathe the
way she lay. I ran in between the cribs and felt of her
little arm that lay outside the covers—it was as cold as
Baby's was. Her hair was torn and tangled. Some of
it that had been torn out in the struggle was lying on
the blanket and caught in the sleeve of my dress—I found
it there next day. I didn't know what I was doing
then. I ran out of the room and called their mother
to come in; my screaming frightened her so, she did not
move, but stood still, shaking. I caught her by the
hand and dragged her towards the room. Before I got
there, I fell down in a faint, and I don't know anything
that happened after that for a good while."

There was a pause: you could have heard the rustle
of a leaf.

"Tell us what you remember when you came to
your senses."

"I was lying just where I fell: Matilda, the Shinnecock woman, was crying over me. I saw people in the
room. The first person I saw to know was the doctor;
he was stooping down over the baby. The mother of
the children sat there between the two little cribs; her

head leaned against the wall: she was like ashes; she had a hand on each of the cribs. She looked at everybody that came near. I thought she was going to die. I got up and tried to go to her. After that I can't remember very much, my head felt so light, and I couldn't seem to think of the same thing long at a time."

"Throw your mind back, and recall, if you please, some of the incidents of that day. Who came to the house?"

"The grocer's man came twice, and a boy from the Neck with fish, Matilda's boy, if I remember right. There was a woman also, who comes every week to wash; she came at seven o'clock, and went away late in the afternoon. And old Andrew was there for a couple of hours in the morning, splitting wood. That was all, except a man who came along and asked for something to eat. Matilda gave him something, and he went off down the lane. Oh, yes; Naomi Emlyn came after breakfast; and their man stopped at the gate to bring some letters, which hadn't come the night before. There was nobody else that I can recollect."

"That is all," said Mr. Bell, sitting down, with a glance in the direction of the prisoner's counsel.

Mr. Hardinge got up to cross-examine her; he was very deliberate. He put his hand on the back of a chair, glanced at some memoranda that lay before him, and turned toward Sophia.

"You have said, I think, that you have known the prisoner since the early part of June?"

"Yes."

"Your relations with him during this time were pleasant?"

"I didn't have any relations with him. I didn't have anything at all to do with him."

"How was that, seeing him so often?"

"I don't hold I'm bound to have pleasant relations with everybody that I see very often."

"Well, I suppose you mean us to understand by that, you weren't an admirer of his, exactly?"

"You may understand what you like."

"Your sex are sometimes hard to understand. Here is a young gentleman, of good address and high breeding, coming to the house every day. He was civil, I've no doubt, to everybody in it. Why didn't he please you, if I may ask the question?"

"I don't admit there was any such person as you describe coming to the house every day."

"Then describe the person that did come, if you can do it more correctly. You certainly had better opportunities for judging."

"A common Irishman, lifting his eyes to his betters, was the man I saw; and I saw him for nothing else, from the first time that he darkened the door till the last time that he went out of it, leaving our children dead behind him."

Sophia's words fairly hissed; her angry eyes were fixed defiantly on the lawyer, whom already she detested.

"Can you in any way account for this aversion?" he said.

"We can't always account for the way we feel towards people," she returned, rendering it, by a glance, a personal tribute to her interlocutor.

"Was he—presuming—overbearing—in his manner towards you?"

"I should think not; he wouldn't have tried that twice, you may be very certain."

"Was he ever disrespectful to your mistress?"

"Disrespectful! In one sense, no; in another, yes."

"Explain to me both senses, will you?"

"He wasn't disrespectful in his way of talking to her; if she had been the queen, he couldn't have been humbler. He *was* disrespectful in daring to speak to her at all, in daring to come near her, in daring to think she might possibly look at a low fellow such as he."

"Then you know something to his disadvantage? Something about his birth and parentage?"

"No, I don't know anything about them. I don't want to know. I've got my eyes and all my senses, and that's enough for me."

"But we're after facts just now. If he wasn't uncivil to you, nor disrespectful in his way of talking to your mistress, perhaps he was unkind and irritable with the children, and that turned you against him?"

"No, he knew too much for that. He always had them after him. He was petting them enough to make you sick."

"The instincts of children are said to be correct. How did the children act towards him? Did they show any of the aversion that one might be led to look for?"

"No, I can't say they did."

"Never from the first?"

"No; little things like them couldn't know much about the real character of people; they liked to be petted; natural enough they should."

" Perhaps he bribed them and brought them toys and sugar plums ?"

"I never saw them, if he did."

" Then their great fondness for him was just the result of his kind and affectionate ways with them ?"

"I don't say what it was the result of."

There was a wrangle of objections several times during her examination, but the judge did not sustain them, and Mr. Hardinge, with a look of satisfaction, glanced down again at his memoranda, and resumed.

"I understood you to say, the night of the murder, you were sitting in the dining-room with your sewing, while your mistress and the prisoner were in the parlor, talking. What led you to go out on the balcony at the time you did ?"

" Because I wanted to, I suppose ; I wasn't bound to sit in the dining-room all night."

"Are you in the habit of sitting or walking on the balcony in the evenings ?"

"There's no reason that I shouldn't if I want to."

"But are you in any such habit ?"

"No, I'm not."

"Then it's clear you were out with a motive. It was too dark to sew there. You were very anxious to get through a piece of work, you said. Why did you leave it and go out ?"

" My mistress looked frightened when she came to get the wine ; I wanted to see if anything was wrong."

"But she hadn't called you when she passed you, had she ?"

"No."

"Then you went to peep in at the parlor window, I suppose ?"

"There wasn't any peeping about it, I looked right in."

"And when you looked through the slats of the blind door; was that peeping or did you look right in ?"

"I looked in; you can call it peeping if you like it better."

Mr. Hardinge saw that he had made a point, eaves-dropping not being popular with juries.

"Now," he said, "if you please, let us go forward beyond the time when you overheard from behind the blind-door, the last words of your mistress and the prisoner, to the time when you were shutting up the house. In your testimony just now, you make no allusion to the doors that lead down-stairs from the rear of the house. How many are there ?"

"In front, there are no doors; you come up outside by the balcony steps on to the balcony, and by the front door into the little entry. At the back, there is only one way of getting up from the kitchen—that is, by the kitchen-stairs, into the open chamber between the rooms."

"Do you know whether this door has a fastening ?"

"Yes, it has a bolt."

"Do you keep this bolted at night ?"

"Yes, always."

"Was it bolted on that night when you went to bed ?"

"I suppose, of course, it was; but I can't swear positively."

"I'm surprised, you have remembered everything else with such distinctness; you are a very excellent

witness—not one in a thousand like you.   Can't you
remember about the bolting of this door?"

"I told you that I couldn't."

"Would you have felt it safe to leave it open?"

"I always wanted it fastened."

"How did you happen to be so careless this time?"

"I suppose I was tired and sleepy; it was late.   I
don't know whether I looked at it or not.   I can't remember everything."

"Whose duty was it to shut it?"

"It was Matilda's."

Mr. Hardinge looked down at his paper again,
shifted his position a little, and went on.

"During that day," he said, "a number of persons
were at the house, you mentioned.   Were they all people that you knew about—people that bear a good
character in the neighborhood?"

"Yes, I believe they do.   I've known them all
summer.   It's a very respectable, quiet neighborhood."

"There wasn't anybody that you hadn't seen before, and that wasn't perfectly respectable?"

"Nobody but the man that came in and asked for a
drink of water, and then for something to eat."

"You hadn't seen him before?"

"No."

"Describe him to me."

"He wasn't very remarkable looking.   I didn't pay
much attention to him.   He was a dirty sort of fellow,
sunburnt and shabby.   I think he wasn't very tall; he
was thick-set."

"What was the color of his hair?"

"Oh, I don't remember.   His hat was pushed down
over his head a good deal; I don't think I saw his hair."

"Have you ever seen him since?"

"I haven't."

"Should you know him again?"

"I think I should."

"Describe what he did."

"I was pressing out some collars for the children, and stood with my back to the door. He knocked, and when I didn't answer, he came on into the kitchen. He stopped when I asked him what he wanted. He said, a glass of water; he spoke thick, like a German. I told him to go to the pump, there was a cup there. When he had got his drink he came back, and came half across the kitchen floor before I noticed him, and said he was hungry. I don't like foreigners, and I was going to send him off, when Matilda, who was in the buttery, called out there was some pieces that she was going to throw away. So I said to give them to him. I told him to take the pieces outside and eat them. Then I went upstairs with the collars. When I came back he was in the kitchen again, sitting by the stair door; I almost tumbled over him when I opened it. I told him to go away, and he got up and went."

"He had been in the kitchen some time?"

"Ten minutes, maybe."

"Were you afraid of him?"

"No, of course not."

"You have a good many tramps, I suppose?"

"No, I don't remember another one all summer."

"I wonder it didn't make more impression on you; have you thought about it since the murder?"

"Not particularly."

"That is all, I believe, that I shall trouble you to tell me now." He sat down.

11*

CHAPTER XIX.

BEING DULY SWORN.

" the heart hath treble wrong,
When it is barr'd the aidance of the tongue."
Venus and Adonis.

" I am cut off from the only world I know,
From light and life and love, in youth's sweet prime.
You do well telling me to trust in God ;
I hope I do trust in Him.   In whom else
Can any trust ?   And yet my heart is cold."
Shelley.

THE court adjourned for an hour at noon.   I was taken into an adjoining room, where I lay down on a sort of hard settee.   The colonel made me take a biscuit and some wine.   Sophia, who was a good deal shaken by the morning's work, went out into the air, and walked up and down, and tried to steady herself. Mrs. Emlyn, with all her superb health, was sensitive and excitable in a high degree.   She could not bear to leave me, and yet her nerves were all unstrung.   The air of the court-room, she said, was all the trouble.   I begged her to go out and get the air with Sophia. The colonel, who was tender as a woman, stayed and watched over me.

" What is coming next ?" I asked him.

" The doctor's testimony."

" And who next ?"

"You, I am afraid."

"I can't be there through the examination of the doctor. Can't I stay here, and go in after, when I'm called?"

He assured me that I might. I don't know how it happened, perhaps it was exhaustion, perhaps a gift from Heaven, but I fell asleep. My sleep was profound and dreamless; I knew nothing till I found some one bending over me.

"I am afraid you'll have to wake now," said the colonel. "Your name will soon be called."

When we went into the court-room, and took our places again, there was for a moment the same hush that I had noticed in the morning when we entered. The doctor's testimony had evidently been professional and rather tiresome; the people had been yawning and lolling. They looked much enlivened when we came upon the scene. They sat up, and leaned forward and gazed intently. The doctor's cross-examination was just ending. He was held for a moment in the vice of Mr. Hardinge's pertinacity. The doctor would not yield the point that a longer time than three minutes was necessary for the extinction of life under the circumstances described. He continued firm. I could see there had been a strong point made in favor of the prosecution. He finally was permitted to leave the stand, and my name was called.

I did not feel any of the agitation that would have seemed inevitable. I certainly knew that there was a great deal depending upon what I said; that certainty seemed, strangely, a sort of strength. The colonel led me along the narrow space between the judge's platform and the table at which the lawyers sat; he seemed to fear

I might fall any moment to the floor ; he looked back anxiously at me, when by reason of the narrowness of space he had to go in front. He supported me as I stepped up upon the raised place upon which was the chair, and stood beside me, a little at the back, all the while that I was kept there.

The attorney for the prosecution rose. When I was sworn and had given my name and residence, I was told to look at the prisoner and say if I knew him. I turned my eyes towards the seat where I had seen him ; certainly I saw nothing. I said yes.

"Your acquaintance with him began when ?"

" About the twentieth of May, I should think."

" Were you acquainted with the family in which he lived, before you came to South Berwick ?"

" No."

" Had you any knowledge of him, or of his family, before you met him there ?"

" None."

" Had you any knowledge of the Emlyn family before this date ?"

" I only knew that there was such a family, and that I had hired a house from them."

" You were on good terms with them all after you became acquainted ?"

" Yes."

" You were entirely ignorant of the antecedents of the prisoner ?"

" Yes."

" How often were you in the habit of seeing him ?"

" Almost daily, through the Summer."

" Where did you generally see him—at your own house ?"

"At my own house very often, or at the house of Colonel Emlyn."

"Were his visits at your house business visits, visits of necessity?"

"No."

"They were then purely friendly, social visits?"

"Yes."

"I would ask, if you encouraged these visits?"

Mr. Hardinge. "The witness must state what was said or done."

Mr. Bell. "What was his manner towards you?"

"Always gentlemanly and considerate."

"Was it the same to others?"

"Yes, according to my observation."

"Was his manner just the same to you as to others whom you saw him meet?"

"No, it was different."

"How so? Will you explain?"

"It was naturally different with the Emlyn children, who were his pupils; and with Colonel and Mrs. Emlyn, who were so much older; and with people whom he met whom he scarcely knew."

"But you felt he was more friendly with you?"

("My learned brother is slaying the slain," cried Mr. Hardinge. "The testimony of the woman Sophia is enough. We know he was her suitor.")

I took the cue from this interjected sentence, as I was meant to, and said:

"Yes."

"Was this acceptable to you?"

"I was glad to have him for my friend."

"Was his manner indicative of anything more than friendship?"

"It may be."

"Did you make any objection to its being so ?"

"I don't remember."

"If he had asked you to marry him, and you had been free of other ties, such as the care of your children, would you have married him ?"

Mr. Hardinge sprang to his feet. "Your Honor, that is *not* evidence. It is bad enough to endure such baiting of a suffering woman, when it is kept within strict legal bounds; but I deny that the counsel for the prosecution has the right to call for an opinion in the nature of a mental operation."

Mr. Bell. "My brother told us this morning he was not retained to defend the lady."

Mr. Hardinge. "I have no fee in my pocket to defend her; but I have a feeling in my heart—a feeling such as every man has in his heart, when he sees a woman, whose sufferings should make her sacred, unnecessarily put upon the rack. Your Honor, it is questionable, bringing her here at all. But, since she is here, let us be merciful to her. Why, your Honor, any man upon that jury may think for himself how would he treat the mother of his little child that had died; died peacefully, and by natural causes, in her arms, when everything had been done to save it. At the end of four short weeks, would he not think she did bravely, if she consented to see a few dear friends that came to mourn with her; if she went down-stairs, and, in the seclusion of her home, went again about her ordinary duties? And if he persuaded her to go out with him once more into the sun that would never shine again upon her baby, would he not take her into green and quiet lanes, or drive with her where they would meet

fewest people? It is only four weeks—and think of
this young mother, after her unspeakable bereavement,
called to face this crowd of strangers! The law demands no such sacrifice. I would rather let ten murderers go free, than have upon my conscience the in-
flicting of such torture."

Mr. Bell. "Your Honor, I'll make a bargain with
the gentleman, for whose tenderness of heart I was not
prepared. If he will waive the cross-examination of
this witness, I will stop at the point I am now, and
engage not to recall her."

Mr. Hardinge. "That will not be possible——"

Mr. Bell (interrupting). "Sir, you are hoist with
your own petard. My question did not please you;
that was all the trouble. I appeal to your Honor to
sustain me, and let the examination go on."

Mr. Hardinge. "I will agree to confine myself to
just half the questions you have asked already, if you
will waive the direct examination."

Mr. Bell. "I will agree to nothing of the sort.
Your Honor, am I at liberty to insist upon the answer
to my question?"

The Judge. "I must sustain the objection made
by the defense. The witness is excused from answering what calls simply for the statement of what existed
in her mind."

Mr. Bell (resuming). "Did he ever ask you to
marry him?"

"I don't know—I understood that he—desired me
to."

"Did you tell him that you would marry him, except for the obstacle presented by your children?"

"No."

"Did he say to you that he knew that they stood between you ?"

"Something like that."

"Did you deny it ?"

"I didn't deny it, or affirm it."

"Didn't you allow the impression on his mind that such was the case ?"

"I don't know what his impression was."

"Didn't he appear to continue to believe it ?"

"I don't know; he didn't refer to it again."

"What reason did you give for not accepting him ?"

"I don't remember giving any."

"Did you tell him you didn't like him ?"

"No."

"Didn't you give him any reason ?"

"I don't remember giving any."

"Simply that you would not ?"

"Yes."

"Had you known all summer that he wanted to marry you ?"

Mr. Hardinge rescued me from this; and Mr. Bell, not well pleased with his progress, turned from this part of his programme.

"After you were left by the prisoner on the night of the second of September, did you stay on the balcony till the hour stated by the witness, Sophia Atkinson ?"

"I did."

"How were you occupied ?"

"I was doing nothing."

"From nine to nearly half-past twelve ?"

"Yes."

"Where were you when you heard the scream given by this witness ?"

"In the parlor."

"State what she said to you when she came from the nursery."

"She said, 'Come and see your lover's work,' or words like that."

"Did you go?"

"She caught my hand and took me with her."

I was growing so white that every one looked alarmed; Sophia darted from her seat, and held the salts up to me; Colonel Emlyn gave me a glass of water, with which the zealous deputy had been armed since I went upon the stand. It had grown warm from being so long poured out, and made me feel a little sick.

"Not to harrow your feelings," said the prosecuting attorney, a little conscience-stricken, "I will rest here, simply asking you if the witness Sophia Atkinson's testimony was heard by you, and if you fully corroborate it; I mean, as concerns the condition of the room, and the appearance of the children as they lay?"

"I heard what she said; it was all correct."

"Very well. Then I have nothing further to ask." And he sat down.

I don't know whether it was the judge, or who, offered me a respite for a little while, till I should be able to go on: I felt very confused and ill for a moment or two, but the opening of a window, and perhaps the salts, made me feel better. I said earnestly:

"I want them to go on; I am able to answer."

This was repeated to the judge by Colonel Emlyn, and by him to Mr. Hardinge, who left his place and came nearer to me. I think he wanted to get where I could see the expression of his eye. He probably perceived that, by reason of my weakness, I could scarcely see any distance from me; my body fell so far behind my mind in this dire strait. This gentleman knew his opponent's witnesses much better than he knew them himself. Of course, being summoned by the prosecution, I had never had an interview with him. I felt that he saw everything in my mind. I was never so entirely under the influence of any one before. He held me with his eye; he guided me almost without the interpretation of words. Jugglery and mind-reading will never seem wonderful me after this.

I saw, by a certain tension of the muscles of his mouth, that he felt the moment critical. A strength came to me with the knowledge; my illness and faintness were all passed away.

"I will not trouble you with many questions," he said, deferentially and quietly. "I would first ask you to make clear to me one or two things in the bearing of the prisoner. Have you observed him to be a high-tempered man, ready to take offense, easily made angry?"

"No, it seems to me not."

"Was he irritable and passionate with his pupils and with little children, or the reverse?"

"The reverse."

"Have you ever seen him under the influence of great disappointment, acute suffering?"

"Yes."

"Did it make him morose, angry—what we would call a dangerous man?"

"No."

"Did it give him the appearance of a man who was desperate, reckless——?"

Before he had finished the sentence, he saw from

my eyes he was going wrong; he adroitly changed it into " reckless of the rights of others, bent upon revenge or success in his own way ?"

" I cannot say he seemed so to me."

"Now, I must ask you to revert to the evening of the second of September. After he had left you, you went directly to the balcony ?"

" Yes."

"From where you sat, could you have heard any one moving about in the house ?"

"In the parlor I could. I doubt whether I could have heard anything in the rear of the house."

"You heard nothing then from within the house?"

"Nothing."

"Nothing from without, about the premises ?"

" Yes, once."

"Please tell me about it."

"It was not long after I heard the whistle of the train, and saw the lights pass out of sight, I heard a slight rustling in the bushes by the gate ; then in a moment I heard the latch lifted very softly, and dropped again as if some one were trying not to make a noise."

" That was all ?"

" That was all."

" You heard no steps, no voices, nothing ?"

"Nothing.

"You heard nothing further all the evening?"

"Nothing."

" Was the night still ?"

" Very still."

" You are very positive about this noise ?"

" Very positive. It startled me. I got up and went to the dining-room window to see if Sophia were still

there. I thought she might have gone down through
the kitchen and out for something. I knew Matilda
was in bed. Sophia was sitting by the lamp, sewing.
I saw she had not heard it, for she had not even looked
up. Then I went and sat down again by the railing,
but I heard nothing more."

"This was about what hour?"

"The train should have gone at nine fifteen. It
was ten minutes late. I heard the sounds at the gate, I
should say, about ten minutes after that. I cannot be
positive, of course, but it was not long after."

The relief and satisfaction in Mr. Hardinge's eyes, I
hope was not apparent to any one but me.

"At what hour did you go into the parlor?"

"It was after twelve."

"Tell me something about the occurrences of the
next half hour, if you are able: I mean, prior to your
going to the nursery with Sophia."

"I sat still, and heard Sophia go about and shut the
doors and windows. The lamp had gone out and I was
sitting in the darkness. Sophia came into the room
several times; I knew she wanted me to go to bed. I
heard her go up-stairs to Matilda's room. She came
down and shut the window in the open chamber between the rooms. Then I heard her go to the door of
the kitchen stairs. She found it unbolted, and made
an angry exclamation, something about Matilda. She
slid the bolt as if she were vexed."

"You remember this distinctly?"

"As clearly as possible."

"This door shuts off all communication with the
lower part of the house?"

"Yes."

"Then it had been open all the evening?"

"I suppose so. The Indian woman must have left it unfastened when she came up-stairs: neither Sophia nor I had been in that part of the house since she went up to bed."

"Did you say anything when Sophia made this exclamation?"

"No, she did not address herself to me; it was simply an exclamation of annoyance at Matilda."

"You were quite wide awake at this time?"

"Oh, yes; that was the reason I did not want to go to bed. I knew I could not get asleep."

"After, when Sophia appeared in the door-way, and gave you the alarm, will you try and remember exactly the expression that she used?"

"She said, 'Come and see your lover's work.' She said it over and over wildly. I could not forget it; it was always in my mind for many days."

"Did her statement have any influence upon you?"
Objected to.

"Did she repeat it to others at that time?"

"In the course of that night and during the following day, I heard her say things to the same effect before other people."

"She then showed a strong prejudice against the prisoner?"

"Yes."

"How long had she expressed aversion to him?"

"From the time that he began to come to the house as a frequent visitor."

"Had she ever expressed open enmity to him?"

"Yes."

"Mention some instance."

"The day before she told me she should leave the house if he came into it again."

"Had he ever given her a cause for feeling so?"

"Not intentionally, I think."

"Had he ever said anything to indicate enmity to her?"

"I never heard anything of the kind."

"Those are all the questions I shall have to ask you now," he said, bowing, and returning to his place.

CHAPTER XX.

FOR AND AGAINST.

" When thou fearest,
God is nearest."

THE next morning the attorney for the prosecution
called first Colonel Emlyn, and then his wife. The
design was evidently to obtain from them proof of the
utter ignorance they were in concerning the antecedents
of the prisoner. He also drew out from Colonel Emlyn
that he was not on good terms with the prisoner when
they parted, but no question was asked which would
permit the witness to explain the cause of the estrangement. He also obtained from him that the prisoner
was a man of resolution, force; that he carried out his
purposes; that he maintained authority in the school-
room. The direct examination was short; the cross-
examination established the good character of the prisoner, his uniformly irreproachable conduct during the
ten months he had been in their house; his gentleness, his courtesy, his rather unusual aversion to giving
pain, his forbearance with the faults of children. Mrs.
Emlyn vehemently threw in several inadmissible statements, which were not accepted as evidence, but which
may have had their effect upon the jury. Colonel Emlyn
was told to state the cause of the coolness which existed
between the prisoner and himself at the time of his

leaving the house. He answered, it was because he did not want to part with him; he considered his going a serious loss to the children; he desired to retain him for at least two years longer in his family. He was asked to state the reason given by the prisoner for his abrupt departure. He had given no reason. The witness had his theory for it, but was not allowed to state it.

The next witness called was the post-master of the village. He testified to an interview with the prisoner early in June, in which the prisoner had given him a slip of paper, containing a name which he had forgotten, saying to him, that if any letters came to that address, he would oblige him by laying them aside, and giving them to him personally. He had received the impression that the prisoner had meant him to be silent about it, though he could not recall anything that he had said to that effect. He had treated the matter confidentially, and had not spoken of it till he heard about the murder. Two or three letters had come to the address given him; he had put them aside and handed them personally to the prisoner. That was in the early part of the summer. Since then, no letters had come to that address. The prisoner's letters latterly had come two or three in one envelope, with double postage, as if inclosed and forwarded to him from some point. They were invariably addressed Bernard Macnally, and, as far as he could recollect, were in one handwriting. He was unable to recall the name on the slip of paper the prisoner had handed him; the paper had been mislaid; he had searched in vain for it. He should know the name if he heard it. It was a long name; there were several initials. As the letters had ceased to come, he had not minded anything about it;

he had a poor memory for names. The letters that had
come to the address given him had been foreign letters,
from somewhere in Great Britain. He could not be
sure of anything else. He had noticed at the time, but
had forgotten.

The cross-examination was short and unimportant.
Though the post-master hadn't a strong memory for
names, he was not weak in other things, and Mr. Hardinge could not get anything out of him but what he
chose to say. He admitted that the occurrence was not
without precedent. That he had on more than one
occasion had the same favor asked him by perfectly respectable young men, but that he had known that it was
just some "lark," and that there wasn't any deception
meant that would do anybody any harm.

Then Sophia Atkinson was recalled, and was shown
a pocket-handkerchief, and asked if she had ever seen
it before. She testified that she had, that she had seen
it on her mistress' throat, and afterwards found it on
the dressing-table in her mistress' room; that she knew
it to be the property of the prisoner, from her mistress
mentioning it as such, and making search for it. It was
not at all like any handkerchief that any one in the
house owned. She could read the initials worked on
it, but she didn't know how they went in order. The
letters were L. M. C. B. or M. C. B. L., or any way
you chose to put them.

Mr. Hardinge made it appear, on the cross-examination, that she had purloined the handkerchief, and kept
it concealed, notwithstanding the many inquiries that
had been made for it.

Penelope Emlyn, recalled, was shown a book, and
asked to identify it. She recognized it as a book which

12

she had seen in the prisoner's possession. It had been brought to her by one of the children, to establish the fact that that day was the tutor's birthday, and to ask a holiday. The prisoner had not denied that it was his book, nor that the day was his birthday. The words written on the fly-leaf were: "To L——, on his fourteenth birthday, with his mother's always faithful love," and the date below. The volume was a worn and shabby copy of the *Book of Common Prayer.* She was asked to identify another book, a copy of the *Tragedies of Euripides,* from which a portion of the fly-leaf was cut out. This book had been lent her by the prisoner, as well as many others. Several of them had no name at all written in them. In many, there was a mutilation of the fly-leaf, as in this. She was not cross-examined.

The Indian cook, Matilda, was next summoned. She was much agitated, and gave a confused account of the incidents of the night. On the direct examination, she testified to having closely attended to shutting up the kitchen, and bolting the door of the kitchen stairs when she went up to bed. She described my coming to her and rousing her, and sending her out to call the neighbors. Her account of the finding of the children's bodies was unimportant and confused.

On the cross-examination she admitted that she was dreadfully tired and sleepy; that she had actually dropped asleep sitting by the fire; that the striking of the clock roused her, and she started up, and took the candle and went away up-stairs, hardly knowing what she did, for fear of being scolded by Sophia, who had told her she must go to bed as soon as she had done her work. She admitted she was afraid of Sophia, who scolded her "considerable." She couldn't say whether she fastened the outside kitchen door or not ; whether she bolted the stair door after her or not ; she was just dead sleepy ; she hadn't slept hardly any the night before ; she dropped asleep almost before she got undressed when she got up-stairs ; when her mistress woke her, she still had half her clothes on ; she knew what an oath was ; she had been converted ; she went to meeting regularly ; nothing would tempt her to tell a lie if she knew what she was doing. That was the reason that she wouldn't swear (again) that she had fastened up the doors, because she couldn't tell *for sure.*

Here the prosecution rested their case and Mr. Hardinge opened his.

His first witness was the baggage-master at the South Berwick station. He testified to the checking of the baggage by young Emlyn, and to the arrival of the prisoner, who reached the station at sixteen minutes after nine. He said to the prisoner, " You'd have been left, if the train had been on time." The prisoner had answered, " No, I shouldn't, I was listening for the whistle all the time. I should have hurried ; if it had blown while I was half a mile off, I could have caught it." The train was late ten minutes. He walked up and down the platform, talking with young Emlyn, sometimes stopping and talking with him and with some other men who were standing about. He was grave, and didn't seem in his usual spirits, but he was bound to say, he didn't seem " flustered," or like a man who had just been committing a crime, and was getting out of reach of justice as fast as he knew how.

The witness was right in saying " he was bound to testify thus, and so." He was bound by his sturdy, sober-minded, American conscience, and not by any predilection for the prisoner. In fact, the defence had this great disadvantage all the way through. The prejudice against Macnally was bitter. South Berwick was in a part of the country where few Irish had settled, and those of the lowest class. There was a jealousy of intrusion that is only seen in such isolated neighborhoods. The population was almost without exception native; they were thrifty and intelligent, and looked with scant favor upon the coming of strangers, even of their own nationality. Colonel Emlyn had overcome this feeling by his unassuming ways, liberality and common sense, and was at the end of four or five years looked upon as a worthy and important member of their small community. But Macnally had never been a favorite—they didn't know how to take him. They weren't used to jokes, being stolid and shy. His merriment seemed to them a disrespect. They were jealous of an Irishman who dared to walk as he pleased over their sacred soil. Sophia's bitter tongue had not been idle. No trifling pleasantry of his about the rural population was allowed to rest with one telling. The stories circulated, and the prejudices roused were numberless. It was from a community so affected that Mr. Hardinge had to recruit his witnesses. They seemed like "Spanish volunteers," led along in chains. I began to see that he would have to spin much of his web of evidence out of his own clever brain.

The next witness was the conductor, who knew the prisoner quite well by sight; thought he might have spoken to him sometimes at the station as his train passed through. He had all summer known his name; known he was the tutor living at Colonel Emlyn's. He noticed nothing special in his manner on the night of the second of September; except that he didn't go to sleep as the other passengers had done. The train was an hour and forty minutes late, owing to a freight train running off the track. He had been awake whenever he came to him to punch his ticket; he remembered particularly the last time when he came through the car; the prisoner had his ticket in his teeth; a little piece was gnawed off of it.

"When I .looked at it he laughed and said, 'Your train goes so confounded slow, we shall have to make our breakfast off our tickets.' He didn't seem in a hurry, no: he looked to me like a man who was in trouble more than like a man who was afraid. He was wide awake and knew what he was about though; he was in the train the last station that we passed before we entered the city. I took his ticket then, and that's the last I've seen of him till I saw him here in court."

The cross-examination did not make much of him. He admitted there was something about the prisoner that made him notice him, but he was in the habit of noticing the faces of his passengers. He didn't look like a man that was running away; he was bound to say that wasn't the impression that he made on him. He couldn't say exactly how a man that was running away would look: he should think he might look hurried and restless. This one didn't look that way: he wasn't looking behind him, and opening and shutting windows, and watching who got in at every station. He looked tired and used up, and yet as if his mind was too full of some trouble to let him go to sleep.

The next upon the stand was the telegraph messen-

ger who handed the prisoner a dispatch from Colonel
Emlyn, as he stepped out of the car at the depot. He
testified to the consternation and agitation of the prisoner when he read the message. He staggered, and the
witness thought he would have fallen if he had not put
out his hand, and helped him to a seat. He seemed
dazed, astounded. He took the paper and tried to read
it for the second time, but seemed to be very faint and
ill; then he handed it to the messenger and said—"Read
it to me—I must have made some mistake—read it
slowly—I want to understand." The witness read it to
him—it was as follows:

"The two children at the cottage found murdered
in their beds an hour ago. Come instantly back. Take
my advice—come back voluntarily; it will be in your
favor, if you do.—Edward Emlyn."

The witness described his pallor and consternation,
his sending him to the ticket-office to see what was the
earliest train back, his anxiety to know at what hour
exactly the dispatch was dated.

The cross-examiner asked how he dared to go to the
ticket-office and leave him, seeing, by the despatch,
that he was a suspected person.

" I kept my eye on him," said the astute messenger,
determined not to have his shrewdness doubted.

The attorney for the prosecution wished, sarcasti-
cally, that all the witnesses for the defence might be as
strongly persuaded of the prisoner's innocence, and dismissed him.

The officer who arrested him was the next brought
forward. He had received the dispatch, at the Cen-
tral Office, just twenty minutes before the arrival of
the train. He had made all possible haste to get to the

depot, and had entered it just as the passengers were coming, in a body, through the gateway, from the cars. If the train had been on time, there would have been no hope. He spotted his man in an instant, from the description he had had. He saw the messenger go up to him with the dispatch, and knew somebody had got before him, and had given him warning. So he came close, and stood ready to prevent escape, if he attempted it. But he corroborated the former witness's account of his amazed and overwhelmed condition, and the lack of evidence to show any inclination to escape.

On cross-examination, he said he must acknowledge he had arrested prisoners who were just as innocent appearing, and who had turned out the worst sort of scamps. He could believe anything of prisoners, pretty much, he said; classing them, evidently, in his mind, in not the most discriminating way.

After awhile the prisoner had got over his shock, and had seemed to take in the situation and to rouse himself; and he had never seen him give way since then, much as he had seen of him.

Yes, he acknowledged on the cross-examination that he was of Irish parentage; he wasn't ashamed of it either; he didn't care what the prisoner was, he was a perfect gentleman.

"Don't you think all Irishmen are perfect gentle men?" said the prosecuting lawyer. Which wasn't evidence, but which was effective.

After he left the stand, I was recalled. I wasn't expecting it at the moment, and was a little agitated, but soon recovered my composure. Mr. Hardinge again came near the stand and spoke in a lower voice than when he questioned the others. He said:

" I made it a point to ask you as little as possible about the details of your going in the nursery that night, after Sophia gave you the alarm. I now find myself obliged to ask you, did you find anything deranged about the room, excepting, of course, the condition of the cribs ?"

"I do not remember anything displaced ; it may have been so, easily, and I not have seen it, in the state of mind in which I was."

"Did you find anything out of order in any other room ?"

"Yes."

"Tell me about it, if you please."

"Sophia dropped the light as she fell; I had to grope about to find the matches. I went across to my own room, and stumbled over something lying near the door. When I got the matches and struck one, I found it was a footstool that generally stood beside my closet door. It was dragged out from its place and lay over-turned near the entrance to the room. The first thought that I had, was that some one had been robbing the closet, but I did not think of it a second time. I don't know whether anything was out of order in that closet; every thought was for the other room."

" Was anything missing from any other room upon that floor ?"

" There was something missing from the nursery. It was not anything of any value to—to any one out-side."

" Describe it, if you please ?"

"It was a toy—belonging to the youngest child—and one of her little shoes cannot be found."

"Where was the toy kept, and what was it?"

"It was broken; a little toy lamb—with a bell around its neck—the Baby would never go to sleep unless she had it in her arms—it was in her arms that evening, when—when—I saw her last alive."

"You—" began the lawyer.

"I cannot talk about it—let me go," I exclaimed, getting up and making a step forward, overcome by an anguish that was uncontrollable.

Sophia darted forward to my help.

"Let me go—let me go out," I said, "I cannot bear it any longer."

The lawyer pushed between her and me, and helped me down the step from the witness-stand, and supported me through the clerks and lawyers, past the prisoner, out into an ante-room. As he went he managed to whisper a few words in my ear, the only ones that I ever had the chance of having with him through the whole trial.

I lay down on the hard settee in the ante-room. I would not go away; but lay and listened to the progress of the case, which I could hear with tolerable distinctness. The defence had, one after another, three South Berwick men on the stand. They testified, with very fair unanimity, to the seeing at various times during daylight of September second, a man unknown to the neighborhood, corresponding to the description of the tramp who ate his bread and butter outside the kitchen door of the cottage, in the morning. The last time he was seen was just before twilight, by a fisherman, who was coming up from one of the fish-houses on the beach, below the Old Town Pond. The witness had been there to stow away a seine he had been

mending; he was coming up the road when he noticed
the man striking off towards the lane that debouches
in the farm-yard of the cottage. He noticed him particularly; he thought he was a rough-looking chap; he
wondered where he came from. He didn't speak of it
to any one; it passed out of his mind. He didn't connect it with the murder, even when he heard of it next
day.

"Why?"

Well, he supposed it was because he heard right
off who it was that was arrested. There didn't seem
to be any doubt about who did it. He didn't recall
the tramp to his mind till a good deal later; tramps
weren't such an unusual sight—he wished they were.
They didn't often get as far down the Island as South
Berwick, but they weren't a rarity enough to keep a
man awake at night if he had seen one through the
day. It wasn't strange he hadn't thought of it; in his
opinion it wouldn't have made much difference if he
hadn't ever thought of it. He was informed that his
opinion wasn't demanded by the court. He was an
aggressive witness; it wasn't difficult to get him to
admit that he'd hang every Irishman in Sutphen
county if he had a fair excuse. For all that, he wasn't
to be shaken about the tramp; "he was bound to say,"
the tramp was going through the lane towards the cottage just before twilight, on the second of September.
There was a good deal more, but this was the substance
of it in the main. And here the case for the defence
was rested.

CHAPTER XXI.

COUNSEL FOR THE DEFENCE.

"For one minute he turned his eye round on the throng,
An' he looked at the bars, so firm and so strong,
An' he saw that he had not a hope nor a friend,
A chance to escape, nor a word to defend;
An' he folded his arms as he stood there alone,
As calm and as cold as a statue of stone."

Samuel Lover.

WE were late the next morning in getting away from the hotel. Mr. Hardinge had already begun his summing-up, when we came into the court-room. There were more people there than ever: not an inch of standing room was vacant; men were sitting even on the ledges of the windows, but the utmost silence reigned, and the most perfect order. Outside it was a matchless October day; through the windows, none too clear, came in the cheerful sunshine. The air inside was as yet comparatively good. The windows were open from the top, and the outer door was but half shut. Macnally lifted his eyes at the stir of our entrance from the ante-room, but they fell again, and he did not look at us. From where he sat to where I did was not twelve feet; yet I had never met his eye. Generally some one was between us; but to-day we were almost face to face, except that, as he sat, his profile was always turned towards us; he faced a little towards the witness-stand and towards the jury. Mr. Hardinge was speaking, standing just beside him. His eyes were on

the ground, but his face expressed intent attention.
He was pale as the dead, but his still face and fixed attitude expressed the intensest mental force and life, I
don't know how.

The first of Mr. Hardinge's speech, as I have said,
was lost to us; when I began to listen, he was saying
this:

"The importance of this case I cannot over-state.
To you men of Sutphen county, it is the gravest duty
that ever came before you. The records tell us that it
is a hundred years since the death penalty has been enforced in this peaceful, law-abiding place. A century
of peace! the heavens have smiled upon you. Do not
rashly break the spell. I know I need not ask you to
deliberate, to weigh each word, to sift each argument.
I am speaking to men who are used to deliberation and
to thought; the tenor of your lives has taught it to you,
the very blood in your veins dictates it to you. I have
faced many juries in my day: if I had a weak cause I
should say, give me anything but a jury of sturdy, sober-minded American farmers. To-day I say, thank
Heaven I *have* a jury of sturdy, sober-minded American farmers, men who can't be bent by prejudice to say
that right is wrong, even if the right isn't what they
like; men who can throw down the gauntlet to the world
and say, we abide by the written law and by the spoken
truth.

"Gentlemen of the jury, I stand before you to-day
to plead for one who is separated from you in many
ways. He is an alien by birth; he is of a nation you
do not hold in favor. The bulk of his fellow-countrymen established in America are your political opponents.
His education has been different; his way of life has been

different; his religious creed is different. What shall I say? Has not God made of one blood all the nations of the earth? Is he not a man for a' that? Will you let him suffer at your hands because he isn't of your blood? 'The stranger that dwelleth with you shall be unto you as one born among you; * * for ye were strangers in the land of Egypt.' I ask more mercy for him because he is a stranger; I ask you to discard prejudices that are inherent in most of us; I ask you to do him justice, as perhaps you would ask to have justice done to some sailor lad of yours, cast by fate into a foreign prison.

"Gentlemen, this case has been cruelly prejudged and falsified; when I have shown you all, I think you will agree with me. Let me begin by putting before you the theory of the prosecution, and by pointing out a few of its weak points. You are asked to believe that this man before you has murdered the innocent and beautiful children of the woman whom he loved, because he was persuaded that they stood between him and the attainment of her hand. They represent him to you as sane, as resolute; they do not even ask you to believe it was in transport of rage, because, sometimes, one is sorry for a man whose sufferings drive him to extremity, and because high-tempered jurymen might have some sympathy for such a one. No, he has done it deliberately, he has plotted and planned, he is a devil in man's shape; he has belied all that has been known of him, all his goodness and lightheartedness; he commits this monstrous crime, and he goes away, meaning, forsooth, to come back and marry the mother when her days of mourning shall be ended. Gentlemen, I won't affront your intelligence by much dwelling on a theory like this. One asks naturally for a motive for the commission of such a crime. There was every motive that he should not commit it. The prosecution declares that she returned his affection ; that perhaps his poverty and her desire to devote her means and all her time to the care and education of these children, prevented her from marrying him. If her affection for them living was too great to be overcome by all his passion, what would her love for them be, dead by such a cruel death as this ? If there was a gulf between them before, there would be an ocean now. There is no room for such a theory in any man's mind. I declare it to be utterly preposterous.

"Let us look at the evidence, and see how it is sustained. The prisoner is shown to you, by the testimony of all the witnesses, even the woman Sophia, as uniformly gentle, gentlemanly, affectionate to children, tender-hearted, keenly averse to giving pain ; it was impossible from his temperament for him to have done this deed. The mother of these children trusted him, enjoyed his society ; ' I was glad to have him for my friend,' she says, in her testimony. I should believe she was a woman not easily deceived ; her instincts are fine ; she has keen, womanly discernment. What if she cannot love him ? ' Love comes unsought, unsent.' Perhaps her heart is in the grave. She cannot return his affection ; she has to deal this blow, but you may be sure she does it gently. Let us look at the character of the woman Sophia. She loves her mistress—apparently most people love her who come near her—but she is consumed with a jealous hatred of the young tutor ; she sees in him a suitor from the first. She dreads a master in the little household. I am afraid she has been mistress, and ruled it with an iron rule. The

young housekeeper and mother yields to her judgment
in all things, lets her manage matters as she will in the
ménage. It would not suit Sophia to have a master
enter ; she will fight against it. She doesn't mind the
weapons that she fights with. She does all she can to
prejudice her mistress, but she makes little headway
here. Her mistress, with all her gentleness, knows her
own mind upon the subject, and, we may well believe,
keeps her own counsel, too. You have heard the history of the pocket-handkerchief. Desdemona's didn't
pass through hands more treacherous ; she steals it from
her mistress' room, hides it till she sees a fitting moment to produce it to the prisoner's hurt. She isn't
above eavesdropping either, this estimable servant.
She can pry not only into her lady's boxes and drawers,
but into her secrets, too. She listens outside the parlor
window, to the broken-hearted lover, who goes away
forever from the woman who likes but cannot love
him, who pities, but who cannot help him. She sees his
pallor, his agitation ; she gloats upon his wretchedness.
Crouched down, gazing through the blind-door, she
reports to us his manner and appearance, as he went for
the last time out of the little cottage, where, for a
happy summer, he has fed his hopes. Trusty, faithful
creature! She can swear falsely, too, or forget amaz-
ingly. Recall her testimony about the stair door, left unbolted. Two witnesses, her mistress and Matilda, prove
her false about it. Then remember the brutal words
with which she flings the awful tidings into the poor
young mother's face. 'Come and see your lover's
work!' Even in that appalling moment, when her
nurslings lie dead before her, her consuming hatred
rises up above all other feelings ; one can almost be-

lieve the Scripture story of demoniacal possession acted over in the nineteenth century.

"I ask you to put at its true value the testimony of a witness ruled by such a deadly passion. I deny that she can see even the smallest detail in an unbiassed light. Hatred and jealousy, such as she stands convicted of, put her out of the pale of public confidence. I ask you to throw out her testimony, and to render your verdict as if she had not spoken.

"Of the medical testimony I must speak briefly. The professional gentlemen have told you the causes of the death of the two children. They agree that, while life might be extinguished in three minutes, it is difficult to imagine such dexterity, such cold-bloodedness. The prisoner, having said his last good-bye to the mother, just on the threshold turns back, and says: ' Mayn't I go in and look at the children before I go ?' Their room is on the same floor. He knows the ways about the quaint little cottage ; he goes in to give them a good-bye kiss, for he is going from America forever on the morrow. The hands of the clock point at five minutes before nine ; the lady notices it, the maid notices it ; they think that he will miss his train. They are both within call. Fancy him going through that deadly work, not knowing at what instant the nurse's black eyes may gleam in upon him ! He has three minutes to make sure that both are dead. He comes out cool and steady, passes through the hall, past the mother, past the stealthy nurse, out into the street, and takes his way coolly to the train, to miss which is to meet death. Escape is all his thought now. Does he hurry ? Does he come, pale and panting, on the platform steps ? You have heard the testimony of the railroad employées. No man was ever cooler, graver, quieter. They start. The train is delayed on the way nearly two hours. Does that fire him with impatience? Why does he not spring off at some of the many halting-places, and strike off across the country, reach the coast, and get away upon some out-bound vessel? Gentlemen, I will not waste your time over such a theory as this; it is too palpable a folly.

"Let us go back to the cottage, where the young mother sits, thoughtful and silent, on the dark balcony. She is thinking of many things; of the sorrow that she has had to cause; of the pleasant Summer that has ended in pain to one whom she has cared for and respected; she thinks of her children; she feels she has her little brood under her wings, though the night is dark and somber. Perhaps her mind goes into the past, recalling a face and voice that she will never see and hear but in dreams again. No wonder she is absorbed; no wonder that the light sounds of the intruder's tread in the darkened rooms beyond the parlor escape her ear. The lynx-eyed nurse has left her post; she has gone to the front window, and is stealthily gazing out upon her mistress, wondering what her feelings are, now that she has sent away her lover. No wonder that she heard nothing; she is absorbed indeed. At what moment the tramp entered from the barn, where since twilight he probably had been concealed, it is difficult to say. It seems probable to me he followed shortly after the sleepy Indian woman, whom he had been watching through the window. He opens the kitchen door, steals across it, follows the woman through the stair door with which he had acquainted himself in the morning. He gropes about and enters the first door he

finds, which is that of the lady's bed-room. While
searching for plunder here, he hears a step; it is Macnally's, going to the children's bedside. He hastily
conceals himself inside the closet. In a few minutes
the step goes out, silence reigns again. He steals out,
across the dark, open chamber, into the room where the
children lie asleep. He busies himself in searching
about for money or valuables; he is not a practiced
housebreaker; he is a clumsy brute of a tramp; ignorant,
but rapacious; probably not long in the country; not
familiar with the ways of households here. Some sound
he makes near the bed of one of the children rouses her;
she sits up, looks around. He starts toward her; she
makes a little cry, which rouses the other, who stirs in
her sleep. He is standing between the cribs; terror
seizes him; if they make an outcry, he will be caught.

"It is a short work to silence the little throats; he is
a coward, a brute, little better than an animal; human
life, so easily crushed out, seems to him little in com-
parison with the chance of detection and a few months
in the county jail. He has had enough of the attempt;
he is thoroughly frightened; he stumbles his way out,
creeps down the stairs, goes softly out the kitchen door.
It is a very dark night; he makes his way along the
little path; brushes against the lilac bushes that stand
beside the gate. From the silent balcony above, the
mother looks down and listens. She hears the gate
open very softly, and then shut. She little knows who
has passed out, and what ruin has been left behind.
She goes forward across the balcony to see where Sophia
is—if she has heard it. No, Sophia has resumed her
sewing and her stolid silence. Sophia has not heard it, she
is intent on other things than sounds like these. The

hours pass. The two sit there silent, characteristically employed, one in quiet retrospection, the other in sharp manual labor, and fierce, angry thoughts. You know the rest. You know the first words that the woman speaks when she beholds the appalling sight; it is the index to the whole. She has a force, a power of her own; she bends people to her way of thinking in an unusual way. She is convinced in her own mind; I do not say she is not; she leaves no room for doubt in any mind as to who has done the deed. She hounds them on to search for and arrest Macnally; she is in authority, in a certain way, in the stricken house; they defer to her; no one has any other theory to oppose to hers; it is as she says. And while, with vixen fury, she points them to the discarded lover, the brutal murderer, dull and slow of wit, goes safely off to swamps and woods and bays, where he may take his time, and get away securely. The house was not properly searched; the traces that might have been found were, in the confusion, lost. I do not blame the local officers exactly. I know what is the force and fire of such a woman's tongue as this. We do not know exactly what things are missing from the house. In the dismay and anguish none of the inhabitants can tell what may have been abstracted. The mother alone has yearned for the little broken toy; the mate of the little shoe that is now her dearest treasure. *When we know where those two things are, we shall know who is the murderer.* Till they are brought into the court, gentlemen, these children came to their death by the hands of a person or persons unknown. Nothing else is possible.

"There is one more point I must touch upon, gentlemen of the jury, and I have done. A great emphasis is laid by the prosecution upon the fact, if it is a fact, that the prisoner at the bar does not give you his true name. They imply that he is an adventurer, a man whose antecedents will weigh him down if he presents them. They say, he dares not tell the truth about himself, or he would tell it, to save him from the gallows. I will tell them something that he dares do; he dares risk the gallows rather than stain, even by an accusation of crime, the honored name he bears. For some youthful folly, some petulance of home-control, he comes to America, and, in his new-born independence, he drops the surname by which he would be identified, and is known by his baptismal name alone.

"That was an unwise thing to do; don't let your boys ever do it! It's all very well if nothing happens, but if it does, see the scrape it gets one in. It looks badly. I acknowledge it. I have pleaded with my client to disclose his family name. I might have as well have pleaded with Plymouth Rock. 'If I perish, I perish.' I like the generous surrender of himself to the consequences of his boyish folly, but, professionally, I strongly disapprove. '*C'est magnifique, mais ce n'est pas la guerre.*' He sees in fancy the agony and dismay of mother, sister, father, when the cruel news is brought; he thinks of the distance, of the long days of suspense before the end is reached; he will not bring such sorrow into the home he never should have left; they shall never know he was accused of murder; that he stood at the bar of justice, to plead for life; that he dragged down a hitherto unsullied name into the slime of criminals and prisons.

"Gentlemen, we many of us have sons. I have a boy, God bless him! now going through the fire of early

college life. I believe he is a good boy; I believe he
will be the stay and support of his mother and sisters
when I am dead and gone. But for all that, I wouldn't
guarantee that he'll keep free of folly and entanglement
while he is in his fiery, foolish years. I've paid some of
his debts for him already. I am afraid I shall have to pay
some more. It isn't even on the books that he mayn't
some day take the bit between his teeth, and walk off
across the ocean with only the formality of his middle
name. If he does, and gets into a scrape, though he's a
good fellow, I sha'n't expect him to show the pluck
that this young fellow shows, and refuse to appeal to
me. I'm sure he'd send a speedy telegram across the
ocean, and call upon me to get him out of his entanglement. It would be the wisest way, though perhaps
not the most heroic.

"Gentlemen, we have all been young; let us not be
hard upon the faults of youth. Let us show the in-
dulgence to this young stranger that we would have
asked for ourselves; that we would ask for our sons, if
they should ever, by complicated imprudence and misfortune, fall into the strait that he has fallen into. I
leave his case in your hands with confidence and a sense
of full security."

CHAPTER XXII.

COUNSEL FOR THE PROSECUTION.

"All my spirits,
As if they had heard my passing-bell go for me,
Pull in their powers, and give me up to destiny."

Fletcher.

I DREW a deep breath; it seemed to me the matter was ended. I was not at the pains to listen very attentively when the counsel for the prosecution rose, and began his summing up. (Not the suffused and light-haired Mr. Bell, who had conducted the examinations, but the senior counsel; senior, but still young.) I listened, as we listen to things of secondary moment in a play, when we know how it is all coming out. His manner was a great contrast to the other speaker's, his voice a very inferior affair. He spoke conversationally, as if he had his finger in the button-hole of every jury-man. I began to see he wasn't "addressing them" as across a gulf, but that he had a hold upon them, as being one of themselves; when he sneered at the opposing counsel, he sneered from their side of the fence. Sutphen County is famed for being very clannish; it was not impossible that every juryman before him was more or less nearly related to him by birth or by connection. He was the rising lawyer of the county; they were all proud of him. It was possible that they wouldn't want to see him lose his case—a case, the like

[286]

of which had never been before the bar of Sutphen County since it had been a county, and had had a bar.

"It's been a great treat, I'm sure," he said. "We're not used to such fine speaking here in this part of the country; and I, for one, have been quite carried away by it. I'm sure I can answer for all of you, that you've been very much pleased—very much pleased. When we put Tom Turner up for surrogate again, we'll know who to send for to stump the county for him." (Tom Turner was a very weak candidate for surrogate at the last election, who had been overwhelmingly defeated. There was an audible titter.) "I almost think I should vote for Tom Turner myself, if he spoke for him. I assure you, he quite carries me away. But, I'll tell you, there's one thing I come back to, after I've been carried away by this extraordinary tide of talk, and that is, Facts. And I don't know but I'm a little stubborner after I get back to them, than before, for I am just a trifle ashamed of myself for being taken off my feet that way. Facts, gentlemen of the jury, facts are what the law undertakes to deal with; not theories, nor flights of fancy.

"Now, this tramp business, gentlemen, you'll excuse me if I call that a very decided flight of fancy. I shouldn't like to call it anything else; the counsel's a stranger in these parts, and he's anxious we should be particularly good to strangers. He quotes the Bible about it, you know. Well, we'll call it a flight of fancy. That poor, stupid Dutchman, who was seen around that day by several witnesses, had about as much to do with the murder as my dog Major had. Now, that lane from Old Town Pond is a highway in everything but name. You all know as well as I do, people go across there every day in the week without being bound to the Detmold farm-house; I suppose we must call it the cottage now—quaint little cottage, and all that sort of thing. It's a mighty damp, rickety, old farm-house, in point of fact, but since it's been occupied by city people, it's politer to say it is a cottage. The folks that have been in it this year must have got used to having foot passengers going through the yard, night and day. The place was shut up so long, everybody got in the habit of going along that way from Wickapogue and thereabouts; it cuts off half a mile or so. The tramp had as good a right as anybody to go through (that was no right at all, but he'd be as likely as any one to take it). He went through, most likely, when the family were in at tea, or maybe he struck off to the village through the fields before he got to the farm-yard. Again, the motive of the tramp was burglary, and no burglary has been committed; a footstool has been overturned and a couple of worthless articles are missing. We won't waste time over that. It speaks for itself.

"Now, a little about that kitchen stair door. Matilda's story was a plain, straightforward one, on the direct examination. You don't expect a poor Shinnecock half-breed to stand up against a city lawyer's befogging questions. On the cross-examination she contradicted herself, as any one of her gauge of intellect would do. She shut that kitchen door and bolted it; she would have done it by force of habit, if she had been fast asleep. Sophia trusted her, and that shows she'd never failed to shut it up before. The lower part of that house was shut off from communication with the upper, as fast as bars and bolts could make it. A noisy little poodle, who never let a stranger enter the gate without barking himself into fits, lay silent on the rug, and never lifted up his voice. The rear was all secure ; the front was guarded by two wakeful women, in full possession of their faculties. Gentlemen of the jury, nobody got into that house from the rear that night ; you know it as well as I know it, notwithstanding this distinguished lawyer's flight of fancy. Who got in from the front, and how did he get in? You have heard the story so many times, it's scarcely worth while to tell it all again. Bernard Macnally, or the man that's passed among us by that name, was the last person to go into that room where the children lay. No other person *could* have got in, no other person did get in ; it wasn't prejudging the murderer, when the work was seen, to say whose work it was. Nobody else had a chance to do the work ; no one else had a motive to do the work.

"The counsel for the defence has given us a good deal of talk about motive. He says the prisoner hadn't any motive. Well, I say he had. Different men need different motives to push them on to doing things. This man is a cool hand. I think he may have been in so many tight places before, he has got pretty well used to tight places, and that sort of experience gives a man courage. He knew he could do it ; he had done as risky things before. He is a man of force, there's no denying that. He knew this widow loved him ; I don't want to say anything against her, but she doesn't come quite up to our notion of good conduct in this county, if she let him be hanging round her all sum-mer in the way she did, if she didn't want to marry him, that's all. But she did want to marry him. The only thing in the way was the children. She hadn't

13

money enough to support this gay young gentleman,
and do justice to the children, too. I've no doubt she
got a little good advice from Sophia Atkinson. Well,
she made up her mind at last she'd do her duty by the
children, and she sent him off.

"You're not to believe Sophia, because she listened.
Pooh, whoo! What woman can you believe, then?
I'm not sure but a man would have listened under the
circumstances.

"Now the rear of the house is all shut up, dark as
a pocket, and as tight. The prisoner has said good-bye
to his lady-love. I should have thought he would have
been thinking about nothing but that. But he asks to
go and see the children, too. He goes in, by the only
entrance one could get in, to the nursery. When he
comes out, Sophia sees him. He looks white and bad;
he walks past the mother of the children without a word;
he doesn't offer to touch her hand. I shouldn't think he
would! He goes away; he knows he has time. He
trusts to luck; he's had pretty good luck so far in his ex-
ploits, perhaps. He is a cool hand, remember. It needn't
surprise us that he shows no fright and nervousness till he
is arrested. We may know all about that sort of thing if
we will look over the police reports. I contend this man,
of whom we know nothing, absolutely nothing, till ten
months ago, is a member of what we call the criminal
class. It isn't a small class either, if we are to believe
all the reports. We live in the country, and it is hard
to believe in such depravity. I could cite you twenty
cases that I have come across in my reading, that have
in them a great deal that is parallel. He means to go
to Europe, stay away awhile, and come back for the
widow and her nice snug fortune, when things shall be

smoothed out a little. I don't say this is a pleasant theory, but it is strictly in accordance with the facts.

"But, in many ways, this case has narrowed down to a contest between two witnesses. If you believe Sophia Atkinson, you believe there was no possibility for any one to enter the rear of the house. If you believe her mistress, you are forced to admit there was. If you believe, again, this latter, you believe some one went out the gate, meaning to get away without attracting observation. If you believe Sophia, you believe no one could have done it without her quick ears hearing them go out. The counsel for the defence says you mustn't believe Sophia, because she listened, and because she kept that handkerchief with half the alphabet embroidered on it. Oh, yes! and because she didn't like the prisoner from the first, and thought him a bad lot. Well, do you know, it strikes me those are just three counts on which you ought to trust her. I don't blame her for listening. Her mistress was young; she had been her nurse before she was her children's nurse; she saw she was being entrapped by a bad fellow; she watched day and night to save her. The handkerchief (which, gentlemen, is one of a set found in the prisoner's trunk) was something tangible to show he wasn't Bernard Macnally, no matter if he was a perfect gentleman, and all that sort of thing. She kept it in a safe place, till she could use it to convince the younger woman of the mistake that she was making. And I don't blame her very much for not liking him from the very first. I think it's to the credit of her judgment that she didn't. An intelligent American woman of her age, who has been trusted all her life by the family that she's lived with, can't be

pooh-poohed off the witness-stand by the flight of
fancy of even a distinguished lawyer from the city.
Sophia Atkinson is the sort of witness I like; she's the
sort of woman I like; I'd like her in my family. If
she's ever out of place, I hope she'll remember my address. If I had a lot of young daughters, ready to be
fallen in love with by adventurers from Ireland, I'd
like to have her round. She'd suit me to a T.

"Now, as to her mistress as a witness. Gentlemen, I
don't like to say anything that isn't flattering about a lady.
I am sorry for the sufferings she has undergone, as sorry
as the counsel on the other side. Perhaps I'm not as
easily overcome by personal attractions as he is; we don't
think so much about things of that kind in the country,
maybe, after we marry and settle down. But I must
say, there are things I don't understand. That gate, for
instance—why didn't Sophia hear it? She was almost
as near. It came in so pat, that gate. It was a god-
send to the defence. I don't know where the defence
would have gone to have hunted up a theory but for
the lifting of that gate-latch. Then that bolt on the
door of the kitchen stairs. It's remarkable the lady
should have remembered it so long—just that little circumstance. It wasn't as if she was shutting up the
house herself; it wasn't as if anybody had suggested,
for days after the murder, that it was of the least importance in the case. Her remembering it so very
clearly is a thing that—well, that I can't understand
exactly. Only on one theory. Now, don't be shocked,
gentlemen. I don't want to be impolite. But I feel
a sort of certainty of one thing. She didn't remember it
till she saw it was a necessary thing to be remembered.
Don't be shocked; I can't help it. It was a strong

temptation. You see, she wants to save him. She—well, she's in love with him, gentlemen, and you know what that means. You know it means, with a woman, that she wouldn't stop at anything. I'm sorry for her. It's an awful thing all round. An infatuation of that sort will outlive everything. You know the law won't receive a woman's testimony for or against her husband. The law knows a woman can't be trusted to tell the truth when it comes to hurting a hair of the man's head that she loves. Now, I don't pretend to say this lady knows she has—well—misstated facts a little. I don't say she would deliberately say what wasn't strictly true. But she wants it to be true so dreadfully; she thinks about it, and thinks about it, and ends up in believing it herself. You can't trust a woman in love; there's no way out of that. It introduces a nice moral question. It's just the sort of thing my brother for the defence could spread out, till you didn't know head from tail of it. It isn't in my line, you see. I wish I could retain him to expound it to you. But as that's impossible, we'll have to let it drop.

"Gentlemen, let's go back a minute to that parting between the prisoner and this lady. You've heard a great deal about it; but I ask your patience while I repeat to you the words which Sophia Atkinson testifies to having heard him say, and which her mistress doesn't deny he said. They're just these. I ask you to bear them in your mind. You remember he had asked her, desperately, at the last, why he must go away, and she had told him, he must go. Then he said (please remember these words), '*It is your children stand between us, you cannot say it is not. You aren't willing to trust them to me, whatever you might be willing for yourself.'*

Whenever the defence talks to you about motive, just turn those words over in your mind, and see what you can make of them. I tell you what *I* make of 'em. I make of 'em motive enough to hang him high as Haman. That is all. I'm not going to talk to you any more about it. People on the east end of Long Island don't have to be talked to all night to make 'em understand a thing. I suppose it comes of living so near the beginning of things; they get an earlier start.

" Now, gentlemen, I believe I have come to the last point I want to draw your attention to. In the judgment of the law, a man's previous character goes for a great deal. Once establish that a man accused of any crime has walked a steady, straight road in the sight of all men for a lifetime, and you've as good as cleared him. A man's life, I say again, goes for a good deal, and it *ought* to go for a good deal. Men don't break out all of a sudden into murderers and thieves. It doesn't come upon 'em like the small-pox, unless they've had it in their system. Now, gentlemen, let's look at this man before us. Ten months ago, he rose out of the earth, or dropped down from the sky, into the Emlyn family. Colonel Emlyn,—now, I've a great respect for Colonel Emlyn, he's a neighbor of mine, and we get along first-rate together—but I wouldn't set him to take care of my family exactly. He advertises for a tutor, and along comes this one. He is a taking young fellow; he talks the colonel into engaging him without a word of reference. He doesn't know whether he dropped from the sky, as I say, or burrowed his way out from the ground. He doesn't ask. He takes him. He brings him home, makes him one of the family. In fact, I don't know but he makes him the most important member of his family. He has the best of everything, he's made a sort of pet of, he's a privileged person, he's introduced to the friends of the family.

"Well, what does the young man do, in return for all this sort of kindness? I'll be bound the Emlyns don't keep back anything from him—they're not that sort of people. Things are talked of freely—their family connections, what they did last year and the year before, what they're going to do next year. Does he return the compliment? Not a bit of it. He talks enough, Heaven knows, but he's exceedingly careful not to talk about himself. At the end of ten months, the people he's been living with can't tell you, though they rack their memory to do it, of a single word that he has dropped about his home, his people, his life before he came to them. They don't know—anything about him. They're ladies and gentlemen, and they don't pry into what he doesn't choose to tell them. The best they can say is that they found him reticent. Reticent! Well, he's the first Irishman I ever knew that was, even about his debts, and the bad whisky that he'd drunk, and the bad morals of his grandmother. No, gentlemen, he isn't a common Irishman, he's an uncommon Irishman; if he wasn't, we'd have had an immigration law that would have kept him out a good many years ago. This man, Irishman as he was, knew how to hold his tongue. Here, at the foot of the gallows, he knows how to hold it still. These kind and hospitable people never got him to betray a word, in all the familiarity of every-day life. He could make jokes, and turn somersaults, and quote Greek and Latin, and shoot and fish, and play with the children, and

make love to the widow; but he couldn't tell them
'iver a ward' about himself. They tell you he was
amiable. Of course. Why shouldn't he be? Even
Sophia tells you he didn't bang the children about
and complain of the biscuits when he came to tea. I
shouldn't have supposed he would. It wasn't in his
programme. He was trying to make people like him,
and to get a footing. He succeeded pretty well.
They were all infatuated with him.

"The whole testimony for character that the defence
can bring, extends back a distance of ten months. Ten
months is a good while for some things, but for others,
it's rather a poor showing. If a man can't behave himself for ten months, it's a pity. If he can't let you look
back into his life more'n ten months, it's a pity,
greater still. The counsel for the defence gives us dexterously to understand, he is of a very fine family.
Well, I'm sure I don't say that he isn't. I'm not much
posted on the ways of fine families on the other side;
but all I can say is, if they're all of 'em given to turning somersaults, climbing poles, going about barelegged,
driving through the streets with warming pans over
their shoulders, I'm sure I'm glad they don't emigrate
to this country in any greater numbers. I'm just as
well satisfied they should stay at home and look after
their peat and potatoes.

"No, gentlemen. The counsel for the defence assures
us that if the prisoner could be induced to roll up the
curtain of his past life, we should see such a Phœnix
that we'd all drop down on our knees and ask his pardon for having imagined it possible that he could do
anything unhandsome. *My* impression is that if that
curtain could be got to move, there'd be revealed to us

such a jail-bird that every man of you'd be on his feet quicker'n wink, and after him while there was breath enough to follow.

"Gentlemen of the jury, don't let that jail-bird slip through your fingers; don't let his counsel have the laugh on you; he knows as well as I do that fine words don't butter any parsnips. We've had a century of peace in Sutphen County. If we want another, let's make it understood it isn't a healthy place for jail-birds and the like of them. Let's show the world (for this is going to be a celebrated case,) let's show the world we're men enough to do our duty, and sharp enough to see it, if we do live on the far end of a sandy island, half way out to sea. Sutphen County wants no advice from city people. Sutphen County can manage her matters for herself. She knows the law, and she has the pluck to carry out its penalties when she sees it must be done. (Looking at his watch.) Bless my heart, I've talked just about twice as long as there was any need. I suppose I needn't have opened my lips. I guess you'd made up your minds upon the matter long before I began to talk to you about it."

And he took his seat as if he were going to open the stove-door to put more wood in, or had sat down to consult his account-book about the winter wheat. He came in very fresh; he hadn't laid a hair in this sharp pull against the city lawyer. All this told upon the audience. My heart died down within me. I couldn't see the jurors' faces. But I had seen a sort of smile pass sometimes over the faces of the three judges. I had detected hearty sympathy in the eyes of all the crowd. Sometimes I had looked with terror towards Mr. Hardinge, and had been reassured. He

looked satisfied and undismayed. Occasionally he had
glanced my way, as if to steady me. He dared not
give me a look, but his eye, as it passed over mine, gave
me a world of succor.

It was late in the afternoon. The court had adjourned ; the judge's charge would be given in the
morning—and then—and then—the verdict. The people were loath to disperse. They stood about in groups
and talked with eager gesticulation. I could hear now
and then a few words. They all went one way. But
they were not the jury. But the jury was made up
of such as they.

How we all lived through that night I don't at all
know. Mrs. Emlyn was so restless that I knew she
would be ill. The colonel looked like an old man. It
was hard for people who had led such quiet and well-
guarded lives. Even Sophia took to walking the floor,
and could not lie down, or sleep, or eat. I believe I
was the quietest of them all, and wrote the first letter
of the day to poor Naomi, left behind in feverish
anxiety at Happy-go-lucky. Nobody had thought
about her and Ned that day. In fact, there had been
no time, and no one had had the resolution to do anything that required an effort of will or memory, or
even of physical force.

CHAPTER XXIII.

IN THE JUDGMENT OF TWELVE MEN.

" The days could somehow drag themselves
    Like wounded worms along:
  But I know not how we lived those nights,
    Save that God made us strong."

                                        Faber.

THE next day opened raw and chill. The rosiest
girls in the court-room had blue lips and noses;
the men outside stamped their feet to keep warm; the
horrid fluted stove inside was beginning to give out hot
air, a smell of heated iron, and an abundance of coal
gas. The crowd was greater than ever, and more restless. Before the opening of the court there was a great
deal of vehement talking, though low, but the volume
of it together made a jarring, rough sound that tortured my ear.

When the prisoner was brought in (we were seated
first) he passed directly in front of us. He even had
to step over the bottom of my dress as it lay upon
the floor. But he did not lift his eyes, nor look at any
of us. It seemed to me like some horrible spell of en-
chantment; we had been all these days within the same
four walls, listening to the same words, thinking, of
necessity, many of the same thoughts; and not once
had our eyes met, not once had I heard the sound of
his voice; the face and figure that met my eye were

[299]

strangely, awfully changed, and yet the same. It
seemed to me such a combination of woe, and shame,
and horror had never come into one lot before. It
was like some horrible revel of the fancy more than
like a fact; he and I compelled to sit and listen, day
after day, to the unveiling of our thoughts, to the tor-
turing into diverse meanings the most sacredly secret
words that we had ever uttered. In the gray dullness
of this chill, real day, it all seemed more unreal and
more hideous than ever. . . . The crier had droned
out his formula, " Hear ye, hear ye;" and in the pause
that followed,

Mr. Bell rose in his place, and said, "May it please
your Honor, since the adjournment of the court last
night, a most important piece of evidence has come to
my knowledge. It was not through any neglect of
those engaged in the prosecution, that it did not come
to light before. It was, I am ashamed to say, due to the
connivance of the officer who arrested the prisoner,
that this important link in the chain of evidence was
not supplied to us before. The officer is, as you remember, an Irishman; his sympathy for his countryman was
greater than his sense of duty. As this miscarriage is
due in no way to the prosecution, and that the ends of
justice may not be defeated, I ask permission to offer
this evidence now. I have the man's affidavit, and the
corroborating testimony ready. It will not detain you
many minutes, and I ask permission to proceed. The
importance of the testimony cannot be overstated."

Mr. Hardinge started to his feet. " In all my legal
experience, your Honor, I have never heard a parallel
to this. It strikes me as an outrage that cannot be
overstated. I protest against it, and deny that the

prosecution have any more right to present a piece of
evidence after they have summed up their case, than
they would have to present it six months hence at the
next sitting of the court. My brother must have devised this way to make his case immortal; one will
never know when it is ended. Your Honor, let us
hear no more of this, in the name of justice, and of
law."

Mr. Bell blushed a deep blush of wrath, and made
a testy answer. The judge, with deliberation, made a
pause in the discussion, and ordered the jury to be taken
out of court. They accordingly filed out into the jury
room, burning with curiosity, no doubt; and in the
silence which followed the closing of the door, Mr.
Bell resumed his argument. I looked in vain for comfort from my friend, the lawyer, now; he forgot me, or
had none to give. He was quite pale, and one could
see all his senses were enlisted in the fight. You might
have fired a cannon off beside him, and he would not
have heard it while his opponent was speaking. I was
so benumbed I could not follow them. I don't know
what was said on either side. I only know that after a
great deal, the judge gave permission to the prosecution
to read the affidavit of the officer, and amid a deep
silence the following was read:

" I, Michael Denny, being duly sworn, depose that
on the morning of the third of September I arrested
the prisoner at the bar." (Then followed the account
of his arrest about two o'clock in the morning, at the
depot, and the circumstances of his detention, etc., at
the police headquarters till the departure of the next
train for South Berwick.) " It was my duty to examine
him and to make an inventory of all the articles found

upon his person. I had him in the waiting-room of
the headquarters. There was nobody else in the room,
only the officer stationed outside the door. I knew
what the prisoner was accused of. I found in the inner
pocket of his coat a child's shoe. I didn't believe he
did the murder. I was sure of it. I knew, though, in a
minute, it would look bad, his having the little shoe
about him. He was standing by the window, I was
away from it. I said to him, 'That won't do you any
good. Pitch it out of the window.' He refused to do
it. I made a move to do it myself. It was a high
window overlooking the street. He put out his hand
to stop me. Just that moment I heard a noise outside
the door, and I drew back, and stooped down over the
valise, where his dressing things and all were. I had
already made the inventory of them, along with the
other officer. It was he that was at the door and now
came in, and another man with him. When I heard
them come in, I pushed the little shoe down into a sort
of pocket that there is inside the bag; it was so little
it didn't seem to take up any room; you couldn't feel
it if you passed your hand over it, not thinking. The
other officers came up, and we finished the inventory of
what he had on. Then they were detailed to take him
up by the train. I never thought of the shoe again. I
meant to have taken it out of the bag the next time the
others went across the room, or anywhere. But it
passed out of my mind. I have been very busy. I
never thought of it again till I heard the counsel yesterday talk about it in his summing up. Then I was uneasy
for fear somebody would find it. I made an effort to
see the prisoner. Last night I got in for a minute,
with an officer. He watched me all the time, I could

see. I knew he distrusted me because I was an Irishman. I couldn't get a chance at the bag, but I suppose he saw that was what I was at, and afterwards they searched it, and when they found this, and saw it wasn't in the inventory that I had sworn to, they brought me up about it. That is all I have to say."

"Your Honor," said Mr. Bell, when he finished the reading of the affidavit (he spoke hurriedly and rather venomously, as if he feared not being allowed to get in all he wanted without being interrupted), "your Honor, I have here the shoe which the opposing counsel told us yesterday would identify the murderer. It was found as alleged in the affidavit, in the prisoner's possession."

And he placed upon the table before him the Baby's little shoe. I gave a faint cry at the sight; I could not help it. The court-room was so still, it sounded from one end to the other, faint as it was.

"You don't need other identification," said the lawyer, "the mother has told you, perhaps involuntarily. But to leave no doubt, I will show you its mate."

And he signed to Sophia, who came forward and put into his hand the shoe that, within a half-hour, she had taken from my trunk at the hotel. I had seen the deputy give her a note, and had seen her leave the court-room, but had been too engrossed to wonder why she went.

"I ask," said the counsel, "that these be put in evidence; that the case be opened to admit testimony of which we were defrauded by the dishonesty of the prisoner's countryman."

He laid the little shoes together on the table, then lifted them to bring them nearer to the judges' range of vision. He seemed to gloat over them. They were little slippers, made with a strap that buttoned round the ankle. They were worn and creased, and so very little. I put my hands up before my face. It killed me to look at them, and to see him touch them.

"Your Honor," said Mr. Hardinge, in a cold, hard voice. "don't let us degenerate into melodrama. We are in a court of law. I contend the absolute impossibility of admitting any evidence, no matter of what force or pertinence. I have already proved this to your Honor. I now ask you to throw out this testimony as utterly impertinent and worthless. If it had come in the regular course of the case, no one would have given it a second thought. It proves nothing. It fits in to nothing. When I said yesterday, that when those articles were found we should have found the murderer, I meant, and the counsel knows I meant, when we found them in the possession of a burglar. Your Honor, this man is not a burglar; the prosecution doesn't present him as a burglar. His having that shoe doesn't prove anything but his affection for the little child that wore it. We know he had been in the room. We don't gain anything by this proof that he had been there."

"We gain one thing," said the senior counsel, rising to his feet. "We take a nail out of that tramp's coffin, and put it in the prisoner's. If we could only set that foot-stool back in its place now, by natural means, I think we could screw down the lid."

"Your Honor, this is no time for trifling; human life is a thing too sacred. Don't allow this to continue."

"I only ask," said the senior counsel, quite undaunted, " that my brother's words have full force with you now. I only desire to recall to your mind, that we heard in court yesterday from him the unequivocal statement that when that toy and that shoe should be found, then and there the murderer would be found. If it was law yesterday, it must be law to-day. I can't turn and twist about so quick as all that. I believed him yesterday. I keep on believing him. If it doesn't prove anything new about the prisoner, it proves something about that man of straw, the tramp. It proves, your Honor, that he didn't exist, and that Bernard Macnally is the man we're looking for, if anybody had any doubt before."

" Your Honor," cried Mr. Hardinge, "don't let a man be hung for the zeal of a blundering officer, and for the chance word of his counsel! I plead with you to sift these facts before they reach the jury; to remember the inflammable nature of human prejudice; to think of the awful burden that would lie upon those who had departed from the rigid impartiality of the law, in such a critical moment as this. If, guilty, he should escape, the law, and not the administrators of it, would have to bear the blame. If, innocent, he should be saved, the law could alone be lauded. It has passed out of our hands; for or against, we have done our best; all human effort is sealed now forever; if that testimony is admitted, the law is violated. A trust has been betrayed; the divine character of justice has been sullied. We are but human; we can see but a little way. We must work within narrow rules, and then trust that they will develop the Divine Will and order. I would never stand at the bar, to plead for or against a fellow-mortal's life, if I did not believe in Divine

Justice working through human agency, humble and
imperfect, but struggling on through generations of
honest effort, to break a channel for the truth. To me,
the law is sacred; break it lightly who dare! I protest
with all my soul against this wanton outrage of it."

And he sat down, almost as pale as the prisoner beside him. My head swam. I could not follow them;
I did not know what they were talking about. I knew
it was the crisis. Once or twice I saw the prisoner lift
his head and look at the judges; he did not seem more
white and self-controlled than before, but I thought his
eye shone with an intenser light. Even the children in
the crowd knew it was a crisis; there was a stillness
that frightened me. It seemed endless—the fire of
those opposing tongues, on which the crowd hung
breathless. I had lost the power to follow them; they
were in the region of the law, pure and simple, now,
and the words were unfamiliar, and my brain had been
on the strain too long. At last there was a pause; the
judge said something; there was a hush; then the
deputy moved forward, and opened the door of the
jury-room. The crowd, bewildered by the technicali-
ties of the discussion, did not understand any more than
I at first; but, gradually, a low, angry murmur spread
among them, as the jury filed back into their places.

"What is it?" I said, catching Colonel Emlyn's
arm, who stood beside me.

"They don't like it," he said.

"Don't like what? I cannot understand."

"The judge has thrown out the evidence," he answered. "He has sent for the jury; he is going to
charge them now."

That gave me new life; but fears began again.

The judge had done his duty in the face of popular clamor. Would it be possible for him to keep on through all, with no concession to prejudice? He had had the law to sustain him in throwing out the testimony which, it was plain to see, was worth nothing, as evidence, but everything, in its influence on the jury. It was another question, whether he would dare to throw the weight of his influence for the prisoner, when it came to matters outside the stern walls of the law.

He was a plain speaker; his use of language was rather limited, but he had a sound legal mind, and a way of putting things that was impressive. If he had had more words, he might have got bewildered among them, for it was evident he was not a ready speaker. But his very poverty of language was forcible. His ideas stood out like Greek statues, undraped. His charge was throughout impressive; intelligible to the meanest understanding, respectable to the highest. It was impartial, in a certain way: he reviewed the case critically; when he got through with that part, you would have been at a loss to say to which side he leaned. But the great strength of his speech was the injunction to them to beware of prejudice, to remember, the rendering of the verdict according to the law was all that they were answerable for. It was not whether they believed the prisoner guilty or not; it was, whether the evidence that had been placed before them proved it. He warned them not to add one jot or tittle to it in their minds to fill up any space left vacant. Did that evidence show that Bernard Macnally had killed the children, or did it leave it an open question? If it left it an open question there was but one thing for them to do.

His few words to them on the solemnity of their
duty were almost startling ; the language was so simple,
the truth so strong. He dismissed them to their deliberation with a wish that they might, one and all, be
guided by that Divine Wisdom which was given liberal-
ly and without upbraiding to those that asked for it.
The words sounded very real.

Then began the time of waiting which I had so
dreaded. An irresistible irritability took possession of
me. I could not bear a word, a sound. I would not
let them speak to me ; I would not go out into the ante
room. In fact, I had such a dread of losing control of
myself, that I feared any physical effort. The lawyers
went out; the prisoner went away with an officer and
his counsel. The judges withdrew into another room.
The people on the benches beyond us fell into chatter
and restlessness, doors opened and shut. A young
woman near me ate an apple ; the smell of it made me
ill; the sound of her crunching teeth made me almost mad.
She had cheeks as red as her apple. Two or three young
men came and sat on the back of the bench before her.
They talked and laughed, and alluded to the trial, and
tilted themselves backward and forward, and she told
them to " Behave," and to " Stop their nawnsense."

The cold, raw wind blew in in gusts when the doors
were opened. A tree close up by the window near us bent
and tapped against the pane, and moaned and rustled, and
tapped again. Two men leaned against the railing just
behind Macnally's empty chair. They looked at it, and
seemed to hold it in abhorrence. They talked in low,
angry tones; they said something about lynch law, and
the rights of communities to protect themselves. Then
the stove. How shall I ever forget it, and its horrible

heat and gas. Sophia went away, and came back with something mixed in a glass, and held it to my lips, and bade me drink it. I hated her and it, but I drank it. I suppose it was something soothing, for I felt better and quieter in a little while.

I have no idea about the length of time. It may have been one hour, it may have been three, when there was a stir, a murmur, an excitement. People all came back to their places. The jury came back into their seats, the three judges resumed theirs. Amidst a pause, which seemed to me interminable, the foreman rose, and addressing the judge, said they had not agreed on one or two points, and had come back for further instructions. He indicated the evidence which they needed to hear again. The clerk was ordered to read what I had testified about the opening and shutting of the gate, about the shutting of the stair door by Sophia, and her exclamation of surprise that it was open. All of my testimony was read upon this subject. The clerk read it in a perfunctory way, in a loud voice, and with no expression. It might have been a bill of lading. It gave me such a strange sensation to hear my words hurtling about my ears in such a fashion. But as to strange sensations, one might think I had exhausted them before this time. The jury expressed themselves satisfied, and were conducted out again. The people all relaxed their rigidity of quiet, and began to move and talk a little.

"It all comes down to that," said a man outside the railing near me. "I knew it would. If they believe her testimony they'll clear him. If they don't, he's bound to swing. There's no getting out of that. They've got to convict him, it's as clear as day."

"Her testimony won't go for that, with the jury," said his companion, taking out his knife and pricking a sharp line along the bench before him. "What's-his-name showed all that up. You'll see. He hasn't got a chance."

"What did they come in, and have the testimony all read over to them, if they didn't believe it?"

"Oh, some dough-head couldn't remember what she said, that's all. Blamed if I remembered it myself, hearin' such a lot of stuff."

Macnally and his counsel did not go away again, nor the judges. There was a general feeling that the decision would not be long deferred. Mr. Hardinge's face was set and anxious. He did not attempt to look at or reassure me. The lawyers for the prosecution were whispering together in a confident manner. The judge looked stolid, his assistants solemn. Every time there was a sound in the direction of the jury-room, the turning of a door-knob, or the pushing back of a chair, there was a sensation in the crowd, and then a murmur of disappointment. Mrs. Emlyn had gone out long before, utterly unable to bear it. The colonel sat faithfully beside me. Sophia, whose face I never looked at now, sat on the other side, rigidly still. I had just one feeling; good or bad, I wished they would give their verdict *now*. I could not bear the strain another minute. It seemed to me the difference between life and death had dwindled into something that you couldn't see. I didn't care. I only asked a certainty.

It was not long—I don't believe more than half an hour, when a stir from the direction of the jury-room showed that the moment had come. The alert deputy was seen opening the door, and putting back chairs and

benches before the coming of the dealers-out of life or
death. I don't suppose there was a pulse in all that
densely-packed assembly that didn't throb quicker at
the thought of what we had arrived at; slow and old,
quick and young—each one was stirred on beyond its
usual beat by the awful possibilities to which we had
come up.

The jury came in, with stumbling, heavy boots on
the bare floor. When they had taken their places, the
clerk stood up, and, in his loud, unmeaning voice,
called out their names, to which, in various tones,
they answered. Then, in the same mechanical voice,
he asked if they had agreed upon their verdict. The
foreman said :

" We have."

A dark shadow fell upon the face of Hardinge. I
suppose his best hope had been a disagreement. The
prisoner was ordered to stand up. He stood up, firm
and straight, and lifted a steady glance to the face of
the man whose next breath would slay or save him.
Merciful Heavens! how do people live through moments such as these?

The clerk said, as if he were reading off a chattel
mortgage :

" Do you find the prisoner at the bar guilty or not
guilty of the crime for which he is arraigned ?"

" Not guilty !" said the foreman, standing up.

An inky black tide seemed swirling over me. I
put out my hand to save myself from some unknown
horror, and sank senseless to the floor.

When I next became conscious, I was lying on the
bed in the room we had occupied at the hotel. The

first few moments were very confused and painful, but
I gradually recalled what had passed, and gathered my
wits together.   I felt smothered and hot; the room
was dark—it was night; there was only a faint light
burning by my bed.   The smell of kerosene irritated
me; the weight of the blankets oppressed me.   I
pushed them back.   Sophia, who was sitting somewhere in the shadow, watching me, came forward.   I
told her I wanted some water, and she gave it to me.
Then I said:

"Where is Colonel Emlyn?   Ask him to come
here."

"It is late," she said, evasively.   "Wait till morning."

I had heard steps in the next room.   I knew that
he was there.

"I want him now," I said.

She went to the door and spoke, and he came in,
looking anxiously at me.

"You may go away," I said to Sophia.   "I want
to speak to him alone."

She exchanged a look with him, and went away
into the next room, not shutting the door.   I motioned
him to shut it, which he did, and then came back and
stood beside the bed, looking down on me with solicitude and pity on his worn face.

"I don't remember everything," I said, pushing my
hand behind the pillow, and trying to raise my head.
"Is he cleared?"

He nodded.   "Yes, he's safe."

There was a moment's pause.   "Where is he now?"

"He went right away with Hardinge."

"Did you speak to him?"

"No. I hadn't a chance; I was taking care of you. You—were ill, you know."

"Did Mrs. Emlyn?"

"No, she had gone out of the court-room. She was here at the hotel."

"Did anybody speak to him?"

"Not that I know of. There wasn't any time, you see, Hardinge hurried him off. He didn't think that it would be wise to run the risk of any trouble. There was a good deal of feeling about the verdict."

"He will be going away—to Europe. I must see him. Colonel Emlyn, you will have to send for him."

He gave me a look of pity. "Don't bother about anything now," he said. "You are too ill."

"I am not too ill. I must see him before he sails. You must go and send a telegram at once."

"It is too late," he said, uncomfortably.

"How do you mean, too late? Isn't the office open? Take it to them, then, and make them promise to send it the first thing in the morning."

"It's too late, my poor child. He's—he's gone, you know."

"Gone? Yes, I know, from here—he went this afternoon after the verdict; but you can catch him; telegraph Hardinge—everybody—don't lose a minute —tell him _I_ want him—he must come—"

"My child, that was two days ago; he sailed yesterday morning—I had a line from Hardinge—"

That black tide was crawling over me again. I put out my hands to save myself from the dark unutterable suffocation, and was swallowed up in merciful oblivion.

14

CHAPTER XXIV.

THE TINKLE OF A TINY BELL.

"—— Left more desolate, more dreary cold
Than a forsaken bird's nest, filled with snow."

Wordsworth.

"Once the hungry Hours were hounds,
    Which chased the day like a bleeding deer,
And it limped and stumbled with many wounds,
    Through the nightly dells of the desert year."

Shelley.

IT was two years later. Sophia and I were on a railway train, drawing near, for the first time since those sad days, to the great city which had been our home before we went to spend that summer at South Berwick. The two years had been passed in a little Canadian village, where Sophia had relations. When I began to recover from the fever which succeeded the days of the trial, it was necessary to take me somewhere, the farther away the better, the doctors said; the greater change the better. The Emlyns would gladly have kept me with them; their kindness was unbounded. But I felt too stricken to bear the touch of even such tender hands as theirs. I was out of place where there was life and youth and hope. I knew it was not right to darken any household with my sorrow; my good friends had already borne too much of it. When Sophia, one day, spoke of this far-away little village, where her

[314]

relations lived, I grasped at it. It seemed to me more like the rest of the grave than anything that I could get this side of it.

"Let us go there," I said.

The quiet, the utter seclusion, the unfamiliarity of everything, the keen, bracing cold of the climate, all combined to heal me of my wounds. At the end of two years I was alive, I was sane, I was well. Sophia had grown restless under the long quiet. I did not want to be selfish. I told her we would come back.

During the two years, the Emlyns had gone abroad. At first I got frequent letters from them, but latterly they had written very little. Colonel Emlyn's health had been a cause of great anxiety to his wife. The excitement of the events of that last month at South Berwick had been very severe upon him at his age. He had never been willing to return to Happy-go-lucky; the place was shut up and offered for sale. He was restless, and suffered from loss of memory, and from sleeplessness; I could see Mrs. Emlyn felt a sword was hanging over her. I did not write often to them, for two causes; first, that it was acute pain to me to write a letter, and secondly, that I thought it really kinder to let all that was connected with that dreadful time die out, and not to bring myself up at all to him in his present state.

And about Macnally. Colonel Emlyn had been very kind in trying to satisfy my desire of getting a letter to him. But after many weeks, my poor letter had come back to me. No trace of him could be found. In the hurried parting between him and Hardinge, only some vague promise had been made of writing; he had given no address. It was not to be expected that he should write to the Emlyns. Colonel Emlyn, with all his de-

sire to save him, had had but one conviction from the
first; and he was too honest a man to be able to hide
it. That he had not given him his hand when the verdict was pronounced; that he had not in the time that
intervened between that and his sailing, made some expression of friendship or congratulation, was enough to
account for his silence towards them. No doubt he
was convinced that there was no dissenting voice; that
no one believed in his innocence of all who had been
his friends that summer. But that he had no word for his
counsel, who, humanly speaking, had saved his life, was
less accountable. The expenses of his trial had all been
met by the salary which he had not touched during his
ten months at Colonel Emlyn's, and by remittances,
which, no doubt, he had received in the last letters which
had come, and of which he had spoken to me. There
was no obligation upon him to write, but the sense of
gratitude to one who had spent so much effort in his
service.

"I own," wrote Mr. Hardinge, in answer to Colonel
Emlyn's inquiries, "I did look for a line of acknowl-
edgment from him when he should have reached
home, but none has ever come. In fact, my dear sir, I
don't, at this moment, know whom I defended, any more
than if I had done it in a dream. But for the strong
impression that the man made on me, I should begin
to feel some doubt of him."

For me, there was but one conviction—that he was
no longer living.

It was a cloudy day in late October; the very last
day of the month. Our long journey was drawing
near its end; an hour more, and we should be in the
city. Sophia was in the seat beside me. I was next

the window, looking out over the broad river, now gray with the approach of evening. The jar and noise of the cars was considerable, but not enough to make it difficult to talk with the person sitting next you. I had something to say to Sophia. I had been thinking of it for a great many days, and had chosen this moment for the saying of it. It was easier to say what I wanted to in this place, than in a quiet room. For one thing, we need not look at each other as we talked, and there was no possibility of showing agitation on either side. (It is necessary to explain that Sophia and I never alluded, in any manner, to the cause of the desolation of our lives. After the children's clothes were packed away, and their books and toys put out of sight, there was never a word uttered between us that would have indicated to any stranger the fact that they ever had existed. Her wound was only less grievous than mine. It was an instinct of self-preservation that kept us silent. If we were to live, that was the only way to do it. We must make a new routine for ourselves, and keep to it. It was the only chance of keeping from despair.) So it was with great effort that I spoke, looking out of the window as I did it.

"You will be very busy to-morrow, I suppose, settling the rooms, and all that. I never was much use in doing that. I'm going to take the chance, and go away for a day and night."

She gave a start, and said:

"Go away?"

I scarcely had been out of her sight an hour since I had been all she had to care for. No wonder that she started.

"Yes," I said, as firmly as I could, "I want to go

to South Berwick. It has been in my mind a great while. This is the best time."

"You'd better wait till you're rested from this journey," she said, hoarsely, "before you take another."

"No; I am well enough for it. I will go in the morning. There is a train at eight o'clock. I looked it out in the paper yesterday."

There was not another word said. We sat in utter silence, side by side, as the cars rushed on into the twilight. The plan, which I had told her so quietly, had been maturing in my mind for weeks; it scarcely ever left my thoughts. The desire to see the children's graves before another snow fell on them, had grown so strong, that I felt as if she must have known it, in our daily life together. She had expressed no emotion; but her face, when we came out into the light of the depot, after leaving the cars, showed the traces of strong agitation. Sophia's face had grown older in these two years. It had come to go well with her prematurely-whitened hair. She looked a woman of fifty, who had seen trouble, and whose heart had known how to ache. She was more silent now, and her silence gave a deep look to her eyes. Those still vehement feelings of hers left a mark upon her face—the more that they found no vent from her lips.

She prepared everything for my journey, and was up in the gray dawn to get my breakfast for me and to see me go, but no further word was spoken between us of the object of my going.

The day was raw and cheerless. A bleak wind was blowing and the clouds were racing over the sky, sky and clouds all gray and leaden. All around the horizon there was a streak of light as if a great chalice of gloom were being let down slowly over the earth and the light being gradually shut out. The men in the cars buttoned up their coats, and huddled round the stove and pointed out, and said, that looked like snow, and "Winter had set in smart and early. A snow-storm on the first day of November was a thing that didn't often happen." I thought of the little graves, with the grass and weeds of two years on them, hidden from my sight by the falling snow. Ah! The dreariness of that long, cold ride! The dreariness of the landscape, the dreariness of the sky!

When I got out of the cars at South Berwick a keen and cruel wind was blowing. I could hardly stand up against it. The snow, which had begun to fall, struck my face with sharp points. I could not walk to where I wanted to go in this state of weather. There was a man there with a wretched, covered vehicle, which I hired, and told him where to drive me. It seemed to me so hard and cruel that I could not go alone; that this lean, curious man should have to go with me, and see for what I went. There are some disappointments that have peculiarly sharp stings, and I have always noticed that such as these are the hardest to bear patiently. I had borne greater things without murmuring; to-day, the cruel weather, the hard grinding necessity that some one should witness my first visit to the graves of my children, the total difference between what the visit was now and what I had so long dreamed it would be, gave me a stronger sense of rebellion than perhaps I had ever felt before. . .

The man behaved better than I thought he would; he drove his rough-coated, big horse up and down the road a little distance off, and did not seem to look at me, but beat his long arms across his breast and engaged himself in keeping warm.

When I got in the wagon again he drove me towards the village. I asked him whether any one lived in the Detmold farm-house. No one, he said. It has never been rented since—since the folks that had all that trouble moved out of it two years ago last September. I think it began to dawn on him who I was. I told him if he knew who had the key to drive to the place and get it, I wanted to go in the house. He knew; and we drove to the house and I held the reins over the back of the heavy winter-coated horse, while he went in and got the key.

While the wind and the sharp hail and snow were beating in my face, we drew up to the door of my poor, desolate little home. I stood by the gate, benumbed with the cold, blinded by the sleet; I could scarcely see where I went. I remembered that I didn't want the man to stay; I took out my purse to pay him. With a strange rush of anguish there came over me the recollection of that bright May noontide when we first drove up to our new home, and when I had eagerly gone in, with the children at my side, forgetting to pay the man for bringing us, till recalled by Sophia. I counted out the change. The man put it in his pocket, and, re-mounting the old carriage, trundled away in it.

The gate latch was so rusty, I could scarcely move it; the path so overgrown, I stumbled through it. The balcony steps were unsteady; one or two shingles were loosened from the front of the house. The vines had trailed over the floor of the balcony, and a heap of dead leaves were blown up into a corner where the trumpet creeper made a shelter for them. On the railing of the

balcony in front, there hung a little board, on which a bill,
"For sale," or perhaps "To let," had been nailed. Whatever it was, many storms and winds had defaced it, and no
one could read now what it announced. When I bent
down to try to fit the key to the lock, my hands shook so
from cold and agitation that I could scarcely do it. The
snow, which was coming in gusts, sometimes ceasing altogether, sometimes driving through the air in thick drifts,
stopped a moment now, and I could see, and opened
the door and entered. If there had been a coldness
that drove the blood to my heart, outside, there was a
chill that seemed to congeal it there, inside. Why had
I come? I asked myself. The shut-up rooms felt like
vaults; dust and desolation was spread over all the
familiar place. It all seemed a mockery, so real and so
unreal, so changed and yet so grossly the same.

"Why had I come?" I said, again, turning my eyes
away from a branch covered with long, gray moss, still
hanging over the mantlepiece, where cobwebs and dust
were thick. The ashes were all taken away from the
cheery little Franklin; the andirons turned and standing parallel, the fender put up in a corner. The table
was shoved up against the wall; the chairs stood
blankly around; a dim, ghastly light came in through
the warped and yawning shutters.

I had promised myself that I would not go into the
nursery. The dark middle chamber was darker than
ever; it smelt of mildew and dust, and the uneven
floor creaked as I trod on it. The wind howled through
the many cracks about the boards, and a little heap of
snow had already sifted in through the chinks of the little, dim and dirty window. I pushed open the door of

14*

my own room. The bedstead was piled with pillows and
bolsters; the dressing-table was bare; the chairs turned
up, one upon the other. The poor little curtains were
still hanging, limp and draggled, at the window, beside
which stood the big three-cornered chair, in which I
used to sit, with Maidy mounted on the stool, looking
out at the bird's nest in the old cedar tree. I wondered
whether the old cedar was still standing, whether the
birds had built in it again. I pushed open the shutters
and then put down the sash, and sat down in the old
chair, and leaned my face on my hands upon the
window-sill, and looked out.

Yes, there stood the cedar, rough and gnarled and
bent, and in it—my heart gave a sickening throb —was
the bird's nest as of old. "A forsaken bird's nest
filled with snow." The tree rocked with the pressure
of the wind; the dead leaves of the vine about it, fell
with every gust; but the nest clung there, empty, useless, undesired. The young and living brood that once
had filled it—where were they? The animate gone,
the inanimate left. My desolation pressed down heavier
upon me, as I gazed at these familiar, unmoved things
of nature; the old boxwood below the window, where
the children played; the cedar where we watched the
bird's nest; the grape-vine where Naomi swung them.
I felt as if they should have perished; as if it were a
cruelty that they should stand while the years passed
over them, and all that dear and precious flesh was
hidden under darkness and decay.

As I sat gazing out, there came upon me a vivid
recollection of that morning after Baby's illness, when
I was sitting there with Maidy, looking at the birds,
and Macnally had come by, with his fishing-rod upon

his shoulder. I recalled Maidy's eager pleasure at the sight of him; I could see his lithe and graceful figure as he swung himself up into the branch and held out the shells to her one by one. Every word that we had said came back to me. I saw again Ann Day come out with her basket of clothes; I saw the dark flush pass over her face, as she watched the distracted parent bird; I heard her muttered curse, and saw her go angrily away. Since it occurred, I had never remembered before the incident of the strangled birds found below the nest that afternoon. A great pressure of great events had pushed it out of my mind. Now it came back to me with a keen clearness. I remembered that at the time, I had felt sure that Ann had done it. I had been able to account for it by the insane impulse to level all maternal happiness to her own dreary desolation. It had affected me, at the time, but I had forgotten it.

A sudden illumination filled and stunned me. It was Ann Day's maniac hand that had robbed my nest of its brood. It was that poor crazed brain that had risen up at the sight of my too-full arms, and had dragged their treasure out. Every circumstance that I could recall confirmed it. I heard, as if just spoken, Sophia's words as she came into the parlor where I sat in the darkness, brooding over Macnally's going:

"Ann Day went away without her money to-night."

The unexplained fact that Rex had not barked; the lack of evidence that any burglary had been attempted; her familiarity with the house; her accustomed noiselessness—all these things flashed before my mind in a moment. I got up from my seat, a sort of fire running through my veins. If she should be dead; if it should be impossible to prove it; if this injustice must go on forever! I knew now why I had come. But my word and my conviction would do little if I could not get some proof.

I hurried out into the snow, now driving in thick sheets past the house. The road to Ann's cottage was a lonely one. I shortened it by crossing some fields and going along a lane. It was a desperate battle with the wind and snow. When I came in sight of it, I was so nearly exhausted I had to stop and rest. I was preparing myself to find it vacant, to hear, when I should go back to the village, that she had gone away, and that all trace of her was lost. When I got within a few rods of the house, I saw a thin curl of smoke rising from the broken chimney. Then, whoever might be there, it was not empty.

It was a wretched hovel, patched up in every way to keep out the cold sea winds. There were some kettles and a tub beside the door; a dingy rag or two fluttered from a bush at the end of the house. I stood on the stone before the door, and knocked. An almost inaudible voice within answered. I entered. The room was so low and so dark I could scarcely distinguish anything for a moment. Something moved on a low bed beside the stove. I picked my way across the room, and stood at the foot of the bed. It was a scene of indescribable squalor. The figure on the bed was covered with all imaginable rags, crowned with an old piece of carpet; the window above it was stuffed up with a sheaf of straw; the smell from the stove was very coarse and disgusting.

"Is it Ann?" I said. "I have come to see Ann Day. It's so dark I can't tell."

A head was turned over a little towards the faint light of the opposite window.

"Yes, it's Ann Day. What are ye wantin' wi' me?"

I now recognized her face. She did not look much changed, except thinner, and she had an expression of physical suffering—suffering which quite engrossed her thoughts. She moved herself up a little in the bed and looked at me. I came around to the side of the bed and stood very near to her. She recognized me, but it didn't seem to affect her much; she was much more interested in a pain which had resulted from her turning over.

She talked a little, answered all my questions quite intelligently. She had been ill, she said, off and on all the fall. She had been very bad since the day before yesterday. She wouldn't let folks know, because they would make her go to the county house. They had been trying to get her there all the winter before. She wasn't going for 'em. She'd stay where she was, if she died for it. I saw from her gasping way of speaking that she had some sharp trouble about the lungs. She had fever, and the agony in her side was great when she tried to move. I tried to make her comfortable in the wretched bed. I gave her a drink of some hot thing on the stove that she had been trying to prepare. Then I drew a chair up by the bed and sat down on it.

"Ann," I said, "I owe you some money, I want to pay you;" and took out my purse. Ann was always greedy of money; she looked up eagerly and watched me.

"Why did you go away that night without your money?" I said.

"Eh?" she said, her face darkening a little.

"I would have paid you," I went on. "You know I always pay you, no matter what happens. See, here is your dollar."

Her fingers closed greedily over it.

"And there's another thing, Ann," I said. "I want that little lamb of Baby's. You ought not to keep it away from me, it belongs to me. I always thought you were an honest woman, Ann."

"Sure and I am an honest woman," she said, hotly.

"Well, is it honest to be keeping away from me what's my own?"

"It can't do you no good."

"You might as well say that little pink calico frock of your little girl's couldn't do you any good, because you couldn't use it. What would you think of me if I got hold of it and kept it, and wouldn't give it back to you?"

A dark flush rose to the woman's face,

"I am an honest woman," she muttered. "I never kep' a.happorth that I didn't own. I've got nothin' on my conscience. You can see my bank-book. I've got no call to steal."

"That's what I always thought till I find you won't give me back the little lamb that's mine. Give it to me, and I'll think you are an honest woman." She muttered and turned restlessly on the bed; this time the pain the motion gave her did not engross her wholly.

"I was always good to you, Ann. I always treated you well. Give me what is mine, and I'll be content. The lamb belongs to me. The one that keeps it is no better than a thief."

"I'm no thief," she cried, "I earn my own bit and sup. Nobody can say I don't."

"Very well, I won't say you don't, if you give me what is mine. I'll always be your friend, but you must give me what is mine."

I saw her put her hand under the bolster, and take out something; she kept on muttering, looking at me distrustfully. "It'll be all right, if you let me have it, Ann. You're so sick, you don't want anything upon your conscience."

"I never took a happorth from anybody. I can die in peace," she said, in gasps, for the oppression seemed growing very great. I saw it was a key in her hand. I leaned forward, and gently, swiftly got it into mine. She still looked at me with distrust.

"Where is it?" I said, getting up.

"In the box anent the chimney-piece," she said, pointing up the stairs.

I climbed the stairs, which shook at every step. The attic, when I reached it, was so low I could not stand upright. The light was so dim I had to feel my way along, till I came to the bricks of the chimney. There beside it stood an old hair trunk; there was a little ray of light coming in from a single pane of glass set in the gable of the house, this was all I had to see by. The wind was roaring outside, the snow was drifting in through many broken places in the wretched roof. I knelt down before the old box, and felt with my hands for the key-hole. I heard the woman moving in her bed, down-stairs; I wondered if she had repented and would follow me up-stairs, and with the strength of fever, attack and injure me. My only companion in this far desolate spot was a mad woman; no wonder that my hands shook as I tried in vain to find the lock.

At last the key moved, with a strong effort. I

lifted the lid, and put down my hand. As I moved slightly the things inside, a faint tinkling sound struck my ear. I gave a cry, as my hand touched the fleecy covering of the poor little toy that my Baby had held against her breast when she fell asleep for the last time. I moaned and pressed it to my lips. It seemed to me that all my agony and yearning had come back as at the first.

A hoarse call from below recalled me to myself. I started up, but before I shut down the lid, I assured myself that there was nothing else that concerned me in the trunk. There was the old bank-book; there was the precious little pink calico gown; the bundle of clothes with the name pinned on them. That was all. I shut the trunk and locked it, and made my way down the rickety stairs.

Ann was sitting up in bed with a disturbed and threatening expression. She had evidently attempted to follow me, but her pain had come on and made it impossible. I just showed her the lamb, and then put it out of sight, and sat down and tried to soothe her.

"Accusin' an honest body," she kept saying. I knew that nothing could be gained to satisfy any mind but my own, by what I could get her to say to me alone. So, after a few moments, I told her I was going away, and would come back, to bring her some tea and sugar, and some things to make her comfortable. She still looked unreconciled to me. I went hurriedly.

The snow had ceased falling, and the sky was not so dark. I went to the nearest neighbor, and got a horse and wagon, and a man to drive me. Then I went to the village doctor, and to a magistrate. I explained what I had discovered. They were alert and interested, and in a very

short time we were all at the door of the poor creature's
hovel. She was angry and stubborn when she saw the
men ; she thought they had come to take her to the poor-
house, which was the object of her greatest dread. Not a
word could be got from her. She turned over with her
face to the wall, and clutched the bed, as if to resist
being dragged off from it.

"Now, look here, Ann," said the doctor, sitting
down beside her, "we've gone through all this before. I made up my mind, last winter, I wouldn't send
you to the county house, no matter who said that you
ought to go. I've come to give you medicine and to
help you to get round again, so as to take care of yourself. This lady here promises to pay for taking care
of you while you're sick. Nobody wants to take you
away from this house, while there's anybody'll take
care of you in it, that's sure."

Ann's only answer was to turn her head and give a
threatening look at the magistrate, who stood behind
him. It was difficult to re-assure her about him, though
happily she did not know his office. We all sat down,
after the magistrate had brought in a few armfuls of
wood for her, to show his good will, and the doctor
dexterously began his cross-examination. I don't know
how, exactly, he managed it, but the results were all
we could have asked. Of course, the testimony of an
insane woman would have been worth nothing in
a court of law ; but, thank Heaven, we were done with
courts of law, and poor Ann's only tribunal would be
a higher one, and it seemed to me that it was very
near.

She evidently was distressed and uncomfortable
about the murder, but it was not at all upon her con-

science. The detaining of the toy from me was a much more serious matter in her eyes, as approaching to the recognized sin of theft. She defended herself warmly, and affirmed she hadn't known I wanted it. That led her to speak freely of the children, and of her taking it out of Baby's arms. She remembered the night, its stillness and darkness, and the time the train went out, and when Matilda went up-stairs to bed, while she looked in the window. It was all confused and rambling, but there was enough to satisfy any mind that was capable of judging, even without the proof that I had found hidden in the trunk up-stairs. She had no power to give her motive ; no power to distinguish between right and wrong; she seemed to have no remorse for what she had done ; a dumb instinct of fear and apprehension had led her to keep out of the way while search was being made, and to resist us now when we probed incautiously.

It was a strange study, that shattered mind. We sat beside her for an hour or more. The magistrate, withdrawing himself from sight a little, wrote down every word she said. At last the doctor and he went away, leaving me to care for her till some one else should come. Before night, the power to give even the poor, fragmentary story we had got from her was gone. Delirium and fever came, and the clouds closed in forever round the broken mind and heart.

She only lived two days more. I staid with her until the last. When I soothed and bathed and held in mine the poor hands that had dealt me such a mortal hurt, I thanked God that He had given me the chance to do it. I prayed Him to forgive her for even her unwitting sin ; I loosed the bands that, perhaps, **only** the sinned against can loose. As I knelt beside her in the dark, dreary hovel, with the night wind roaring outside, and the fire burning low within, her moans grew fainter, her breathing softened ; "me foine ghirl —me foine ghirl," she murmured, "it's all roight wi' me, it's all roight."

The hand in mine relaxed ; her head fell back. I knew it was all right with her at last, poor soul !

These incidents made a great sensation in South Berwick. There had been no doubt of Macnally's guilt before. It came like an awful revelation to them, the nearness they had been in to the shedding of innocent blood. They accepted the facts simply, and honestly acknowledged their mistake. My one desire now was to get this news to the ears of Macnally, if he should be living still. To that end I did everything that lay in my power to give it publicity. But it was little use fanning the flame. It was a burned-out sensation. The local papers, of course, gave it great prominence. But the larger journals, which were the only ones that would convey it far enough to reach him, contented themselves with an insignificant paragraph or two, which might most easily be overlooked. I put advertisements in the papers, English and Irish, but they never met any eye for which they were intended.

Of course, at the very first moment, I wrote the Emlyns. Several weeks passed, and no word came. At last, I wrote directly to their banker in Paris ; in a few more weeks came an answer, inclosing my letter to Mrs. Emlyn, and a very civil note from a clerk, telling me the news which I must have missed during my week at South Berwick, where I saw no papers.

Mrs. Emlyn had died at Naples, after a very short illness. Colonel Emlyn's condition of mind, wrote the civil clerk, rendered him unable to receive or answer letters. The young lady and gentleman who had been under their charge had sailed for New Orleans some weeks before. He was unable to give me their address. The door was shut in my face, in fact. I wrote again, asking that the New Orleans address might be found for me, if possible. But no answer ever came. Probably the civil clerk had left the office. I wrote letters to Naomi and to Ned. But New Orleans is a big place, and Naomi and Ned were small people. It was no wonder that they never got them, with that very general superscription.

My heart was sore with this reopening of past wounds and coming of new ones. The desolation that had swept over all that happy summer was complete. My good friends; how many tears I shed for the one in her foreign grave; the other, in his no less dire oblivion. The two children of their love, set adrift upon the world at an age so tender; how hopeless and dark the mystery looked;

"If thou wert all, and naught beyond, oh, earth!"

CHAPTER XXV.

THE EASTERN MOON.

" The pure calm hope be thine,
　　Which brightens like the eastern moon,
　　As day's wild lights decline."
　　　　　　　　　　　　Keble.

TWO or three years after this, I can't exactly remember when it happened, a great piece of good fortune befell Sophia. Some distant relative left her what was quite a grand fortune for a person in her walk of life. She received the news characteristically. It was quite unexpected, but she bore herself with great equanimity; in fact, towards me, in almost utter silence. After the first glow of satisfaction, a gloom settled on her. I think it seemed to her "on the uprooted flower, the genial rain." What might it not have been, if it had come earlier, and when there was some object in making our lives happy.

After a few days, she came to me, and I saw she had been bracing herself up to the necessary discussion of plans.

"Well, Sophia," I said, with something between a smile and a sigh, " I suppose I am now to take care of myself. You have done it for me a good while. I am not unreasonable enough to feel hurt. You must tell me just what you mean to do, and I am not going to make the least objection."

[333]

She waved her hand angrily, as if she disdained to answer me.

"I am going to lay a plan before you," she said. "It's for you to say whether it shall be carried out. I want something to do. I couldn't be happy to sit down and eat up my income. If you're willing, I want to take a large house, and fit it up, and rent out my rooms, and furnish private meals. The best rooms shall be fixed for you. You won't be bothered about anything; but it will give me something to do. It will be an interest. I can make money—Heaven knows what for—but it will be something to make it." I saw the wisdom of the plan at once. Our small and monotonous life had been very wearing to Sophia. When her work was done, which was all too soon, she had not my resources. She could not put a book between her and retrospect, nor go out and be soothed by a sunset sky or stimulated by a strong wind. She was much more unhappy than I was, in those days. I welcomed the change for her, and gave her all encouragement.

Her face wore an altered look from the day it was decided on. I entered into it with all the heart I could muster. We went out, day after day, hunting houses. At last one was selected—or rather, two. They were large—not new houses—on an avenue that had seen its best days, but was still very respectable. Indeed, a good many people of distinction lived there still; but the tide of fashion had rather set away from it, and had left it quieter, and, consequently, much nicer than many of its more popular neighbors. The avenue was broad. One of the houses was on the southeast corner of a well-built street, on which it opened; the other one was next it, on the avenue, on which was its en-

trance. The rent was reasonable. Sophia took them
on a long lease. A communication was cut between
them. The rooms were large and well-shaped; they
arranged in suites admirably. It certainly seemed a
good investment of her capital. We furnished it pret-
tily, and it was a great amusement. After all, money
does bring a certain *soulagement*.

My rooms were particularly to my mind. The
parlor was on the ground floor of the corner house,
almost level with the pavement; it had three windows;
two on the avenue, one on the street. The houses opposite were low; we had sunshine a great deal of the
day. Sophia insisted upon giving me this room,
though it would have brought her in a little fortune, as
a doctor's office. It was furnished charmingly, though
simply. I delighted in the windows, in the fire-place
(where I burned soft coal), in every piece of furniture
that I got for it. My sleeping-room was on the floor
above. Sophia had my meals served to me in my parlor, in the daintiest manner. The servants were taught
to consider that no one came before me. I had the
best that could be found of everything.

The house filled up. Sophia knew how to keep it
well. She had found her niche. She had no troubles,
no perplexities; she loved to rule, and no one did it
better. Her servants were models, her house grew to
have a certain reputation of its own among people of
high standing. Her lodgers staid with her, year after
year. There were applicants before-hand for any va-
cancies. Sophia's fortune was made. She was steedily
making money, and what was better, steadily growing
more at rest and better satisfied.

And so the years went on. And I? I was happy.

"My indomitable health," as the doctor had said, had borne me up over the tide of misfortune. I was still young. The spring of life had not been broken. My sorrows, as far as I could dare to say so, were not the results of my sins. I was natural and simple-hearted enough to take the reaction when it came, and to lift up my head when the storm had passed. I had wanted to die, but since it had pleased God that I should live, I took life meekly, and tried to be happy in it. And I *was* happy. There was a dear church in which I daily said my prayers, there was a dear hospital whose wards were as familiar to me as the rooms of my own house. And there were my dear sunny windows, and my books, and flowers that bloomed for me, and a bird that sang.

Yes, I was happy. It was a singularly peaceful, secluded life for one to lead in a great city. I had scarcely any acquaintances and no friends, except among the poor and dying ones to whom I ministered. Sometimes the people who visited at the hospital, or whom I met at church, would try to approach me. That was the only morbid thing about me. I could not meet their advances. It would be only ripping open the wound again to make new friends. I resisted all attempts to be drawn at all out of my silent life. I suppose a certain mystery surrounded me. I know curious eyes followed me. Not unfrequently some of the families occupying Sophia's rooms would make inquiries of her; it sometimes happened that flowers or fruit would be sent to me by the more determined ones. But they never succeeded in breaking in upon the sanctity and stillness of my life.

It was now ten years since the death of my children. I was a woman of thirty-four, not old looking for thir-

ty-four. Several years of peace had given me a look
of content, I dare say. The days were wearing on as
usual. I had nothing to dread. There is one element
of peace in that. All had happened to me that could
happen, it seemed to me. If Sophia should die, I
should lose a friend, but it would not be beyond my
strength to bear. If illness came to me, I felt I could
endure it. I had grown so accustomed to the sight and
thought of illness in the hospital, that I did not dread
it as before. If death came—there was no question of
mourning then.

It was an afternoon in late November. I was tired
from several hours at the hospital, but when I came in,
I found my fire blazing, and a very cheerful look about
my room. I was sitting in a favorite deep chair by one
of the windows, a book in my hand, idly looking out
and resting from my long day's work. I felt a trifle
dispirited that day. I had found myself out in a matter,
in a way that discouraged me with myself. I had
found I had a hope, which I had said daily to myself was dead. I could no longer hide it from myself,
that every day, when I walked through those dreary
wards, I said inwardly, I may find him there. Whenever a new case was brought in, I found myself watching eagerly to see the face upon the pillow. I looked
over the lists daily in all the men's wards. I had seen
so many foreigners, so many men of education, lying
there, unknown and friendless, I said to myself, why
not he, if he still lives? There is just one chance in a
thousand. There is no wrong in looking for him. That
day I had seen a face that recalled his so strongly, I
had scarcely had strength to look again. But it was only
to be disappointed; it was not he. I had been un-

15

nerved and unfitted for my work by it.   I reproached myself, and came home heavy-hearted.

So, when Sophia came in and sat down by the other window, as she often did towards twilight, to talk with me a little while, it was quite an effort for me to look up cheerfully and say, " Well, what has been going on to-day ?"

" The second floor front in the other house is let," she said, with a tone of satisfaction.

" Ah ? That's good news.   I hope to a good tenant ?"

" There couldn't be a better, I should think.   He's only too swell, I'm afraid, for me."

" Oh, you'll be equal to the situation.   I'm not afraid for you.   Who sent them to you, or him—which was it that you said ?"

For I was trying hard to be interested, with but very poor success.

" It's a gentleman.   The British Consul sent him to me.   I guess you've heard of him, that is, if you have read the papers."   There was a tone of satisfaction in her voice.   Sophia liked to have distinguished people in her house.

" Why, what is he," I said, " to get himself into the papers ?"

" Well, he's a speaker ; he gives lectures, and makes speeches.   He's all the fashion just now.   He's just come over from England.   He's a great man, according to the papers.   He has written poetry — and things.   Everybody's talking about him, so they tell me."

And Sophia looked more satisfied than ever.

" You can't mean—Conyngham ?" I said, looking up.

"Yes," said Sophia, with importance. "That's the name. Mr. Conyngham."

"Sophia!" I exclaimed, vividly interested. "You don't mean to tell me he is coming here?"

"Why not, to be sure? Do people that write books want more tenderloins and mushrooms than other boarders? I guess my table will do him, if he's only got to write poetry and make speeches. It's the swell people that I am afraid of—swell English people, more than any others."

"I don't care about the swellness of him, though he's all that, I believe. But, Sophia, are you *sure?*"

"Sure as fate," said Sophia, not altogether pleased with my remaining doubts.

"It's the strangest, strangest thing," I said, lifting up a book upon my lap. "This is one of his books I was just reading. I thought, only last night, when I finished the first volume, what would I give to see him, to know what he looked like in the flesh."

"Well, naturally, I shouldn't think you'd hanker much to see him any other way," said Sophia, a little tartly.

"But, Sophia, what *does* he look like? Tell me all about him."

"I can tell you better when I've seen him."

"You haven't seen him?"

"No, he came while I was out at market. Mary showed him the rooms. He seemed pleased. This afternoon his agent came and saw me, and engaged them, and told me who he was."

"Does he bring a servant?"

"No, he only has the two rooms, the parlor and the bedroom. The agent said he might want a good deal of waiting on, but he'd pay me extra for it; he didn't keep a man. It's a very good price he pays; he can have all the waiting on he wants. I can't get on with people that put on airs, but I don't take it he's the kind that does."

"I should think not! But—well, when does he come?"

"To-morrow afternoon; his baggage is coming in the morning."

"Well, Sophia, be sure you take a good look at him and tell me what he's like. I can't help wondering—wondering—what the man would look like that had written that book."

"Why, don't you like it?" said Sophia, a little uneasily.

"Like it! Ah—I've more than liked it. It's stirred me to my depths!"

"Well," said Sophia, getting up, "it always strikes me people must be a little soft that go on that way about books. Strikes me I wouldn't let anybody hear me talk that way if I was in your place."

"Do you think it would disedify Mary and Buttons? I'll be very careful. There's nobody else that's likely to come in range of my observations."

Sophia was jealous of my books, as she had nothing else to be jealous of, except the hospital. Poor soul, there was a time when she was very glad to see me take to them, but she had forgotten that.

The next afternoon, when I came home, I thought with lively interest of the new arrival. I entered always by the door of the street; he would go in by the avenue door, consequently, I saw no trace of his arrival. Sophia did not come in, as was her habit, during the hour before dinner. I missed her less, because, with the book in my hand, I sat by the window as long as I could see, and then sat with it in my lap before the fire, wondering, pondering, with my eyes fixed on the deep glow of the coals. It was a strange chance that had brought that writer under the same roof with one to whom his books had been so much. But—with a sigh—it wouldn't be much of a chance, strange and wonderful, to him. No doubt he was well used to finding flatterers under every roof, and I must prepare myself for being disillusionized. I had heard people of common sense always were disillusionized when brought face to face with genius, and I was a person of common sense, Sophia notwithstanding. No doubt he would be short and stout, material-looking and dull-eyed. Ah, yes, I must be prepared for this. I much preferred it to long hair and a poetic look. He was sure not to have that; he was too great a swell, according to the papers. I didn't mind the swellness, as I had said, one way or the other. That was an accident of birth or temperament. But I earnestly wished he might not be stout. My mind dwelt upon his waistcoat.

When my dinner was brought in, I asked the maid about Sophia.

Oh, didn't I know? She had told Buttons to tell me as soon as I came in. She was taken sick that morning when she came in from market, and was in bed with the worst-kind of a pain in both her ankles. She was very bad.

As soon as I had eaten my dinner, I went up to her. She occupied a room on the top floor of the house, as cold and cheerless as possible. Nothing would ever induce her to do better for herself: even in summer, when her house was nearly empty, she still struggled up to this dismal spot.

I found her very suffering, and necessarily pretty sharp. I took the matter into my own hands, and had a fire made up in the tiny little grate, and sent for a shade for her light, and put things in some sort of comfortable order. Also, Buttons went privately out to get the doctor. She growled at all these things, but I think it pleased her to have me care for her. I sat down by her, and waited for the doctor. All her cares were very heavy on her. It was useless to reassure her; she wasn't used to being ill. She was determined in her own mind that everything should go wrong.

"That man's dinner," she said. To think of his first dinner going up without her being there to see to it. She had smelt the soup burning all the way up to the fourth floor. She knew for a certainty he would go away in the morning.

"Did you see him when he came?"

"See him? No, of course, I didn't. He had to come, with nobody to show him to his room, Buttons standing on his head because there was a fireman's procession in the street, Mary flustering away because Mrs. Graham had rung her bell, and Elza, scrubbing out the bath-room, found him standing over her shoulder, and saying, 'Can you tell me where I'll find my room?' The clean sash curtains weren't put up. The fire wasn't made in the grate; he had to ring his bell to order it. There's just one thing about it. He'll go away to-morrow, and I'll have my rooms upon my hands. And it'll be a while before the British Consul sends me any body else; I might as well give up the house, if I can't keep about and see to things myself."

It was no use to argue with her, though, of course, I tried to do it. I only hoped the doctor would be encouraging when he came. But he wasn't encouraging to me, at least, when I followed him down stairs and asked him his opinion. She was in for a long illness, he was afraid. It would be a wonder if she got out of her room all winter; inflammatory rheumatism was not an easy thing to manage in a person of her temperament. He advised me to encourage her, and not let her know how ill she was, and keep her from fretting about the housekeeping.

It was certainly good advice; I had been anticipating him, however; but Sophia was not encouraged. We had our hands full, Buttons and Mary and I, for the next two or three days, in keeping her encouraged and in reassuring her about the house. I gave up the hospital, of course, and had to spend a good deal of the time in her room. (A good deal of the time I was ordered out of it.) Virtually, much of the direction of the house came on me; I tried to spare her in everything.

My interest in the new great man did not abate exactly, but I had not very much time to think about the matter. He did not go away, however, as Sophia had predicted, but seemed, on the contrary, to be establishing himself for the winter. Notes with magnificent monograms were coming all the time. Carriages were driving up to leave cards, or bring important-looking gentlemen to call. Buttons gave up the boot-blacking and the knives, and did little else but open the front door and "run of arrants" for the stranger; an inferior boy was found to take his place down-stairs.

One day, sitting in the window, I saw a carriage drive up. The footman took a note, and brought it to the door. I saw a girl's face at the carriage-window— the sweetest, most earnest, enthusiastic face. She looked up at the house with such a world of expression in her eyes. He, the hero of her dreams, the genius who had enthralled her soul, lived there, behind that red-brick wall, with its plain, square windows and white shades. How could they look like other red-brick walls and windows? The house was transformed for her; she devoured it with her eyes; her gaze lingered on it as the carriage drove away.

Pretty young thing! it made me a little ashamed of my enthusiasm for his books though, since I had such immature company in my enthusiasm. I couldn't understand how they could have appealed to an imagination so young, a heart so inexperienced. To me, they would have been written in a dead language at her age; at least, so it seemed to me, as I recalled myself. But, in some matters, we sometimes do our youth injustice.

That afternoon I took a collection of papers upstairs to Sophia, and, sitting down, proceeded to amuse her with the divers descriptions, histories, and criticisms of her interesting lodger. It really eased her pain considerably. She took a personal pride in his successes.

"Now, Sophia," I said, "we'll skip his parentage; there's half a column of it. I'm sure we don't care who his great-grandfather was, and his distinguished uncle that married Lady Somebody. It's evident they're all vastly above us. We concede it. But they weren't, oh, joy! titled people—only landed gentry, and all that. Now I'm happier. I can get along with landed gentry, and not surrender my independence altogether. But titled people! How could I bear the weight of it. Now we come down to something personal. Ah! we'll read that."

"Read all," said Sophia, snappishly, "if you're going to read any. I hate skipping about so."

"Well, we won't skip any more after this. You shall have everything Jenkins has to say about your lodger. Now listen. (I *can't* go back among his ancestors.) 'Leonard Conyngham was born about the year 18— (why can't they be accurate on a point so vital!) on the family estate, near Mallow. (I wonder in what part of Great Britain Mallow is. I must look it up on the map.) He is one of a large family; one brother has distinguished himself in the army, another in the navy. A third is a prominent barrister. Two of his sisters have married into the nobility, one being the wife of Lord Massy, and another married to Sir Gerald Austen.' (Sophia, do you hear that! 'It's a very fine thing to be brother-in-law.' I *knew* he was more than 'landed gentry.')"

Sophia showed so much irritation in her face that I suspended my pleasantry.

"'It will be seen by this, that our illustrious visitor is entitled to the highest social consideration, entirely apart from his distinction as a man of letters and an orator. The suddenness with which he attained his present height of popularity may be accounted for by a little retrospect. These particulars have been furnished us by one well acquainted with his family history, and may be relied on as entirely accurate. Young Leonard showed very little of the genius which has since distinguished him during boyhood and early

15*

youth. He graduated at Dublin University without
much distinction as a scholar. (Why Dublin University? I should have preferred Oxford, it seems to
me, if I had been a 'landed gentry.') His family were
anxious that he should enter the church, for which he
had been designed from childhood. This he refused,
and an estrangement from them was the result. He
then threw himself into some political movement, with
more generosity of spirit than worldly wisdom. The
country was in its usual disturbed state; his party
was unsuccessful in its attempt; he was obliged to flee
the country, and for several years his family were in
great anxiety about him. About seven years ago he
returned from Australia, where he had been laying up
the stores of experience and adventure from which he
feeds his marvelous fancy. He then resumed his place
at home, and devoted himself to the study of the law.
But it may easily be guessed he did not stay long
in bondage to this exacting mistress. He was meant
for higher things than pleadings and practice. The
publication of his first book took the public by storm.
His maiden speech in Parliament, to which he had been
returned, was equally a bomb-shell. Two such gifts
are rarely allotted to any one man. At once an orator
who can thrill crowds with the fire and eloquence of
his tongue, and a writer, who can hold them with the
magic subtlety of his pen, we do not hesitate in saying,
Leonard Conyngham stands foremost among the younger
men of the nineteenth century, and has before him a
future which can only be limited by his own failure
of will and steady purpose.' Hear, hear!" I cried, laying down the paper. "Sophia, that's very fine writing.
But he is undoubtedly a great man, and as long as he

pays his bills promptly, I wouldn't think of turning him away because he's so distinguished."

"I don't know what you see so much to laugh about," said Sophia, rather tartly. "Everybody's paying him all the attention they know how."

"Of course they are, and they're quite right about it. He is a very remarkable sort of person, I am sure. Here's a long article in the *House Journal*. It tells you all about his dinner engagements, the receptions that have been given him, the *on dits* about him, his personal appearance. Ah! it seems he isn't short and stout. Hear this: ' He is rather slender, below middle height. His hair is dark, his eyes are very brilliant, rather deep-set. His expression is one of profound melancholy.'. Think of that, Sophia. What if he has dyspepsia? Perhaps the biscuits don't agree with him. Fancy if you are anyway responsible for that profound melancholy. Don't you think you'd better speak to the cook about it? Isn't it possible that her baking powders may have alum in them? I feel that you cannot be too careful with such a great man in the house. But hear; there's something else that's very interesting. He is very inaccessible, the paper says."

"The street cars pass the house," cried Sophia, angrily. "That shows how much good there is in newspapers."

"It doesn't mean that, I think, you know. It means he is hard to get to go to dinners; he avoids people, and all that sort of thing."

"I don't know about that, I'm sure," said Sophia, subsiding. "It's no odds to me how often he goes out, his dinner's always ready for him here. He pays for it, and he's entitled to it."

" And I'm sure he likes it, else he would go out
oftener, and eat other people's dinners," I said, molli-
ently. Sophia didn't know about that either, she was
sure.

" And here's a melancholy account of a distinguished family that had a reception for him, and he
wouldn't go. The young lady of the family was so
heartbroken she refused to come down-stairs. I wonder
if it was that pretty girl I saw here in the carriage?
And as to the balls he won't accept, and the breakfasts
and the suppers and the dinners that he will not eat,
really, it's a crying shame! They'd keep a poor family till the youngest baby came of age. It shows a
want of heart ; it shows a want of principle, if one may
say so."

While I was thus endeavoring to divert Sophia
from her rheumatism, Mary came to the door. She
was blushing and looked excited. She handed Sophia
two tickets and a check.

" Well ?" said Sophia, sharply.

Mary explained that Mr. Conyngham's agent had
just called and asked for her. He said he wanted her
bill for the two weeks' board. She had told him her
mistress was sick, and couldn't see him. Also, that she
never made out bills. The ladies and gentlemen
always sent the money in when it was due, and when
they went away for good, she gave 'em a receipt in full
if they wanted it ; but she wouldn't be at the pains to
make out bills for people every week. The agent said
it was a mighty poor way, and she'd get in trouble if
she didn't look out ; but he wrote her a check, and put
the roll of bills back in his pocket. Then, when he

was going away, he seemed to think of something, and
turned back and said :

" Here's a couple of tickets ; give 'em to your mistress, and tell her maybe she'll be well enough, by to-
morrow night, to go and hear Mr. Conyngham."

Sophia looked almost pleased as she turned the tickets over in her fingers. "Much good they'll do me,"
she said. And she told Mary a long message to take to
the laundress, as if she weren't gratified at all. But
when the girl was gone, she handed the tickets to me,
and said :

" You must take one of the servants with you, and
go to-morrow night." I laughed at the idea and begged
her to excuse me. But before the night came, I found
she had set her heart upon my going. I resisted quite
firmly at first. It was the sort of thing I did not feel
at home in doing. I often went out at night, with a
servant, during a Mission every night for nearly two
weeks, and on Festivals, and at many other times.
But this was different. I should see the world ; I did
not want to go. And yet it was selfish to resist Sophia,
who was feverishly set upon it ; and it was, after all, a
thing which might give me great pleasure. Though I
had taken the tone of ridiculing the august lodger, I
did not forget that he had thrilled me deeply, that I had
often longed to see him, to know more of him, before
I found him under the some roof.

Also, I was very weary of being in the house so
much. Sophia was infinitely more tiring than a whole
hospital. There, I had the recompense of feeling that
I could give comfort. Here, when I had climbed up all
those weary stairs to Sophia's dull room, I was quite at
a loss to know whether I brought pain or pleasure. On

general principles I continued to go and do my best, however. I had a great longing to go to the hospital; the sight of that face, which I said to myself again and again was not his, had given me a restless desire to go. I might be missing some chance which would never come back again. But when I had sent for the servants and given them their orders for the day, and had mounted to Sophia's room, and done what I could for her comfort and cheer, the day was too far gone to admit of a journey to the distant hospital. I had scarcely time to get my usual walks, and my books were effectually routed, which was no doubt a satisfaction to Sophia, if she knew it.

Therefore, when the evening of the lecture came, I was more ready than I should have supposed it possible, to embrace the opportunity of getting a little diversion and fresh air.

CHAPTER XXVI.

THE LECTURE.

> "What I do,
> And what I dream include thee, as the wine
> Must taste of its own grapes.   And when I sue
> God for myself, He hears that name of thine,
> And sees within my eyes the tears of two."
>
> *E. B. Browning.*

MARY was detailed to accompany me.   Sophia was more interested than she would acknowledge ; she wanted me to have a carriage ; she dictated to Mary what she should wear, to look at once respectable and menial.   When we got out into the clear, frosty, star-lit night, I wished that it had been five miles instead of five blocks that we had to walk.   The great man's carriage was standing at the door, waiting for him ; therefore I dared not lose the time, and we walked directly to the hall.   It gave me a strange feeling to be going in out of that clear, still grandeur (for "the streets were dumb with snow," and the night seemed silent, for a city night) into the gay, gas-lit place, filled with bright faces and bright dresses.

The agent had paid Sophia the compliment of pretty fair seats.   We had to walk a good way down the aisle, now filling up with chairs, to our places, Mary following me with my wraps.   The house was very full, and crowds were still coming in.   When we

[351]

had got into our seats, I found that we were separating a large party, or perhaps it was only two parties who happened to meet. Beside me was a young girl; on the seat before her, a young man—very young; and a line of people in front of us, who seemed to belong to him; and directly behind us, more, who seemed to know them. The way in which they talked over and through us was quite remarkable to me; they seemed to think, because I was not talking, I was not hearing. The very young man in front leaned over, and talked about the lecturer to the young girl, who was impatiently looking at her watch.

"They say he is always a little late," she said.

"That's his airs," said the young man. "People will put up with anything from him. There never was anything so ridiculous as the way he is run after."

"I don't blame anybody," said she, with an abstracted air. "He is the most perfectly satisfying man I ever met. When he has been speaking to you, you never seem to lose the sound of his voice; it goes over and over in your ears—it is such utter music. And his eyes, ah! I never felt as if I were being looked through and through till I met them."

"Come, now!" cried a matter-of-fact little voice behind me, which indicated black eyes and a small, trim figure. "Come, now! how many minutes did he talk to you the other evening at the A——s? For, I suppose, it's there you met him."

"It was necessarily there, for it's the only place he's been," she said, loftily, not giving the statistics called for. "He went there, because of some family obligation. He has only been to a few dinners, and one supper at the club. You can see he hates society; he is suffocated with its inanity."

" Bah !" cried the brisk voice at my shoulder.

" Airs," said the very young man in front.

" As you will," said the young woman, who evidently courted misinterpretation. " I don't suppose it concerns him or surprises him that everybody does not understand him."

" As long as you, and the eleven thousand other virgins do," cried the little spitfire behind my chair.

" Really," said the other, " I'm *sorry* that you take it so to heart. If he should by any chance be at the F——s this week, I'll manage to present him."

" He would be suffocated; don't think of it."

An admonitory and motherly voice, also behind me, checked this sharpness, in a very low tone, and then went on aloud.

" Have you heard much about him from the A——s? One doesn't attach much value to what the papers say."

The young æsthetic person was only too glad to be permitted to tell all she knew on the subject, which, of course, had the weight of an authorized version, coming from the A——s, who were his family's friends. Her statements did not differ materially from the newspapers however, except for the sun-flower-and-peacock-feather-iness of the descriptive terms. All that I gathered that was of any fresh interest, was that his profound melancholy, his utter disillusion, as she called it, was the result of some mysterious occurrence in his youth, of which his family had not the liberty, or perhaps, the power, to speak.

" But does he seem unhappy, gloomy, in ordinary life ?" asked the mother of the sharp tongue, over my shoulder.

"No-o, I can't say he does. He makes jokes and all that—but one sees the underlying bitterness."

She of the incisive tongue gave a little laugh It was probable she would have said something signally unsympathetic, but that, at that moment, we became aware that the vast audience was composing itself into an expectant silence. The young people about me grew instantly absorbed. I was so cured of my enthusiasm by this burlesque of it in others, that I found more interest in watching the young girl beside me, and for a few moments, I did not look up at the speaker. Notwithstanding her æsthetic affectations, she was quite genuine in her admiration; her eyes glowed, her breath came quick, she bent forward to catch his words. I wondered how much of this was the effect of contagion; he was simply the fashion; girls were going mad about him, as they did about singers and actors; they talked and wrote and dreamed themselves into love with him. It was a curious study; this girl, at least, and the girl I had seen in the carriage window, were genuine about it. They were wasting a good deal of womanly feeling on a man who, to say the least of it, wouldn't give them half a thought for all that they gave him. I quite enjoyed the girl's quickening color, as his voice grew clearer, and met our ears more distinctly. I rather envied her the possibility of the emotion.

Then I turned my eyes from her with a sigh, and slowly fixed them on the speaker. Our seats were a good way from him. I had no glass; I could hardly distinguish his features. I don't know why, but after he had spoken a few minutes longer, a strange feeling came over me; the past came back in those vague, dumb yearnings that no lapse of years can kill. I was not thinking of what he said. I had not yet given my attention to him and to his subject; I was not following him. But I was thinking of scenes and days long past. I was standing by the waves and feeling the salt spray on my face; I was sitting in the ruddy light of the drift-wood fire, and listening to Shamus O'Brien.

It is impossible even now to me, to tell the subject of the speaker's words. In any intellectual way, I had lost the thread; I had not begun with him, I was not thinking with him. From that I know what an orator he was, that by and by, a detached sentence or two he uttered thrilled me through and through; and as he went on, I listened, entranced and breathless as the girl beside me.

It was one of the lower tones of his voice that sent a sudden, blinding thought flaming through my mind. I leaned forward, I tried to see his face. I was too far away; my agitation did not help me. I could not distinguish a feature. The glass of my neighbor was lying in her lap. I took it up, scarcely asking her. She was too engrossed to do more than glance impatiently at me, and to look up again at the speaker.

I turned the glass at hazard; it fitted my eye, and I steadied it on his face. I gave a low cry. The glass fell from my hand.

By this time the girl was gazing intently at me; for the matter of that, the others too.

"You know him?" she said, under her breath.

"I am ill," I said, "I—I—must go away."

Mary, very much frightened, had half risen. Every one was looking at us.

"How can you get out," murmured the young girl

beside me; "through the aisles and all, it is so crowded."

The lady behind me thrust a bottle of salts into my
hand. Mary held it up to my face. A few impatient
words from some disturbed people in front of me
steadied me a little. I made a gesture to Mary to remain. I might as well be there as anywhere. I could
only die, wherever it was. The horrible physical
sensations that succeeded the sudden shock of recognition seemed to me like death. The crowd terrified me,
they were so thick around me. I felt that I should
smother if they did not give me air. I seemed to feel,
by a cruel trick of memory, the same sickening sensations that had overcome me in the court-room.

When last Bernard Macnally and I had been face to
face, what a different crowd, what a strangely different
scene. All that was the same was I, who sat stunned
and silent then as now, with faintness and tremor, and
a failing heart. Ah, what a gulf rolled between us!
What barriers had risen up! Not a scaffold, but
a throne, on which an admiring world had put him;
not death, but oblivion; not shame, but praise. Oh,
that I had found him stretched helpless, friendless, pen-
niless, upon a pauper's bed! Ah, that *that* had been
the face, not this; that that had been the scene, not
this. Its garish lights, its thunders of applause, its
meltings of emotion, how terribly far they all seemed
to push me out—out, shivering, into the darkness and
oblivion from which I had come in! I longed to creep
away and hide myself. But I could not go. Cruel
and hard, the crowd hemmed me in, unheeding. I and
my wound were things of the past. I must take myself away; here there was nothing but the stir of grand

emotion, but the glitter of high pomp, but the thrill of mighty genius. I must take myself away. I was altogether out of place. I—why had I not died? Why had I nourished up my poor little life of peace, to have it killed again, with no possible healing to come after. I lived, and from now, only to suffer, only to cause him suffering if he ever knew it. His wound was healed; his life was at its brilliant noon; all the reparation I could make him was to keep out of his sight, never to recall to him the fearful suffering that I had been the means of bringing on his life. I had, unwitting, done him worse wrong than his worst enemy could have done him. Now, witting, I must have the courage not to do him any more.

The face that I had seen had not been one to pity. Pity! I had spent ten years of pity on him; night and day, one prayer had underlaid all thought, all work, all speech; a prayer for mercy on him, whether he should be among the living or the dead. Now—God help me!—I was the one to pity. His face, changed in a subtile sort of way, older and deeper-marked, was warmed with the glow of genius, strong with a sense of power. Where was my place now—mine—who had been bound to him with such bonds—yoked to him with the memory of such suffering? Ah, my place! It was not anywhere in the compass of his vision. If there was an humble spot far away out of his sight and the sight of those who surrounded him with their adulation, I might kneel on and pray for him. But it seemed to me, in that first moment of bitterness, that I had no longer any need to pray for him. He had all, he was all. God had more than answered all my prayers. By and by I should be thankful; God would be patient; I could not be thankful now. I knew it would all be right in time. But, oh! for the narrow cot in the dreary hospital ward! Why had not that prayer been answered? Why—why—? Oh, my Lord, bear with me!

At last they were going; the people drew long breaths after the tension of the past hour; murmurs of deep feeling, a flush on almost every cheek, life in the dullest eyes, all paid their involuntary tribute to the voice whose echoes were yet in their ears. Even the lad before me seemed sobered and less trifling for the moment. The young girl beside me turned her shining eyes upon me; she had not lost thought of me, I know.

"You are better?" she said.

"A little. It will be all right when I can get into the air."

But instead of getting better, it was getting worse. The stir, the noise about me, the necessity for physical effort, all brought back my faintness. The lady behind me saw my pallor, and leaned over, and talked encouragingly to me. But the young girl had but one idea; what was her hero to me that the sight of him had overcome me so? She remained in her seat, though her companions had risen.

"You—you have heard Mr. Conyngham before?" she said, with the directness and ignorance of youth.

"She is too ill to talk," said the older lady, with a glance at my tortured face.

"I thought, perhaps," she said, with the persistence of a one-idead person, "that she knew him, and that suddenly seeing him had made her ill. Was it so?"

"I want to get into the air," I said, turning from her, and struggling to my feet.

The elder lady gave me her hand, and her kind aid. Mary, excited, and rather helpless, kept the crowd off on the other side. We got out, I don't know how. The air revived me.

"It's horrid," I said to the kind lady, when she was satisfied to leave me, "the feeling faint in a crowd. It has happened to me several times in my life. I am so sorry that I had to trouble and disturb you."

I hoped she would tell the girl, and make her know I had been often so before. What if she met him again and told him of the incident?

The stars shone down cold and keen upon that miserable walk. When we were just nearing the house, a carriage drew up with rush and bustle, at the other entrance. A man sprang from the box, rang the bell, and returned, and opened the door. I caught sight of Macnally as he stepped out and passed quickly into the house. It was several minutes before they heard our ring.

"They're so taken up with waiting on the other door, and you look fit to drop," said Mary, pulling again at the bell. "They might attend to somebody else but him, I think. But to be sure it *was* beautiful, wasn't it? Ah—there's that boy."

And, to hurry him, she pounded a little on the panel.

CHAPTER XXVII.

THE CORNER ROOMS.

"Love is subtle, and doth proof derive
   From her own life that Hope is yet alive ;
And bending o'er, with soul-transfusing eyes,
And the soft murmurs of the mother-dove,
Woos back the fleeting spirit, and half supplies ;
Thus Love repays to Hope what Hope first gave to Love."
                                Coleridge.

THE next morning I did not dare to go up to Sophia. The dark circle round my eyes, and my white face, would not escape her criticism. I must make up my mind what I meant to say before I saw her. So I sent her word that I had a headache, and that when I felt well enough I would come up. I wandered about my room aimlessly and feverishly. All the little occupations and interests of my daily life wearied me. I tried to pull the dead leaves from my flowers and to give them water, to feed my bird, to put the books and ornaments in the order that pleased my eye. It was generally a happy hour's employment, with the sun pouring in upon my pretty room. To-day I threw myself down in my chair and knew that it would be an interest no more. There was one interest ; what was that ? Listening for the opening and shutting of that other door, waiting hidden behind the curtains for his going out. I hated myself, but on such things as these my interests must centre while the same roof covered us. I knew myself so well; I had gone through so much. I knew what had been and what would be, with a grinding certainty that left small space for hope.

At last he went out, passing out upon the sidewalk, but a few feet from where I watched him. He walked with a firm, quick tread. His face had a pre-occupied expression, but I failed to find on it the melancholy that was ascribed to it. You would have called him still a young man. The slightness and grace of his figure, and the way he carried his head, were sure notes of young manhood. He wore no beard. The lower part of his face was firm, almost firmer than one liked. I should have said he had forgotten how to laugh, though he might still know how to smile. The expression of his mouth was different from of old, more changed than the expression of his eyes. It was a large, though well-formed mouth, with an upper lip that curled a little, though it was not very short. In other days there had been the greatest sweetness in the curves and movements of his mouth; there now, if anywhere, was the look of melancholy of which they talked. His face was always colorless; his nose was very straight and perfect; his eyes seemed to me much deeper set, and more shaded by heavy brows, than they had been when I had known them first. His broad, high forehead was very white, the short-cropped hair that scarcely admitted of a parting had touches of gray all through it.

After he had walked quickly out of sight, with the clear, fresh morning air in his face, I resolutely set myself to find some occupation. I sent for the servants, as usual, and gave them the orders which the day

16

required. I went to the store-room, and gave out the stores they needed. I heard their complaints, and undertook to convey to Sophia whatever it was impossible to solve without her. I had never loved these details, but since Sophia's illness I had found a certain pleasure in doing something distasteful for one who had served me so long and so unselfishly. Now, even that was gone; it was all hard duty, and I hated it.

When there was nothing else to occupy me, I started slowly up the stairs. I knew, sooner or later, I must face Sophia. I should not gain courage or cunning by delay. When I reached the second-story hall, I paused to look out a window. What should I say to Sophia, if she asked me to describe him; how dissemble my emotion if she made me talk about him? The door of a room stood open; to gain quiet and time for thought, I wandered in. This suite I knew was vacant. I pushed the door shut, and sat down in the window.

My parlor, as I have said, was the corner room of the corner house. This room was its counterpart on the floor above, with a hall bed-room adjoining. At one time these rooms were let as one suite with those Macnally now occupied, which adjoined them, in the avenue house. The connections between the houses, which Sophia had had cut originally, were one through the lower halls, at the head of the basement stairs, and another at the top, through two of the fourth-floor rooms. But when a large second-story suite was wanted, several years after, she had had a door cut from the parlor of the corner room into the front bedroom of the house on the avenue. It had been used for a year or two by the family who took it then. After they left, she found the rooms rented more profitably in smaller suites, so the door was fastened up; and an extra closet being desired in the bedroom of the house on the avenue, she had one built in front of the door. All these circumstances came into my mind, as I sat by the window. I had a curiosity to know whether the door had been nailed up or not. I turned the knob— it was locked. I could not tell whether it was nailed till it was unlocked. Sophia's key-basket was in my room. I don't exactly know what I meant to do. I went down-stairs and got it, refusing to think.

When I came up, I closed the door that led into the hall, went across the room, and pushed away a sofa that stood against the door. The key fitted readily into the lock, and turned. I pushed the door; it yielded— it was not nailed. I stopped a moment to think. I knew there was no one in the rooms occupied by Mac- nally. The last two weeks had shown that his invari- able practice was to go out between eleven and twelve, and not to come back before five. I knew the servant had arranged his rooms, and had gone out of them; I heard her in another part of the house at work. I don't know why I wanted to go; it was nothing; there was no harm. I would go in. I pushed the door open. A piece of muslin had been hung over the door, under the pegs which were nailed across the top. It was perfectly dark; the closet-door was shut. I opened it carefully, and listened. The room was vacant—the only sound was the ticking of a clock. Then I took out the key of the corner room, and dropped it in my pocket, and pulled it shut after me; and then, with a beating heart, pushed open the closet-door, and found myself in the rooms occupied by Macnally. My first care was to go across the room, and quickly slip the bolts of both the doors that led into the hall.

Then I stood still, and tried to control my agitation, and to look about me. The room used as a parlor was large, with two wide windows looking on the avenue, where the morning sun streamed in. The fire-place was on the side of the room adjoining the next house beyond. The bedroom was separated from the parlor by large, double doors, which were, however, kept open; and curtains, now drawn back, hung before the entrance. The furniture was unobjectionable, the carpet dull and unobtrusive. Everything was in scrupulously neat order; but it seemed the dreariest and most unhomelike place. It looked like a man's room—a man *en voyage*, too. On one side of the table lay a heap of newspapers; on the other side, a heap of books; in the middle, a heavy portfolio, tightly strapped. On the mantel-piece stood a box of cigars and a match-safe. The fire had been raked down, and put out, and freshly arranged to light. The chairs stood with their backs to the wall. It was a dreary place. The bedroom (but I merely glanced at it) was as orderly and as dull. A handsome dressing-case, with brass lettering—L, B. M. C.—upon it, stood on the bureau; two trunks stood in prominent places; the wardrobe doors were shut; the bed well made, with snowy linen; it was anything but a room that belonged to anybody. It was a room to stay in for as short a time as possible, and to go away from without a feeling of regret.

And this was the sort of life to which he was condemned, a man with the sensibilities, the tastes, the affections which make home dear. But for the love that he

had spent on me, but for the fate that had linked him
with my terrible sorrow, he need not have been a wan-
derer, a homeless man. I knew he would bear that
scar upon his heart forever. I knew he would never
lift a child in his arms without a pang. I knew fire-
side delights and merriment would always give his heart
an ache.

There came a subtle little solace in a thought I had;
there was something I might do yet, beside say my
prayers for him. I might, for the weeks or months he
staid here, make these rooms something more like
home. With poor little natures like mine, there is
such comfort in having something to do, when sorrow
presses. It is so terrible to fight out a sorrow, a temptation, with your hands idle in your lap. My heart
revived when I looked about the room, and thought of
all that might be done to make it pretty. I had a
plan; it matured in all its details with such rapidity. It
never would be found out, for the chambermaid was a
mere machine, with no more powers of observation than
a Universal Wringer. She would never ask how the
things came there. She would dust them and put them
back with equal interest, whether they were mummies
or royal Worcester porcelain. As for Macnally himself, he would feel them—like a man, perhaps, he would
not notice them.

It must be done gradually. To-day, it would suffice
to bring up the lovely table-cover from my own room,
to put a shade over the lamp upon the table, to put
away on the book-shelves all but the morning papers
and two or three books that looked as if they had been
freshly read; to fill a glass with violets and put them
on the mantel-piece, where they would show their dim

outline in the mirror, and shed their delicate perfume on the air. I pulled the chairs about in more becoming attitudes; I moved the great chair up before the fire; I brought a footstool from the other room, and put before it; I draped the curtains with a different expression. It did not look like the same room; and yet the changes were so slight, they would be felt, not noticed—by a man, at least. I longed to see the effect when the fire should be burning, and the shaded lamp shedding out its soft light. But that I could only see in fancy. My work done, I slid back the bolts of the two doors that led into the hall, and went back quickly into the closet, which I examined carefully. It was not used, save for a gun-case in one corner, and an empty portmanteau in another. There was a second large closet at the other end of the room, and a wardrobe. This one, apparently, was not needed, for the man of fame was evidently not a man of luxurious pretension. The sheet, when it was dropped inside over the door below the pegs, looked like the wall. No one would think of questioning it, on a cursory glance. I listened well that the corner parlor was empty, pushed open the door, and got safely in the room, locked the door, and moved the sofa back.

Now I felt stimulated enough to go to see Sophia. I felt quite equal to my part. I found her more fretful than usual, because anxious about me. I had quite a high color on my cheeks, and she suspected either deception or a fever—she was divided between the two. She took hold of my hand unexpectedly as I was arranging her pillow, and decided it was fever.

"I shall get up to-morrow," she said angrily, "doc-

tor or no doctor. I'm not the kind to lie still and let
other people do my work. I'll get up if it kills me."

Heaven forbid! I thought, as my heart sank. What
should I do if she did get up? I tried to persuade her
I had nothing to do that tired me. "If I weren't doing
this I should be going to the hospital."

Then I did not get exercise enough; I was used to
the fresh air. I promised her I would go out every
day to walk. I would begin that very afternoon. I
would have promised her anything; my heart was in
my throat; what if she should persist in getting up!
She didn't say she wouldn't, but I hoped she was a little less firm about it.

"How about the lecture?" she said suddenly, turning her eyes full on me.

"Didn't Mary tell you?" I said; "the crowd and
the close air and everything made me faint at first.
And after that I couldn't pay much attention. I was
afraid I should be faint again and have to go out, and
how I could have done that I can't imagine, for the
aisles were crowded; you never saw such a crush. I
don't believe there was standing room for another person. The audience seemed perfectly carried away with
him. He has a wonderful voice. I wish I could have
listened to him attentively, but when once one gets the
idea that one's going to faint, it's all over with one's
listening."

"What does he look like?" she said, with her eyes
still on my face.

"We hadn't seats near enough to see his face with
anything like distinctness. I hadn't a glass. I bor-
rowed one from the lady next me, but I only kept it
for a minute. There isn't much satisfaction in a glass

if it isn't fitted to your eye; turning and twisting and lengthening and shortening; sometimes I think it's rather worse than none at all."

"Then you didn't see him?"

"Yes, I saw him, just a glance. I should say he looked like the descriptions of him in the papers. I should say his face must be very fine, if you could watch it while he spoke. Next time the agent presents you with some tickets, I hope he'll have the grace to give you better seats."

"Next time I'll go myself. You're a poor hand to do anything but read books and go to hospitals."

I could not tell whether she had any suspicion of the truth. She always had suspicions, but they were frequently quite wide of the mark. I knew she distrusted me, and felt there was something hidden, but I hoped it was that she fancied I was more ill than I admitted, or that something in the house had gone wrong, that I was keeping from her.

The result of her suspicions and her frettings was, she was much more ill before the day was over, and put herself back several weeks in her recovery. It was growing no easy task to soothe and please her. She worried about everything, whether it were doing well or ill. She would have dismissed every one of the servants, if I had not interfered. They were all excellent in their way, and did their work with surprising fidelity, considering how much they were left to themselves.

But the most fruitful source of anxiety was the standing empty of that second-story corner suite of rooms. Such a thing had never happened to her since she took the houses. Here it was the first of December, and one of her best suites of rooms bringing her in nothing. At this rate she couldn't pay the expenses of the house; she was running behind every month; something must be done.

It was in vain I assured her that she was making money every month; that I was keeping her accounts with all the care I could, and that I knew there was not a cent owing, and a comfortable amount on hand. And that she ought to be very thankful to be getting on so well, when she was not able to look after things herself.

That gave her no comfort. Something must be done about it. I must put an advertisement in the papers. I remonstrated. It took from the dignity of her house to advertise the rooms; she had never done such a thing before. It would be a direct loss of prestige. Then I must write for her to the British Consul, and to one or two of her former patrons. That I engaged to do, devoutly hoping that they wouldn't know of anybody.

Those rooms once occupied, my plans must fall totally to the ground. Even if I could get a pass-key to enter from the hall into Macnally's rooms, I was not mad enough to run such risks. I never went into the other house, nor into any rooms but my own, and any servant meeting me on the stairs would have cause to wonder what had brought me there.

My pretty bubble danced along the ground; much as it pleased my fancy and soothed my dreary hours, I could but see how little chance there was that it could please and soothe me long. When Sophia got out of her room it would vanish, or, if the corner rooms were taken, it was gone. But the more fragile, the dearer it became.

16*

CHAPTER XXVIII.

CONSTRAINED TO HEAR.

" Or is it over ? art thou dead ?
　Dead ! and no warning shiver ran
Across my heart, to say thy thread
　Of life was cut, and closed thy span !

" Could from earth's ways that figure slight
　Be lost, and I not feel 'twas so ?
Of that fresh voice the gay delight
　Fail from earth's air, and I not know ?"
Matthew Arnold.

A WEEK had passed. Every day I had been in
Macnally's rooms. By twelve o'clock they were
in order, and the servant was out of them, and did not
come near them again, till she came in to light the fire
at five, before his return. I had full liberty, but I
could not feel safe, or anything but agitated and uneasy.
When my own rooms were locked, it was understood I
had gone out, and no one was troubled as to where I
went. As I was entitled to frequent the hall and staircase of the corner house, on my way to my sleeping-
room, which was on the second floor, no one had cause
for speculation if they met me there. Mr. Conyngham's notes and cards and letters were always kept by
Buttons, and presented to him in a bunch when he had
come in in the afternoon, and the rooms were rarely
entered through the day.

The rooms had improved under my agitated hands.
A stand of plants was in one window, an odd-looking

little writing-table in the other. A better rug lay before the grate; on the mantelpiece stood an odd India
vase, always filled with flowers which looked at themselves in the mirror. On the other side of Macnally's
little travelling clock I put a low brass candlestick with
a red candle in it, and beside it a brass match-box with
a serpent on the lid. His books increased every day.
I put them in order on the shelves. I saw with satisfaction that he had taken more books out of his trunks,
and added them to the others, and that he brought out
a handsome inkstand, and seemed to be settling himself
a little into place.

The table now pleased me. He dined on it, so all
the things had to be taken off at meals, and therefore
there could be but few. But the cover was rich-toned
and soft, and a pleasure to the eye. The lamp was
solid and simple; a couple of books always lay on it,
the two or three I knew, by instinct, that he was reading, and a paper knife, a new magazine, and a bowl of
blue cloisonné for the day's harvest of cards and notes
of invitation. The table stood opposite the fire-place,
the wide easy-chair between; it seemed to me there
must be an alluring suggestion of quiet evenings, and
easy, unhurried mornings.

The houses opposite were low; the morning sun
poured in at the windows through the soft, pretty
hangings. I took care that the lighting of the fire
should never be forgotten in the afternoon at five.
Mary was most trustworthy, but every morning, when
I gave my orders, I reiterated, " Never forget to take up
Mrs. Graham's tea at five o'clock, and to stop on your
way and light the fire in the second story front rooms."

I don't believe she ever forgot it. I often heard
the crackle and the splutter of the coal from the corner

room, where I had paused to listen if my orders were strictly carried out.

I had strange feelings those stolen moments that I spent there, glancing at the books that he had just laid down, touching the chairs, the furniture that he had touched an hour before; smelling the scent of his just burned-out cigar; turning over the cards and notes that his eye had just passed over. They were strange, I cannot say happy, moments. I hated deception. I doubted sometimes if it were right or wrong. If it were wrong, it could only be as an injury to me, if ever any one should know. There could be no moral wrong, and for the motive that had moved me to it, and the hope that I had brightened even a few hours for him, I was willing to bear all the criticism that might fall on me, if ever it were known. But the constant watching against discovery, the constant agitation that contact with these inanimate things brought me, made my life anything but one of peace. I suppose my face showed my restlessness and damaged health. Sophia watched it narrowly and fretted herself worse every day about me.

The day of which I speak had been a very deranged one in the house. Mr. Conyngham had begun the contrarieties by going out an hour later than his ordinary custom. That had disappointed the maid of the hour she usually gave to the arrangement of his rooms. Then Mrs. Graham, a very exacting young matron, who had the third-floor rooms, had had a luncheon-party, and had taken the time of all the servants she could lay hands upon. Sophia probably would have seen justice done; but I had no authority to interfere. At three o'clock, Mr. Conyngham's rooms were still untouched. At half-past three, the maid rushed hurriedly through them; and at four, left them superficially arranged, and went to do the rest of her neglected work. The old lady who had the back rooms on the second floor of the corner house was enraged that the cleaning of her windows had been neglected on account of the irregular festival of Mrs. Graham. She sat all day with her doors open, to waylay the chambermaid, who had refused to come to her when she sent her word about the windows. While her door was open, and she was on guard just inside, I could not get into the corner room. I had some fresh flowers to put there, and a waste-paper basket that I had been embroidering. I was most impatient of her vigilant watch.

It was half-past four when the arrival of a visitor obliged her to descend from the watch-tower. I took the opportunity to go into the corner room, and through the closet to the other rooms. There I found more to do than I had thought; the maid had left things in very indifferent condition. I hurried through the arrangement of the flowers, and restored things to order as quickly as I could; but, doing my very best, it took a good many minutes. The room was a little chilly. I knew Mary was still up-stairs, for I heard her voice distinctly talking with the Grahams' waiter. The fire would not be lighted if I did not do it. I struck a match; in a few moments it was blazing cheerfully. I went to put the waste-paper basket under the little writing-table in the window; as I did it, I glanced out. The carriage that Mr. Conyngham always came home in was driving from the door. He was then already in the house. A fury of terror seized me. I sprang to the door and unbolted it, then hurried across the room, and got into the closet just as the parlor-door opened.

But, unimagined situation! As I was eagerly turning the knob of the door that led into the adjoining room, I was arrested by the sound of talking there.

"And where does this door lead to?" said a thin female voice.

"Oh, to nowheres in particular," answered the voice of Buttons, as he slipped the bolt and shut off my escape. "'Tain't used for nothing. *These* is the rooms that goes together."

I heard her ask more questions, and appeal to some one who was with her. I was in an agony of fright. Through the door, which I held a crack open that I should not smother, I saw Macnally, and a gentleman with him. They were now seated near the fire. I could see them distinctly by its blaze, the curtains into the bedroom being drawn quite wide apart. If there had been any emotion strong enough to conquer my fear and shame, it would have overcome me when I recognized in the stranger Mr. Hardinge. I never can express half of the guilt and degradation that I felt; it had no proportion to the wrong that I had done. I could not forgive or excuse myself, now that I saw of what I had been in danger every day. Every feeling seemed to dwindle to nothing before the instinct of self-preservation, the womanly defence that nature gives us. At that moment I loved no one but myself, I cared for nothing but to escape from my intolerable dilemma. The motives that had led me into it seemed contemptible.

It was impossible not to hear what was being said by the two men sitting at the fire. I could not miss a word, a syllable, scarcely an expression. They were talking of something that had occurred the night before. Mr. Hardinge had gone to him after last evening's lecture, and spoken to him. He had, he said, a fear that he would not be glad to have him know him.

"Far from it," said Macnally. "I have been thinking every day since I came of looking you up. I should be a most ungrateful brute if I hadn't meant to do it. I have been here less than a month, and I have been much occupied, but not enough to drive out the thought of what I owed to you. Of course it was an effort, breaking the ice, and going into things that one would be glad to get out of one's mind forever; I'm sure you understand."

"Of course; and that's why I hesitated to speak to you last night. All these years I have said the same thing to myself, when I have wondered that I did not hear from you after you went home."

"You got my letter from Liverpool, when I landed?"

"No, I never have had a word from you since I left you on the steamer."

"I can't account for it—but—yes—perhaps I can. When I landed at Liverpool, I was on the eve of a terrible fever. That letter to you was the last thing I remember. I got to my room at the hotel; I remember my head was so bad I could scarcely tell the servant what I wanted, but he brought me ink and paper at last. I wrote to you. My feeling was I was going to die, and that must be done before I was past thinking. When the letter was sealed and directed, I sent for the man and gave it to him, with some money for a stamp. It was a supreme effort. I think it probable I sank down then into the stupor which was the beginning of my illness. The man probably pocketed the money and mislaid the letter, or else I had misdirected it in my confused condition. One is as likely as the other. You must have thought me a bad fellow."

"I always felt there must be some excuse. I had an idea that you weren't—living, perhaps. Were you long ill?"

"A good many weeks, I fancy. I was at a strange hotel; my things weren't marked, you know. They just took care of me for charity's sake. A good Sister of Mercy nursed me; none of my people knew anything about it. I—well, I might as well tell you, I owe it to you. I had been a little hardly treated at home, I thought. I had been an idle fellow, self-willed too, I suppose. But it doesn't seem to me they went the best way to work to get it out of me. However, I don't pretend to judge. I don't think I should have been so stubborn if they'd been more lenient; as I look back, I don't see that they were quite justified. When I got over my fever, I was not over my resentment, quite. I was despondent and purposeless. I resolved I would not go home. I had still a little money left. I sold some things I had, paid the expenses of my illness, and took passage for Australia, where I staid three years. At this moment, no member of my family knows that I ever was in America till now; none, at least, but a little sister who was faithful to me always, and to whom I always wrote from here."

"That accounts for your never answering my letters, sent at random, to be sure, nor seeing my advertisements about the discovery that was made two years after, at South Berwick. You do not know of it?"

"Yes, I know of it; after my return to England, I saw a paragraph in an old paper. It seemed an accident that I should have found it. I never could get hold of any fuller statement, though I looked through many files of papers; but I had not the advantage of a date to fix it. What I saw was a mere paragraph in a torn scrap of paper, the name of which I did not know."

"Why did you not write to me?"

"I—I—hated to open the old wound again. It's always hard to me to speak of things that have gone deep. It's a bad trait, I know. It's got me into the worst troubles of my life. I'm always promising myself to begin a reformation."

And he looked up to his companion with the old sweet smile of South Berwick days.

"Well, you may congratulate yourself you have begun the reformation now, I'm sure," said Mr. Hardinge.

"I'm going to carry it a little further," said Macnally, a constrained, pained look succeeding the smile. "If you can tell me anything of the other actors in that terrible drama, I shall—be glad."

"I'm sorry to say I can't tell you very much. The poor young mother I know nothing of, except that she went to Canada, after a few weeks or months. I think she can't be living, or sane—one would almost wonder if she were, after what she had gone through. I think the more that she must be dead, because, at the time of the discovery at South Berwick, she did not come to me, or make any sign. I should have thought she would naturally have come to me, hoping I might tell her something of you, or get to you some message from her. It was a painful case—a painful case."

There was a long silence; Macnally sat gazing into the fire. At last he said:

"The woman, Sophia: I wonder if one could hear anything of her. She is not the kind that dies," he added, with a short, bitter laugh.

"No," responded Hardinge, "she had fire and ven-

om enough in her to outlive a dozen generations. She's
living, you may take your oath of that."

"I wonder what would be the best way to go to
work to find some trace of her?"

"Advertising, I should think, or application to some
detective agency. If you like, I'll see what can be
done."

"If you would, I should be very glad of it."

Mr. Hardinge took out his memorandum-book.
"Sophia—Sophia—do you remember the name? Of
course, though, I've got it on the minutes of the trial."

"Atkinson," said Macnally, briefly.

Mr. Hardinge wrote it down, and put the book back
into his pocket. "And the poor Emlyns," he said;
"you know about them?"

"No," returned Macnally, briefly again, and I saw
his face darken.

"Mrs. Emlyn died very suddenly, in Naples. She
had but a few days' illness, the result largely, I suppose,
of her devotion to her husband and her anxiety about
him. He was, you know, very much broken down by
the excitement attendant on the trial; he was losing his
mind fast, but the poor lady did not live to see him a
total wreck. The decline in his mental condition was
very rapid after her death; in a few months he was
hopelessly imbecile. I believe he is still living, very
tranquil and harmless."

"And how about the children, Ned and Naomi?"

"They were sent to an uncle in New Orleans. Ned
was married last year. He is a fine young fellow, and
will make a good lawyer. He's persevering and manly.
And Naomi is quite a beauty. By the way, she's in the
city now. She has been very much admired."

"Pretty little Naomi!" said Macnally, with a sad

smile. "She was always faithful to me; she proved my only friend."

"Shall I send her word about you? or shall I give you her address? I could get it easily, though I can't recall it at this moment."

"No, oh, no. I shall like to meet her without preparation. I wonder if the child would know me."

"I'm quite sure you wouldn't know her, if you think of her still as the child. She must be—fully twenty-three. She is a young queen, tall, like her aunt, and quite commanding."

"I have a fancy that I should know her eyes; I shall like to test my memory. You say she goes much in society? It will give me an interest—I will go out more. You don't think it's possible she would know anything of—the others?"

"No, I think there is little chance. She would have told me if she had had any news of them. She scarcely ever fails to speak to me of that time whenever I may meet her. Young as she was at the time, it made a very deep impression on her mind."

There was a little pause. Mr. Hardinge got up to go away.

"I'm going to ask you," said Macnally, a little awkwardly, as he rose, "not to let—anybody know of my identity with that unhappy man you saved from the gallows, not even little Naomi. I've a great aversion to its being known on the other side; and to tell the truth, I've a great aversion to sensation as connected with myself in any way. It couldn't do any harm, I know; but I am sure you understand how painful it would all be to me if in any way the rumor should be started."

"I can understand it perfectly, my dear sir, and you

may be assured of my strict silence. But, you'll excuse me for saying so, you will have difficulty in keeping it a secret, unless people have short memories.

" You knew me easily, then ?"

" In a moment."

" I felt I was so changed. I depended on that, and on the chance of not being seen by the few people who were familiar with me then. It seems so long ago, and it seems as if it were such a secluded, narrow path I walked."

" Well, let us trust you won't meet any Sutphen County people. Sutphen County! The name always gives me a kind of shiver. Do you realize how close a shave that was? Two minutes before that jury came in, I would not have given sixpence for your chance."

I saw Macnally's face grow white as the firelight played on it. An almost imperceptible shudder passed over him, but he did not speak.

" But for the testimony of that poor young creature," went on the lawyer, " you must surely have been lost. You never knew what anxious hours I had lest she should fail us. If she had lost her reason, or had become hopelessly ill, or had wavered but a hair's breadth in her testimony, there would not have been a ray of hope. But I needn't have feared. A woman never breaks down till she has nothing to hold up."

At this moment the servant came in, bringing coal. Mr. Hardinge held out his hand, and Macnally followed him out of the room. The servant continued busy about the fire. In a moment Macnally came back, and threw himself into the chair before the fire. The woman went away, closing the door behind her. Macnally sat fixedly gazing into the flames, as if to read there the riddle of his life. He lay back in the chair, his head a little bent forward, his look deep and intent,

not as men dream and wonder. The room was very
still. There was snow on the ground outside, and the
passing wheels were muffled. His face was half turned
towards my place of concealment. If I had made any
noise he must have heard me. If I had made any
movement he must have seen me.

He never stirred; I think it must have been a long
half hour. I had a chance to burn well in upon my
memory that pale profile, with the bent head and the
intent eyes; the relaxed figure that was so motionless;
the hand that was so slender, still and white. The
firelight shone, now broad and ruddy, now flickering
and yellow; but its changes never moved him from
his fixed position.

At last Mary came in to arrange the table for his
dinner. He turned a little restlessly and pushed his
chair a trifle nearer to the fire. My terror was increasing; in a moment the chambermaid came into the
bedroom. If there were anything she kept in this
closet, I was lost. She went to the washstand, poured
fresh water in the pitchers; lit the gas above the dressing-table, pulled down the window shades. Mary, by
this time, had arranged the table and put on it the
lighted lamp, with the shade upon it. Then, glancing
around to see if everything were in order, she turned
and left the room.

As the chambermaid came again to the wash-stand,
she muttered, "There, I've forgotten my towels," and
putting down her pail of water, went out of the room,
looking out the key of the linen closet on the bunch in
her belt, as she went. I knew the linen closet was on
the floor above. She went out, leaving the door ajar.
There was a bright light over the dressing-table; I had
to pass full in front of it, before Macnally's eyes, if by

chance he lifted them up from the fire. But it was the only moment, before the woman should come back.

I remembered he would have heard the maid moving about in the room, and my movements would be less likely to attract his notice. I pushed the closet door open; and in the strong light of two gas-burners, walked across to the hall door, and out of it. He had not seen me; there was no sound of his even turning in his chair.

When I got to my own room, and sank down and hid my face in my hands, I asked myself three questions—Was it possible anything would ever tempt me to do this thing again?—Had I been punished or rewarded by what I had overheard?—Was I further from or nearer to Macnally than I had been before?

"Nothing, nothing," I answered, to myself, with passionate protestation, "would ever tempt me to do this thing again."

I *had* been punished by what I had been forced to overhear. I remembered that he had never once spoken my name. That he had said these were things that he would be glad to get out of his mind forever. No, he had not forgotten, his was not a nature to forget; but he would be glad to forget if it were possible. The memory of me was only fraught with torture to him. The wound had been too deep to heal; it might be silent for long intervals, but it broke out now and then, with undiminished pain. Through me his life was desolate; he strove against me as against an enemy. He would be glad to forget forever what he had so far only succeeded in forgetting fitfully. Ah! bitter hearing! Then his words had planted another thorn. Naomi Emlyn, a young queen, now in her fresh womanhood and perfect beauty, tenderly remembered as "his only friend," was to be sought out. She surely would be "an interest" to him. To meet her, he was going more into the world. For my own peace of mind, I should better not have done that little piece of eavesdropping.

And again, had this evening's occurrence put me further from or nearer to him? It had cut both ways. It had put me further from him than even all these years had put me. It had made it impossible for me to hope for any recognition. His happiness seemed to depend upon oblivion, and if I had a duty, it was to save him from a re-opening of the wound, and to further his attempt to find in something new an interest. But the sight of him, the nearness to him, the sound, close to my ears, of his unapproachably sympathetic voice—what had they not wrought upon my heart! I had thought the years had disciplined me. I had fancied that all was dead within me but the hope of Heaven and the thought of duty. What would I not have given to have recalled the life of peace that his coming had spoiled! It would take years to bring it back again. Never, it seemed to me, while I knew he lived, could I be at rest again without him. But lately, it would have seemed to me that to know he was living would have been happiness enough; living, if even lying on a narrow cot in some ward of Charity Hospital. How perverse and ungrateful I had become. He was living, he was at the height of fame and prosperity, he was not ill satisfied with life and its results; and I was passionately wretched, because I could not claim a part in his life any longer, because the door was shut between us, and I could not touch his hand or meet his eye.

CHAPTER XXIX.

SOME DEAD FLOWERS.

" No longer roseate now, nor soft, nor sweet,
But pale, and hard, and dry as stubble-wheat."
E. B. Browning.

" Dear as remembered kisses after death,
And sweet as those, by hopeless fancy feigned,
On lips that are for others; deep as love—
Deep as first love, and wild with all regret;
O Death in life ! the days that are no more."
Tennyson.

I KEPT my resolution for a few days. I only saw him from the window, going in and out. I walked much. I tried to keep myself from thought by busy occupation. Sophia had nothing to complain of in my devotion to her and her duties. I even found a day, once in the week, to go back to the hospital. But, all I succeeded in doing was wearing myself out, and leaving thought still master.

Mr. Conyngham's cards and visitors increased; his goings out increased. Several days in the week Buttons brought down word he would not dine at home. On many nights I heard him come in after midnight. Had he found Naomi Emlyn yet? The papers were daily chronicling his doings. He was lecturing very often; sometimes he was gone for a day or two, lecturing in other cities. It was my constant hope the corner

[384]

rooms would be rented. I even sent an advertisement of them to the papers. Many people came to see them, but they were not taken—now for this reason, now for that. I longed to see that temptation closed upon me; but, while those rooms were vacant, I was not sure of myself—I might be tempted to go again into the room which I had declared to myself I never again would enter.

About this time there appeared in all the papers an advertisement addressed to Sophia Atkinson. I took pains that it should never meet her eye. The servants did not read; but the lodgers—one or two of them—noticed the advertisement, and sent it to Miss Atkinson, with their compliments. I was fortunate enough to intercept the papers, and take them to my own room first; and so Mr. Hardinge's efforts for his client were not crowned with much success. His detective, also, I had the good fortune to see in the hall, as I came in one day, and to throw completely off the track. I convinced him that this Atkinson was a very different one from the Atkinson whom he pursued. By a fortunate mistake, her residence, in the directory, was put down as the number of the house on the street, and not the house on the avenue. It was also put in, S. Atkinson, and not Sophia Atkinson. So Sophia nursed her rheumatism up-stairs, and Mr. Conyngham, unsuspected, kept his rooms below.

One day, it was a rainy, in-door day, I had had less possibility of occupation than usual, and had taken out my water colors. There was an unfinished sketch of a bit of the South Berwick beach, having for background an opening in the dunes, and a distant glimpse of green meadows and purple hills beyond. I finished it; it

17

was a characteristic view; it seemed to me no one could claim it for any other spot on earth. A sudden impulse seized me. I scorned my resolution; the corner parlor door stood open as I went up-stairs to my room, with the picture in my hand. I pushed through the door; in another minute I was in the forbidden rooms.

I had forgotten to say, that over the corner where stood a little table with cigars and ash-stand, I had hung an engraving, and under it, a small and insignificant photograph of some favorite picture, I can't recollect at this moment what. These two had hung low, and I had, in other unconventional places, put one or two more. The walls were rather dark, and they had a good effect.

I hastily took out the photograph from its frame, and put in its place the little water color I had just finished, and hung it exactly as it had hung before. Why did I do it? It would be hard to say. It might never attract his notice. It might even be that he would look at it and never see a suggestion of the spot I meant. I did it, perhaps from an impulse to escape from the resolution that I had made to hide myself from him, to defend him from the past. It was a perverse and passionate resistance of my own decree.

When I had put the little picture in its place and given a glance back at it, I hurried out, to escape from reason and from self-reproach. As I passed his dressing-table, I saw lying on it, beside a crumpled handkerchief and a pair of gloves, a couple of dinner cards and some withered flowers. It was evidently the contents of his pocket, emptied out the night before when he came home. The chambermaid had left them, not knowing where to put them. I glanced down at the cards. They were exquisitely painted. On one was written, Miss Emlyn; on the other, Mr. Conyngham. My heart gave a throb. Then he had met her; they had been side by side for hours, last night at dinner. I would take my little sketch away: South Berwick was recalled enough. But no; it should stay. I would go away, and never come back into this cruel room again.

But what were my resolutions worth? Not long after, it was a wild and stormy evening, I was sitting in my window, looking out; the light within was turned low. The people struggled past around the corner where the wind met them full, with heads bent down, and umbrellas bent and twisted. I liked the fierce beat of the rain upon the pane. I liked anything better than soft moonlight and calm days of sunshine; I was too restless to like things that were at rest. While I looked out, leaning my forehead against the glass, I saw Mr. Conyngham come out and get into a carriage. A man held the umbrella over him and opened the carriage door; then got up beside the driver on the box, and they drove away. I don't know what there was in the sight of his departure that gave me such bitter thoughts. It was in such contrast to my loneliness, to my misery. I thought of the gay scene to which he went, the adulation with which he would be met. I remembered Naomi would be there, no doubt. Naomi, whose eyes he thought he must remember, who had been "his only friend!" The world was at his feet, if he wanted it; love, perhaps, and a life-long devotion was stretching out its hands to him to draw him from his life of cold seclusion; and I, ah, what lay before me in the dreary years to come?

I turned from the window, and shut out the storm

and darkness. I opened my portfolio, and sat down beside the lamp. From a folded sheet of paper there fell out a bunch of flowers that had been pressed, stems and roots and leaves and all. Sudden tears sprang to my eyes at the sight of them. They were little pink flowers that I had gathered at South Berwick the year before, when I had spent a day there, in the latter part of August. The country people call them " meadow-pinks," I don't know what their correct name is. They are a little star-shaped flower, of a soft yellowish pink, with brown and yellow centers. They grow in salt-mead-ows, and no doubt are very common, but I had never seen them anywhere but at South Berwick, and they were en-tirely associated with the place. In masses, they are very beautiful, and they were often the ornament of my little tea-table at the cottage ; in a low glass dish, against the dark mahogany, they were lovely. I was very apt to wear them in my dress. Ned and Macnally never crossed the meadows without bringing me a bunch. They did not grow very near us, a mile or more away. It was quite a circumstance to get them, but I was seldom without them. When we were driving, it was an excuse to prolong the drive, to go and get some. I knew Mac-nally had often walked miles out of his way, to bring a handful to me. I could see him now, standing in the door, in his blue-flannel clothes, with his game-bag over his shoulder, his cap in one hand, the flowers in the other, his face eager, bright, and yet almost shy, if I were sitting alone in the parlor, and there was no child to pick up in his arms and make a turmoil over.

They were my flowers, *par excellence;* every one got them for me, brought them to me, associated them with the thought of me. These I held in my hand were

excellently pressed, they had retained their color and
their shape, even to the roots and leaves. I put them
aside, and tried to recall no more pictures that they suggested to me. It was late when I went up to bed: I
had my portfolio in my hand. The corner door was
open. Why could they not keep that door shut? I resolved to lock it and to carry the key up to Sophia. In
the meantime, I pushed it open, and went in. It was
only eleven o'clock, there was plenty of time before he
should come back. A sudden impulse seized me, and
I went stealthily in. There was light enough in his
parlor for me to make my way across the bed-room.
The lamp was turned low, the fire gave out rather a
fitful glow. His chair was by the table, standing as he
had left it; a half burned cigar lay on the ash-stand on
the table, a book half-closed was beside it. A note,
torn open carelessly, lay on it. The envelope had the
initials N. E. on it; the address was in a woman's
hand.

I took a handful of my flowers, and shut them in
the book; put another lump of coal on the fire,
smoothed out the table-cover, which was drawn awry,
straightened the rug, and put the footstool before the
chair, then went away.

The next morning, about nine o'clock, I had to go
into the other house, to ease Sophia's mind about the
condition of a window-shade in the upper hall. It had
been reported to her in a damaged condition. She
could not sleep for thinking of it. She would not take
the word of the servants about it; I must go and look
at it myself. I rarely went into this hall; it gave me
rather an uncomfortable feeling, and I dreaded meeting
any of the lodgers, who always eyed me with more in-

terest than I liked. As I got near Mr. Conyngham's
door I caught sight of some one standing in it, and the
figure of Buttons in front, again, of that. All that I
could do was to step back behind a wardrobe, which
hid me from sight in an angle of the hall. Buttons
was a little waif whom I had found in the children's
ward at the hospital several years before. He was at
least fifteen now, but he looked barely nine. He had
a tiny, well-made figure, and a tiny, acute face. I had
persuaded Sophia to get him a suit of brown clothes
with brass buttons, and to take him into her service.
It was a very good investment; he never outgrew his
clothes. He was quite useful, and a distinguished ornament to the establishment. The apron that he wore
when about his menial work was so absurdly little, it
looked as if it had been made of a pocket handkerchief,
but it came below his knees. His intelligence seemed
preternatural because of his size. His accent was South-
ern, with flowers of Hibernian eloquence engrafted.

Mr. Conyngham was saying to him:

"I want to see the—person who keeps the house.
Will you go and say so to her?"

"She's ill, sah, can't see nobody; much oblige, sah;
very sorry, sah."

"I am sorry, too. You are sure it is impossible?"

"Sartain sure, sah. She ain't see nobody for this
month and more. She's quite an old lady, she is, and
she's got the rheumatism very bad."

"What's her name? I think I have forgotten it."

"Her name, sah? Missatkins, sah."

"Sacketts? Miss Sacketts, did you say?"

"Yessah, Missacketts, sah. That's what her name is."

Buttons made dreadful work with people's names;

he made no account of a syllable or two, more or less; it had been quite a hindrance to his usefulness as a hall boy, but I blessed him for it now, and remembered with relief that he habitually deprived Sophia of the last two letters of her name.

"Sacketts, Miss Sacketts?"

"Yes, sah."

"And who else lives in this house? Can you tell me any of their names?"

"In *this* house, sah?"

"Yes, in this house. On the floor below, who is there?"

"There's an old lady, sah; she have a son, sah. They very nice people, sah, they have live with Miss Sacketts a long while."

"And here, on this floor?"

"There be two ladies, sah; they have the back rooms, like you have the front. They be maiding ladies; they come last year, they did."

"Are they—young ladies, at all, either of them?"

"*Oh*, no, sah," and Buttons grinned a little. "They be quite maiding; they be settled, both o' 'em. And the floor above, there's Miss Graham, sah. She's got some children, sah. Miss Graham she's a very little lady; she's got black eyes and speaks up sharp. She makes 'em all stand round, she does. Mr. Graham's very nice gentleman. He don't say much 'bout things no way. And up-stairs o' all that, there's where the help sleeps, and where Miss Sacketts has her room, and one gentleman lodger who don't take no meals. I do his blackin' for him, though, and he pays me very handsome."

"And there's no one else in this house?"

"Nobody, sah, in *this* house, but what I ha' been tellin' you."

"Very well; that is all." And Mr. Conyngham turned back into his room and shut his door.

Christmas was approaching; for two days before it, he was away. On Christmas eve I broke my resolution again, and made his room bright with some holly, a spray or two of mistletoe and a glass of fresh flowers. I did not know that he would come back, but late that night he came. On Christmas Day he went out early to church; he crossed the street just as I was coming out the door, when there was scarcely light enough to see. For the rest of the day, he was shut up in his room. He had a great many calls from gentlemen, who took advantage of a leisure day, but he did not see any of them. There was no lack of flowers and daintily-done-up packages; Buttons was a busy man that day. I heard Mary say to one of the other servants, that his meals had come down almost untouched. In the evening, I heard him walking up and down his rooms, up and down, for an hour together. It had been a raw, cheerless day, and the evening had closed in with mist and rain. The wound had begun to smart again. Who does not pity the homeless man, to whom these days of festival are torture? The world cannot supply the want. Nothing but little arms around his neck, a tender hand in his, the blaze of his own hearth, can make the earthly side of Christmas fair to him. If all are sorry for such a man, how much more the one whose hand has dealt the wound; the one whose misery it has been to make his life a blank. I was glad when Chrismas Day was over, with the thoughts it brought to him and me.

CHAPTER XXX.

CAP AND APRON.

" The thirst that from the soul doth rise,
Doth ask a drink divine;
But might I of love's nectar sip,
I would not change for thine."

Ben Jonson.

TWO weeks after Christmas Day, he went away again (there was nothing else that marked the lapse of time to me that winter). The time of his return was indefinite. He left word that his letters were to be kept for him, that his agent would call from time to time to get them, and to make the payment for his rooms, which were to be kept in order, ready for him to occupy at any time. From the papers, I learned he was in Canada. I suppose all the world learned it from that or other sources. There was a cessation of cards and invitations. Buttons had slack times, and but for the inflation of his mind, might have returned to the knives and boots. But having been Mr. Conyngham's gentleman, he refused to decline upon that occupation, and became a little pert and troublesome in his idleness.

Sophia was improving slowly; if the foggy, moist, January weather had not been against her, the doctor thought she might have been down-stairs by this time. Several weeks passed—three, I think it was. The house seemed silent and dead to me. I went about my

17*

daily occupations with a dullness of heart that fore-
boded ill for the future. I had begun to think that he
would not come back; or that his coming would be
but the prelude to his going away entirely.

The day had been wet and foggy, but, towards
evening, it had turned cold; and now, at half-past ten
o'clock, it was snowing thickly. I sat reading by my
lamp. I had heard the bell of the other house ring
sharply several times; no one answered it; it was now
quarter to eleven. I looked out. The lights in both
halls were turned low; the servants had evidently gone
to bed; the house was supposed to be shut up. Whoever it was, tired of ringing at that bell, came around
to the door of our house, and rang sharply there. I
could not let any one stay outside on such a night; I
opened the door. It was a snow-powdered boy, with a
telegram addressed to "Miss Sacketts." I paid the
charge, and hurried to the lamp with it. It read:

"Train due at ten o'clock. Have supper ready for
me. L. B. M. CONYNGHAM."

It was already, as I have said, quarter to eleven. I
hurried to the kitchen, where I had not been half a
dozen times before. There I found the cook asleep
before a good hot fire. The laundress had been dozing
in a corner, but was just rubbing her eyes and getting
up to go to bed. "Where were all the other servants?"
Buttons had gone to bed with a toothache hours ago.
Mary and the chambermaid had gone out to a party, to
be away all night. Mrs. Graham's waiter never staid
after nine o'clock, unless she had company, and needed
him; and the two women who attended to the other
tables also lodged abroad. What was to be done?
The laundress was a starched, middle-aged creature,

whom I had never liked. She did her own work well, but had never been known to assist in that of any other servant. She was feeling particularly bitter about the party, too, to which the women were gone, whose duty she was asked to undertake.

I soon found it was useless to urge her to arrange the room, or wait upon the table. She flatly refused to do it, and seemed disposed to be impertinent. The cook, who was a vast, good-natured negress, bestirred herself in a slow way, and began to prepare some supper. It was not possible to ask her to carry it up; it was doubtful whether she could get up the basement stairs; she never had attempted it since she originally came down them, and she had increased in bulk considerably. Her few outings were made by way of the area-door, which was double, and which was always opened on both hinges to let her pass. She lodged in some obscure, unexplored portion of the basement, cooked *à merveille*, and was always good-natured, when the demand upon her was not unreasonable. She tried to bring the laundress to reason; the best that she could be made to consent to do, with the persuasion of both of us, was to open the door for the gentleman, when he rang, and to carry the tray of supper up, and set it on the table that stood outside his door.

"Oh, well," I said, "that will do; he can take it in himself, no doubt."

My own resolution was taken. I hurried up-stairs to the linen closet, where I knew Mary's fresh caps and aprons were, took one of each, as well as linen for the table, and let myself, by the closet door, into Macnally's room.

The rooms felt chill and damp. I lit the fire, the

lamp; turned the gas low above the dressing-table.
There were fresh towels and fresh water on the wash-
stand; there was not much dust. In a moment the
parlor seemed transformed by the glow of the fire and
by its ready warmth. I laid the table with shaking
hands. I knew where the china and glass were kept,
in the closet outside the door. There was a screen that
Sophia had devised, that was put before this closet, and
the table where the tray was to be put. Even if the
house were not asleep, this would make it safe for me;
I could move in and out of the room without observation, and the house was so still, owing to the lateness of
the hour, and the snow-paved streets, I could hear the
laundress three stories off, if she repented and came
up the stairs.

I arranged the table with glass and silver and some
flowers, to have a very nice effect. Then I moved the
lamp to a side-table, and drew down the gas, and put a
heavy shade upon it. There was also a shade upon the
lamp. Except for the glow of the fire, there was no
light shed about the room; that thrown by the shaded
gas upon the table did not extend beyond the circle of
the cloth. I moved the chair up by the fire, arranged
the footstool before it, put on the side-table below the
lamp, the cloisonné bowl of notes and cards that had
accumulated since he had been away, and placed beside
his plate three or four letters that had come that day.

It was now half-past eleven. There came a ring at
the door. I grew pale with fear that the laundress had
grown stubborn and might not go, but after a moment,
I heard her mount the stairs and go slowly to the door.
Then I heard Macnally's quick step on the stairs, and
her heavy one going down the basement stairs, and a

bang of the basement door. I pushed open the door a little, that he might get a gleam of welcome from it, and withdrew into the closet just as he entered the room. He said " Ah !" in a tone of satisfaction, as he glanced around the bright and home-like place. He shook the snow from his coat, put down his bag inside the bed-room door, took off his ulster, and then returned and walked round the room, and looked about it as a man does who has made a home of a place, and is glad to get back to it once more. He glanced at the notes and cards with little interest, took up the letters, laid back two, and read one.

In the meantime, I had gone into the corner room, and was putting on my cap and apron by the glass. Mary was slender, and about my height. My dress was black and unobtrusive. I felt reassured as I glanced at myself in the dim light. Then I went back softly and listened. Macnally was in the parlor ; so, with a beating heart, I stepped out into the bedroom. But the peril was so great, I resolved the heart-beats should be regulated, and they were. He had left the parlor door open when he entered from the hall. It was important that this door should be shut, or the laundress would see the preparation of the table, and know I had been in the room. I went quietly out into the hall through the bedroom door, and shut the parlor door from the outside. It was just in time. I heard the heavy-footed Hebe coming up the basement stairs, and I returned to the shelter of the bedroom door. She put down the tray with an ostentatious clatter of the dishes on it, and turning, went stolidly down the stairs again. Then I came out into the hall, set the screen before the table and the parlor door, opened it, took a covered dish in my hand, and went trembling in.

It rather steadied me to find my entrance was not at all observed. He had thrown down his letters and was walking about the room again. I saw him take up the lamp from the side table, and go over to where the little water-color sketch of the beach hung, and gaze at it long and fixedly.

By this time I had got the things all upon the table. When he put back the lamp, he knocked the shade off it. As he turned away, I hurriedly replaced it, and then stood back in the shadow. I hoped he would see that his supper was ready. I had not taken it into consideration that I should have to speak. Instead of noticing the preparation for his meal, he went to the writing-table, brought a portfolio to the light, and sitting down, not in the chair placed for him at the head of the table, but in one he pulled up for himself, hastily scratched off a little note, put it in an envelope and directed it. Then he got up, pushed back his chair, and said,

"Have this sent for me to-night, will you, if possible. Or, if not, the first thing in the morning."

He handed it to me without looking at me, but as I took it, his eye fell on me as he turned away. I was conscious that he had looked at me, but I had been very much in shadow, and my face had been turned away. I had been prepared, from what I had heard Mary tell Sophia once, that he would not notice me. She said he was a very nice gentleman, but he wasn't like most other gentlemen; he didn't notice servants when they waited on him, and though always civil, never talked to them. Mary was very pretty, and had, no doubt, been used to a different line of conduct in other nice gentlemen whom she had waited on.

Instead of sitting down at the table or noticing that it was ready, he threw himself into the chair before the fire, and sat gazing at it while the minutes passed. I moved about the room, or stood back in the shadow, my agitation increasing every moment. Presently he said, without turning his head,

"Will you put another piece of coal on the fire!"

The fire was sending out a ruddy glow just then. The movement brought me right into the heart of the light, and into range of his steady gaze. But I went quickly forward, took the coal from the scuttle, threw it hastily on the fire, and drew back again out of the light. Still he sat gazing on into the same spot and did not move; then I made a feint of going out into the hall and putting another dish on the table, and then I said, in a voice that sounded strange and unnatural in my own ears,

"Your supper is on the table, sir."

He did not look up, but moved back his chair and took his seat in the one placed for him at the table. This one was a dining chair, with rather a high back, and arms. He leaned back wearily in it. I had gone back, and stood behind him. He drew a dish towards him, took up the carving knife and fork, cut a bird in two and put it on his plate. He took some salt on his plate; he took up a piece of bread. The toast under the bird seemed to strike him; he pulled the dish back again and took it upon his plate. He did not have a traveller's appetite, apparently. I was watching keenly, and he was playing at eating, trying to like his food, and not tempted, now it was before him. I remembered

hearing Mary say to one of the servants that many
days she took away his dinner, almost as she had carried
it up to him. I was afraid he was ill. His long journey surely should have given him an appetite. The
sort of solicitude I felt for him, took away my appre-
hensive feeling about myself.

"Will you give me the wine?" he startled me by
saying at last. The wine was within easy distance of
his hand, if he had stretched it out. But I suppose he
was in the habit of being waited on. He held his wine-
glass in his hand; I went around the table, took the
decanter up and took out the stopper, then came a little
nearer to him, and lifted it up over the glass to fill it.
I gave a stealthy glance at his face. He did not look
up, his eyes were fixed on the glass. The decanter was
rather a heavy one; my wrist shook a little. I glanced
down; it gave me a sudden terror to see how strong
the light shone on my hand, and how white it looked.
I had, too, forgotten to take off my rings!

I was on the right side of the table; with his right
hand he was holding the glass. I made a little awkward effort to tip the decanter down, and the wine
began to gurgle out and fill the glass.

At this moment, his left hand made a panther-like
spring, and grasped my wrist. I uttered a cry, and let
the decanter fall upon the table; and the odor of the
spilled wine always comes to me as I remember that
strange scene. He started to his feet:

"What does this masquerading mean?" he said, in a
hoarse, harsh voice.

I had put up my other arm before my face, which I
bent down and hid completely from him. He caught
the wrist of this arm (still holding the other in a

fierce grasp), and drew it away from my face. I lifted
my head, and for a moment our eyes met.

Then he relaxed his hold upon my wrists, gave a
sort of gasp, and, staggering back, sank into his chair.
I was stunned for a moment; I put my hand up to my
temple. Then as I saw the horrible whiteness of his
look, and the closing of his eyes, I gave a cry, and
threw myself down on my knees beside his chair.

"What have I done," I cried, "what have I done?"
and I caught his hand and tried to warm it. He moved
his hand a little and opened his eyes and tried to speak.

"Oh, forgive me," I cried passionately. "I never
meant you should have seen me. I would have died
first. I thought you would not know me. It is too
cruel—I have done so wrong. Don't look at me if it
hurts you so!" and I put my head down upon the arm
of his chair, for his eyes only rested upon me for a moment, and then closed again as if the sight were insupportable.

"It seems cruel," I went on incoherently, with tears,
looking up at him; "it seems cruel, but it really was a
sacrifice—and I did not think that you would know
me. All winter I have kept out of your sight, and I
never, never meant you should have had the pain of
seeing me. I had vowed to myself you never should.
It will be ungenerous if you let it make you ill, when I
did not mean to do you any wrong, when I only did it
for a kindness. I was so sorry for your lonely coming
home. I—I—have been so sorry for you always," and
I began to sob.

He made a fierce effort to overcome the faintness,
and tried to speak. "I shall be better—in a moment,"
he said.

I started to my feet and hastily poured a glass of wine, and held it out to him. He drank it with an effort, and as he gave the glass back to me, our eyes met, and the thought of the last time when I had stood before him, while he drank off the wine I had poured out for him, flashed through both our minds.

"That was a long while ago," he said, leaning his head on the back of the chair, and looking up at me.

"Yes," I said, uneasily. "But you needn't think of that time, if it makes you ill. You needn't think of anything—you can be as if I hadn't had the misery to come and trouble you again. I will go away, and you can forget it all, and be like other happy people. You have everything, you ought to be happy. Remember, I meant it always—it ought to make you forgive me— I never meant to bring it all up again. Give me the credit of that, at least. I don't think I have been self-ish."

"You forget," he said, brokenly, "I don't know— anything—"

I was standing before him; I saw his eye rest on my apron; I thought I saw a look of disgust pass over his features. Of course it was not, only the physical pain that his recurring faintness gave. But, stung by my mistaken thought, I tore the cap and apron off, and threw them on the floor.

"I am not a servant," I said, with a little bitter laugh. "I only put those things on to come and wait on you because there was no other way that you should have anything to eat to-night, when you came home. You don't know about it—but this is Sophia's house. Sophia had money left her; she is a rich woman now, for a person of her class. She has had these two houses for a good many years, and I have always lived with her, and had her prettiest rooms, and been quite in luxury. She doesn't know you're here—she's ill—I've kept it from her, that you might have peace. I've hoped you might feel a little as if it were a home. I knew it couldn't last—it was not selfish in me—what were a few weeks or less? I know you think it was unwomanly in me to come into your rooms.—Yes, perhaps it was. I never meant to do it. I always felt ashamed. I thought you'd never know, and the rooms looked so dreary the first time that I saw them.—It was all a sudden impulse to-night; the servants were all gone to bed but one; she brought your supper up and left it at the door. I thought you'd never know me, I kept the room so dim. It was your fault; you should not have caught my hand. You never need have known me if you had not."

"You don't understand," he said, with effort, pressing his hand against his heart; "if I could—"

"I do understand," I cried, with fresh tears. "I understand it all. I have made you ill. I have always done you harm. I wish I had been dead before I came up here to-night."

He stretched out his hand to me; I had gone back a few steps from him, but I came nearer again, and took his hand.

"It's very hard for me to see you look so ill," I said, falteringly. "Can't I get you anything? Isn't there any medicine you take?"

He shook his head, and lay back in his chair, holding my hand in a faint grasp, and looking at me with deep, unmoving eyes.

I grew restless under his steady gaze. His recognition of me had been all pain, all anguish ; he had yet to utter the first word, give the first glance, of pleasure. I thought of all my doubts, of all that had pained me, as I had watched his goings out and comings in. I thought of Naomi Emlyn. I knew that the note, even now in the pocket of my apron, was addressed to her. I had indeed been an unwelcome apparition. It was his deep and unforgetting nature made him so strongly moved at sight of me. Perhaps he had only recently made up his mind to believe me dead, and to fill my place, and this was the moment I had chosen to come back. It was torture to have all these thoughts, and stand beside him, and feel his faint fingers clasp my hand.

"It agitates you to see me," I said, constrainedly, and I loosened my hand, and drew a little back. It wasn't a difficult matter to do ; I couldn't see that he made any effort to hold it longer. A swift red overspread my face, as I turned a little from him.

At this moment I heard outside the door, steps and voices and the bumping of a trunk against the floor, then a loud rap. I sprang forward, caught up the cap and apron from the floor, and disappeared from sight. I heard the door open as I hurried through the closet. The expressman and the laundress had not had the good manners to wait till they were told to enter. It was well for me that I had heard them when I did.

CHAPTER XXXI.

A WOMAN, NOT A SHADE.

" Kiss me for my love!
    Pay me for my pain!
  Come! and murmur in my ear,
    How thou lov'st again!"
                        Barry Cornwall.

IT was about eleven o'clock the next morning that one of the servants brought me a note from Mr. Conyngham. Of course, I had known he would come, and was prepared for it. I read it hastily over, and told the servant to say I would be glad to see him.

Yes, I was quite prepared to see him. I was dressed—not in a cap and apron. There are some scenes you can't go through in a short dress, and mine was long. It was only a black cashmere, but it didn't look like Mary's. I had a bunch of violets at my waist; I had spent an hour about my hair, which hadn't any gray in it at all, but was as soft and brown as ever.

The snow was falling outside thickly before the windows—great, soft flakes, which darkened the air. The hangings were drawn back a little; the room had a great many flowers about it; there was a warm glow from the fire on the hearth. The room was large, but the ceiling was not high. It looked filled and warm and mellow with rich tints. I pushed a chair I liked

between the fire-place and the window, and sat down
there. I was knitting the pale gray stripe of an afghan,
and I kept my work in my hand. There was a quick
knock at the door. I said, "Come in," and Macnally
entered. I got up, and he came across the room to me,
and took my hand. He looked pale, but not ill, as he
had done the night before. I sat down, saying:

"You are better, I am sure, to-day?"

There was no use ignoring last night, though I should
have been glad to do it, if I could. If I could only
have remembered what I had said to him when I threw
myself down before him on my knees! It would take
a very long dress and a very composed manner to
obliterate that miserable mistake.

"I'm afraid," he said, "I gave you some anxiety
last night. It's unlucky that I get those attacks when
I have any sudden—surprise or anything."

"I should think," I said, looking down at my knitting, "that if you have any trouble of the heart or anything like that, you ought to be careful and avoid excitement. Speaking, and all that, isn't it bad for you?"

"You mean for the excitement of it? Oh, that's
not the sort of thing that hurts one—," and he smiled
a little faintly.

He did not sit down, but stood leaning against the
mantel-piece, just beside me. He had an affinity for man-
tel-pieces. I seemed always to remember him standing by
a mantel-piece and looking at the fire. But he was not
looking at the fire now, he was looking at me, I could
feel that. I tried to think of something to say. I had
meant to be so calm, so reassuring to him. I had meant
to make it so easy for him to explain everything to me.
But here I was, changing from red to white, and my

breath coming in such a suffocating way. He did not
speak. It seemed to me he might have spoken, he
might have helped me; one ought to feel sorry for a
woman. I went on with my work. What should I
have done without it? At last I remembered something to say: it was the thing that gave me most control.

"Oh, that letter. I hope it won't make any difference. I just found it this morning in the pocket of—
in my pocket. Here it is," and I took it out and gave
it to him. He took it indifferently.

"It's just as well," he said. "It doesn't make any
difference now."

No, of course not. I could see that. There would
have to be such a different story now, it was just as
well it didn't go. But I must help him about that.
How should I begin?

I pulled a long thread of the worsted off the ball,
to knit more freely. It slipped through my fingers as
I laid it in my lap, and rolled away across the floor.
He did not notice it or pick it up. I did not dare to
go after it myself, I was so afraid of losing the little
self-control of manner that I had. All this time I did
not look at him, but I felt he leaned a little towards me.
In a moment he laid his hand upon my wrist, and held
it firmly.

"Put down your work," he said, in a low voice,
"and look at me. Have we nothing to say to each
other, after all these years?"

I drew my hand away. "I hope you will forget
last night," I said.

"Why should I forget it?" he asked.

"There were many things to—to—make me—You

must remember a woman will do a great deal from compassion. I shall always feel I owe you reparation—but that doesn't mean—"

He had released my hand, and stood in his former attitude, and did not attempt to say a word. It was insupportable this silence, and his eyes upon me.

"That shade," I said confusedly, "I want it down. The light hurts my eyes."

He did not notice what I said; I don't think he heard me. I got up uneasily, to go and pull it down myself. As I stood up, I turned a little towards him; I glanced into his face; I met his eyes, full of an agony of love and disappointment.

"Ah," I cried, "you *do* care! Why could you not say that you—were—glad?" Then, with a sudden passion, I flung myself into his arms with sobs. "I will not live any longer if you go away again. I have borne all I can bear. I have died a hundred deaths. You may kill me if you go away again. I will not—will not—live to suffer any more alone."

* * * Why could he not say that he was glad? Ah, "glad" does not come in a moment, after such long-dying deaths. I think he held me in his arms with more of agony than joy at first. The pain had been so deep-branded, a sudden bliss could not obliterate it.

* * * "Make me glad—make me believe in it," he said, faint again, lying back in a deep chair, and holding out his hand to me. Then I knelt beside him, and held his hand against my lips, my cheek.

"If I could only blot it out," I said; "if you only could forget—"

"I cannot," he said; "I cannot forget the pain or anything. It is my misery that I cannot."

   *   *   *   That afternoon, we were still sitting in the low, pretty parlor. The streets were all muffled with the snow, which was falling yet in soft clouds before the windows. The street lamps were just being lighted; upon the hearth the fire was making a deep glow.

"I did not think," he said, "you would have looked so young and well. I am trying to understand it. I am *afraid* you have been happy."

"Ah! that is just what has tormented me, as I have watched you going past these windows. There never was any drag or dullness about the way you walked."

"I acknowledge I have liked my work. There is a satisfaction in being able to do things."

"And being praised for it."

"No, I never cared a straw about that. It's the work itself that pays you: the praise gives you a feeling of dissatisfaction. That's about books, I mean. Oh, of course, when you're face to face with people, and speaking to them, there's a fascination in finding that you have the power to move them. Yes, I've liked that. I'm Irishman enough to be inflammable."

"Ah! well, I didn't blame you for not looking dull or weary when you went past the windows. I tried to tell myself I was very glad about it. But for all that, it's been pretty hard these two months. It has been like being shut into a dungeon without light or air, and knowing that *you* were in a crowd of people dancing and making merry overhead."

"Ah! save the mark! Such making merry! You needn't have been afraid. At home I could not bring myself to endure it ever, I felt I was such an alien. Here I had an incentive to going in society. I had

18

sometimes a fancy that you might have drifted into that sort of life."

"I!"

"I felt you might, if you were living, have come under the eye of some one—like Boughton. This is not a reproach—it seemed to me you might have married. I always thought of you as passive and passionless. I couldn't hope if you were living, your loveliness could be hidden. Somebody would see you and want you; there was nothing now. Why not—it was all equal. This was only one of the thousand fancies that I've had; but it gave a little life to the dreary crowds and crushes of this—forgive me—dreary, crushing city."

"And you looked for me *there!*"

"Yes, and then for some one who could give me news of you. I heard Naomi Emlyn was here, and I found her out. She could not tell me much, as you know. She will be so glad. I feel as if it were selfish not to have got her word to-day. She is such a beautiful young creature. The yellow-brown hair, and the eyes and the sentiment have all deepened; one rarely sees a woman so attractive."

I had loosened my hand from his.

"You will let me bring her here to-morrow?"

"I—I don't receive visits. It would derange my plans a little. One must have a rule, and keep to it, you know."

"But Naomi! whom you always loved so much. I thought it would be such a pleasure to you."

"Oh, not particularly a pleasure to me. She has outgrown the affection I had for her. I should have to make up a new one to fit her now. I haven't seen her since she became this beautiful young creature.

The last time I saw her she was rather a tomboy, and had to be sent away to wash her hands before she came to dinner. She also used to bother me with questions. I used to think her sentiment was a great nuisance; if it's deepened any, I should like to give it a wide berth."

"You're not," he said, stooping down and looking in my face, "you're not, by chance, a trifle jealous of our pretty Naomi?"

"You're not," I said, "by chance, a trifle jealous of that anonymous gentleman, married to the passive and passionless woman you described?"

"I? oh, I wasn't jealous of him. I never have been jealous in my life."

"Well, then, no more have I."

"Ah," he cried, turning my face so that the fire-light shone on it, "now I begin to believe it is all real. You are a woman and not a shade. I owe Naomi thanks for that! Did I tell you? She's to be married after Lent. I wrote only a few days ago to London for a wedding present for her. I don't believe you can fancy what it is to be."

"I don't want to fancy," I said, getting my face out of the light. "I wish you would stop talking of her."

Horrid as it is to be jealous, I don't know but it's worse to be ashamed and disgusted with yourself for having been jealous without any reason.

* * * * * * * *

"There is one thing I want to ask you," he said, later on, that evening. "Remember, it isn't a reproach."

He got up and walked about the room a little. I could see it cost him a great effort. "Those dreadful

days—there in the court-room—why didn't you—say a
word to me?"

"How could I? You did not give me a chance;
you never even looked at me. Besides—I couldn't—
before every one."

"I don't mean that. I knew you couldn't speak to
me. But why didn't you say something for me to
understand, when you made your answers? There was
not a word; I didn't know whether you believed the
worst of me, or not. I knew you didn't want me—
hung—but you can't understand the horror of that silence. It seemed to me if you *had* cared, if I had had
the place that you have given me now, then was the time
to have been brave and to declare it. I couldn't see how
you could have helped it. I—but I ought not to have
begun to talk about it."

"Yes, you ought," I cried. "Thank Heaven you've
given me a chance to tell you. I thought you understood—I never dreamed you didn't. It was Mr. Hardinge; I never said a word but as he led me. I never
took my eyes away from him. He gave me the cue
for every word I said. He would not let me be—anything but cold towards you. It was for the effect upon
the jury. Don't you see, my testimony would have
gone for little if they had believed I—I—cared for you
that way. I supposed he would have told you; that
you'd talk it over with him."

"He wouldn't be likely to talk to me about *you*."

"Why didn't you ask him?"

"Ask him! ah!"

"It would have saved you a great deal, if you could
have overcome that reticence."

"Yes, it would have saved me ten years of tormenting doubts. For if I had been sure—as you were—I might have been at rest. There were all my convictions on one side, my heart's fixed faith; and on the other, a silence like the grave; not one word from the hour I told you till this day—everything, everything against my hope but just my hope itself. Ah, well! It's past now. We won't talk about it any more."

* * * "Sophia," I said, sliding down on my knees before her bed, and taking hold of her hand "I haven't been up here all day, and I'm going to tell you the reason. I've got something to tell you. Don't take away your hand." For she had restlessly moved her hand away. My taking it seemed a most unnatural proceeding to her. I don't believe she had ever let me hold her hand before since I was a little girl and she took me out to walk. "Sophia, I've got to tell you who Mr. Conyngham is. He is Bernard Macnally. I've known it since the night I went to hear the lecture. I didn't tell you; there wasn't any use."

She gave a violent start, and turned her eyes upon me with a piercing look.

"I never meant that he should see me. I had resolved he shouldn't ever know. But last night he saw me, and he knew me in a minute. He isn't changed—towards me—Sophia. He came to America with just that only hope. He has been all these weeks in Canada trying to get some clue of where we lived when we were there."

"And you?" Her voice was thick and hoarse.

"I never have felt but one way."

"Then go, and leave me to die alone at last." And she turned her face to the wall, white and working with emotion.

"No," I cried, catching at the hand that she had snatched away; "no, Sophia, I am not going away to leave you altogether. You shall live here and keep your house the same, and we will come back and this shall be our home whenever we are in America. Sophia, he wants to see you. He wants to thank you for all you've done for me. He knows I shouldn't be alive if you hadn't been so good and faithful to me through my trouble."

A sort of hiss broke from her lips.

"He isn't—angry about anything. If there was anything to be forgiven, he forgives it with his whole heart. You were mistaken; he knows anybody can be led into a mistake. You *won't* be hard about this, and spoil my happiness to-day? Think how much you and I have gone through together, Sophia. Be as good to me in my happy days as you have been to me in my wretched ones. You can't be sorry that this has come to me after all my misery. You must know he will be good to me always. Why can't you look at me, and tell me that it pleases you to hear it?"

"Go away, now," she said, faintly. "I don't feel well enough to talk. Wait till to-morrow morning."

I had to wait.

CHAPTER XXXII.

A FAIR LAND.

" Because, in this deep joy to see and hear thee
  And breathe within thy shadow a new air,
  I do not think of thee—I am too near thee."
                                        E. B. Browning.

THE next day, Macnally said to me, with simplicity,
" When shall we go to church and be married?
To-morrow?"

"Oh, no, not to-morrow."

"Well, the next day?"

"That's Friday."

"The next?"

"I don't like Saturday. It's the swell day to get
married, and for that reason nothing would induce me.
And, of course, we wouldn't be married on Sunday,
since I don't wear a cap and apron. Next week we'll
begin to talk about it."

He was an Irish lover, and he began to talk about
it long before, and I had to make some sort of promise
for the following Thursday. That week, what happy
walks we had together. He made me tell him all
about the way I had spent my days, and take him to all
the places I had been in the habit of going to, even to
the streets where the poor people lived whom I had
visited. I showed him where I went to take my walks,
a corner where I came to see the sun set, down a street

where there were rows of trees, and some sky and a little river bit, beyond. My city and his city were very different places. There was no danger of meeting any body that he knew in mine. We had very free and happy hours together in the open air, as well as in the pretty, low parlor. For that week, I don't know what became of all his dinner engagements and things like that. I am afraid he was a little rude to some of his good friends. I am quite sure he never even answered any notes. He was an Irish lover, as I have said, and he didn't allow himself to be diverted from the matter that he had in hand. There was an engagement to lecture, which was a little more serious. I would not go to hear him; nothing would have induced me then. The loss of a whole evening was quite out of the question to him; so the lecture engagement was broken, not dishonorably, of course, but at a considerable loss of money. I can scarcely fancy two people more indifferent to sacrifices of *that*. Fortunately, there was a good deal to sacrifice with.

    * * I even took him to the hospital. I am sorry to say, he didn't enjoy it at all, but stood as near the door of the ward I was in as he could get, with a contraction of the brow, and a most uncomfortable expression. He had all a man's dislike of painful sights, and a poet's sensitiveness, I suppose, besides. At first, when I went in, I felt guilty, being so happy among the children of woe; but in a few minutes, the old love of ministering to them came back to me. I almost forgot him, and staid a long, long time in my favorite ward, as engrossed and eager as ever. When I came away at last, I am afraid he saw I had been away from him in every sense. The scene was so unspeakably repulsive to

him, that the thought of my being part of it was insupportable. He could not bear my dress should touch the door as I passed through it. When I stopped for a moment in the great, dark, sounding, stone corridor, to speak to an orderly whom I knew, going up to a surgical ward with some evil-looking instruments and a roll of bandaging, he actually took me by the arm, as if to force me away.

"Can't I speak to the poor fellow?" I said; "he's one of my most intimate friends."

We passed out under the stone archway, into the sunlight and fresh air, through ranks of wretched workhouse women waiting for official orders. A wan woman, thinly clad, with a pallid baby in her arms, passed out before us. The crutches of a boy, blue and thin, thumped on the pavement in front of us.

"Poor wretches! They're discharged," I said, hurrying forward to them.

"For heaven's sake, give them this money, and come away," he said.

I gave them the gift, which was lavish and absurd, and then went back and took his arm, and we walked down towards the boat, which was to take us to the city. The sun was just setting; the sky was clear and rosy; a strong wind was blowing across the island. Between this stone-built, hard-paved, barren city of sorrow, and that city of tumultuous life and luxury to which we were going, the icy river was flowing, all lit up now by the tints of sunset.

"You don't like it, I'm afraid," I said.

"Like it!" he exclaimed, hurrying me towards the boat. He held my arm under his as if in a vice. "And

18*

this is the sort of thing you've been doing! Thank heaven—"

"Listen," I said, stopping, and trying to take my arm away. "There's one thing I might as well say now and have done with it. There sha'n't be any— Thursday—remember, if you don't promise me that I may always go to all the hospitals I want to, all my life."

"Go to as many hospitals as you like, only don't ask me to go with you," he said with a groan, resigning himself.

"Oh, with pleasure; I don't want you to go. You're very much in the way; but you may give me lots of money always. That would be so nice. How much money do you think you've got altogether? I never thought to ask you."

"I hope you'll leave a small percentage to pay the household expenses. The rest, of course, belongs to the cripples and the small-pox patients."

"Oh, I'll spare enough for all that. I hope you are very rich. I wonder that I didn't think of it before. Do you think you could give me fifty dollars for a feast for male ward No. 6, on Thursday?"

"A thousand, if you won't ask to go there for a fortnight."

"Oh, well, that's reasonable. No, I won't ask to go for three weeks, if you say so; at least, not till we come back."

* * * Macnally had said to me, earnestly, "Get Sophia to consent to see me before we go away. I should somehow feel better about it if she would."

But it was of no use asking her. On Wednesday night, late, I went up to say good-bye to her. I found her looking pale and changed. For the past ten days she had been stiller and quieter than I had ever known her. She seemed to have withdrawn from us, and to be holding bitter communion with herself. It frightened me to see her so. I asked her if, even now, she wouldn't let me stay at home till she was better.

"No," she said, and her voice was not feeble. "I am no worse. I don't need anybody."

"Macnally wants to know if you won't see him for a minute. He desires it very much, before we go away."

She shook her head.

"I don't feel well enough. Tell him—it's all right."

That was the nearest that we got to it; but for her, it meant volumes. I was always glad to recollect those few words.

She allowed me to kiss her, and she held my hand tight, for a moment. * * *

On Thursday morning, I went out to church in the gray twilight, accompanied by Mary. This last was a concession to Macnally's wretchedness about my going out unattended at that early hour. I heard the door of the other house shut, just after we got out into the street, and I knew that he was following us at a little distance. We were to be married after the seven o'clock celebration. The sky was growing lighter about the east. It was going to be a still and lovely February day. The streets were silent, the houses shut; a few hungry little sparrows fluttered about the pavement, hunting crumbs; a dog shivered before a door, outside of which he had been shut all night. Poor little dog! It was my wedding-day; I hoped he would get in and find a cheerful welcome waiting for him. It was my wedding-day, and I felt happy, for the faint rose tints that I saw creeping up in the eastern sky, through the bare branches of the trees.

I had not seen Macnally since the morning before. I had told him I must pack my trunk, and that there were many things that I could not do with interruption. I knew he would not join me till before the altar, but I heard his step half a block behind me.

* * * Who cannot fancy what that hour was? I almost forgot him, as in the hospital. When the few people had gone out of church, and only the one or two were still upon their knees who were going to stay and pray for us, I saw the priest was waiting, and that Macnally was standing at the chancel steps. I seemed to be coming out of a far land; the land I came to was not fairer than the land I left—"pure lilies of eternal peace whose odors haunt my dreams." * * *

When we came out of the church, the air was full of sunshine and the streets of life. Merry children ran past us on their way to school; window blinds were opened and curtains drawn, and flowers looked through the glass and drank the sun. One could see the buds were reddening on the bare gray trees as the sun shone through them; one felt, in everything, even in the not warm air, "the first blind motions of the Spring, that show the year is turned."

THE END.